THE CURSE OF ETERNITY

THE CURSE OF ETERNITY

MICHAELA CUNNINGHAM

Published by Michaela Cunningham
265 Main Street #74, Danbury, CT 06810
www.michaelacunningham.com

First Printed in the United States of America

Library of Congress Control Number: 2025914777

ISBN 979-8-9915751-0-2 (hardcover)
ISBN 979-8-9915751-1-9 (paperback)
ISBN 979-8-9915751-2-6 (e-book)

Cover illustration and design copyright © by Kim Dingwall, www.kimdingwall.com.
Scene break illustration copyright © by Black Bird Designs, www.blkbirdesigns.com.
Interior design and typesetting by Sabrina Milazzo, www.sabrinamilazzo.net.
Copyedited by Kait Waterhouse, www.kaitwaterhousewrites.com.

For Sabrina,
the most magical person in my life.

"*Do you not think that there are things which you cannot understand, and yet which are; that some people see things that others cannot? But there are things old and new which must not be contemplate by men's eyes, because they know—or think they know—some things which other men have told them.*"

Abraham Van Helsing, Bram Stoker's *Dracula*

— 1 —

FORGED IN BLOOD

A SHARP CHILL CLIMBED MY SPINE, AND I SPUN—MY BLADE RAISED AGAINST the monster at my heels. The human face was an illusion in the darkness, but the undead man's sharp canines aimed at my jugular ruined any chance of mercy from me. My machete sliced across flesh and sinew, right through the spinal cord.

With its nerves disconnected, the vampire dropped like deadweight. Returned to the corpse it was meant to be—for now. Except there wasn't time to cart the sucker off to a big bonfire and roast s'mores over the dusty remains. Because he wasn't the only checkbox on our to-slay list.

Shouts followed a loud bark to my right, and I turned. My sandy-haired older cousin had his machete stuck in the crook of another vampire's arm. Unphased by the sharp instrument causing clotted blood to drip down her elbow, the vampire raised her arm. The action pulled Andrew closer despite his attempt to plant his boots and pull back. Instantly, I advanced.

A pale hand with a silvery hue reached for my older cousin's face, and I brought my blade down on its wrist. Growling in frustration, the vampire turned to me, and I swung. Her hair swished across her shoulders right before her head promptly parted ways with her torso. Flecks of dark blood splattered my face, but Andrew ducked away just in time to avoid the gore. A high-pitched familiar cry snapped my attention to the other side of the shadow-drenched room.

The tension in my shoulders eased when Olivia swung her machete down onto her opponent's exposed neck, the undead's previously severed hamstrings preventing it from standing to retaliate. Andrew's younger sister, still a year older than me, looked up from her task with the terror of the hunt shining from her wide blue-gray eyes. Golden blonde hair in a pixie cut framed her oval face, as splattered in vampire blood as my dark brown curls pulled back into a ponytail.

Our hunting dog, Stake, tore the head from the shoulders of Olivia's felled vampire, ripping through the connecting sinews. Thankfully, the sturdy Jack Russell Terrier was trained to keep the head as far as possible from the dismembered bodies. I stopped midstep when Andrew darted in front of me on his mad dash toward the fight ongoing at the center of the room.

By the time he got there, it was over. Johann Harker slashed across two vampires' throats in quick succession. *That's what they got for underestimating my old man's lightning reflexes.* The blue-gray eyes I'd inherited met mine as the thump of the final vampire hit the abandoned building's dusty cement floor. Exhaling slowly, I lowered my machete and wiped the sweat from my brow.

Between the four of us—and Stake—we took down five vampires in the span of a few minutes. Hence why hunting was a group affair, even in the best of circumstances. The afterglow of victory brought a smirk to my lips.

"What's our inventory?" Andrew asked, his back straight and eyes scanning the room. He counted over the corpse-like bodies twice. *What a kiss-ass.*

"That's what I was about to check," Johann said, huffing as he unlatched the walkie-talkie on his hip. "Checking in on dingo squad—over." His voice came out muffled on the devices attached to Andrew, Olivia, and myself. Silence answered us for several moments. Anxiety squeezed my chest, until a crackling rough voice replied.

"Small skirmish, got six pieces of tinder to burn." Uncle Alaric's jovial tone made me grin, and the whooping of a baritone voice followed in the background before he finished, "Over."

"That's about what I expected." Johann sighed the words, and gestured with his machete for the rest of us to get a move on. Andrew promptly jumped into action, but Olivia and I took the time to sheathe our weapons before following his lead in moving the undead heads further from the bodies.

The problem with vampires was that they struggled to stay dead—although the struggle was mostly on our part. With enough time, the magick keeping them animated would glue their heads back to their bodies. I'd never seen it happen, but I wasn't keen to, either. While we piled them up face-down in the corner of the grimy room, Johann gave Uncle Alaric and the Tsosies his overall take.

"The building's been scoured between the eight of us. Can't imagine there's any more still lurking. A colony of eleven is massive as it is. Over," Johann said, and sheathed his machete.

"Seems more like two separate colonies that decided to share a haunt," Elias Tsosie replied over the walkie, pausing to exhale what I imagined to be cigar smoke before it cut out.

While I envisioned Johann's long-time family friend standing around in his blue jeans and gallon hat, puffing on a stogie over a pile of corpses, my combat boot skidded on a slow-forming puddle of congealed blood. Unbalanced, I landed on my ass, and caught a snide look from Andrew.

Restraining myself from flipping him off, I settled for a grimace and hauled myself up. The keychain on my belt loop jingled as I patted the dust off my jeans. Great, now I felt sticky *and* grimy. Olivia offered me a sympathetic smile, but my returning expression was more pained than pleasant. Stake's damp nose nudged my hand, and I patted his side before he bounded off to his true master.

"That would make more sense," Johann answered into the receiver as he inspected the piles, probably counting the heads to make sure we didn't miss one. Apparently satisfied, he turned his back on the corpses and started for the door, still hanging off its hinges from when we'd busted in earlier. "I'll head to the truck for a wheelbarrow and the tarp. Want to send Caleb out to bring in your barbecue? Over."

"He's already on it—Alaric went with him. Figured a white man at his side would keep him from getting harassed this late at night. Can't be too careful this deep into Albuquerque," Elias said, and his booming sardonic laugh followed. If I strained to listen hard enough, I swear I could hear it from the other side of the empty building.

"Radio back when we're loaded up, if we haven't crossed paths by then. Over and out." Johann hitched the walkie-talkie to his hip, and not a peep sounded from the other end. My father turned to the three of us, his gaze weathered, but the creases around his eyes deepened when they landed on me. Frustrated, my fingers twitched, and I bit the inside of my mouth to keep it shut.

"You kids stay here. Keep the room secure until I get back, and if there's trouble, you work as a unit." His unwavering tone left no room for argument. Not that any of us would have bothered.

"We know the drill, Dad," I said, frowning. Even when I was eighteen and fresh on the hunt, he never needed to tell us what was common sense. That was three years ago. Really, I'd only been hunting for two and a bit years…until more recently.

"Reminders never hurt anyone," Andrew muttered, and my teeth clenched. Of course, he just *had* to say something.

"Stay sharp, I'll be back." Johann raised a hand in parting as he turned to walk out, Stake on his heels. Their steps were silent through the empty corridor beyond, leaving an eerie stillness behind until Olivia broke it with a gentle sigh. Posture stiff, I counted to ten before whirling on Andrew.

"What the hell was that? 'Reminders never hurt anyone,'" I mocked, and Andrew rolled his eyes.

"Andy…" Olivia's inflection turned cautionary, and my jaw tightened. Like usual, he ignored her, instead striding to the corner to stand possessively beside the pile of heads. His gaze met mine, unrepentant. I was in for it.

"You realize that *thing* almost sunk its teeth into you tonight, right?" he accused, and before I could so much as take a breath, he was already spouting off whatever idiocy his brain could come up with. "It's hard enough bringing you along the last few weeks when you're sloppy, but *none* of us want to deal with the consequences if you get turned into one of those monsters." Andrew's boot nudged the slackened jaw of a head, and I seethed.

"It *got behind me.* It happens!" I shot back, struggling to keep my voice down. "Besides, I wasn't the one whose arm almost got crushed!"

"I had that under control," Andrew said, his outward demeanor unruffled, but his arms crossed over his chest defensively. I exhaled a derisive laugh.

"I saved your ass. Me, the screw-up. And you just can't admit it."

"Maria—" Olivia started, but Andrew's barely contained vitriol was quicker.

"No, *you* can't admit that you're still rough around the edges. God, I don't even know why Johann brings you along. There's a reason Ethan stays home. If you're not an asset, you're a liability."

"Seriously, you're comparing me to Ethan?" I scoffed, genuinely offended. Their younger brother had never shown interest in picking up a machete in his life.

"Eight months is a long time away from the hunt," Andrew stated, his words like a slap in the face. My hands shook, and I balled them into fists. "Not to mention the shit that went down before that."

Old guilt flickered into fresh rage, and I looked to Olivia. Eyes averted, her small pale hand rubbed the side of her neck. The motion seemed subconscious, but a deep part of me cracked. I started for the doorway, clenching my teeth together so I wouldn't scream.

"Where are you going?" Olivia whispered urgently from behind me, but I didn't turn.

"For a walk," I muttered.

Soft steps shuffled after me, but then Andrew said, "Just let her go. Johann already declared the place thoroughly cased."

"It's still not safe," Olivia replied, and I could imagine her blue-gray eyes widening in dismay as I stepped around the door hanging off its hinges.

"She's got her walkie." Andrew's tone took on a finality that was clearly a piss-poor imitation of Johann's self-assured confidence.

Their voices faded, the whispers unheard over the sound of wind against the boarded-up windows along the corridor's wall. My boots scuffed across the cement, and I made an effort to quiet the noise. I didn't know where I was heading, except that it was opposite to where Johann's Ford F-250 and Elias's Dodge RAM 1500 were parked across the street on Richmond Drive.

On the corner was Route 66, and the noise of traffic would cover up whatever disturbance our hunting might have made. That was one benefit of living in Albuquerque. Nobody questioned it when we walked down the street with machetes on our hips, and the New Mexico desert was a relaxing drive away. The perfect place to burn the undead corpses into ashes.

Turning the corner, I exhaled heavily in an attempt to calm down. As if I didn't already know I had messed up, Andrew seemed determined to never let me live it down. We typically avoided each other at home, as much as any family could while living under the same steeple. My head throbbed as the adrenaline ebbed away. Through a surprisingly intact window, the moon waned between sparse clouds drifting past.

A tiny nagging part of me—that seemed to open like a chasm at the worst times—wanted to believe that Andrew was right. As a kid, I'd thought my family's legacy was incredible. Then I grew up, and got bitch-slapped by my first vampire. If the last eight months of on-and-off therapy taught me anything, it was that the mental scars cut deeper than the scratches littering my thick skin, all thanks to my ancestor.

Being descended from the legendary monster hunter, Van Helsing, sounded cool growing up. The secret tale passed down through generations told of his 'triumphant' victory over the original vampire—Vlad Dracula the Fourth, son of the Impaler. Back when Romania was still split into Wallachia and Moldavia, and long before we'd immigrated to America.

Except, when Helsing finally ended Dracula's reign of terror over the continent, it didn't eradicate the threat of vampires entirely. The first vampire's bid for power might have died with him, but the monsters he'd created since his inception were still undead and kicking. That's why my family's legacy, our typical weekend activity, involved exterminating the parasitic species that reveled in feeding, raping, and murdering innocent people.

It's what I was born to do, my calling. At one point, I'd done it proudly and without failure—until I fucked it up.

My steps slowed, nearing the next bend, and my intake of breath panged with morose hurt. Whether I liked it or not, I could bleed and die like any other human. Just like everyone else, I had to live with my consequences. No matter how much it killed me.

Guilt from both the past and present stung my chest on my exhale. Walking alone left me cooled off, but angrier with myself. Shaking my head, I turned around, intent on heading back— when a shadow to my right emerged from a stairwell.

"This place is not safe, miss," a deep voice warned, and my fists shot up. Eyes narrowed, my right foot slid back in a defensive stance as the silhouette of a tall man in a leather jacket emerged. Except he wasn't human, that was obvious from the silvery pallor of his skin.

Under the indirect moonlight filtering in from the nearby window, a shimmer danced across the angular side of his face and the exposed flesh of his outstretched hand. The vampire moved closer, his expression falsely innocent and both hands raised in a placating gesture while he spoke with an Eastern European accent, "Please, allow me to escort you out. You are not safe here."

The vampire's stalled approach gave me the moment I needed to withdraw my machete. His dark eyes glanced at my blade, and then his black eyebrows rose with obvious surprise.

"Oh, perhaps you are, after all."

Without hesitation, I rushed him. My blade swiped in an arc, aiming for the head, but the vampire stepped aside with a blur of speed. *Shit, his accent*—all the oldest vampires were from that region. The monster had speed and experience, meaning I needed the surprise of proximity. So I moved in, stepping into his space and aiming my machete for the torso. Vampires might not feel pain, but if I could bleed him out then his actions would slow.

The bastard dodged again, and for a split second, I warred between frustration and confusion. Because he moved further away, backing up several steps which I admittedly struggled to keep up with.

"If you would only listen—" he said, quickly cut off when I slashed at his head—or where his head was a millisecond ago. The vampire stepped aside, his expression so exasperated it only pissed me off more. "You are being obtuse."

Okay, that did it.

All of Andrew's tauntings echoed in my head, and my blood boiled. Fresh adrenaline fueled my onslaught. The hum of my pounding heart in my ears was deafening compared to the shush of my blade slicing the empty air beside the vampire's head.

This one was *fast*, and a sinking realization left me woozy. I wouldn't be able to take this one down on my own. Terrifying peace settled in at the thought, and I forced my focus not to waver while the vampire eluded my every strike.

In a last-ditch effort, I extended my arm past my usual safeguards. The sudden reach struck true, and my blade made contact with the vampire's throat. Dark red blood oozed from the nicked skin in clotted streams. *Yes! Finally—oh fuck.*

Inches separated us when the vampire glared down at me. Panic slowed my hurried retreat, and he suddenly grasped my right wrist. His grip tightened, forcing my fingers to loosen on my machete's handle. At first, I figured he'd snap my tougher-than-average bones.

Then he yanked me forward and I stumbled, off balance, my chest nearly touching his. Fear pounded through my skull, and my lungs stilled while I stared into his eyes—so clear up close, almost as black as a raven's wings.

His other hand rose in a flash, covering my mouth and nose. On instinct, I inhaled, breathing in a sweet, powdery texture. The edges of my vision turned foggy, darkness closing in with each thrum of my beating heart...

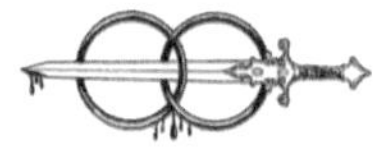

An ache pulsed through my forearms, and my awareness flickered to life. Stinging pain tightened my shoulders. My tongue felt thick, like it was wrapped in cotton, and I swallowed hard before forcing my eyes to open. Every flutter of my eyelashes was sluggish, and it took several blinks to figure out that I was staring down at my lap. Still clad in my bootleg jeans, and my gaze roamed to my black combat boots, the laces tied how I'd left them.

Cool air raised the hair along my upper arms, around the straps to my red halter top. *Where did my denim jacket go?* The loose ends of my hair tickled my collarbone, so my hair tie must not have made the trip here. With effort, I looked up. Iron shackles clamped around my wrists held my arms above my head. The chains connecting either side were slung unceremoniously over a wall sconce. *Wait,* my brow furrowed, *where am I?*

It wasn't the warehouse, that was for sure. Cozy furniture surrounded me, with a writing desk on my left that stood opposite a row of bookshelves, and an antique dresser positioned against the right wall. Atop its sleek, solid oak beauty was a silver platter with a decanter, a bottle of red wine, and a single polished glass. *What the hell?*

When I tried to move my arms, pain iced through my veins. I bit back a scream. Holding completely still, I eyed the shackles a little closer. Etched markings circled the iron—magick sigils. The discomfort ebbed the longer I stayed stationary, fading into pins and needles while the blood drained downward.

Squeezing my eyes shut, I opened up my other senses. Beyond the hum of an air conditioning unit pumping out dry air, voices were murmuring in the next room. One was strangely familiar, while the other came through hazy, like over the phone. Both of them sounded masculine.

"If anyone can do it, you can, Drake," the deep, staticky voice said with a tinge of humor.

"Must you always taunt?" the other replied—and his accent rekindled my memory while goosebumps crawled over my flesh.

Startled, I pulled at my restraints only to be shot through with scorching agony. A groan passed my lips as my head bowed, trying to curl into myself. Except the shackles wouldn't let me move far. After several deep breaths, my ears stopped ringing.

"Then I will handle it," the vampire said from the next room, his tone flat.

Heart pumping in my chest, I listened close to hear the call-ended beep. Despite the vampire's silent footfalls, I sensed his approach. The air conditioning switched off, and I stared at the only doorway in or out as the vampire's tall figure entered the room.

2

DYING TO SURVIVE

"IF YOU'RE GOING TO KILL ME, WHY DON'T YOU JUST GET IT OVER WITH?" I demanded, but my false bravado was painfully obvious by the sweat on my brow. The vampire's returning stare was unexpectedly miserable. Maybe he thought I'd beg for my life. I wouldn't give him the satisfaction.

"This exchange need not be so hostile," he replied, his accented voice as smooth as silk. Like the light poised before an angler fish's fangs. "My intent was never to harm you."

I glanced pointedly at my restrained arms above me.

"This—" He gestured at my aching arms. "Is merely a precaution for communication."

"You want to *talk* to me?" My voice hitched up an octave, and I cleared my throat. "Is that part of your sick fantasy, or something? Have a chat before you drain me dry?"

"There will be no 'draining' of anyone this evening. The other hunters you were with saw to that," he answered, apparently unbothered.

I straightened my spine the best I could.

"My family's going to find us, you know." I glanced at the doorway, like they might bust in unannounced. The vampire's stare never wavered from my face, and I schooled my features firm. "They won't let you get away with whatever you're planning."

"You act as if you know me, and I assure you that you do not— Miss..?"

I snorted. "Go to hell where you belong."

The vampire approached, faster than I'd anticipated, bringing his striking pale features into sharper focus. His straight black hair barely shifted with his smooth stride. Eyes almost as dark stared down into mine, mere feet away, and I swallowed. It wasn't unusual for vampires to be attractive, but it sure was annoying.

He'd removed his leather jacket at some point, and the light gray T-shirt he'd worn beneath was now on full display. Stretched taut across his built shoulders, which I definitely wasn't noticing while I glanced from his face to the hem of his dark-wash jeans. My brow pinched. *This guy seriously wore dress shoes with denim?*

When he shifted on his feet, I looked up. Bruise-like circles beneath his eyes shimmered in the room's dim candlelight, evidence of his living human facade. The whole thing was an illusion. Like a mirage, trying to convince the mind that all was fine and dandy despite the obvious threat. I knew better. I'd seen them in the sun.

What I'd never witnessed before, on a vampire's face anyway, was an apologetic expression. That was new, and strangely...disarming to my rapid heartbeat.

"Your 'family' will not find you here. I have covered my tracks well enough. However..." He grasped the antique desk's wooden chair and dragged it noiselessly across the carpeted floor. As he sat directly in front of me, his dark eyebrows pulled together. "I am prepared to release you, as long as you agree to convince your fellow hunters to leave me be."

"Excuse me, how stupid do you think I am?"

"I never said you were unintelligent—"

"Right, so we'll just 'leave you be' to eat whoever you please. Capture a hostage and you think you get an 'all you can eat' free pass?"

"Fortunately for you, and the rest of the public, I abstain from human blood," the vampire said, and I was too baffled to reply. Yeah, like I believed that—but admittedly, this was the strangest interaction I'd ever had with an undead. He leaned back in his seat, appearing relaxed with one leg across his knee. "I am aware this must be a peaceable arrangement."

My eyes narrowed. "Such a pacifist, chaining up a woman."

He huffed, which must've been a choice since he didn't exactly need to breathe. "As I said, merely a precaution. It would be unwise to allow a descendant of Helsing to roam freely around my residence."

"Observant," I remarked, and his shoulders rose and fell.

"The one who destroyed Dracula is notorious, legendary even, to my kind. As are those who carry his bloodline."

My frown deepened. "But you don't want to kill me?" Sure, vampires would sometimes keep people around as their own personal vending machines, but then why was he stopping to chat?

"No," he answered slowly, "I am disinterested in murder."

"You expect me to believe that you're not with the colony I was hunting? Your 'kind' has been leaving a bloody trail all throughout Albuquerque!" A horrible thought sunk to the pit of my stomach—but no, my family and the Tsosies couldn't be dead. I couldn't believe he'd be able to take out all of us. The vampire's silence turned deafening, spiking my anxiety.

"I assure you, I played no part in that. Nor did I even know they had come to this city until I smelled their 'colony.'" The vampire shifted, his gaze diverted to the closed drapes on the far wall. "I was only passing by when I glimpsed you through the second story window. I thought you were an innocent person, unaware of your proximity to monsters. Then I smelled the blood on you, and when you withdrew your weapon… It became obvious you were the hunter, rather than the victim."

When I scoffed, the vampire's gaze returned to mine. No longer exasperated and sincere, his features hardened, clearly irritated.

"What will it take for you to accept my words?" he demanded, voice quiet, but I was already biting my tongue. Nothing I could say would make this better. "Perhaps some time alone will aid you in collecting your thoughts." The vampire stood in a blur, and my heart jumped into my throat.

"Because that'll work!" I blurted, and he paused. "Leave me here, chained up like an animal, and I'll come to heel? You're as bad as any of them!" It was stupid to argue, but I could handle a fight. Being left defenseless, on the other hand? I stifled a shudder.

The vampire stood stock still, but I looked away before he could see any terror in my eyes. All I had to do was wait, just until my family could find me—

"Alright, I will release you."

What did he just say? My attention snapped back to the vampire, but my spine pressed into the chair when he moved closer. Then he stopped, like he'd sensed my discomfort.

"And you must promise not to fight me." Dark eyes stared into mine, close enough to reflect the blue-gray of my irises. "Do we have a deal?"

"Sure," I answered with conviction, my heart pounding. The vampire pulled out a key from the back pocket of his jeans. A shiver skittered down my arms when his cold hand brushed against mine to unlock the shackles. Unsurprising, since vampires couldn't create their own body heat, being mostly dead.

My left wrist came free, and I gasped when my hand fell limp onto my lap. Pins and needles itched down my arm, the blood rushing in a torrent. Another loud turn of the key rang out from the second shackle, freeing my other hand. Before I could so much as take a breath, the vampire's face appeared inches from mine.

"I will not hurt you unless you force my hand," he warned, and straightened up.

Flexing my numb fingers, I stood. While I tracked his reaction, he measured mine in return. When he pivoted toward the doorway, I took my chance. The only way to incapacitate an undead was to traumatize their spinal column, so I aimed my knee for the base of his back. Too fast, he spun around to catch my leg— and raised it high.

Unbalanced, I toppled backward. My hip hit the floor with a thud, and I rolled onto my front to push myself back up. When I rose, the vampire was waiting, shaking his head in disappointment, and my ire ignited. Grabbing for whatever I could, I yanked an old landline telephone free from the wall and chucked it at the vampire's head.

He dodged it, but the corners of his eyes tightened, his jaw clenching at my destruction. Desperate to distract him, I reached for something else, an old teacup, and threw that next. This time, he caught the cup in his right hand, and tossed it onto the cushioned armchair I'd just vacated. The vampire approached one step at a time. Until I was backed up against the wall opposite the door, our position forcing me to glare up at his irksomely handsome face.

"I did warn you," the vampire muttered, raising his hand. I flinched, but he was only holding a bunch of sand. On impulse, I charged him, ducking down under his arm to elbow his side. I struck true, and the blow shoved him aside long enough for me to make a mad dash for the door. My booted foot crossed the threshold before his hand clamped down on my arm, sending another flash of needles through my magickally-frayed nerves.

He yanked me around to face him, and I threw a punch at his straight nose. In a blur, he blocked it, catching my fist in his grasp. Hands occupied, I drove my knee into his abdomen. The vampire took the blow, only to release my arm and grab behind my knee while pulling my fist in an arc. Twisted around, I was thrown to the floor when he let go.

Before I could regain my wits, he was on top of me, pinning me down with his hands gripping my forearms.

"Ow," I groaned, blinking through the aches.

"Are you alright?" the vampire asked, holding me still beneath him. His needless breathing stayed even while I gulped down air.

"No," I spat, abandoning both my pride and dignity.

"I would charm away your discomfort, however, if my charms worked on a descendant then I would not have bothered with such theatrics." Figure hazy with speed, he released me and stood. This legacy was a bitch, but at least I would heal fast.

"I'll take the pain over the mind violation, thanks." I sat up, winced, and eyed the vampire—now at the other end of the room by the antique dresser.

"You truly despise me."

"It's nothing personal," I replied through a huff. "I hate all murdering parasites."

The vampire inclined his head, as if to say I had a point. Then he turned to the forgotten wine glass, and filled the decanter. Despite his vulnerable position, I figured I'd end up right back where I was if I scrambled for the door. I needed to play this smarter with less brawn, more brains—not my specialty.

"Drink this." He turned around, offering a glass filled with dark liquid. "It may 'take away the edge,' as they say."

Wary, and still on my 'must stay sober at all costs' step in the program, I shook my head. Annoyance oozed from him as he set the glass back down, but his brow pinched with curiosity.

Outmatched, and alone, I mustered up some anger of my own to keep from shutting down. "What?"

"Well, I can hardly allow you to simply walk out of here and discover my address."

"You're still talking about letting me leave?" I balked, and his head tilted.

"I said that I would, did I not?"

There wasn't much I could say to that, so I changed gears. "What was your plan, anyway? Get me to hear you out and then walk me blindfolded to the bus stop?" To my surprise, the vampire's eyes closed briefly before rolling. His posture shifted from one foot to the other. *Was he…being sheepish?*

"Unfortunately, I had not anticipated the effects of the faery dust. It was never my intention to abduct you, yet it would be dangerous to leave you incapacitated where we first fought…" The way he spoke, his apologetic timbre and serious demeanor, almost made me believe him.

"So this is…your house?" It felt strangely awkward when he nodded, especially since I desperately wanted to be anywhere else. Then I shook my head. I could *not* be getting caught up in this vampire's story. This place must belong to some long-dead owner the vampire murdered. That made more sense than— "Wait, you used faery dust on me?"

"Indeed." The vampire scooped up a purple pouch from the floor near the wall.

His movements blurred until he stood before me, offering the bag and its contents. Hesitantly, I accepted it, and he retreated, giving me breathing room. The pouch's material was velvety, but the silvery powder inside felt like a strange mixture between soap and sand.

"I thought perhaps, if you remained uncooperative, I might use it again and leave you at the local hospital this time."

"No thank you." Without thinking, I tossed the bag back to him. *Damn my manners in returning people's property!* This wasn't a casual chit-chat, even if the vampire kept acting like it was.

"Perhaps we ought to go with your idea, restricting your vision?" Leaning back against the wall, he crossed his arms over his chest.

"Not freaking likely," I muttered. The vampire shrugged with a wave of his hand.

"I can, quite literally, do this forever," he said politely. "I suggest you make the choice so we may end this stalemate."

"Fine," I snapped, out of options and losing faith in any back-up arriving. "But if you try anything—"

"You will be quite as ineffective as before, yes," he cut across. Chewing on my lower lip, I debated my options one last time. At least this way, I was free. Which was better than the chains, even if I couldn't see.

"Throw a paper bag over my head and let's get this over with," I grumbled. Across the room, he opened the top drawer of the antique dresser to pull out something long and made of fabric, *a scarf?* "How kinky," I murmured dryly.

Ignoring my crude remark, he offered me his hand, and said, "Now, please refrain from attempting to bite me."

I eyed his pale fingers before hefting myself upright on my own. Except the sudden vertigo put me off balance, and I stumbled. The vampire's hand took mine, steadying me, and I recoiled.

"I've got it," I said, my eyes narrowing as the vampire took a step back before making a spinning motion with his pointer finger. Teeth clenched, I obeyed while every fiber of my being screamed *don't do it*. Goosebumps cropped up all over my body as he placed the thick length of fabric across my eyes. I winced when he tied the knot in place, pulling at the roots of my loose shoulder-length hair.

"Apologies," he said softly.

"Yeah, yeah, where am I going?" Truthfully, I wasn't totally blinded, but everything further than a few feet away was hazy. He took my hand again, startling me, but I didn't pull away. Mostly to maintain the illusion that I was impaired, but my pulse thundered when his cold callused hand exerted the smallest pressure to lead me forward.

An unusually polite vampire, he may be, but I still didn't like this.

We took a turn past the doorway ahead before shuffling across a stretch of carpeted floor. Then a second door creaked open.

"A step," he instructed, and I crossed over a ridge in the floor. My boots crunched over grass while my heart raced. The click of a car door's locking mechanism made me jump. If he was lying about where he was taking me, at least I knew how to tuck and roll to get out of a moving car. Even if I had to break through the window to do it.

"Inside," he said—*bossy, much?*

"And here I was taught never to take a ride from strangers," I muttered. His answering chuckle almost made me smirk, but then I frowned. *He's the* bad *guy, remember?*

The passenger seat was cool to the touch, made of a comfortable leather. Aside from the bubblegum-scented air freshener barely overpowering the used cigarettes in the ashtray, I couldn't make heads or tails of the car's interior features. When the engine roared to life, the noise settled in around us like the car lacked any sound dampening. *A classic model, maybe?*

It started forward a short way over gravel before pulling out onto an asphalt road while a train's familiar chugging rumbled by. *Okay, so he must live near a rail line.* An increasing number of streetlights affirmed that we were returning to Albuquerque, and thankfully not heading out into the desert.

"Where are you taking me, anyway?" Buses might not be active after midnight, but I'd walk home if I had to.

"Back to where I found you. Unless you are lacking in vehicular transport and would prefer me to drop you elsewhere?"

"I'll manage." *Vehicular transport?* Yeesh, this one was old.

"It was never my intention to interfere with your work," he assured, the same hesitant, apologetic cadence returning to his tone.

"I'm sure my family finished up just fine without me." The bitter words left my mouth before I really thought about it, and my fists clenched, itching for my machete. Chagrin washed through me. Here I was, with yet another monumental failure under my belt. Seriously, after so many months of rehabilitating into my old life, I end up being helped out by an enemy?

The charity of it, if the vampire could be believed, was excruciating. How proud my ancestor would be, knowing that his great-great-great—however many times 'great' granddaughter—was a recovering addict might be bad enough, but this took the cake. Alexandru Dracula, aka Abraham Van Helsing, spent the better part of three centuries on a vendetta to destroy his younger-brother-turned-first-vampire—Vlad Dracula—and I couldn't manage against one lousy undead.

It wasn't like Vlad didn't have it coming, he did attempt to murder Alexandru to usurp the Wallachian throne. At least, that's how the story went. How Helsing lived for three centuries to slay Dracula at last was the real mystery. Supposedly, the archangel Michael gifted him immortality, strength, and speed to rival Dracula in order to end the vampire's reign of terror over Eastern Europe before it spread to the rest of the world.

Not that I strictly believed in that story. Especially since it involved Dracula having gained his vampirism from the devil himself. No matter what the truth was, my family and I were still 'blessed' with superhuman enhancements. Our duty was to eradicate the vampires Dracula made in those three hundred years, the ones who fled the old continent when their ruler was snuffed out. Some legacy I upheld, where I got regularly bruised and battered by the undead.

Part of me wished the vampire had killed me. At least I'd have died with my dignity.

Silence stretched between us through three stops at the deserted lights before the vampire suddenly said, "What do you call yourself?"

Considering everything that had happened tonight, that struck me as an oddly normal question. I could have ignored him, but my name wasn't exactly rare.

"Maria." No need to give him my last name since 'Harker' was much more identifiable. "And you're Drake, right?" I glanced sidelong at the vampire as his knuckles tensed on the steering wheel.

"I did not realize descendants could overhear cellular telephone conversations so clearly," he remarked, uneasy.

"Don't underestimate me," I warned, and grimaced when he smiled.

"I would not dream of it," he said, like it was a private joke, and I had to catch myself on the dash when the car stopped short.

Growling under my breath, I ignored his brief chuckle and lifted my blindfold. The sign for Richmond Drive SE was dead ahead. *The bastard really brought me back?* He'd even left the car's doors unlocked. I immediately grabbed the interior handle, but hesitated. Wary, I shifted to stare him down.

"Now what?" This couldn't be it.

"Now you exit, and we part ways," he answered, a strange edge of dejection in his voice. Whatever it was, I wasn't asking twice.

Leaving the scarf on the seat, I climbed out of the low car and onto the sidewalk. Something clattered against the pavement beside me, and I spun to find my machete in its sheath, lying undamaged at my feet. When I bent to pick it up, the car's engine revved. It took off in a hurry, leaving a cloud of exhaust that obscured its make, model, *and* license plate as it turned the corner. A shaky breath passed my lips, worn from all the adrenaline.

Beneath the waning moonlight, a chill breeze slithered over my bare shoulders as I turned toward the warehouse—and froze.

Down the street, a figure only a couple inches shorter than me emerged from the shadows cast by a main entrance's overhang. My grip on my machete relaxed when the streetlight illuminated their dark brown complexion and the short black hair on their head. A curved blade with a bone pommel was held tight in their grip while small chestnut eyes took me in over an upturned nose and very full lips.

The walkie-talkie strapped to their torso crackled when they turned it on, and I nearly winced when Laura Tsosie spoke into it. "Guys, I found her."

3

STORIES TO TELL

"HEY, LAURA. UH, HOW'D YOUR HUNT GO?" MY ATTEMPT AT BREVITY FELL flat under Laura's scrutinizing stare.

"Where the hell have you been?" they demanded, and I actually winced when they advanced. "Everyone's been off their rocker since you stopped answering your walkie—where the hell *is* your radio?" Laura's attention shifted to my bare shoulders. *Damn it,* I'd be hard-pressed to get anything by Laura even if they weren't descended from those blessed by Naayéé' Neizghání.

As Elias told it, the legendary Diné monster hunter had recruited and trained one of the Tsosies' forefathers to battle against the evils of the world. While the Tsosies' own unique bloodline lacked natural immunity to a vampire's charms—like ours did—their strength, speed, and innate senses passed down through the lineage more than made up for any potential weakness.

Although *our* progenitor was supposedly saved by an archangel, it never mattered much to me how we'd been 'gifted' our abilities. End of the day, monsters needed slaying. That's what vampires were, after all, and the Tsosies' ancestors had fought worse. *Bet the undead didn't anticipate that when they expanded to the Americas.*

Before I had a chance to get my thoughts in order—boggled as to why the vampire had returned my machete but not my jacket and walkie-talkie—a familiar high voice called out.

"Oh my gosh!" Olivia's strained squeal followed the soft sound of her footfalls across the concrete sidewalk. She rushed past Laura, who hadn't moved, and threw her shorter arms around me. With my sheathed machete in one hand, I awkwardly patted Olivia's back with my other. My older cousin pulled away only to stare up at me with tears brimming her wide blue-gray eyes. "You scared us half to death! I can't believe you bailed on us without so much as a heads up—"

"I didn't bail!" I retorted, not bothering to keep my voice down.

"Then where were you?" His gruff voice deepened with concern, and I automatically straightened up. Olivia stepped aside, leaving room for Johann to approach unimpeded. Hesitating, I glanced at Laura, who was mumbling into their walkie-talkie.

"I got kidnapped," I blurted, and Laura stopped mid-sentence to look at me. Olivia's mouth popped open while I stared up into Johann's blue-gray eyes. "A vampire got the drop on me, and carted me off to a nearby building." My voice was cool, casual, but my pulse raced. "It was close, I had to play possum for a bit, but I got 'im." I swallowed hard under Johann's scrutiny.

His expression softened despite his gaze continuing to assess my body for injuries. Then he stepped forward to sling an arm around me. Tears pricked my eyes while I hugged my only living parent.

"Thank God you're alright," he whispered. When I nodded, his unkempt beard tickled my face.

"So you really weren't…" Olivia glanced from me to Laura as Johann stepped back and shot her a vehement look. The accusation in Olivia's eyes, mimicked by Laura's brief shrug, set my chest ablaze.

"No, I really wasn't." This was why I lied. Not because it was smart, or safe. For fuck's sake, that vampire was still out there, living who knows where in *my* home city. This whole night was my mistake, but I didn't need to give my family anything else to use against me—

"So where's the body?" Laura asked, walking closer on a very slight limp. Beneath the hem of their capri pants, a puckered pink healing scratch ran down from their knee to their ankle. My family weren't the only fast healers. "Dad already went with Alaric and Andrew out to the desert to burn the ones *we* got."

"My Ford's still parked across the way," Johann said, shrugging out of his massive jacket to hand it to me. "As long as the head's a ways from the body, we've got time before it reanimates—"

"I already burned it," I stammered, sweat prickling my neck while I fumbled with donning his denim jacket. "Idiot had me in some basement boiler room. Once I lopped the head off the sucker, I dragged the body into the kiln. But, I mean, toting a head down the street wasn't exactly an option…" My throat bobbed on a swallow, but they were listening to my hasty lies. "There was some lighter fluid and a box of matches—I guess the vampire was a smoker—so I managed on my own."

Thinly-veiled panic set in at my attempt to weave between truth and tales. Except Johann's impressed expression put me at ease, and simultaneously twisted my guilt like a knife. I chewed on the inside of my cheek under Laura's dubious stare, echoed by Olivia's fretfully furrowed brow.

Not wanting to be questioned further, I added, "So Andy went with Uncle Alaric, huh?" The prick probably didn't care an ounce that I'd gone missing. So much for my hope that any of them would have found me…

"Yep," Laura answered, turning heel to stride up the sidewalk. Olivia went to follow, but paused when Johann placed his large rough hand on my shoulder.

"You shouldn't have gone off on your own like that," he said, his gaze steady on mine like an x-ray. "You know the rules. I won't have you on hunts if you can't keep to the code." My throat ached, but I managed a nod.

"Andrew was taunting her," Olivia piped up in my defense, but she closed her mouth when I widened my eyes at her.

"It's not because of him," I said, hoping to all hell that Johann wouldn't think I was incapable of controlling my emotions. My father's salt and pepper eyebrow rose, and I stammered, "Okay, he pissed me off. But it won't happen again." Mostly because I wouldn't let them stick me with Andrew next time. Johann seemed to deliberate, and then ran his palm over his weathered face, smoothing back his short hair with a sigh.

"It won't happen again," I promised quietly.

"It better not," he said, but my heart lightened to know he wasn't banning me from future hunts. I breathed a sigh of relief, and the corner of Johann's mouth lifted in a knowing smile. "Come on, kiddo, let's get home." Our fearless leader turned to follow Laura, whose athletic figure dashed across the street without looking either way.

Olivia sidled closer as we fell into step together. "What happened to your hair tie?" she whispered, and I compulsively ran my fingers through my ratty knots while the wind tangled the dark strands further.

"Got lost in the scuffle." I patted my pocket, unconsciously checking for my phone which I already knew was stowed in Johann's truck, and then froze. Whirling, I looked this way and that to be sure I hadn't dropped it on the sidewalk. Except the barren streets were just that—empty. "Shit!"

"What's wrong?" Olivia's eyes went wide, worried, and Johann stopped on the other side of the road. His hand reached for his machete. I waved him off, my brow furrowing in disappointment.

"My scrunchie isn't the only thing missing after the fight," I explained, sullen, and Olivia glanced down at my belt loops. It felt weird without the weight, so I strapped my machete's sheath to the belt around my hips while we crossed the road.

"Your lucky keychain is gone," Olivia said, and I nodded, grouchy. "Should we search the building you killed that vamp in? Maybe it's somewhere between here and there…"

Fear laced with guilt spurred me to reach for her shoulder as she turned, already scanning the nearby buildings.

"No, it's okay," I blurted. "I'm exhausted. I'll come back tomorrow to look for it."

Avoiding her gaze, I trudged up the sidewalk toward the F-250. The truck's interior light came on, illuminating the parking lot when Laura opened the door while Johann shuffled things around on the truck's bed. Then the hood closed with a shuddering thud, and Caleb emerged from around the front. Our gazes met, and his concern was palpable through his kind deep brown eyes.

"Man," Caleb breathed the word, closing the distance between us with several long strides. "Are you okay, Maria? I'll knock Andrew's lights out for being such a—"

"I'm good," I assured, and smiled. Caleb Tsosie's signature lopsided grin lit up his copper complexion, and my shoulders relaxed. Long black hair fell in waves around his shoulders, clad in a red T-shirt covered with grease stains and darker splatters, the latter courtesy of a now really-dead vampire's blood. The Harkers and the Tsosies had been thick as thieves since Johann and Elias, Caleb and Laura's father, learned that they were both hunting the same things.

That was way back in the day, and now the Tsosies were practically family.

"The fluid's alright, Caleb?" Johann asked, walking around to the driver's seat. Laura appeared to be back on their phone and riding shotgun, as per usual.

"Looks fine," Caleb replied.

Exhausted, my smile faded on my way to the back seat. Olivia and Caleb hung back a step while I climbed in, but I glimpsed the curious glance they shared. When Olivia shook her head at him, I gritted my teeth. Even one of my best friends thought I'd run off to party.

In the window seat, I scooched over to make room for Olivia in the center and Caleb on the far side. His considerable height forced Laura to move their seat forward. The truck's engine started up, practically purring. My brain tuned out the story Olivia relayed to Caleb of my noble victory over a wayward vampire. To avoid his curious, worried stare, I closed my eyes and relaxed into the seat.

Comfortable as I was, my mind wouldn't stop whirring. I would *not* break my family's trust a second time. After everything, I couldn't lose their belief in me—*again*. I said I'd eradicated the threat, and damn it, I was going to make good on my word. Except, the more I thought about the last few hours, the less sense I could make of the whole night.

I must have fallen asleep on the ride home. Because I had to be dreaming if I was starting to consider that maybe—just maybe—the vampire was telling the truth.

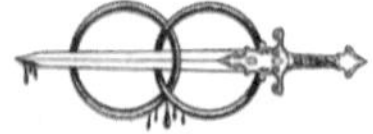

Light filtered in through my east-facing window past sheer curtains, and the sun's rays glared across my analog clock's glass surface. I chewed on the inside of my cheek while watching the little red hand ticking away atop my nightstand. It wasn't until both hands stood straight up, officially making it 'afternoon,' that I hauled myself off my decadently soft pillow.

Then the aches hit me, vibrating all the way up my side and through my funny bone. My exterior was healed, but a fight still stung the next day on my sore muscles. Regret laid heavy over my chest, twisting my heart and lungs as I debated telling everyone the truth.

It would make hunting the vampire a lot easier if my family was involved. They'd come up with a plan, and deduce his whereabouts with a radius of probable locations based on how long it took the vampire to drive me back. Even taking into account that he might have obscured the route on purpose, the Tsosie family had a network in Albuquerque as old as the clay dirt, which would help us track the sucker.

All I had to do was admit that I'd lied.

Chewing on my lip all morning might have left a permanent dent, but at least it stopped me from shouting in frustration. Because the extent of my uselessness was irritating. Not only did the vampire beat me more than once, he'd *driven me back*—relatively unharmed.

That's the part that really crushed me, because I couldn't figure it out. Okay, so he said he didn't drink people-blood—was that even possible for the undead? Despite the stack of books on lore sitting in our family's library, I was clueless.

Years of at-home lessons with my cousins to 'know our enemy' hadn't proved fruitful in my case. The whole time we were sitting around the dining table, meant to be studying up on vampire history and anatomy, I was sharpening my machete.

It's not like I hated learning or reading, I just couldn't wait to get out there and live it. After all the stories that Grandpa told us growing up, tales of his and our ancestors' brave efforts taking out vile monsters, I wanted nothing more than to be a part of that. Until I turned eighteen, and joined my first vampire hunt.

Maybe if Mom was still around… Nope, I was *not* going down that sinkhole. I patted my face with my cold hands to wake myself up, and promptly shot up out of bed, aches be damned. Wincing, I limped over to where my dresser stood, shoved against the wall opposite my bed. The ceiling fan high above was stationary, unnecessary with the temperate springtime air drifting in through my open window.

What had once been one of several offices that belonged to the Holy Trinity Church had since been transformed into a modern bedroom—at least, what was modern in the 1930s when my great grandfather bought it out of foreclosure. Sure, we'd gotten weird looks growing up in Thomas Village, as the family of woodworkers who lived in a church.

Hence the vanity by the door, which had been a handcrafted birthday present from Johann when I was twelve. My dresser was a family hand-me-down, built by my grandfather back in the '80s. Regardless of what our neighbors thought about us, this was home. Had been for generations, and we were here to stay.

Fully dressed, I shambled out into the long stretch of hallway. At the end was the closed door to Johann's study—our family's 'library' and where Uncle Alaric managed the woodworking store's finances. Behind me was the stained-glass window, haloing my shadow in a rosy glow as I made my way to the third door on the right. Bright sunshine pooled over the hardwood floor where it met the kitchen's tile.

I raised my hand to cover a yawn, and smacked into something hard.

"Ow!" I rubbed my forehead.

"Ugh, damn it," Andrew grumbled.

"Language, Andrew!" Aunt Susan scolded from her position before the stove, and the spicy scent of sizzling sausages made my mouth water.

"Watch where you're going next time," Andrew muttered, without looking at me, and bypassed me into the hall. I rolled my throbbing eyes when his bedroom door slammed shut.

Sweat beaded Aunt Susan's brow beneath her dirty blonde hair, tied back in a knot. Beside her, Ethan's begrudging frown was second-rate compared to Andrew's permanent sneer, but the brotherly resemblance was there. My younger cousin's hair, almost identical in color to his mother's, shifted across the rim of his prescription glasses.

"You know, people who wear glasses should be exempt from doing dishes. They keep fogging up," Ethan complained, taking a dish in rubber-gloved hands before ruthlessly scrubbing it. The pinkish pallor he'd inherited from his mother flushed red with a huff. "In fact, it should be considered child abuse to force me into this."

"You're part of this family, and you've got no job otherwise, so you're helping out," Aunt Susan chided. Ethan's retort died in his throat, miserably shaking his head. Attempting to get in and out for my caffeine fix *without* alerting the media, I tip-toed around the kitchen island. Then the back door opened.

"Oh, good! You're up. I was going to come check on you," Olivia said, her smile brimming, which immediately garnered Aunt Susan's attention.

"Oh, dear, how are you feeling?" she asked me, her thin eyebrows pulling together in concern over her dark blue eyes. Ethan spared me a glance, and then went back to his chore.

"I'm fine," I assured, stifling a wince when I reached up to grab a mug. "Just a little sore."

"Yes, I expect so." Aunt Susan nodded, returning to her cooking but clearly discomfited. "If you ask me, you're all too young for this 'hunting' business."

"So dramatic, Sue," Uncle Alaric called out from the backyard, a moment before he entered the kitchen behind his daughter.

Olivia moved aside to make room while her father went to the sink, probably to wash varnish off of his beefy hands.

Ethan took the opportunity to vacate the space, several dishes left unwashed, since Uncle Alaric was as broad as a bodybuilder and just as muscled. My uncle wasn't as tall as his older brother, Johann, but their similarities were obvious despite their polar opposite demeanors. Affable emotion twinkled in my uncle's blue-gray eyes as he winked at me, and his bushy mustache twitched.

"Heard everything that happened. Sounds like you had a hell of a night."

"Something like that," I replied, my gut twisting. To avoid telling another lie, I brought my cup of black coffee to my lips and drank deeply. Blissful caffeine zinged through me, courtesy of Johann's specialty beans imported from who-knew-where. Aunt Susan gave Uncle Alaric a gentle smack with the kitchen towel.

"A 'heck of a night' is one way to look at it." Aunt Susan never swore, or took the Lord's name in vain. Maybe being a lifelong Catholic had also made it easier for her to accept our family's legacy—or she was just a tough lady to begin with. Except she melted like butter when Uncle Alaric turned to her, and planted a kiss on her rosy cheek.

"Are you sure you're okay?" Olivia whispered, momentarily distracted by Ethan silently heading out the back door, his pack of Marlboros and lighter in hand. Frowning, her stare quickly returned to boring into my skull like she could decipher my well-being through sheer willpower.

"I'm fine," I ground out, quiet under the murmurs of Aunt Susan and Uncle Alaric's open flirting. "I wish you'd stop asking me. You all fought vamps last night, too, and I'm not hounding y'all with a thermometer and stethoscope."

"That's different," Olivia said, imploring, like I was being un-reasonable. "The rest of us had each other's backs. You were *alone*. It must have been awful." Her honest concern cracked my irritation, pushing the unease and guilt back to the forefront. Had that been how she'd felt—alone—abandoned? I swallowed down the rest of my coffee, eager for a change in topic.

"Where's my dad?" I glanced from the adjacent dining room to the alcove beside the refrigerator, which hosted our washer and dryer.

"He's still in the shed out back, I think, working on the lat-est commission," Olivia said, but by the look in her wide eyes, she wasn't done with our conversation. "I was thinking, if you wanted to go back together to look for your keychain—" Her offer was cut short by the ringing coming from my pocket.

Grateful for the distraction, I fished out my phone and checked the Caller ID. Sweet mercy was being delivered. Forc-ing a smile, I sidestepped Olivia to head back into the hall.

"It's Everly, I should take this," I said, and Olivia nodded. On my way out, I caught her frowning down at the floor. Heart heavy and sinking, I answered the phone with a sigh. "Hi, Eve."

"Hey, Maria. What's going on?" Everly's bubbly high voice brightened my mood, even if she did sound concerned.

"Well, lots, actually." I couldn't tell my family the truth, but Everly… She was the one person outside of my family, and the Tsosies, who was in-the-know.

Everly giggled. "I had a feeling. That's why I called."

"You're an angel," I assured. "Mind if I stop by to vent?"

"I'm at the shop right now, getting things set up for business," Everly answered, obviously giddy about her new venture as a self-employed entrepreneur. "But I could always use the extra hand."

"Great. Thank you," I stammered, my heart racing at the relief of being able to come clean to *someone*. Hopefully in doing so, I'd figure out the next step in hunting down my secret vampire. I cringed at the thought—*he wasn't* my *vampire*—and added, "I'll see you soon."

— 4 —

NICE FUCKING DISGUISE

THE DOOR TO MY SILVER FORD TAURUS SHO THUNKED CLOSED, PARKED IN the lot off of Carlisle Boulevard. Glancing past the barbershop next door, I smirked at my best friend's business front. Cheap white print across the glass door read 'Professional Psychic, Everly Nice' in bold font. I knew the stenciled letters were inexpensive because I helped stick them to said door last week.

It was nice having my best friend from high school back, since she'd been staying with her parents on some Army base up in Alaska for the last few years. After saving up from doing odd jobs, she managed to find a place to live and work in Albuquerque at the start of the year. Smiling, I pushed open the door and called out, "Eve? I'm here."

"Oh, thank the goddess," squeaked a voice from behind a tall stack of cardboard boxes.

I rushed forward to catch them, relieving the load from a pair of very freckled pale arms. Everly stepped back, and I peeked around a cardboard flap while she clapped dust from her small hands. At barely five feet tall, not including the volume from her curly red hair, Everly was a sight for sore eyes in her light-washed jeans and sky blue spaghetti-strap tank.

Her bright green eyes widened, thin red eyebrows high on her heart-shaped face when I easily hefted the stack with one arm.

"I *almost* forgot how strong you are." Everly beamed, revealing slightly crooked canines—nowhere near as sharp as the ones I'd often seen.

"That's pretty bad for your brand," I mocked in good humor, glancing pointedly at the 'Psychic' neon sign behind a shelf of Tarot cards Everly had drawn herself. She rolled her eyes.

"Memory was never my strong suit. It's foresight that I excel at," she retorted, and I bounced my eyebrows in concession.

"Alright, where do you want these?"

"Just over there is fine." Everly pointed to a bare stretch of wall beside a cozy armchair. Its startlingly familiar shape made goosebumps crop up along my arms while I set the boxes down in a row one after another, careful not to jostle her array of baubles. When I straightened and turned, Everly's knowing eyes narrowed. "What's wrong?"

"Okay, I take it back, you're good." I stifled a sigh, *where to begin?* Thankfully, Everly was patient. She hopped up onto the reception desk in the corner, over half as tall as her, and made herself comfortable beside the unplugged laptop. Avoiding the armchair, I slowly paced from one end of the work-in-progress shop to the other. Then I blew out a long breath, and told her everything. From the fight with Andrew, to being dropped off by my mortal enemy—or immortal, technically. Everly's red eyebrows rose, nearly disappearing beneath her bangs.

"Wow, that's a lot. Are you alright?" Her concern didn't offend like my family's dramatics had. Mostly because Everly wasn't 'superhuman' like us. Able to glimpse snippets of the future, yeah—but for her, a bruised elbow took a week to heal.

"Yeah, physically I'm fine. It's just my head that's going crazy." Tired of standing, I decided to sit on the floor. Moments passed in silence, both of us speculative, but then Everly opened her mouth.

"Do you believe him?"

At first, I didn't know who she was talking about. "The vampire?" I clarified, and she nodded. *Leave it to Everly to voice the same question that kept pulling me up short.* Averting my gaze, I rubbed the back of my neck. *Was* it actually possible for a vampire to abstain from human blood on purpose? I thought back to last night, and the vampire's face surfaced in my memory.

Beyond the classical good looks I pretended didn't sway me, his expression had seemed so sincere. The way he pleaded for my understanding… Even when he threatened to leave me in chains, there was something about it that gave me the impression he was strangely…lonely.

When I'd barked back at him, he'd only hesitated for the briefest moment before remorse won out over his obvious frustration. Of course, he'd probably been around for ages, so maybe he was just a great actor. Less confusing memories were suddenly catapulted to the forefront, of the broken victims my family and I had found over the years.

The bodies drained of blood, missing persons finally found, but too late. *That* was the reality, not some pretty story cooked up by a bored, psychopathic monster who probably just wanted to mess with a young vampire hunter.

"Nope," I answered at last, but my teeth clenched when Everly smiled. She promised she wasn't telepathic, but the way she seemed to *know* what I was really feeling surpassed even our close friendship. That, or my face was obvious. Clearing my throat, I stood and brushed the dust off my jeans. "I'm going to find out where he's holed up, decapitate his undead ass, and then have a sweet bonfire out in the desert." Easier said than done.

"And how are you planning to do that?" Everly's amusement shifted to curiosity. At least she wasn't worried that I couldn't handle myself. Granted, Everly had never seen a vampire before, let alone fought one. Still, the faith in me was nice.

"I heard a train pass by right when he drove off the driveway and onto the road," I explained, motivated by my singular clue. "It only took about fifteen minutes to get back to Richmond Drive. All I have to do is map out the city's train routes in relation to anywhere fifteen minutes away from the warehouse." I *had* picked up a thing or two from my family.

Everly's eyes widened appreciatively. "That sounds like a lot of work."

"Yep, but I know just where to start," I said, and my grin slowly strengthened.

"And where's that?" Everly played along, biting her lip to keep from smiling.

"The library."

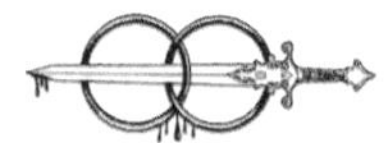

I probably could have gotten all the same information at home using my computer. Except that ran the risk of my family popping in on me unexpectedly, and the last thing I wanted to do was skirt more questions with outright lies. It was easier for everyone if I kept the plan between me and Everly, for now. Because she'd already proven to me that what happened last year—what I'd *done*—hadn't killed her respect for me as a person.

She'd been there for me through every way-too-long message I sent her during my recovery process last summer. Even a few thousand miles apart, her responses were a hell of a lot more supportive than how my ex-boyfriend handled my rehab admission. *That* relationship imploded well before I'd gotten out. Good riddance, my family had said. After what had happened, I didn't blame them.

Not like I'd have been able to tell my ex the truth about me, anyway.

I drummed my thumb on my faded steering wheel, patiently waiting at a traffic-heavy red light, but my depressive thoughts were more draining than the stop-and-go. The only person 'in the know' outside of my family, and the Tsosies, was Everly. After she announced her veganism when we were sixteen, I grew progressively more guilty about her passionate soap-boxing over my family's 'hunting excursions.'

It wore me down so much that I just blurted out the truth to her. At first, I thought she might call me crazy and storm out of my bedroom *and* my life altogether. I hadn't counted on her having a secret of her own—that she practiced witchcraft. Telling the truth had brought us closer together, each other's first true confidantes outside of our blood relatives.

That friendship was priceless, which might've had something to do with why my two ex-boyfriends and one ex-girlfriend were so jealous of it. Lying to them about my weekend activities sucked, but a part of me, deep down, always felt that they wouldn't have understood it. Knowing that things wouldn't progress beyond a 'good time' was what hurt the most.

My designated therapist at the rehab center had 'inferred' that my issues with substance abuse stemmed from an inability to form deeper connections with others. In layman's terms, I had *trust issues*—big whoop. The rest of my family, and the Tsosies, kept the same secrets but never failed as hard as I had.

I cut the engine to my car in the Main Library's back parking lot. Breathing out a sigh, I closed my eyes while the car's internal heat climbed from a lack of air conditioning under the New Mexico sun. *What the hell was I doing?* Hiding things from my family was a *great* way to earn back their trust.

My eyes opened as I snorted, and flung open the car's door to exit. One way or another, I needed to research the railroad lines to get a lead. Whatever I found out, I would take the information back to my family and fess up—*today.* The brick canopy above the library's entrance kept the double glass doors shaded, cooling my neck as I yanked open one side.

I inhaled the familiar scent of aged paper, and my shoulders lowered an inch. It'd been a while since I'd come here, at least a few weeks now. Honestly, I missed the days spent catching up on my fiction reading list. Those were the only books I could stand, the ones with inevitable happy endings where the bad guys got what was coming to them. As long as it never veered into the realm of blood-sucking or necromancy.

The pull toward the 'Mysteries' aisle was tantalizing, but I made an effort to head for the 'Local References' sign board in the far corner beside the boring non-fiction section. My focus trailed across the spines, until *Railroads and Railroad Towns in New Mexico* caught my eye.

I pulled down several resources, figuring I'd cross-check the established roads with the ones currently in service. *That* I could search for on the library's computers. If that didn't work, then I should at least be able to estimate which railway lines were active between Friday nights to the early hours on Saturdays—and make an educated guess about where they were in relation to the warehouse on Richmond Drive.

On my way to the circular tables in the middle of the floor, I stopped mid-step. My attention landed on a well-read classic by my favorite author. *The Hound of the Baskervilles* poked out from the section bearing all of Sir Arthur Conan Doyle's works. The computer bank was only around the next bend... *It couldn't hurt to take a break for a few minutes, right?* I set down my stack of books to snatch up the novel off the shelf.

Exhaling in delight, I sank to the floor beside my self-assigned reading material. Only one chapter, then I'd get back to my research. Except that turned into two, and by then the story was getting good. My gaze roved over the fine print as the pages flew between my fingers.

Until a disembodied woman's voice spoke over the intercom, *"The Main Library will be closing in thirty minutes."*

"Shit!" I hissed, my spine cracking when I finally straightened up and looked out the nearest window. The sun had descended considerably, but welcome rays still brightened the space. Grimacing, I glanced at the stack of books on railroads. I hadn't even cracked one open. In a huff, I stood to replace the novel in hand. I could check out my books before closing, and verify information on the internet at home, even if I had to sneak the material into my bedroom—

"A Doyle fan. I should have presumed such from your inability to leave well enough alone." The voice came from the other side of the shelves, deep and rich with his Eastern European accent. Startled stock-still, I slowly lowered my hand.

This could *not* be happening.

Pulse racing, my fingertips touched the handle of my machete. My eyes narrowed, tracking a tall silhouette's movements as he strode up the next aisle, only to casually stroll around the bend of shelves.

"What the *hell* are you doing here?" I demanded in a whisper.

"What has the world come to that a vampire is no longer allowed to move freely as he pleases?" His response was almost inaudible, but the gentle smirk that graced his shadowed lips was obvious.

"It's light out," I remarked, grasping at straws for my reasoning—hang on, *I* wasn't the one being questioned! If the out-of-state baseball cap and large-framed black sunglasses he wore was any indication, he was well aware of the time. Paired with his black leather jacket and dark-washed jeans, barely any of his skin was in direct sunlight.

Under the fluorescents, his human illusion remained intact while he strode closer, brandishing a book in one hand—*The Da Vinci Code* by Dan Brown.

"I happen to be here for the same purpose as you, I suspect. Checking out a book." His dark eyes glanced down at the stack of literature behind me, but I didn't dare turn to follow his gaze. Instead, I squared my shoulders, and he murmured, "A detective, indeed."

"You didn't think I'd give up that easily, right?" I shot back, irritated by his handsome face—his expression *way* too relaxed, considering the sharp object resting against my hip. If we weren't in a public place, I'd have drawn my weapon on sight.

"Truthfully, no. Though I did hope that your animosity would ebb somewhat with my confessions." The slight smile on his lips grew taunting, and my face warmed.

"You may have let me go, but that doesn't mean you don't hurt people," I muttered, but my brow furrowed. Here he was, right before me, and all he could muster up in the face of my conquest to kill him was *amusement*?

"I assure you that I do not. In fact…" He leaned in, and a narrow ray of dying sunlight fell across his striking features. His ordinarily pale complexion thinned, tinged to gray across his cheek which hollowed beneath the sun's rays. Skin stretched taut over his sharp cheekbone, and I swallowed. Behind his sunglasses, his eyes turned bloodshot until streaks of red dominated the white sclera. I refused to let him unsettle me— "I wager that I can prove it to you."

"What?" I staggered back a step, almost tripping over my stack of books. "And why the hell would I believe you?"

"Because the truth is rather more convincing than my word alone," he answered. When I kept my mouth closed, the vampire's gaze flickered between me and the railroad research. "It would also prove more fruitful than your foolish errand to attempt to locate my whereabouts through sleuthing."

"I'll take my chances," I retorted, mentally kicking myself for having such a mediocre comeback. Especially when it seemed to only make him smile wider—revealing the points of his canines until the sun dipped an inch further, and we stood in the shadows together.

"In that case, I wish you luck." He tipped the edge of his cap, like some old-fashioned gentlemen. "Until next time, Maria." The way my name rolled off his tongue sent unexpected shivers up my spine—the kind I associated with sensing a vampire's bloodlust. Except this time it felt…different.

Before I could do more than open my mouth an inch, he strode past me. I felt a brush against my hip, but by the time I fully spun to follow him, his silhouette had disappeared around the corner. Heart racing, face red, and brain a discombobulated mess of frustration, I jumped when the lady on the intercom echoed throughout.

"The Main Library will be closing in twenty minutes."

Scrambling, I picked up my night's reading material and hurried through the library. It took an annoying amount of time to check them out, waiting on several others who didn't decide which books to take home until the last minute. Foot tapping, I chewed on the inside of my cheek while the librarian stamped my books one at a time before scanning them out.

Finally out the door, and far too late to determine which direction the vampire might have gone from here, I trudged up the sidewalk toward my parked car. When I fished into my back pocket for my keys, I found something else that wasn't there before. A piece of folded paper came out with my clattering car keys.

Confused, I manually unlocked my three-decades old car and shoved the thick railways books onto my passenger seat. The door thumped closed while I hurried to unfold the note. Written in scrawling cursive that reminded me of signatures on the Declaration of Independence, a phone number was inscribed above two words—

'Call me.'

— 5 —

MASK OF LIES

YEAH, LIKE I WAS GOING TO FALL FOR SUCH AN OBVIOUS TRAP, WERE MY thoughts for the last eight days. Now that I was surrounded by scattered pages of printed railway maps and pencils reduced to nubs from using my high school math compass, I was starting to reconsider. Apparently, my naivety knew no bounds.

It'd been easy to figure out that whichever train had passed through at close to two in the morning last Saturday *hadn't* been on any of the public transit routes. A quick look-see at the Alvarado Transportation Center confirmed that. What they *couldn't* answer was which train might have been on a set of unknown tracks in a vague, general vicinity of where I described when I couldn't even tell them which direction the train might have been going.

Explaining that I'd been blindfolded at the time, acting like it was some dumb prank I'd agreed to, had only earned me the classic side-eye while the conductors clearly thought I was losing it.

Then there was the fact that any trains carrying cargo claimed by a private enterprise were not strictly public knowledge. Something about 'preventing terrorist attacks.' Because I didn't have a badge or laminated card to show off—and it's not like I could *charm* them into divulging information like a vampire could—I was shit out of luck. As it turned out, I was as useless at the research as I was when fighting the undead bastard.

Our brief conversation at the library replayed in my head, and I bit my lower lip. His cocky attitude, certain of my impending failure, was at odds with the pleas he'd made for my cooperation back in his 'house.' It could have been the lower level of an apartment, for all I knew. Frustrated, I crumpled up the papers detailing types of trains by the sounds they made. I chucked the wad at my growing wastepaper basket.

Brow furrowed, I sucked on my teeth and glanced at the note by my sock-clad feet. I still hadn't consulted my family about this dilemma. Mostly because I wanted to prove to that irksome bloodsucker that he shouldn't underestimate me. The least I could do was find his address before fessing up to my family…

Days of reconnaissance throughout the city left my eyes tired from driving and my brain in shambles with growing despair. No matter where I went, which train tracks I followed, I couldn't recognize a damn thing. Even when I retraced the turns I thought the vampire had made when he drove me back to the warehouse, I'd only ended up on I-25 going south into nowhere.

Based on how long it took to drive me back, he couldn't possibly live further out… This city wasn't even that freaking big, and I was still stumped. I rubbed at my aching temples while glaring at the note. *'Call me'*—what a cliché. Snorting to cover my annoyance, I snatched up my cell phone and dialed the damn number. The worst that could happen was that it was a fake.

At least, that's when I thought he wasn't actually going to pick up.

"Hello?" An Eastern European accent, thick like he'd just been woken up, spoke out of my receiver. Seconds ticked by, my breath held, and then I closed my eyes.

"Hi," I said, voice tight, and waited—but not for long.

"Ah, Maria." His tone turned amused, and the way he said my name—like we were old friends or something—made me dig up the memory of our exchange in his car.

"Drake," I replied, perfunctory, and he had the gall to chuckle.

"I am pleased you telephoned, though I assumed you would be unable to resist the mystery." Rustling crackled over the receiver, like he was getting out of bed, and I glanced at my window. Of course, it was the middle of the afternoon. The sunlight might not kill them, but they're a hell of a lot less conspicuous in the dark.

"Where are you?" I asked, straight to the point and hoping he'd divulge either out of boredom or over-confidence.

"Was your reading material insufficient?" Drake shot back, and I wrinkled my nose.

"Fine, you got me," I admitted, flushing as the back of my neck warmed, and I stood to pace my bedroom.

"Think of it this way," he said, and I frowned at his bemused timbre, "you must have developed extensive knowledge on a subject you would not have otherwise given its due time."

"If trains bored me before then it'll be too soon if I never read about another one," I snapped, and mentally kicked myself. Why the hell did he get a rise out of me so easily? It was worse than with Andrew, who always treated me unfairly compared to his brother and sister. With Drake... My pride took a hit every time I was forced to acknowledge he might be right. Even if he did laugh at my snark.

"Perhaps now you will reconsider my suggestion," he said, and hesitated. "I may not tell you my residential address, but I can offer my whereabouts for this evening."

"So you can lure me into a dark alley?" My eyebrows pulled together. "I don't think so."

"It is a well-lit, public space, I assure you."

I inhaled deeply, glancing at my closed door, locked from the inside. It's not like I couldn't verify the address on my phone, but if it's around people then it'll be a double-edged sword. He might not be able to cart me off so easily, but I also couldn't behead him if I got the chance. Since I wasn't any kind of government personnel that could trace phone calls, I had no other options to get to the bottom of this. *Unless I admitted to my family that I'd lied…*

"Fine," I said through an exhale, and my pacing stilled. "Where?"

"A pub in the city. Its signpost reads 'Two Fools Tavern.'" He almost sounded relieved, or I was imagining the way his accented voice softened. "I will arrive at seven o'clock. As long as you are alone, I will meet with you."

"Why are you doing this, anyway?" I asked, genuinely too confused to feel conflicted.

"Because," he said, as serious as the first night we met, "I rather enjoy residing in this city. If I prove to you that I am not a threat, then I will not be forced to leave." Melancholy laced his words, and I blinked unseeingly at my window.

"Okay," I stammered. "Tonight, then."

"I look forward to it." His tone returned to its normal, unfortunately attractive cadence—like he didn't have a care in the world—a moment before the call ended.

The phone beeped while I pulled it away, and then stared down at my bright screen until it faded to black. What the hell had I just agreed to? Pulse beating fast, I ran a hand through my curly hair, and resumed my pacing. Suddenly, it was like the room didn't have enough air in it. So I yanked on my boots, fastened my machete to my hip, and headed out.

One arm was through the sleeve of my gray jacket—a sad replacement for my lost denim one—when I stopped short in the doorway. The lingering smell of smoke wafted up the hall, from where the stained-glass window at the end was cracked open. Rolling my eyes, I walked down until I stood before Ethan's closed door at the very end, nearly opposite Olivia's.

While Olivia's bedroom door had a flowery embroidered sign with her name on it, Ethan's was plain except for the scratches across its front from when we practiced throwing knives as kids. A deep sniff confirmed my suspicions, and I pounded on Ethan's door. The loud rock music playing inside cut off a moment before it opened.

"Yes?" His thick dirty blond hair stood on end, wet from a recent shower, and he pushed his square-framed glasses up his straight nose. Crystal blue-gray eyes stared back, innocent enough, but I knew better. My lips pursed when I leaned into his room, pointedly glancing at the smoking ashtray propped on his open window sill.

"You really should stop doing that, or at least take it outside," I chided, and Ethan snorted. While he backed into his room, I hovered at the doorway.

"You sound like Liv," he remarked, and I shrugged.

"Maybe you should kick the whole smoking thing altogether. You wouldn't want to end up like me." The comment was ridiculous in truth. It didn't take cigarettes to get me into the harder stuff, since I'd never actually smoked—tobacco, anyway.

"Duly noted." Nonchalant, Ethan lifted his smoking cigarette to his lips and took a drag. Staring me dead in the eye, he exhaled a cloud of smoke and said, "So what's got you all riled up?"

My back straightened. "What?"

"That line between your eyebrows is going to permanently wrinkle if you don't get over whatever's bothering you." He rocked back to sit in his desk chair, poised before three monitors and a desktop computer thicker than my thigh—and I wasn't skinny. Stifling a frown, I rubbed at the spot above the small bump in my nose ridge.

"What do you care?" I asked, diminished, and Ethan shrugged, turning to face his many screens.

"I don't. It'll only make me look better by association in our family photos."

"Fine." I sighed, racking my brain for a way to make any of this shit translatable without fessing up. "I just agreed to see a guy I met at the library." *Technically, all true.*

"He must be pretty boring if he hangs around the library." Ethan pulled up a game on his computer, his gaze focused.

"He's pretty damn interesting, actually," I piped up, and then blinked. Why the hell was I defending him? No, I was arguing for my *obsession* with getting payback from the vampire. That was it.

"You gonna go on your date dressed like that?" Ethan glanced over his shoulder, his stare disapproving, and then returned his attention to his first-person-shooter game.

"What's wrong with it?" I looked down at myself. A white T-shirt and denim jeans was classic 'me.'

"It's a bit bland for meeting up with such an 'interesting' guy." Ethan's short laugh clued me into his teasing, and I rolled my eyes.

"Stop smoking in the house, or I'm telling Olivia," I warned, and Ethan grinned over his shoulder, displaying a sliver of the *Metallica* print on his T-shirt.

"No, you won't. Close the door, thanks, Maria."

Before I had a chance to build up any steam for a good comeback, we both flinched at the sound of Aunt Susan's voice calling down the hall.

"Ethan! The washing needs hanging up. I'm going out for groceries, have it done before I'm back!" Her words were followed by the kitchen door closing shut, the closest path to the little parking lot out back where we kept our cars. A grin spread across my lips when Ethan sulked, hurriedly putting out his cigarette so his mom wouldn't see the smoke while she was outside.

Grumbling to himself, he passed me in the hall with a grimace. As he turned into the doorway for the kitchen, I couldn't help but look down at my zipped-up jacket and jeans. The combat boots were a must, but if I was really going out on reconnaissance—to a bar, no less—maybe Ethan had a point and I should work harder to blend in.

What the hell did people who drank on Sunday nights usually wear? Car keys in hand, I ditched my idea to scope out the location ahead of time. Butterflies tumbled in my stomach for absolutely no reason. *What the hell was I doing...*

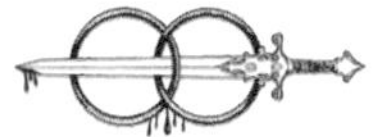

The Sun Pointe Apartments complex where my best friend lived wasn't new, as evidenced by its faded beige exterior under the harsh Albuquerque sunshine. Heat hit my face first when I exited my Taurus, forcing me to shade my eyes with my palm. Squinting, I strode up to the light blue door on the ground level.

Identical windows rested on either side, the blinds drawn, but a black cat lounged on the sill to the right. Since it was still light out, I didn't worry about banging on the door to make sure I'd be heard over the heavy music playing inside. I scoffed at myself while I stood, waiting.

Because I shouldn't have let Ethan's comment get to me. Especially since it was *so* far from a 'date' that it wasn't even funny. Who cared how I dressed? Oddly, my thoughts turned to the vampire—Drake, if that was even his real name. What the hell did going to a bar have to do with proving his innocence?

If he thought he'd be able to slip a sedative into my glass, then he would be sorely disappointed—emphasis on the 'sore.'

The door opened, pulling me from my internal concerns into external reality. Equally worrying considering the bright smile plastered across Everly's freckled face.

"Hi," she said, stepping aside so I could escape the slow sunburn to my neck.

"Hey," I replied, a bit stiff while I glanced around.

The place was cozy, with a brown suede couch and boxy television that I'd help Everly carry in two weeks ago. Although her roommate had been living here for a few months, the tall goth woman was exceptionally minimalist. At least, she hadn't deigned to decorate anything outside of her bedroom.

By the sly expression on Everly's heart-shaped face, the direction of her thoughts was obvious. With Olivia at work putting together bouquets made of flowers or fruits, and Andrew inside the church this afternoon—lurking around for someone to annoy, probably—my phone call with Everly had to be brief before I left, giving her the same vague story I'd told Ethan.

Which meant that my best friend thought she was helping me get ready for a date. Oh, how this would really put a rock in her cauldron, or whatever modern witches used.

"Listen—" I started, but promptly stopped when the music cut off, and the door at the end of the hall opened.

Dressed all in black, sporting a *Type-O Negative* T-shirt, Addison Dawkins emerged from her room. Short black hair shifted along her defined jawline, framing her extremely pale face where silver piercings reflected light off her lips and nose. Hazel eyes lazily glanced my way before she disappeared behind the partition which hosted the kitchenette.

Everly opened her mouth, probably about to loop in Addison, and anybody that would listen, about my epic conquest for love.

"Come with me," I said, grasping Everly's hand and pulling her up the short hallway.

Across from the full bathroom was Everly's room, small compared to mine, but she still managed to cram a million books on witchcraft into the space. Once inside, with Everly gamely following along, I closed the door behind us and exhaled. My gaze found Everly's bright green eyes, and her smile vanished.

"What's wrong?"

"I couldn't tell you about it over the phone, but I'm not 'going out' going out tonight," I said, and dropped my voice to a whisper. "I'm meeting with the vampire."

"What?" Everly took a step back, her eyes widening as she plopped down onto her turquoise bedspread. "The one that gave you his phone number? You finally called him!" A hint of righteous glee returned to her voice, and I groaned.

"Alright, yeah, all of my research tanked so I went with Plan B," I bemoaned, shuffling over to drop into Everly's white desk chair. Swiveling back and forth, I rubbed my temples. "It's probably a huge mistake, but I agreed to meet him at some bar tonight."

"A bar? Sounds cozy," Everly chimed in. When I glared, she giggled. "Come on, you're the one who agreed to meet with him, so why the long face?"

"Because I still haven't told my family what really happened," I said, grumpy, and Everly's vindicated teasing eased into sympathy.

"Then why are you here, talking to me? It's not like I can be your backup, or whatever it is your family could contribute to a hunt."

"That's the thing, strictly speaking, I'm not going *hunting* tonight." Face hot, I straightened up in the desk chair. "Stupidly, I sort of agreed to hear him out."

"Wow, that's a bit of a change in tune," Everly said, her short legs absently kicking the air, several inches above the patterned rug she'd laid over the tiled floor. "What do you think you'll do, if he's telling the truth, after all?"

"I don't know…" *Truthfully*, I couldn't even conceive that outcome. The only thing I had any mental effort to focus on was—

"But I-I've never dressed up to go to a bar. Or a 'pub,' as he called it. What's even the difference?"

"Pubs usually serve food, too." Everly nodded wisely, but I wasn't surprised by her sage knowledge. She'd met more foreigners in her lifetime, moving around as often as her family had. Suddenly, she clapped, startling me. A suspiciously satisfied smile pulled at the corners of her full lips. "Never fear, Maria. There's no way I'd let a friend go anywhere without dressing their best."

I nearly choked. "I have my doubts about slipping into any of your clothes, Eve." Her flat chest and narrow hips meant she still fit into outfits from our high school days. I, on the other hand, got my curves from Mom and height from Johann—Dad, whatever. The mental distinction made me frown, but Everly must have thought I was still mulling over my clothing conundrum.

"Oh, don't worry. I've got an idea." Everly hopped off the bed, her strides jaunty on her way to open the door. She peeked out into the hall, and called out toward the front door, "Hey, Addison? Do you have any dresses that Maria could borrow for the night?"

The blood drained from my face as Addison's quiet footsteps preceded her appearance at Everly's doorway.

"Uh, sure, I guess. What's the occasion?"

6

CHIN HELD HIGH

EYES CLOSED, I STRUGGLED NOT TO FIDGET WHILE SEATED ATOP THE TOILET'S lid. My nose itched, but I didn't dare scratch it while Everly swiped eyeliner above my lashes. When I sensed her take a step back, I scrunched my nose and blinked hard.

"Don't do that! It'll smudge," Everly admonished, clicking her tongue in disapproval while she held my chin around the dimple to keep my head straight.

"Why am I even letting you do this?" I asked, not for the first time, and peeked through my eyelashes as Everly turned away.

"Because you usually never let me and I couldn't pass up the opportunity." She winked at me, then puckered her lips like I was meant to mimic it. So I did, rolling my eyes which felt heavier with all the product clumped on. Once she was done applying something to my lips, she smacked hers and I followed suit.

"It's not like *I've* ever had the opportunity, either," I said, a bit sullen at the turn of conversation.

"Exactly, because you only date *losers*." Everly huffed, oddly peeved. True, in hindsight, my ex partners were less than stellar. I squirmed at the uncomfortable thought. Like it was my fault that I picked the worst people for me. My gaze quickly settled on hers in challenge.

"Right, and your usual dating pool is what? Princesses?" I scoffed, but Everly grinned like she had a secret.

"Don't forget, there was that one lady I was talking to online who said her father was an oil baron. That's basically the same thing these days."

"And I remember that one ending *so* well," I said, vindicated, but Everly shrugged. Her face fell, and I internally winced at my teasing comment. Even if she had started it. "I'm sorry—"

"Our petty dating disasters aside," she cut in, focusing on my curly hair while she ran her fingers through it with some kind of gel-like substance, "the *point* was that you never let me doll you up for a night out. So I'm taking advantage of it."

"Yes, because if the vampire tries to maul me then at least I'll look fabulous." I smiled wide, and Everly smirked. Seconds ticked by while she worked, but a glance at my watch revealed I had plenty of time, too much, really. Weird tumbles started in my stomach, like moths made of acid. Nervous, I picked at my plain fingernails for something to do.

"Have I told you that I'm talking to someone lately?" Everly piped up, surprising me.

"Uh, no. Who?"

Considering the blush spreading across Everly's freckled face, it was probably more serious than her tone let on.

"Just a woman I met at Humble Coffee the other day. She's super pretty, and totally took an interest in my Wicca stuff right away. The first thing she told me was that my pentagram earrings were cute." Everly's smile turned shy, and guilt swelled in my gut. How long had I been hogging every phone call with Everly that I didn't know she had met someone new?

I forced my expression to brighten. "What's her name?"

"Courtney. And she's super mysterious, too. I hardly know her but there's been absolutely none of that 'new relationship' awkwardness," Everly rambled, practically glowing. "She's got connections all over the place, too. She promised to take me to that up-and-coming nightclub—you know the one on Central Avenue? There's a line a block long on weekend nights, but we have plans for tomorrow. And she's so cool, she even said that I could bring friends!"

"That's generous," I remarked, barely getting a word in.

"Yeah, do you want to go, or—Oh, um, I'm sorry." Everly bit her lip, face flushed, and my hands stilled on my lap. Like she was embarrassed to have brought it up, her attention fell to the sink where she started packing away her makeup.

"Eve, I'm going to a *bar* tonight. I can handle being around alcohol," I assured, but her bright green eyes were full of uncertainty.

"That's true, I just didn't want to overstep… I remember how you told me you liked to avoid those places on principle—"

"Because I usually end up at night clubs for work, not partying." I exhaled a dry laugh, glad I skirted the words 'hunt' and 'vampire' when there was a knock on the bathroom door.

"We're decent," Everly said, and cleared her throat. Did everyone in my life not trust my word anymore? Discomfited, I stood as Addison opened the door and held out a black length of fabric.

"This is all I could scrounge up without spikes or rips in it, as requested." She handed it over, and Everly cooed at it while holding it up by the straps. Personally, I was dumbfounded.

"Is it still folded up?" I asked, taking the dress when it was offered only to realize that, no, this was the entire length. While holding it up against my bust, I doubted it would cover all of my ass. "This is a shirt."

"It's a dress," Addison stated in monotone, her deadpan stare on my frazzled shock. I swallowed, not wanting to be ungrateful, and Everly shooed Addison out the door.

"Try it on and see how it looks," Everly squealed at me, stepping outside just as her black cat, Bast, rushed into the bathroom meowing her head off. About to argue, I raised my hand to get Everly's attention, but she was too focused on closing the door to the hall.

It clicked shut and, alone except for the feline, I breathed a sigh. Would it be really rude to only pretend I'd tried it on? Maybe marginally better than if I refused it outright... Except curiosity got the best of me, especially when I glimpsed my face in the mirror's reflection. Glitzed and glammed was an understatement. I looked like I was being preened for the prom night I never attended.

Ignoring the silver eyeshadow and dark eyeliner, plus the oddly shiny lips I pressed together, I frowned at the outfit. How was I supposed to get the *thing* on? A handy zipper down the side let me shimmy it up, barely making it over my hips, eons wider than Addison's skinny frame. Somehow, the material managed to stretch to cover my butt and then some.

Then came the question of my machete. Since there weren't any belt loops, I shrugged and strapped it tight around my waist. It wasn't unusual to see weapons on a person's hip this far South. Counting it as an accessory, I bobbed my head at my reflection. Weirdly enough, I liked it. The dress contoured my curves, pushing up my braless breasts to create way more cleavage than I could attain naturally.

There was a soft tap on the door. "How's it going?" Everly called out, and my shoulders slumped. Right, I wasn't *actually* going on a date.

This was too ridiculous, even for me. Forget trying to 'blend in' with the regular weekend night crowd. The vampire would have to deal with my T-shirt and jeans. I was about to unzip the dress, and then hastily wash off the makeup, when Bast started scratching at the door. Mewing like I'd been holding her hostage for the last five minutes, she darted out the second I cracked the exit open.

"Oh my goddess!" Everly shrieked, placing a hand over her heart while she stared me up and down. Panicked, I tugged down the dress' hem.

"I was about to take it off," I mumbled, my face burning when Everly stepped into the bathroom to get the full three-sixty degree view.

"No way!" she hissed, like I'd suggested we skin her cat. "You look so good! There's no way you can *not* wear this tonight."

"But I'm meeting with the vampire!" I whispered, voice straining, and Everly waved a hand like that was a small, unimportant detail.

"Isn't this way better, though? Think about it, he'll be easy pickings if he's too distracted by how hot you look." Everly's gaze roamed from my face to my bust appreciatively, like she took personal validation in gussying me up.

"You're crazy. I'm getting changed, help unzip me—"

Before I could turn to give her access, Addison called from down the hall, "What time did you say you had to be there, Maria?"

"Seven!" I called back, grateful for the hour I'd have left to get unready.

"Uh, you should probably start going, then," she replied, her slim frame appearing outside the bathroom door, and her pencil-thin eyebrows furrowed.

"It's only five-forty," I said, glancing down at the chunky watch on my wrist. Confused, I squeaked when Addison showed me her phone. "What!"

"Daylight Savings happened last night," Everly said, her voice small and eyes wide when I whirled on her. "We sprung forward, I thought you knew…"

"Shit!" I stomped out of the bathroom, rushing to don my cotton jacket—crazily matching my ensemble from my black boots to my backpack purse. "Okay, I've gotta go. How do I look?" Breathless, I faced Everly and Addison. The former brimming with delight while the latter hung back in the hall.

"Like you're wearing makeup," Addison commented, her expression bland, and I gave her a 'come on' look.

"You look *great*," Everly assured, and then her voice dropped to a whisper. "Are you nervous?"

"Not nearly as much as I should be," I admitted, a hand on the door while Everly scooped up her midnight cat to keep her inside the cooled apartment. Silence descended, and I suddenly felt tongue-tied about how to leave things. "I'll call you when it's done, okay?"

"Good luck." Everly nodded, beaming, and I turned heel to rush out the door.

Traffic would be annoying. Teeth gritted, I hopped into my car in record time. The Taurus' engine hummed as I waited to merge onto Montgomery Boulevard, but I hesitated. It wasn't too late to call my family. We could plan an ambush while I distracted the vampire for who knew how long—

'*I didn't want to overstep,*' Everly's words drifted back, circling in my head only to grow louder alongside my family's criticisms. The eggshells they all walked on around me… Hurt, conflicted, but mostly determined to prove them wrong, I stepped on the accelerator.

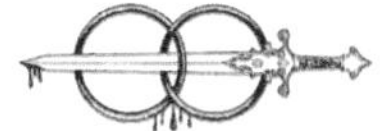

The low rumble of my idling engine cut off. Silence surrounded me in the parking lot, but it felt strange to be parked in my usual spot at my old haunt on Central Avenue. The Cold Stone Creamery's red neon sign illuminated the sidewalk, contrasting the blue exterior of the Two Fools Tavern four lanes away. I'd never glanced twice at the pub across the street before today.

Inhaling deep, I flipped down my sun visor to give myself a once-over in the mirror. The effects of Everly's craftsmanship were marred by my grimace in the face of all that makeup. My eyes closed. I would just have to accept that I'd be sorely over-dressed for tonight.

Why the hell did I let Ethan's snide teasing, and Everly's eagerness to play dress up, get the best of me? The whole thing was so silly, immature, and I stalled by double-checking that I stowed my wallet in the glovebox, along with my phone, before leaving my purse on the passenger seat.

Sure, being without a way to call for help might have left most people a sitting duck, but I wasn't most people. My machete's sheath bumped against my hip as I stepped out of the car. At least my address and my family's contact numbers were safely out of the vampire's reach.

The car locked with a twist of my key as I turned—and nearly jumped out of my skin. Standing a foot away was none other than the undead man himself. Dressed in a simple black button-up shirt beneath his leather jacket and dark-washed jeans, he looked like any other middle class white guy.

It was the sheen across his pallor that gave him away, silvery and ashen, almost anemic. Dark circles bruised beneath his almost black eyes contrasted the slight smile quirking up the corners of his mouth. Like he was trying to hold back his amusement. My whole being warmed with chagrin as I met his gaze, but I kept my back straight.

"Don't *do* that," I said in a huff. Drake's gaze momentarily wandered from my face, and I zipped my jacket higher to cover my chest, readying myself for whatever insulting opinion he might have—

"Apologies, I simply was too impressed to purposefully make noise on my approach," he said, and I blinked. *Was that a com-*

pliment? "Although admittedly, I am partial toward your ordinarily scrappy appearance."

A laugh bubbled up my throat, escaping before I could squash the insane hilarity of this situation. It was too late to turn it into a cough, but I cleared my throat all the same while Drake smiled.

"Perhaps this will return you to your roots." His grin broadened when he raised his hand, my denim jacket in his grip.

"Hey!" I snatched it from him, earning a low chuckle that reignited my ire. "I was wondering where that went. And what happened to my walkie?" I shrugged on the added layer, and suppressed a contented sigh. Feeling more right with the familiar weight on my shoulders, I swept my hair out from the collar while Drake seemed to hesitate.

"The radio?" he asked, and I nodded. His lips pressed together, almost a wince. "It broke on the trek to my domicile. I had hoped to repair it, but alas…" The vampire shrugged, and his seemingly-honest discomfort brought me up short.

"Oh." Not like I'd expected to get it back. When I shifted, a puff of air rose from my denim jacket. It smelled nice, clean in a way I'd never gotten out of my washing machine. *Had he had it dry-cleaned?* Baffled, but refusing to lower my guard, I frowned.

"I was wrong," he said softly, his attention flickering to my midriff before rising to my eyes. "Any attire suits you."

"You're not gonna convince me of anything with flattery," I retorted, but my voice quavered, and he inclined his head in a dignified nod.

"Alas, I promised proof, and so I shall deliver." With a hand extended toward the Two Fools Tavern across the street, he stepped aside. "As is the custom in this country, ladies first."

7

BETTER NOT TOUCH

WARMTH HIT MY ALREADY FLUSHED FACE AS I ENTERED THE PUB, AND glanced over my shoulder at Drake. He'd held the door open for me, and his brief smirk when our gazes met only left me more confused. *He sure did seem self-assured*, but how was a bar full of people going to prove his innocence? Which was a bit of an understatement because this place was *packed*.

Drake walked in, hot on my heels, and the draft from outside disappeared when the door swung shut. Goosebumps crept up my arms while his raven-dark eyes stared into mine for one long moment. Before I had a chance to voice my disbelief at his chosen setting for our meet-up, a deep voice called out.

"Finally made it, Drake!" Hurriedly wiping down the bartop, a middle-aged man with shoulder-length salt-and-pepper hair accompanying a matching beard nodded at us. "Brought a friend?"

"Dire enemy, more like," Drake replied, his smile wide and oddly inviting. It took effort not to gape at how different his attitude was tonight compared to when we first met. Not a shred of animosity or annoyance lingered on Drake's face—even when he looked at me. "Come along, I assure the patrons here do not bite." Cramped as we were, side by side in the entryway, his leather jacket's sleeve brushed my arm when he directed me to go ahead.

"Yeah, yeah," I mumbled, feeling like a fish out of water while I waded past tall tables and the people clustered around them. Everyone held either a glass or snack food in hand—mostly some variety of a chip, fry, or peanut. My stomach rumbled when I passed a full plate of nachos being set down between a group watching some sport on one of the TVs. Thankfully, there was too much noise all around for my gurgling belly to turn any heads.

On our way through the throng, I was forced to stop several times because someone had stolen Drake's attention. He'd turn to offer them a polite greeting or question about their daily lives while I kept a few steps between us, so that nobody thought we were together. If I had to be introduced to anyone else as a 'dire enemy,' I was going to unsheath my machete.

Still, Drake's gaze always reconnected with mine after a few exchanges of conversation. With a parting word, he'd leave one person only to be caught by another a short distance later. Now I understood why he kept ushering us further back, deeper into the pub and away from the hustle and bustle. Already, sweat beaded my neck and chest from the oppressive body heat accompanying the delicious smells wafting from a kitchen in the back.

I shrugged off my jackets as we reached a lone table in the far corner. It was quiet compared to the rest of the place. Maybe because it was the designated 'make out zone,' judging by the couples nearby. A sign for the toilets was pictured with little stick figures, and a couple giggled before they went inside, hurriedly checking over their shoulder like they thought they were being sneaky.

Nose wrinkled, I dropped my folded jackets down on one of the high chairs before scooting up onto its neighbor. A weird pang pulled at my heart, being surrounded by so many lovey-dovey, drunken pairs. Sure, none of them were bound to last unless they came here together in the first place, but that didn't magically erase the lonely ache in my guts.

On the other side of the table, Drake made no move to sit down, instead leaning his forearms on the surface heavily stained by glass rings. A laminated paper was pushed toward me, and I raised my eyebrows at it. When he didn't say anything, I used my index finger to swipe the menu closer.

"You seem popular," I said, watching him closely while my elbow rested over the menu. Drake shrugged, seeming unbothered while scanning the room like he was checking for the exits. *Damn it*, I should've been the one doing that.

"They are people I see here every week. Some are regulars and come each night." His dark eyes refocused on me, and I chewed the inside of my cheek. Somehow, that one sentence felt loaded.

Since I figured I was pretty safe—my back to the wall and plenty of witnesses around—I started to scrutinize the people Drake had spoken with. None of them had any visible marks, not on their necks, wrists, elbows, or anywhere else I could see. There were more discreet ways for vampires to feed, but most didn't bother—and *those* arteries rarely left the bitten alive.

So this was his 'proof' about not hurting anyone. If he could have acquaintances—or friends, if he saw them every day, like he claimed—then clearly he wasn't a threat. At least, that seemed to be where he was going with this. Frowning, I stared down at my hands, loosely clasped together, and moved them to my lap while I mulled it over.

"What would you like to drink?"

Thoroughly gripped by my thoughts, I had to look up to be sure I'd heard right. Except his accent was so distinct that I couldn't have made it up. Especially when his dark eyes bore into mine, questioning.

"Just water," I said, straightening up in my seat, and Drake nodded once, glancing at the menu.

"And for your meal?" His eyebrows rose, and I scoffed.

"I can't afford anything here." Not only because my wallet was in the car, but for the simple fact that my bank account was running dry. There was a reason I liked checking out library books. Maybe it was time to act as receptionist for the Harker Woodworking store again…

"I would be remiss to force a woman to pay her own way." Drake chuckled, like the idea of me buying my own dinner was silly. My teeth clenched, and I bristled.

"Showing off how many people you can stand to get to know, and offering to buy me dinner doesn't change anything." I met his stare without blinking. The implication of his words appeared to finally dawn on him since Drake's smile vanished. Quickly replaced by innocent dismay, the same expression he wore that first night we met. Maybe I wasn't the only one feeling the pressure of tonight's outcome.

"To 'show off' was never my intention," he said, diminished and serious.

"Then how does this prove anything?" I demanded, my palm flat on the menu, but I couldn't maintain my harshness when his attitude so quickly shifted to being apologetic. My shoulders lowered a fraction while Drake seemed to consider my question.

"It does not… I simply did not wish for you to be hungry." His gaze flickered to my stomach before glancing away, like he hadn't meant to look. Just then, my gut decided to betray me with another long rumble. Face burning, I covered my abdomen.

"Oh…" All of the fight went out of me, and I looked down at the menu to hide whatever feelings crossed my face. "I guess I'll take the Macho Nachos, then—thank you." *Damn my manners.*

"I will be but a moment," Drake said quietly, and then moved away without a sound.

I awkwardly shifted in my seat while watching him head to the bar to place the order. Again, he stopped several times when a person here or there pulled him aside to chat. Something about his posture, his expression, troubled me. The more I watched, the better I understood why.

Even when his conversation partner laughed, guffawing at whatever joke or tale either they or Drake told, the same couldn't be said of him. His smile was always polite, content to be there, but missing the general ease everyone else possessed. Maybe because they were inebriated, and vampires couldn't get drunk—as far as I knew, their bodies healed too quickly to stay intoxicated.

Several minutes later, which felt like none at all, he returned carrying a glass of water and basket of nachos in one hand. In his other rested a glass of red wine, reminding me of the very thing he'd offered me that night in his house. He set the food and beverage before me, and I quickly sipped at the water to keep from scarfing down the chips on sight.

Having watched him the entire time, I didn't have to worry about my drink being poisoned. While I picked up a chip, and crunched through several more after that, Drake delicately sipped his wine. Almost like he'd bought it for the sake of it, instead of actual want.

Once I swallowed, I asked, "How come you know everyone here?"

"I come here very frequently," he admitted, and his slight smirk implied it was both an embarrassing secret and a casual fact. "On my way home most nights, I pass down Richmond Drive. Hence our meeting."

"Does the pub usually stay open past midnight?" I asked, trying for sleuth, but Drake smiled. Clearly, he saw right through my attempt to poke holes in his story.

"No, I had lingered for longer than usual to enjoy a smoke or twelve with a few regulars."

"You *are* a smoker. I knew it," I said, proud that I'd at least inferred *something* correct about him. Although his car's overflowing ashtray was a dead giveaway.

"Indeed," he remarked, almost holding back another smile before his expression turned somber. "I overheard the commotion in the warehouse, and smelled the decay of—" He glanced over the room, not to be overheard, and leaned closer an inch. "My *kind*. You may ask anyone here tonight to corroborate. Many can testify to my whereabouts prior to our original meeting. I never had any association with that 'colony.'"

"I believe you," I admitted, surprising myself just as much as him given the way his mouth hung open a moment longer. As his lips pressed together, his throat bobbed on a swallow. *Shit, should I have said that? Even if it was the truth…*

"Thank you," he said, his voice full of unexpected gratitude.

"Don't mention it," I mumbled, and took a swig of my water to avoid saying anything else. Drake's gaze trailed my movement, focusing on my half-empty glass.

"I would happily purchase a more expensive beverage for you. A cocktail, or a mixer?" He smiled, bewildering me when the gesture softened his dark eyes. "I feel like celebrating."

"I—uh, I don't drink anymore," I said, warming at my core for reasons I wouldn't acknowledge. "My, um, program frowns on it." Suddenly, he looked from me to his wine glass. Damn it, I shouldn't have mentioned that.

"Should I return this? I will not be long—"

"No—" I reached out to stop him when he started to move away. My fingers brushed over his knuckles, and he halted immediately. The contact sent a shock down my hand, through my wrist and up my arm as I flinched back. "I'm way past that stuff now, anyway. None of my family will let me live it down, but I'll be damned if I make anyone return their drink for me." My confession left me breathless, struggling to shove down the vulnerability that had bubbled up out of nowhere.

At least Drake sat down again, opposite me but strangely too close after what just happened—or maybe too far.

"They seem to care about you greatly. Your family, that is."

"How do you know?" My skepticism faded as he cleared his throat, and it clicked. "Wait, were you watching us after you dropped me off?"

"It seemed ill-advised to leave a young woman all alone on the desolate streets." Drake shrugged. "When the woman with the large knife appeared, I feared I had placed you in some peril before your familiarity became obvious."

"Laura. *They* are Elias's middle child." *Wait, he'd have no idea who Elias Tsosie was.* So used to being around people who already knew everyone else in my life, I changed tracks. "I met up with my cousin Olivia and my dad after that. Unlike *Andrew*." I rolled my eyes. "Who—even though it was *his* fault I was wandering those abandoned halls—went ahead with the burning party…" I cut myself off to gauge his reaction.

My silence must have been obvious, because Drake's easy smile turned strained, like he knew exactly what I'd been referring to.

"If you fear for my disapproval, I assure you that the disposing of murderers does not concern me." His tone was bitter, uncharacteristic from what little I knew of him. Except his ire didn't seem to be directed at me, or my family of hunters, but at the very thing I *hunted*. An odd kinship glowed in my heart, which I promptly squashed before it could make my face any redder.

"Good to know," I stammered, defenseless against his unwavering gaze. "Um, by the way, talking about things that have been 'disposed of,' you don't happen to have my lucky keychain, do you?"

"The one with the pierced beer bottle cap?" he asked, curious, and I nodded.

"That's it. I'll be wanting that back."

"Certainly," he agreed, and I waited, assuming he would produce it from thin air like he had my denim jacket. "Unfortunately, I do not have it with me."

"Damn," I grumbled, turning back to the nachos to hide my grief. "Just, don't lose it, okay? It has a lot of meaning..." Maybe it was stupid to reveal that to a potential enemy, but it wasn't like he'd care—

"Why is that?"

Really should've expected that one. My eyes closed briefly, and I inhaled a deep breath to prepare for the words about to pour out of me like a dam. Unlike the tears I refused to cry. If he wanted to know, then so be it. Everyone had a sob story.

"It's from the first beer I ever had, when I was thirteen. Olivia snuck them out of the fridge for us while my mom was in the hospital," I explained, and my gaze lowered to my glass of tasteless water. "She was gone two months later. They caught the cancer too late."

Readied for the onslaught—either pity or patronizing comments about how she's 'in a better place'—I wasn't prepared for Drake's response.

"It is unfortunate that she cannot see how beautifully her daughter has grown," he said, voice even, leaving no room to be questioned. Slowly, my gaze rose to meet his. Understanding shone behind Drake's eyes as his head tilted slightly. "That is a true tragedy."

Moisture briefly blurred my vision until I blinked it away. The only people who'd come close to empathizing were Caleb and his siblings, but none of us liked bringing up the topic of our dead mothers. Elias had had to raise three kids into adulthood after his wife, Rosa, passed suddenly from a car accident.

It wasn't like Mom's death. Isabelle De Loera-Harker had died slowly. Drawn out by chemotherapy that just wasn't working fast enough. As per usual, the thoughts threatened to drown me whenever it was brought up, obscuring everything else going on around me. This time, for whatever reason, I managed to focus on the intensity of Drake's gaze.

The nearly black pools of his eyes were stifling, making it too easy to look past the shimmer of mirage concealing what he would really look like under direct sunlight. *Shit,* I couldn't get lost in his allure, so I forced myself to lean away and cleared my throat.

"You don't even really know me," I accused, mild and perfunctory.

"Not so," he replied, straightening up like he'd been unintentionally leaning closer. "I know that you are brave, determined, and—most importantly—a fan of mysteries." Drake smiled, completely at ease while heat flamed my face at being given so many compliments in quick succession. "And, obviously, very selfless." That made me snort.

"Yeah, right. I'm accepting a free meal, aren't I? Running the risk of spilling guac and melted cheese on this borrowed dress." I waved my hand up and down to further illustrate the point, but I didn't expect his gaze to track the motion so closely. My body spiked hot to match my face when he took an unashamed second before looking me in the eye again. Swallowing hard, I tried to turn the conversation around. "So, your name really is Drake?"

"Yes, although admittedly, it is not my given name, but my last," he answered, swirling the barely touched red liquid in his glass by moving the stem with his forefinger and thumb. "In full, I am Ignatius Drake."

"No middle name?" Teasing edged into my tone, and Drake briefly smirked.

"They were not very common when I was born. What about yourself?"

"My middle name is Joanna, but if you try to call me 'MJ' then you'll be on the wrong end of my blade." Despite my honest annoyance about the nickname, Drake laughed.

"I will steer clear of it, though I fear it will be tempting without knowing your family name." The glint in his perceptive eyes was unmistakable, and I took a deep breath.

"It's Harker," I said, burying a wince the instant the name left my lips.

"Ah, how appropriate. Perhaps I ought to have guessed."

Brows raised, I stared him down. "Because of Stoker's work?"

"Indeed, though I glean from your attitude that you dislike its representation?"

"Vampire fiction doesn't interest me. They never get anything right. Even Bram embellished."

"Stories tend to require a level of 'embellishing,'" Drake agreed, clearly amused while I pouted down at my empty food basket.

"What about you?" I asked, my gaze rising to meet his. "What's your story?"

"Not nearly as exciting as your family history, I assure you." He lifted the glass of wine to his lips, hardly taking a sip. Obviously avoiding my prying—which I was *so* not going to let slide after his own probing questions—he surveyed the bustling pub, slowly emptying when the 'responsible' crowd started shuffling on home.

A forlorn expression came over his striking features while observing the people around us go about their lives. Following his line of sight, I watched a group leave through the main door.

"Did you want to go? Catch up with your buddies, or whatever it is you do together," I asked, and my heart jolted when Drake's focus slid back to me. The corners of his lips twitched, not quite smiling, but no longer frowning.

"While I enjoy their company, I confess that I maintain no close relationships with people."

"Why?" I asked, and my brow pinched. After everything he'd been going on about, claiming he wasn't a risk to anyone, it seemed like a major red flag.

"Would you be able to deepen any relationship where you could not be honest and true about who you are?" he asked in turn, and my mind emptied.

Even with Everly, who could practically read my thoughts by looking at my face, nobody had come close to understanding that simple fact. My cousins didn't seem to care. Olivia brushed it off whenever I asked her about people she might be interested in, and Andrew was too hopeless to get a date.

Ethan might have had an easy time hooking up with strangers, but as far as I knew, it never went beyond some fun nights and then deleting their numbers to make space for new ones.

Drake's answers were unexpected, but I'd stopped feeling uneasy in his presence sometime between when we got here and now.

Maybe because I'd been blindsided by our kindred spirits.

"I get that," I murmured after a moment. Lips pursed, I pushed the empty chips basket aside and drank the last of my water. Drake's wine wasn't even half gone, but he didn't seem to care. His attention went to my scraps, instead.

"Would you like dessert?" he asked.

Smiling, I nodded and grabbed my jacket. "If you're shouting, then sure."

Drake's black eyebrows drew together. "You wish for me to speak loudly?" His complete sincerity made me laugh, but I stifled it when the bartender glanced over.

"No, I meant, are you still paying?" Biting my lip, I watched his understanding dawn.

"Yes, as long as bribery aids me in my plea for innocence," he said, smiling like he already knew the answer.

I rolled my eyes, but grinned. "Sure, it'll keep you on my good side—for now."

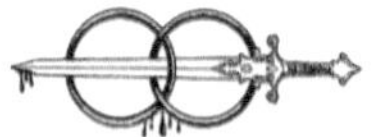

"Have a good night, folks." The woman at the register waved, and I lifted my plastic ice cream spoon in return. She'd already looked tired when we'd entered the Cold Stone Creamery across the road several minutes ago. Deep circles bagged her hazel eyes, her light brown hair pulled back into a hairnet while she'd scooped out my ice cream and Drake paid.

The door swung closed behind Drake, having held it open for me, and I watched him sidelong on our slow walk through the parking lot toward my car.

"Do you always pay with cash?" I asked, curious when I'd glimpsed the stack of large bills in his worn leather wallet.

"It is rather difficult to apply for credit when you are meant to be deceased for two centuries," he replied. I nodded, determined not to show any surprise at hearing his true age, even if my heart betrayed me by pumping faster. Shockingly, he added, "Do you always dress so nicely when you make plans to meet your mortal enemies?"

A giggle threatened to climb my throat, but I forced it down to a deadpan. "Only when they buy me ice cream."

When he laughed, the sound was so contagious I couldn't help but follow suit. The red neon sign of the ice cream shop flickered off by the time we'd stopped. Breathless and light-headed despite the sugar buzz, I leaned back against my car and focused on my melting meal.

"Does this mean that I am cleared of suspicion? Or will I be forced to bribe your good will again soon?" His stare was mischievous while he stood only a couple of steps away. Silence descended, except for the chirps of crickets and the locking of the door to the Cold Stone Creamery. Averting my gaze, I instead watched the employee who'd served me as she veered toward a car parked further back in the lot.

"You're in the clear," I admitted, my attention on Drake as he shifted closer. Voice a whisper, I spoke the truth, putting all of my cards on the table. "I never told my family about you. So, you're safe."

"Truly?" He seemed astounded, and I guiltily nodded, my guts twisting over revealing the lies I'd been telling my people. Then my stomach squirmed for a whole other reason when he said, "Thank you, Maria." For whatever reason, the sound of my name in his accent was mind melting. A shiver ran up my spine, pinned to the spot beneath his unwavering gaze.

"N-No problem," I said, and swallowed. "You won't have to see me anymore after tonight. I'll leave you alone."

"Ah." He paused, and then whispered, "How disappointing."

The moonlight above filtering down through parted clouds wasn't strong enough to break his human illusion. Instead, it lit up his face how I imagined he might have appeared under the sun—before he became what he was. *Maybe it didn't matter.* Because I didn't know his story, or much of anything about him, but that might've made it easier to leave it a mystery.

One that wouldn't intrude on this moment as the space between us shortened. Drake leaned closer, and in a moment of insanity my eyelids almost closed before a scream split the air, quickly choked off. Both of us straightened up, practically jumping apart as I whirled to find the source.

Except I didn't need to see it to know. Chills climbed my spine, pulling me toward the shadows of the lot where a vampire lured the Cold Stone Creamery worker through a mixture of brute force and mental manipulation. Before I could consider any alternative, I was moving.

My machete was drawn as I leaped onto the hood of her car to cross over it, quicker than having to run around it. In my hurry, I was stupid. The noise alerted the monster, already ravaging the poor woman's neck. She sagged against the brick wall the vampire had pressed her against, and the tall masculine figure now sprinted for me.

I braced my right leg back when the enemy reached me in a blur of motion. Senses hyped and adrenaline coursing, I met the vampire's blunt attack with my machete. The blade sliced through the vampire's tanned arm until dark clotted blood ran from the wound. Bone had stopped my blade from piercing deeper, and the vampire used that to his advantage.

The creature's smug grin spread a moment before he round-house kicked me in the gut. I bent double, gasping for breath and angling my machete to keep the vampire's blows from making contact with my skull. Muscles on fire from a lack of oxygen, I stumbled away, trying to put distance between us.

My ankle rolled on a shallow pothole in the concrete parking lot, and I fell over. Pain sliced through my forearm where I hit the asphalt, and I slashed a desperate swing of my blade to ward off the vampire. Except he caught it. Despite the tan complexion, the fingers gripping my machete's edge maintained that same silvery undertone, just like a corpse.

Blood beaded the length of my blade from the vampire's cut palm, but they couldn't feel pain the way we did—the way I *was*. Finally, my lungs expanded, giving me enough clarity to stare up into the murky brown eyes of the thing that was about to kill me.

Then a pop like a wet slap thundered through the air as the vampire's head was torn from its torso. The pavement flooded with grimy blood while I scrambled away. Breath hot and fast, I looked up from the fallen body to where Drake stood, holding the decapitated head between two blood-stained hands.

His expression was furious, all his rage directed at the beheaded, undead man—his own *kind*. Drake tossed the head aside, glaring in disgust at its rolling progress. Stunned, I tightened my grip on my machete's handle and forced myself to stand. At the shift in my movement, Drake's gaze immediately found mine.

Where a split second ago his dark eyes were filled with loathing, now there was only concern—directed on me.

"Are you alright?" he asked, and I swallowed despite my dry mouth.

"I'll be fine," I stammered, but sobered at the low moan from the shadows. The woman was still alive, slowly bleeding out from her neck wound and delirious from having been charmed. I ran to her, falling to my knees and instantly tearing off a chunk of her pink blouse. Wincing at her now exposed stomach, I pressed the fabric down against her punctured throat.

"Will the woman live?" Drake asked, voice urgent, and I shook my head.

"I need my phone. I have to call someone—" With one hand, I fished through my jacket pockets for my car keys. Fumbling, they slipped through my fingers, but never hit the pavement. Drake took them, gone in the blink of an eye before returning moments later. My phone was offered, screen black, and I snatched it up with one slippery hand, soon struggling to swipe it open with the woman's blood staining my fingers.

"Come on," I grumbled, nearly a shriek while I hoped to hell that the woman would make it.

"Maria, I must leave you."

"What? What's wrong?" I looked up just as my phone unlocked, but Drake wasn't there. Whirling, I glanced this way and that, but

I was alone. To keep from hyperventilating, I forced a slow breath and went through my contacts list.

"Unreliable fucking vampire," I rasped, my thumb hovering over the name of the one person I could trust to help me—and hopefully would keep his mouth shut. It took three rings before he picked up, my words a rush before he could speak. "Caleb? I need your help."

8

LIGHT THE TORCH

EXHAUSTED, I WARMED MY TREMBLING SAND-AND-CLAY COATED HANDS over the fire that turned the vampire's remains to ash. Crackling flames obscured the soft thud as Caleb closed his car's trunk, always careful with his '87 Mustang coupe. He shuffled over, across the deserted plain a little ways off I-40. We'd opted to meet halfway between Albuquerque and Cedar Crest, where the Tsosies lived.

Dead flesh crumbled away like dry tinder in the ditch I'd dug. Beheading was the easiest way to incapacitate them, disconnecting the spinal cord so they couldn't move. A stake to the heart would slow them, since it'd make it harder for the vital organ to pump the blood they still needed to survive throughout their bodies. The problem was trying to overpower their lightning fast reflexes and strength to skewer them properly.

Quick decapitation was a more sure method, and it also dried the vampires out, making them easy kindling. Still took ages for the things to actually disintegrate, which was why Caleb and I were out here well past midnight. I flinched when Caleb sighed, my nerves frayed.

He stopped beside me, rubbing the back of his neck below his long black hair, tied up in a bun. Unfortunately, I'd left my scrunchie back at Everly's. The dark curls around my bare shoulders knotted from the desert winds blowing in, but I'd done enough shivering tonight—from fear and otherwise.

Just as I was about to ask Caleb to let me have it, he said, "That was the last of the kerosene I brought, but I think it's pretty much toast now."

"Thank you," I said, having to clear my throat when it came out hoarse. Caleb's warm brown eyes glanced me up and down, then he raised one thick eyebrow.

"I wasn't going to mention it, but you're pretty dressed up for an ice cream run." A grin spread across his full lips, gentle as always. His amusement was contagious, so I cracked a smile.

"Everly was bored. Apparently she's been hellbent on dressing me up for ages," I murmured, my mirth fading as my heart squeezed when I remembered Drake's comment about how I looked.

"Not that I'm complaining, Everly did great work. It's rare to see you this way." Caleb's shoulder bumped into mine, and heat spread through my chest from his affection. Totally different from how I'd felt when I'd touched Drake's hand earlier. This was playful camaraderie, with family. With Drake… Okay, I needed to stop thinking about him.

"I'll pass your compliments on to Everly," I replied, but my forced smirk faded when I found Caleb's expression had lost its humor. His brow furrowed, concern plain across his features even before he voiced his thoughts.

"You shouldn't have taken the vampire on alone, Maria. You know that." His opinion wasn't unexpected, but somehow, it still hurt.

"What was I supposed to do? Let the woman die?" I didn't know for sure if she'd made it, but I called for an ambulance as soon as I'd hung up with Caleb. Bitterness filled my mouth, regretting how I'd had to drag her to the roadside, leaving her there alone so that I could deal with the decapitated vampire before the cops showed up. Once she was loaded in, sirens blaring around the next corner, I'd scampered off to do the dirty work.

Caleb's lips pressed together. Vindicated by his silence, I faced the slowly dying flames, hoping the woman was okay.

"Even Johann doesn't take them on alone. My dad, either. I'm just worried that you're going to bite off more than you can chew. After what happened at the warehouse the other week—"

"I made it back in one piece, remember?" I retorted, face flushed. Deep down, I knew he was right. Both times, the only reason I lived to tell the tale was because Drake was there. If any other vampire had caught me alone in that warehouse… More importantly, if Drake hadn't stepped in to save me tonight, I'd be dead.

Instead of berating me about my impulsivity, Caleb exhaled a long sigh. The shake of his head and quirk of his lips seemed to be his way of conceding that we weren't going to agree. Personally, my energy was too depleted to argue, either.

With the last of the vampire turned to charcoaled bits, I edged away from the fire, morose on the walk back to my car, which sat parked beside Caleb's. I leaned against the hood, and the cold metal chilled the back of my thighs where my dress rode up. Caleb stomped out the glowing red embers before sauntering my way.

When he stopped a few feet from me, I looked up to meet his gaze.

"I'm glad you're alive, Maria," Caleb said, "but are you okay?"

I shrugged, stifling a wince when my ribs stung. "A bit bruised, but I've suffered worse from Andrew while practicing fighting techniques."

"Nothing worse than an older relative you can't beat." Caleb smiled, and I returned the sentiment as he moved closer. His hand took mine, pressing a soft squeeze into my palm before letting go, but his attention was on the dusky horizon the whole time he touched me. Under the moonlight, I thought I glimpsed his cheekbones darken.

"I'm exhausted," I admitted, recapturing his gaze. "I'm sorry for calling you out here so late. You're a godsend."

"I was already up, actually, gaming with Jim and Cody."

"You don't see enough of each other working at the garage?" I teased, but I'd met his coworkers. They were cool. Caleb smirked, his arms folded across his broad chest.

"Nah, but it *was* a long week. You should have seen the old Chevy I worked on. It would be better off as scrap metal." A yawn brought his palm up to cover his mouth, and guilt squirmed in my chest.

"About tonight—"

"I won't tell anyone," he promised, lifting one side of his mouth in a lopsided smirk. "You can trust me."

"You're the best." I straightened up to give him a hug, throwing my arms around his wide shoulders. Warm hands held my waist in return, lightly and not nearly as wholeheartedly as I'd squeezed. Awkwardly clearing my throat, I let go and stepped back. "I'll let you get home, okay?"

"Don't be a stranger." He winked, grinning despite the dark circles beneath his eyes.

Once he returned to his car, I hopped into mine. When we reached the highway, Caleb beeped his horn as we pulled out in opposite directions. The night's events replayed in my head. Between kicking myself at my dumb replies and questioning the trust I'd felt for a *vampire*, what made me flush was neither of those thoughts.

It was the last thing he'd said to me, before all hell broke loose. The way he'd leaned in, his impossibly dark eyes gazing at my lips—high above where my jugular pulsed with anticipation. What would have happened, if the woman hadn't been attacked? If we hadn't been interrupted…

Glad I was alone in the car, I swallowed hard. Nothing good could have come from kissing Drake. *So why did my chest ache so damn bad?*

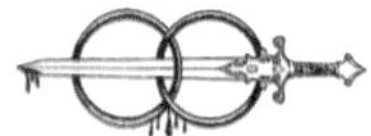

Groggy and sore, the first thing I did when I cracked my eyes open was reach for my phone. Only to be let down when the screen illuminated to reveal several new messages, but none from *him*. A sigh escaped me, and my eyes closed in acceptance. I'd told Drake that he wouldn't have to see me after last night, and that was that.

'*How disappointing…*'

His accented voice replayed in my head, renewing the throb in my chest from my ride home. In all my panic, I never thanked him for saving my life. Conflicted, but determined to focus on the people I already knew and trusted, I chewed on my lower lip and checked my unread notifications.

When I got home last night—early morning, whatever—my immediate priority was to sneakily jump in the shower. After that, before passing out in bed from the spent adrenaline, I managed to text Everly with a brief update. The words I used exactly were, *'Tonight sucked, vamp attacked, (not Drake), I'm going to bed.'*

I probably should have guessed such a vague explanation wouldn't cut it. Her response was several paragraphs long, and I read through each message while the seconds ticked by on my alarm clock. At the end of it, she elected to mention—yet again—her hot date tonight at the club.

Then I checked Caleb's text, and my heart sank. Not because it was bad, just the opposite. Worry laced every word of his message, sent around nine this morning, *'I know last night was rough, but I'm here for you if you need anything. We all are.'* It was typical, the same things I'd been told for almost a year by everybody in my life.

Before the addiction, the incident, and the rehab, nobody talked to me this way. It was only after my most vulnerable moments were laid bare, when everyone got to take a good look at my struggles and whispered behind my back about my treatment and diagnoses. That's when they all started to *care* so much.

Maybe I was being selfish, wishing that they wouldn't spend that energy worrying about me. Anyone should be so lucky to have family and friends so willing to help, accepting and unbiased. Except what nobody seemed to realize was that I wasn't a fragile little thing—not before, during, or after.

The things I'd gone through, the choices I made, they were *my* mistakes that I needed to learn to live with. Nobody could have saved me from the fallout, and it bothered me every day that they all seemed to think I still teetered on that edge. That if one bad thing happened, then I'd fall off the wagon and need to be rescued from myself and anyone in my vicinity.

Tired of their condescending opinions, I decided to stop letting *their* fears control me. Because my instincts weren't permanently impaired, and I'd proven that to myself last night. Even if I never saw him again, keeping Drake safe from my family had been the right call. Emboldened and sure, I flipped back to Everly's contact and dialed.

Her high voice squeaked through the receiver after only one ring. "Gods, Maria! I've been waiting for you to reply all morning. Are you okay?"

"I feel great," I lied, smiling brightly until my cheeks hurt. "I was wondering if that invitation was still open for tonight? Unless you and the new boo want some alone time." Sitting up, I carefully ran my fingers through my tangled hair.

"Y-Yeah, I'm sure Courtney won't mind!" Everly's hesitancy strengthened my resolve. "We're meeting up around opening time. Eight o'clock?"

"Sounds great," I replied, and my thoughts turned to Caleb as Olivia's singing filtered in from the hall. "Is it okay if I extend the invite?"

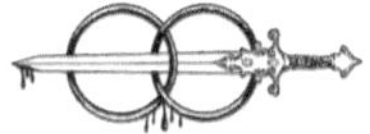

Under the concrete canopy of the parking block on Copper Avenue, my car petered out with a puff when I turned the key. Opening my door, I breathed in the chill night air while my passengers clambered out of their seats. Despite Ethan's griping about not riding shotgun, he managed just fine on the short drive.

Olivia's wide blue-gray eyes anxiously glanced my way, not for the first time since I asked if she'd wanted to 'come with' tonight. Maybe I shouldn't have bothered. At least Ethan seemed excited, straightening out his *Gojira* T-shirt, its black-and-white design pairing nicely with the silver chain around his neck.

Olivia's ensemble was her usual, looking put-together in a frilly pink skirt and matching blouse. Personally, I was glad to be back in my jeans and tank top. Since my cotton jacket was ruined, having used it to wrap up the vampire's head for easy transport last night, and my denim one was ripped along the forearm, I chose to forgo any outer layer in case it was an omen.

It wasn't that cold tonight anyway.

Springtime was like that here, chilling one day then gorgeous the next. On our walk down 5th Street toward Central Avenue, I kept quiet while Olivia and Ethan bantered.

"Yeah, because it's *so* complicated to play the same four notes for an entire song." Ethan's eyes rolled, and Olivia bristled.

"And what do you expect they'll play inside the club? I doubt they've got anything heavier than *Skrillex*." She glanced at his shirt, and her lips pursed.

"That's different, I won't be sober enough to hear it anyway." Ethan grinned, and Olivia's shoulders slumped, huffing but not bothering to dignify his words with a response.

When we reached the crosswalk, the line for The Belphegor wrapping around the block came into view. Distracted by the masses, it took a few seconds to realize Olivia had started staring at me. As our gazes met, she opened her mouth.

"Are you sure about this?" she asked, not bothering to whisper. Ethan walked ahead, obviously uninterested to hear how this conversation turned out. I *could* ignore her, but knowing my cousin, she'd keep pestering until I answered.

"Yes, Liv. I *want* to come out and have a good time with friends." Traffic thinned, and I hurried along several paces behind Ethan. Olivia quickly caught up, sighing.

"But what about the temptation? You know we could all hang out doing something else. Even if Everly is busy here tonight, we could plan something together next weekend. There's a great bowling alley my coworker told me about—"

"Liv," I cut across, seething, and had to take a deep breath while I stared down at her. *She meant well,* I kept telling myself so I wouldn't lose it. "Can we not? Just for tonight, can you please just stop?" I was pleading, obvious by the desperation scrunching up my face. Olivia seemed to recognize it, because she let out a long exhale, deflating like a stubborn balloon.

"Oi! You coming? Caleb's saved us a spot," Ethan called, waving his arm at us once with a disgruntled expression, a contrast to Caleb's genial smile beside him.

Today, Caleb's black hair was braided down his back, courtesy of his older sister Linda, probably. A white T-shirt hugged his muscular frame, pairing well with light-washed jeans and cowboy boots that peeked out beneath the bootleg hem. It suddenly struck me how much he was starting to look like his dad, from the broad shoulders and impressive height to his enviably manageable wavy hair texture.

All the Tsosie 'kids' had a darker complexion thanks to their mother, and though Laura seemed to resemble her the most in appearance, Linda was the one that had inherited Rosa Tsosie's nurturing demeanor. I'd never once heard her complain about stepping up to help take care of her younger siblings when Rosa passed. Thinking about it, maybe that's all Olivia was trying to do for me—help watch my back.

A group of women nearby kept glancing at Caleb while he beckoned us over. I didn't blame them, he was hard to miss. Before things got awkward, I figured I should apologize to Olivia. Except, when I turned to her, the words died in my throat at the sight of her flush.

The red staining her cheeks was a stark difference from her white-faced worry moments before. My gaze followed hers, straight to Caleb, and my eyebrows rose curiously as we met up with the guys.

Caleb whistled low, his tone playful. "You look nice, Liv," he said, but his gaze slid to me before nodding, like his comment was an inside joke about how I'd been dressed last night.

I rolled my eyes, biting my lip to keep from being obvious with a smile. Then I remembered what Drake had said, about preferring my 'scrappy' appearance. A laugh almost burst through my lips, but the pang that accompanied the memory dampened it back down into my chest.

"Thanks," Olivia replied, oblivious to my inner turmoil while straightening out her skirt.

"I don't mean to be a party pooper, but…" Caleb's voice lowered to a whisper. "Will they let me and Ethan in? I think they check ID at the door." His eyebrows rose. *Right,* his twenty-first birthday wasn't until August, nearly a full year younger than me.

"Oh well," Olivia piped up, unconcerned but sparking my annoyance when she shrugged, clearly having thought this whole night was going to implode before it started. "I won't be too disappointed if we have to find something else to do—"

"Everly gave me a code word to get us in fast," I said, restraining my ire, and I forced a smile in the face of Olivia's doubt. "Come on, let's test it out."

Not waiting for anyone, I strode ahead, around the crowd peering over each other's heads on tiptoes to check how long the line was to the front. Before the black entrance door, painted over in red that resembled blood dripping down its surface, a bouncer stood guard. Bald, but young, the Black man was about as big as Caleb, but with a sureness in the stiff set to his built shoulders that gave off the 'don't even try it' vibes.

His brown eyes focused on me when I approached, my confidence and straight back proving myself even before I sidled closer to whisper, "Kali, goddess of destruction." Thin eyebrows high, he silently counted all four of our heads before stepping aside. Thrilled, I grabbed Ethan's hand and towed him inside, both of us laughing while I overheard Caleb jauntily cajoling Olivia onward.

Part of me didn't care if she came in or not. Music thrummed underfoot while strobe lights flashed through the hallway painted black on all sides, including the ceiling. At the end, past figures gyrating on each other against the walls, we emerged into the main room of the club. Bodies swayed to and fro, moving in and out of sync with the rhythm pumping through the place.

A lone DJ head-banged to the beat, electronic-sounding but strangely dark for club music. Then her short black hair and facial piercings came into view. Addison raised both hands into the air, spurring the crowd on while jumping up and down as bass shook the midnight floors. So many colors flashed before my eyes, I was nearly blinded, but still managed to glimpse a petite figure with long curly red hair by the stretch of a bar.

I turned to get the others' attention, everyone's eyes glazed over by the strobing kaleidoscope. My hand found Olivia's, and she jolted until I squeezed in reassurance. Through the din, I managed to mouth my words while pointing toward the bar. She nodded, and Caleb tore his gaze away from the sea of swaying bodies to glean our muted conversation.

Ethan, on the other hand, looked about to waltz off into the crowd until Olivia and I grabbed his shoulders to steer him toward the bar. His grin diminished with our pushing, only to return with vigor when he realized where we were headed. Rows of bottles lined the wall behind the bartop, illuminated by a neon pink and green backdrop which obscured the color of the alcohol inside.

Everly's head turned on our approach, her freckles stark against her flushed skin. Her smile was luminous, love-struck—which made sense when I noticed the woman beside her.

"You made it!" Everly called over the music.

Before I could speak, Ethan shouted, "What are we drinking?"

"Nothing for me." I shook my head, almost regretting it when Olivia's shoulders relaxed. *Did she always have to act like such a babysitter?* "But I promised to buy Caleb a drink."

"What'll it be?" asked the bartender, a man with a bright blue mohawk and equally light eyes. He glanced over each of us, his gaze resting on the gorgeous blonde woman beside Everly for a moment longer.

"Bourbon, whatever's cheapest." Caleb winked my way, and I smirked.

"I'll have whatever she's drinking." Ethan pointed at the bottle in Everly's hand.

"A vodka cruiser," the bartender said, already bustling around.

"I don't—" Olivia started, steamrolled by Ethan.

"Pipsqueak here will have a Bloody Mary." He turned his full brotherly sass on Olivia, who seemed about to argue, but then the drinks were set on the teak bartop, and the bartender moved elsewhere for another drunken order.

"But we didn't pay?" I voiced, my brow furrowed, and Everly's date finally spoke.

"It's on the house for any friends of Eve's." Brown eyes—darker than I would have expected for someone with such light blonde hair—met mine in answer. She was a couple of inches taller than me, towering over Everly who appeared dressed to impress in a very tight, sparkly green number. Meanwhile, the sleek black skirt and ruffled blouse showcasing the woman's figure seemed more fitting for a high-stakes business meeting than a nightclub.

"Guys, this is Courtney," Everly said, giddily waving her hand with the introductions. "That's Caleb, um—Tsosie, right?"

"Yep." He raised his shot glass in salute, and Everly beamed.

"He's a mechanic, and Maria's *other* best friend." She giggled, her focus swinging to my cousins. "Olivia and Ethan Harker are siblings, and of course I've already told you about Maria."

"Harker?" Courtney blinked, and a curious smile froze across her delicate pale features.

"That's our name," I affirmed, and her gaze once again met mine.

An odd feeling swooped in my stomach that had nothing to do with Courtney's good looks. Thankfully, her attention immediately returned to Everly when my best friend exclaimed, "And here's Addison! Addy, are you having a drink? Courtney said she's buying!"

Addison shrugged her thin shoulders, moving between partiers like a fish through water until she reached us. Her slender forearms rested on the bartop, eyeing up Courtney with suspicion until she caught me looking. "Sure."

Olivia had only taken a small sip of her drink when she spluttered, sending tomato juice flying all over my top. "What are you doing?" she shrieked at Ethan, who'd taken a hearty swig of his drink. "You're not even twenty!"

"Bartender didn't know that." He winked, leaving Olivia gaping at him. Ignoring her aghast expression, he backed up into the crowd. "If you'll excuse me, I'm here to actually have *fun*." Under the flashing lights, the music heralded by Addison's stand-in, Ethan disappeared from view. Olivia set her drink down, about to storm after him, but I caught her arm.

"He's an adult, Liv," I reminded, but Olivia's eyes narrowed.

"He could get *hurt*," she argued.

"He's not stupid!" I shouted over the music. "Besides, Caleb isn't drinking legally, either—"

"That's different." Olivia's mouth twisted, her face red and sweaty even before Caleb intervened.

"It'll be okay, Liv. Who hasn't snuck into a club before and got someone to buy them a drink or two?" His genial, easygoing grin was hard to argue with. While Olivia visibly deflated, I had to chew on the inside of my cheek to keep from continuing the issue unnecessarily. Of course, she'd have listened to anyone but me.

"Oh, I love this song!" Everly chimed, her bottle only half-emptied when she took Courtney's hand to lead her onto the dance floor. "Come on, guys!"

"Oh, man," Caleb murmured before downing the rest of his shot. His hand extended to me, but I managed a smile and shook my head.

"I'll catch the next one," I said, giving Olivia a little shove his way. Suave and unsubtle, Caleb caught Olivia and spun her around. They moved into the crowd, Olivia's expression mixed between elation and terror, and I returned to the bar. Addison accepted a drink from the bartender, raising the glass of pink liquid in thanks.

"So," I called out over the noise, and Addison hesitantly turned my way. *Shit, I sucked at small talk.* "Uh, the music sounded great before, when you were up there." I pointed toward the raised stage, and Addison lifted a brow.

"Thanks." Gaze averted, Addison downed her drink in one swallow. A flush blotched her cheeks pink, peeking through the layer of goth-white foundation. "Well, I'd better get back to it."

"Right…" I winced when the glass hit the bartop hard, feeling strangely awkward as she rushed off, soon out of sight.

I was such an albatross… Seemed like nobody could have fun or relax with me around.

Taking a deep breath, I leaned against the bar. The person next to me ordered a glass of red wine, just audible over the noise, and I closed my eyes. It was impossible not to think about last night. The whole evening had become my obsession all day long, wondering why Drake had done or said this and that.

Indebted as I felt for his rescuing me, I hesitated to return to the Two Fools Tavern. He'd said he went there most nights, but would it be reasonable to purposefully run into him? Even if it was just to express my gratitude… A heavy sigh passed my lips, and my eyes opened. Several feet away, my friends and family danced—except Ethan, who occupied the far corner where his attention was focused on a good-looking man.

It was one thing to keep Drake a secret from them because it was the right thing to do. If Drake wasn't hurting anyone, didn't want any trouble, then I'd give him that—protection. To keep seeing him would only fracture things further, creating more gaps in my stories. After everything, if my family eventually found out…

I wouldn't be able to face them, let alone myself.

My brow furrowed when Olivia light-heartedly laughed, watching Caleb attempt the robot. How much longer would it take to prove myself to *her*? What did it mean that she was still suspicious of my ability to stay sober? Did the rest of my family feel that way, too, and were just better at hiding it? Drake hadn't pushed the issue when it came up, trusting it when I told him I was fine.

Lost in thought, I jumped when someone bumped my shoulder. At first, I figured it was an accident, so I moved aside. When a warm hand wrapped firmly around my arm, I turned to face the asshole trying to assault me. My left hand fisted, teeth clenched as I stared up at a tall, silvery blond man whose hair fell straight past his shoulders. Pale green eyes bore into mine, and I was about to shove my fist into his nose—

"You are Maria Harker?"

Spine straightening, my hand uncurled to rest on my machete's handle. "Who wants to know?"

"I come bearing news. Ignatius Drake needs your help."

Stunned, I glanced over to make sure my family was still out of earshot before I faced the stranger full-on. "What the hell are you talking about?"

"He is in danger, resigned to a fate not yet sealed—"

"Who are you?" My eyes narrowed when exasperation crossed his features.

"Someone who has known him well for much longer than you."

"If you're such great *friends*, then why don't *you* help him?" I searched his severe face for tells of a lie, but the resentment behind his unflinching gaze seemed legitimate.

"Because Ignatius will not *listen* to me. He may listen to you."

"W-Why me? How did you even—" Shock, confusion, and concern racked my brain—cut short when the man opened his palm. His grip on my arm fell slack while I blinked down at the old bottle cap keychain, every nick and scratch identical to mine. I took it with shaking fingers, and the man slid a note across the bartop toward me. A small golden marble lazily teetered at the paper's edge.

"Here is the address. If you care for him an ounce, for what he has sacrificed for you, then you will take this to him." He pointed to the orb, his index finger inches from its reflective surface. "Quickly, before it's too late."

I glanced down at the paper and sphere. "What is—" By the time I looked up, the stranger was at the other end of the room.

As he disappeared behind a door, his hair shifted, revealing the sharp points of his ears.

Breath caught, and my heart pounding, I gathered up the note and golden orb in my palm. My steps toward the exit faltered when the music shifted, and I looked over my shoulder. On the stage stood Addison, selecting the next song for the tipsy, high-riding audience. Between her and the bar, my friends and family were grouped together, laughing, soaking up each other's joy.

Just how different had I always been from the best people in my life?

They lived without shame, while guilt and humiliation followed my every step. As bad as Andrew's personal rain cloud he carried with him everywhere. Only one person in recent memory made me forget to hurt—to be ashamed of who I was, what I'd done...

So I turned my back on them, and walked outside into the night's breeze. Stars glittered overhead while I ran toward Copper Avenue, my car keys in hand.

— 9 —

THIS RABBIT HOLE

SHIT, THIS WAS A BAD IDEA. THE TEXT I'D SENT CALEB WEIGHED HEAVILY ON my conscience while I drove south down I-25. Hopefully my message asking him to give my cousins a ride home didn't send them all into a panic. Unexpectedly leaving in a hurry was *not* a good look in the 'staying sober' department, but I had to be sure about what the faery man said.

Really, it shouldn't have been any of my business. By his own admission, Drake was over two centuries old. It was hard to believe, regardless of who he was now, that Drake had been innocent all that time. Surely, when he was first transformed, he'd been as much of a monster as the things I often faced.

Except, as true as that must be, I couldn't fully judge him for it. Maybe because I was tired of people thinking the worst of me for my past mistakes. I had no idea what kind of a world Drake had lived in during those days. Not a clue about where he came from, who his influences were, or why he decided not to hurt people anymore.

The pang in my chest grew as I turned off the Pan American Freeway, taking Exit 220, per my phone's directions. Cold sweat beaded the back of my neck, and I flipped on the air conditioning. The chill that caressed my shoulders wasn't enough to distract me from feeling like a complete idiot.

Truthfully, I didn't know a damn thing about Drake. Only that something about him affected me, making me question my beliefs. It was enough of a gut instinct to make me lie to my family, ignore my legacy, and let him go. As old and capable as he was, I knew in the pit of my stomach that my family and I could've taken him down.

Since that first night, a strange part of me didn't want to. It was exhilarating, meeting someone who didn't know me from before. Who couldn't judge me based on my history. Someone who was already in-the-know, that I didn't have to lie to about who I was and what was important to me.

If I was being honest with myself, I hadn't been trying that hard to kill him since I first fought him in the warehouse. Every time I ran into him, it felt like I was going through the motions, doing what my family would've expected of me. Which was crazy, because I'd always known what he was…but he never acted like the monster I kept accusing him of being—at least, not with me. My hands tightened on the steering wheel. *Damn it, Maria, pull it together.*

Directly ahead down Rio Bravo Boulevard was a set of train tracks, and my insides swooped. This was it. It had to be. Past the desolate tracks, I turned right on Rossmoor Road only to take an immediate left onto Poco Loco Drive—poetic, really.

Dead ahead, my phone displayed the big red bubble showing my destination.

The Rio Bravo riverside picnic area was shrouded in pitch-black darkness around the glow of my headlights. Curious, I slowed into an open parking space and cut the engine. Wiping my sweaty palms on my jeans, I took a deep breath.

True, I didn't have to do this, but he'd *saved my life*. More than once, it felt like. So I exhaled, stuffed my wallet into the glovebox out of habit—hesitating a brief second before tossing the keychain in after it—and climbed out onto the gravel.

The hunting etiquette drilled into me since childhood repeated in my head, *never take anything into unknown territory that we weren't willing to lose.* Misplacing my lucky keychain had been a wake-up call. So I fished the car keys out of my pocket, and subtly left them on the top of my tire, easily concealed by my side fender in the shadows.

All that laid between me and the greenery ahead was my machete at my hip, and the wind raking through the branches. My pulse thundered as I swallowed, and honed my senses while taking in the surroundings.

Quiet landscape surrounded me as I passed the picnic benches and trudged over dry foliage. The whoosh of rushing water echoed from the Rio Grande nearby, seemingly in time with my heartbeat. Clouds overhead moved in to cover the moon, and my eyes widened to see through the dim. A lone figure stood not far off, leaned against a tree, and I froze. Every muscle I'd tensed suddenly eased when the clouds shifted, brightening the space long enough to glimpse a trail of smoke rising high.

My fingers relaxed on my machete's handle, and I took another step across the grass toward Drake. The crunch of my boots over the packed earth caught his attention immediately. His gaze met mine, and despite my hammering heart, I didn't stop walking. In a blur, his cigarette was gone, and he moved closer.

When he appeared directly in front of me, I staggered to a stop, wholly unprepared for the fresh emotion crossing his face up close.

"What are you doing here?" he demanded, and though his words stung, there was something more to his expression. A fear that he'd never shown in my presence, before now. "You must leave. Maria—" Drake reached for my arm, but I stepped back so he couldn't usher me anywhere.

"Your faery *friend* found me," I retorted. Obviously, my 'help' was unwanted. "He nearly ruined everything! My family was in eyeshot, if they'd bothered to look." Something about what I said made Drake halt, his hostility crumbling into confusion. "The faery told me that I needed to come here *immediately*. And that you were in danger—because of me."

Every excuse I'd made for leaving my friends was because I felt responsible for whatever was happening to Drake. Now that I was here, the whole thing seemed like bullshit. Until Drake's pale lips pressed together, concealing whatever thoughts hardened his gaze.

"Aiden had no right—"

"Is it true?" I asked, needling for a purpose that would keep me from storming away. From abandoning whatever I thought I was starting to feel for Drake. His dark eyes searched the distance, glancing over my head and around us. I waited, biting the inside of my cheek to keep from repeating myself.

His eyes closed in a long blink, his jaw tensing, and when his gaze recaptured mine, my heart cracked at the vulnerable uncertainty behind his dark irises. Like I'd broken through his defenses as easily as he was able to pull down mine.

"There are higher powers at play, and I have been summoned."

"Summoned?" I balked. "By who?"

"The *Judecător Imperial*. Please, there are so many semantics, and there is not the time to discuss—"

"What the hell are you talking about?" I stammered, at a loss, but I didn't flinch when Drake placed his hands on the sides of my arms. His grip somehow steadied me, reassuring.

"I have broken a crucial covenant by executing another immortal without due process." His stare was so intense, I couldn't even hope that he was joking.

"Vampires…have laws? But—After Helsing killed Dracula, his whole operation fell apart!" It was what I'd been raised to believe, but by Drake's pained expression, it wasn't the truth. Which meant that everything I knew was about to change.

"That is what they wished for you to think, and it worked. My kind has managed to remain enshrouded in myth, evading persecution by humanity whose modern inventions have *far* surpassed any attempt immortals might make to subjugate them."

"Who is 'they?'"

"Officially, we refer to them as the *Domnitori*." Drake's accent thickened on the word from his native tongue, and goosebumps erupted over my exposed flesh. My hands trembled, and I forced the tremors to stop, swallowing hard and taking shallow, deliberate breaths.

"How could we have never known… Wait, how did you even get caught?"

"There was another vampire nearby, most likely hunting alongside the one we killed. That is why I left so suddenly—except I was too slow to catch them. The summons came for me shortly after." He shook his head, almost distracted. Like he was trying to focus on three things at once. "Maria, I beg of you, now is *not* the time. I will be entombed for my crime at best, turned to ash at worst, but they must never know the reason. Your entire family will be endangered—"

"You're being summoned…because of *me*. Because you took out that vampire to save me." Guilt was a shadow compared to the warmth blooming in my chest, taking root deep in my abdomen. "Why? Why would you risk that?"

Drake licked his lips, an oddly ordinary human gesture that stole my attention. Deliberation crossed his handsome features in the darkness, and my heart pounded.

"Better I than you," he answered at last, almost closing the distance between us with a single step. Inches separated us while I gazed up into his dark eyes. His hand rose, and my breath caught when his fingertips brushed my cheekbone as he swept aside the curls framing my face. A shiver ran down my spine, and for a fraction of a second, everything seemed to stop. "You are so beautifully human, Maria, and I have lived lifetimes longer than I ought."

Breath held, my mind empty, I lunged for him. My arms went around his neck, pulling him closer until our lips met. Shock was obvious in both of us, and my mouth stilled against his when he froze under my sudden affection. I was about to die of humiliation—until he started kissing me back.

The tender swell of his lips on mine sent surges of heat through my core, reinforced by his hands at my waist. Crushed against him, I returned the sentiments tenfold as my fingers threaded through his silken hair, holding him to me. The thrum of my heart against his unmoving chest accompanied my ragged breaths.

Our kiss broke only so I could inhale, but we were like magnets. Every push and pull in sync while I made out with my blood's mortal enemy under the overcast night sky. His tongue exerted gentle pressure against my lips, and I willingly opened. The taste of his venom-laced saliva was shockingly sweet, and I nearly moaned when he held me closer. I'd always expected everything about vampires to be wrong—inhuman.

Except, as our bodies molded against one another with natural ease, I couldn't imagine a single thing wrong about this. Before I could think too hard about the fact that we were in a public park, and that proverbial-but-possibly-literal swords hung over our heads, my phone buzzed in my pocket. A groan rose up my throat when I was forced to pull away. Heat prickled in all the best places, demanding satisfaction.

Unlike me, Drake wasn't breathless when he released me, his touch slipping away. Except his step backward staggered, his expression stunned while his eyes burned, craving something fierce. Drake swallowed, his composure lost, and I suppressed a bud of pride while retrieving my phone. *Shit, why was Everly calling me* now? Brow furrowed, I answered it.

"Hey, Eve, not a great time—"

"Maria! Where are you? Are you okay?" Her panicked voice cut through me, leaving my insides full of ice where warmth had ignited moments before.

"I'm fine, what's wrong?" Just as I spoke, Drake's posture stiffened. His dark eyes narrowed, focused on a spot behind me while his fingers clenched into a fist.

"I've got a really, *really* bad feeling," Everly continued, but my heart had already dropped, and I slowly turned to follow Drake's gaze. "Wherever you are, you need to get out of there—"

"Too late." Drake's voice lowered so only I would hear. Because we weren't alone anymore. I backed up a step, and Drake caught my shoulders before I could bump into him. Then he leaned close, his lips brushing my ear when he whispered, "Follow my lead."

Without hesitation, I nodded, and lowered my phone only to let it drop to the ground. Staring ahead, I stomped on the phone hard enough to crack it straight through. Everly's voice dissipated into the wind, but at least I wouldn't worry about them going after *her*. The man at the center between two vampires stepped forward.

While his buddies were dressed in simple suits, uniform and unremarkable except for their differences in height and hair color, the one who approached was clearly in charge. It was obvious even before a grin split his beige face, the mirth never reaching his piercing green eyes. Brown hair a shade lighter than mine curled beneath a mauve beret, the color matching the gentleman's suit he wore, outdated and old-fashioned.

In the blink of an eye, Drake subtly stepped in front of me.

"Don't let me interrupt your goodbyes," the man-in-charge said. His British accent was a surprise, and I gulped when his sight centered on my face before dipping to glance over the machete at my hip. "Unless your strumpet can't be charmed?"

Drake tensed, his attention flickering between the man and the two vampires flanking him. Then I figured out why the stranger was so weird. Because he was, in fact, a *man.* No trace of vampirism showed in his complexion, nor any sharpness to his canines when he grinned wide like this whole thing was a joke to him. What power could he have over the two behind him?

"She has no part in this, and your orders do not include her, Ezra. Of that, I am certain." Drake's jaw flexed, his ruthless gaze unwavering on the well-dressed man before us. Ezra sighed, twirling a finger like something invisible was swinging around it—when suddenly, there was. A long golden chain looped around his forefinger.

I inhaled a quick gasp at its appearance, absent one second and there the next. *No*—it shouldn't be possible. For vampires to have reorganized after Dracula's defeat was one thing, but to be using a sorcerer as their errand boy meant their political structure was in a whole new ballpark. In a single hour, Pandora's box had opened. *We were all fucked.*

"He has a point," Ezra murmured, glancing over his shoulder at the steadfast vampires behind him. With a shrug, he waved his hand and the pocket watch in his grasp disappeared, fading to nothing. "Plus, we didn't pack any food in the van, did you, boys?"

Neither vampire answered, and Ezra faced us again with a wave like 'let's get this over with.' Drake turned to me, his pointer finger suddenly crooked beneath my chin. Our eyes met, and for an insane moment, I wished I could go with him. Beyond Drake's melancholy acceptance, I glimpsed Ezra's shifty smile.

It prepared me a moment before the sorcerer muttered, "Go get her."

Our hearing equally heightened, and Drake's probably superior, we both whirled, our defensive stances set. The enemy advanced in a blur, one for each of us. Irony at working together with a vampire hit me as I blocked a strike with my forearm, preventing the shorter brown-haired undead guy from punching my head in.

Now several feet away, Drake and the taller blond one jabbed and dodged in quick succession, each landing hard blows but both owning dead nerves to prevent them from feeling the full effects of any impact. I couldn't watch them, instead preoccupied by the kick my opponent aimed for my hip.

Pivoting out of reach, I withdrew my machete in one quick movement and slashed. Instinct must have made the vampire back up in a flash, not nearly as ballsy as the one Drake took out the night before. This one seemed wary of my blade, and I pressed with my advantage while I had it. The best defense was a killer offense, so I swung in an arc, aiming not for the obvious point at the neck, but the backs of the vampire's thighs while I hastily feinted to hop-step for the vampire's flank.

My blade managed to cut through sinew, but not down to the bone. That didn't matter, my unexpected attack striking true meant the vampire wasn't anticipating my tactics. By the time he realized, he was slowed down by his shredded muscles. The vampire staggered, reaching out with clawed fingers to grab my hair.

My teeth gritted when I retreated, and several hairs were pulled out by the root. Scalp stinging, I heaved a harsh breath as a wet tearing sound and noisy crack pierced the night. No scream followed, and when I dared to look, I found Drake standing over the body of his opponent. The blond vampire's head wasn't just torn off—half of its shoulder went with it.

Dark blood coated Drake's clothes, his expression blank when he threw the pieces connected to the head far away. It landed in the shadows beyond a cluster of trees. Nausea swam in my guts at the brutality of the unrepentant gore. This was another level to anything I'd personally witnessed. The kind where life stopped making sense for several heartbeats.

Then my gaze met Drake's, and his horrified expression soon blurred as cold clammy fingers dug into my wrist. My grip slackened, knuckles spasming, and my machete fell while I bit down a shriek. Pain returned me to the moment, and I kicked at the vampire grabbing me.

Close as we were, my knee rammed into the enemy's side hard enough to crack ribs. If the vampire felt it, he didn't show it. My wrist was twisted unnaturally, forcing me to bend with it to keep it from breaking, and I went down on my knees. The earth was hard beneath my jeans as my gaze lifted to the starry sky when the clouds parted.

For one short second, my death played out in my mind's eye. Then there was a snap, and my wrist was freed. I slumped onto my side, scrambling away with my throbbing arm held close to my chest. Drake was on the vampire, whose arm dangled limp on one side. My vampire kicked the other's legs out from under him, already weakened from the work of my machete.

Our opponent went down, his white face neutral and unmoved while Drake grasped his neck in a blur. Then it all stopped. Between one of my heavy breaths and another, Drake collapsed to the ground—his eyes glazed over and unseeing, like a corpse.

"No!" I shouted, panicking when I found that my machete wasn't within arm's reach. My whole body trembled while soft footfalls neared, and my back stiffened. The sorcerer strode to where his lackey was struggling to pick himself up off the ground, but didn't offer an ounce of help. Instead, Ezra went to where my machete laid, near hidden in the unruly high grass.

Chilled sweat ran down the side of my cheek when he approached, forcing me to stare up into his smug face from where I knelt on the ground. Gloved hands held my machete, and his pitying stare was almost mocking.

"I'm intrigued," he admitted, relaxed as anything while I shivered from spent adrenaline.

"You're human," I spat, hoping I was wrong. When Ezra only raised his eyebrows, violent rage filled me with acid. "You're a traitor to your own people. Working for *them*? What the hell is wrong with you!"

"Obviously, you know what Ignatius Drake is, and you fought side by side," he pointed out, and my jaw snapped shut. "Perhaps we are not so different, you and I." A smirk played at the corner of his mouth.

"I am *nothing* like you," I hissed, resolute. Ezra's lips twitched, downturned for the briefest moment. His composure returned as he turned his back on me, walking tall toward the road where he came from.

"Restrain her, we're taking her with us."

Before I could scream for help, or try to run, pain sliced through my whole being. It was so instantaneous, and foul, leaving my mouth sizzling with electricity that prevented me from screeching through the agony. Every muscle went slack. My bones vibrated like they were trying to jump out of my skin.

When cold hands lifted me from the ground, and the vampire carried me away, his limp sent flashes of renewed torture from my fingers to my temples and down to my toes. White hot, invisible nails seemed to be gouging me from every direction. Through the insanity of the psychic pain, sporadic moments of clarity repeated one thought.

I was in deep shit.

— 10 —

A MEANINGLESS IDENTITY

SHIFTING METALLIC THUDS JOSTLED ME AWAKE. AT FIRST, I COULDN'T PLACE where or even who I was. Excruciating body aches set in. *That's right, I passed out at some point after my brain was fried with head-splitting agony.* Something smelled awful. When I pried my heavy eyelashes apart, the slick sensation of sweat covering me from head to toe settled over me like a film.

Great, the bad smell was *me.*

Arms trembling, I flexed my numb fingers, strung up high over my head. I didn't have to look to know that the pinching clamp around my wrists were shackles. My mouth tasted like sawdust when I tried to swallow, but couldn't manage it.

In the dim space, road noise pierced through the cold hard walls. *Was I inside some kind of a vehicle?* My vision slowly adapted to the surrounding darkness, but I startled when Drake spoke before I could even recognize his silhouette across from me.

"I am terribly sorry," he whispered, and despite the exhaustion vibrating through every word, I'd have recognized his accent any-

119

where. "Never did I wish for you to become involved. For any harm to come to you."

Caught way off guard by his quiet sincerity, I blinked several times through the sweat rolling down my brow, and licked my dry lips. It didn't help that my tongue felt like sandpaper, so I cleared my sore throat instead.

"What's going on?" I rasped, and then my sweat chilled like droplets of ice. "Those vampires. They took us, right? I—" Panic threatened to drag me under, but I needed to pull it together. This wasn't the time to break. "What's going to happen to us?"

"We will be executed," Drake answered, and my heart dropped while my brain whirred.

Ever since I started hunting, I knew my life could end at a moment's notice. A razor's edge my ancestors had walked along for generations. Too many had slipped off, *and now I would become one of the fallen*. Then Drake's brief explanation before we were ambushed surged to the forefront of my mind. Apparently, Van Helsing hadn't succeeded as much as we'd thought.

"By the Domnitori?" I suppressed a shiver while my freezing bare arms shook against my restraints. Through the darkness, Drake's gaze held mine as he shook his head. Despite not knowing anything about the vampire overlords, that felt like a relief. A stuttered breath passed my lips, and I closed my eyes. "Then where are we going?"

"To New York," he answered, and my eyes flew open. "It is where the Cneaz resides year-round. Our journey north will only grow colder. I am sorry." His attention flickered to the exposed flesh at my throat, and I could have sworn he swallowed as a chill traced my spine.

"So I'm going to die." I exhaled a rough, hysterical laugh. "And nobody back home will even know what happened to me." For all my daring acceptance of the risks, the hunting lifestyle, I had hoped whatever end I met would be quick. Not dragged out for months in a hospital room like Mom's fate… At least she had had the chance to say goodbye. "Looks like I failed as badly as Helsing did."

"What do you mean?" Drake asked, curiosity lacing his tone. I started to shrug, but the shackles restricted the gesture.

"He was supposed to end Dracula's reign of terror, and he didn't, not really. Vampires are still out there, they continue to hurt people, and here I am." I savored the burn of cold air in my lungs. It meant I was still breathing. "Being carted off by a bunch of bastard vamps who answer to some high-up aristocratic parasite." My jaw clenched, and it was an effort to continue. "Everything my family and I have sacrificed has been for nothing. We didn't even know this kind of threat still walked the Earth."

"If it is any consolation, your ancestor *did* alter history for the better," Drake pressed, and despite our reckless kiss in the park, I couldn't understand why he seemed so intent on reassuring me of anything. "When I was young, I witnessed the acts of Vlad Dracula the Fourth—"

"What?" I squeaked, equally torn between being horrified, and awed. "You… You were alive back then?"

"I was one of the last of his chosen children."

For a second, everything else left my head. Shock overshadowed the pain and aches, disappearing alongside my deep-seated terror. Sure, Drake was old, but I never expected *this*.

"That's—" I cleared my throat. "Impressive." When Drake briefly laughed, the sardonic sound managed to pull a smirk from my cracked lips.

"Hardly, and that is what I am attempting to explain. Most of us still existing today are from the same era. Very few immortals are created in this age, and your ancestor is to be thanked for that." His words managed to warm the center of my heart, that there being less vampires was a *good* thing. It helped, even if it only distracted me from our impending death for a moment.

A memory clicked into place, from before I left my family at the club, and drove to the Rio Bravo park where Drake awaited. In hindsight, he must have known the other vampires and the sorcerer would come for him. Except that wasn't what made me pause. It was another player on the field whose nosy involvement hadn't made any sense before.

Carefully, I wiggled my hips to figure out if that little orb the faery gave me was still nestled safely in my pocket and—miraculously—it was.

Hope surged, my breathing sped up, but I tamped it down before I could give anything away. My hearing picked up every pothole and passing car on the road. I would bet the vampire driving this—*van?*—had superior hearing even to a descendant of Helsing.

Coming up with a plan would have to wait, so I refocused on the conversation at hand, and asked, "How is that possible? And why aren't there any new vampires being made?"

When the van jostled, I stifled a shriek as the shackles pulled at the sores forming across my wrist bones. Drake's brow pinched, concern crossing his features while I breathed through the pain.

"It was made illegal shortly after Dracula suffered his final death, sometime around seventeen-fifty-two." Drake's tone was perfunctory, like talking about what happened almost three hundred years ago was inconsequential. Maybe that's what it was like to survive for so long. The impact of events packed less of a punch.

"Why? Their whole plan was for world domination, wasn't it?" At least, that's what I'd been raised to believe Dracula had been after.

"Once their *voievod,* Dracula, was gone, the Domnitori acted as a council to lead the remaining immortals. Many of them 'saw the writing on the wall,' so to speak. They feared human invention, the acceleration at which it was progressing, and opted to enact a law of secrecy."

"The vampire leaders…fear *us*?" I balked, but Drake nodded.

"Perhaps they can terrorize and torment the few, charm those who fight against them—but the entirety of the human population?" Drake scoffed, his lip curling. "Dracula only believed it was possible because he existed during the aftermath of the Black Death. When humans fell left and right like flies, their numbers in Europe decimated with the ease of neglect. Many of his council came long after, nearing the industrial age, and they were right to be afraid."

Flooded with too many revelations, I blurted, "My… My family always told the story like Dracula was given his immortality by the devil." Part of me needed to know, if only to ground myself, just how much I'd been misled to believe—or chose to ignore. "Grandpa explained that there were three brothers, the sons of Vlad the Impaler…"

Being a story I'd been told since childhood, the rehearsed words flowed easily off my tongue. "The oldest was Mihnea, followed by Alexandru, and then finally Dracula. When the Impaler died, Mihnea was too sickly to take the throne of Wallachia, a failing kingdom already. Except Dracula wanted to rule instead, so badly that he made a deal with the devil for immortality, speed, strength, heightened senses…" Everything that made vampires the monsters who preyed on people.

"He received it, yet it came at a price," Drake continued on my behalf, and my gaze shot to his. Dark eyes bore into mine, and my stomach warmed beneath his unwavering attention. "Consuming the life blood of others was key to maintaining such 'eternal youth.' Under the rays of sunlight, our true ages are revealed which cast us as skeletal creatures—held together by magick and wicked deeds."

A small, sardonic grin tugged at the corners of his mouth. "With his newfound strength, Dracula bested his elder brother, Alexandru, yet lost interest in Wallachia when he set his sights on *more*. Whether that was the continent, or the globe in its entirety, I have no clue. The world seemed smaller in those days."

"Except Alexandru didn't die," I argued through a cough, my parched mouth almost at its limit. The distraction of our conversation was the only thing keeping my thoughts from spiraling, so I clung to my family's oral history instead of acknowledging whatever future laid ahead. "During his final breaths, he was visited by the archangel, Michael, and given a similar version of immortality. But his came with an expiration date. That was the balance, or something. Over the centuries, he eventually took on a new name—Abraham Van Helsing.

"Once he killed Dracula, he aged like any ordinary man. That's how I came to be…" It was how Grandpa always ended the story, impressing onto us, even as kids, that we were part of a great legacy. One which led to Helsing's *great* descendant being chained up in a van, driven across the country by vampires and some asshole sorcerer.

A curse, more like, because how many of us survived into the golden years? My father and uncle were the oldest generation still alive and actively hunting. Grandpa retired ages ago, long after his own brother was killed in the crossfire during a hunt. We had no extended relatives on the Harker side. None of them survived the legacy.

Looks like I landed on the wrong side of my family's history.

"I have been taught a similar version of events," Drake acknowledged, but his whispered words brought the conversation to a close.

A sigh rattled through my lungs while I thought about my family. *Why did they have to push me to this point?* Was this what I deserved for what I put them through last year? Would I never get the chance to earn their forgiveness?

My eyes shut tight, holding back the prickling tears.

"How long—" I cleared my aching throat while my wrists throbbed and empty stomach twisted. "How much longer until we get wherever they're taking us?" It was hard to believe our destination, and maybe it made the situation less real not to name it.

"Enough distance exists between now and then for you to rest—if you can," he tacked on, and my stinging eyes opened. Surrounded by the van's jostle, speeding down unknown highways, my chest shuddered with a suppressed sob.

When I had no one, not even my machete to make me feel safe, Drake's steadfast kindness cut through the chaos inside my head. Somehow, just his presence here with me became a comfort. Maybe because we were both racing toward the same fate, our destinies now intertwined. Whatever the reason, I couldn't shake the burgeoning warmth squeezing my heart while chills skittered over my shoulders and down my spine.

Minutes passed after silence descended between us. Each second punctuated by the same confusing question. *How had I ever considered him my enemy?*

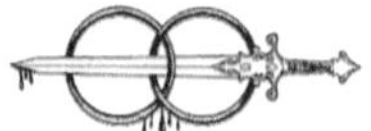

The stale dry air worsened the cotton feeling in my mouth. Staring down at the floor of the van, I couldn't help but stew in misery. Thankfully, Drake only asked how I felt once since I woke from the latest in a series of uncomfortable naps. My non-committal response about wishing for water was answered with more sympathy, but no promises.

Never in my life did I think I'd be this thirsty, or that I'd rather starve for days than go one more second without something to drink—anything, at this point. Through the brain fog, I tried to sort out how much time had passed. *Damn these shackles,* everything from my fingertips to my tailbone hurt.

Picturing my family was the only thing that blocked out the relentless thirst and stomach-growling hunger. How long would it have taken them to realize I was missing? Everyone had been having such a good time at the club… *Everly*—she would have alerted them that something was wrong.

Except, even if they learned right away that I'd gone missing, none of them would have a clue about why or where I'd disappeared to. Unless they decided to scour every street of Albuquerque, the chance of them finding my car before the vampires' trail went cold was too slim to hope for. Even with the help of Elias's fellow Navajo contacts at the police department, nobody could turn back the clock.

The slow acceptance that they weren't coming to save me set in. Everly might have some natural inclination toward precognition, but she wasn't infallible. Hell, nothing she'd ever shown me came close to what that sorcerer could do. Besides, I didn't want her involved if it meant she risked getting hurt.

Secrets and stupidity would cost me my life, but I wouldn't drag others down with me. Somehow, that small ounce of martyrdom renewed my vigor. Sure, I was going to die, but I'd still go down swinging—

The trundle of the van's tires changed their tune. We clearly weren't on the highway anymore, or asphalt in general. When the van suddenly stopped, I lurched along with it. Inhaling a hiss through my teeth at the sharp, stinging sensations bolting down my bound arms, I got my legs under me in time to keep my hip from banging into the interior wall.

Car doors slammed from the front cab. Adrenaline put my senses on high alert. My vision cleared in the darkness while my heart thrummed with anticipation. Drake's posture stiffened, and his gaze shot to the back of the van.

"Prepare yourself," Drake whispered, his low voice triggering my heart to pound. "I will do what I can to keep you unharmed." His dark eyes met mine, and he winced. "As best as I can." Before I could respond, the doors banged open. Light blinded my vision, and I blinked in quick succession.

The scrape of chains followed as cold hands gripped my wrists, and the shorter vampire ripped free the bolt holding them to the van's interior. He held my chains tight while leading me out with a sharp pull. With my legs numbed from the awkward position I'd been in, I stumbled only to fall right out of the van with an undignified grunt.

My ringing ears made it hard to hear, but I registered the sound of Drake's voice, deep with his thickening accent while he growled foreign words to the vampire that had dragged me out. Laid out on the ground, I stared skyward as rocks pressed and poked against my bare arm and into my side. My breath fogged with each exhale.

Closely-grown pines obscured the oppressive clouds above that felt so much closer than the expansive blue skies I'd grown up with. Streaks of orange and pink shot across the sky, fading to a blanket of glittering stars on the far side, *near sunset.* The ringing in my ears abated as my shoulders were gripped firmly by a stranger's hands.

It was the tall blond vampire who lifted me, and I quickly got my knees under myself, followed by my feet. I wobbled, but caught myself before the vampire took the chance to touch me again. When my gaze found Drake's, I stifled a gasp.

It shouldn't have been a shock to see him under the dying rays of sunlight, but it was. Maybe because I'd convinced myself that he was more man than monster on our endless journey here, but the day had a habit of bringing uncomfortable truths to light. His dark irises were surrounded by bloodshot sclera. Red rimmed the lash line of his eyes, sunken into his stark bone structure which was covered by a thinning layer of deathly pale grayed skin.

Deep hollows stood out along his temples and beneath his cheekbones. All of his features, already so angular, turned ghoulish and grotesque. The only part of him wholly unchanged were the straight strands of black hair falling across his forehead and over his ears. As he neared, a step ahead of the shorter vampire who now held his chains, I buried the impulse to back away.

"You cannot die," he urged in a whisper when he passed, inches away from me, and turned his gaze ahead. "If you discover an opening, love—flee."

My breath caught, but I took a step to follow to avoid being pushed around again. Then I looked up, and my stride faltered. Cobblestone created a walkway on either side of the white quartz stones surrounding an enormous fountain. It must have been a dozen feet taller than me, crafted from granite and depicting a horrible image of a bat-winged creature devouring a young woman's throat.

Water poured from torn stone skin, pooling in the basin to reflect the colonial-style porch of the brick building ahead. Several white pillars lined the stoop, as long as my family's entire church. An elaborate solid oak door was set into the surrounding brick, with ornate storm windows on either side, shuttered closed.

Forcing my legs to move, my gaze traveled upward—and up some more. The thing must have been three stories tall, and so long on either side that its end disappeared into the surrounding pines. Shoulders hunched, I climbed the three steps to the stoop and shuffled across the glossy varnished porch.

Goosebumps crawled over my flesh while I tried and failed not to shiver. The human sorcerer was nowhere to be found, and the shorter dark-haired vampire moved ahead to wait before the doors. Drake stopped beside him beneath the stone overhang that held up the balcony above. Now shaded from direct sunlight, he glanced over his shoulder at me and I stared back at his handsome face. His brow twitched, nearly pinched with concern, but then his lips pressed together, and his features settled into a placid mask.

The doors ahead opened, so soundless that I shuddered, but grit my teeth in preparation of what awaited behind them. Inside the manor was another sight to behold, one I didn't even try to take in fully. A grand staircase stood at the end of the foyer, its banister wooden but stained black while a golden runner climbed its white steps.

Marble floors shone under my boots, nearly reflecting the unlit red-wax candles peeking out from the chandelier high above. Paintings lined the wood-paneled walls on either side, many of them depicting men and women in the throes of passion while blood poured from their torn flesh onto sheets or chaises. A brush of air against the nape of my neck indicated the doors were closing. I shivered as the soft glow of dying light from outside vanished.

A lock was bolted shut, and I gave into the urge to look back. Two suits of armor stood on either side of the closed doors, both sporting wolf's head helmets and holding long spears. *Wait,* who had closed the doors?

Foreign words spoken by an unfamiliar voice swung my attention forward. I followed Drake's gaze to the railing at the top of the stairs, separating the second floor from a long drop down. My lips parted, confused and baffled by the gross amount of wealth adorning the vampire who stood at the balcony.

Pale blond hair fell straight to his shoulders while icy blue eyes met mine. A smile flickered across the edges of his wide mouth, hidden too fast for me to guess at its meaning. Golden rings embedded with gemstones clung to his long white fingers. An embroidered long-sleeved vest in a deep royal blue stood out against the pallor of his neck and hands.

The golden necklace hanging to his chest barely stirred as he walked soundlessly down the stairs. In a blur, he appeared several feet away, and I retreated a step on instinct. My back hit the tall vampire escort, and I cringed when a chill climbed my spine. The regal vampire moved closer, and my fists clenched.

"If you touch her, you will find there are no bindings strong enough to hold me, Lucian," Drake said, his voice low with lethal promise while his gaze tracked the vampire. Lucian paused in his approach, and slowly turned his icy stare onto Drake.

"So strange, Ignatius," Lucian began, his accent strong enough to almost make his English unintelligible. "I have never understood why you choose to keep humans as companions. It is beneath your status to roll in the mud with the pigs."

"As a fellow of the old guard, you ought to respect my threats," Drake replied, unmoved, and a beat of silence passed between the two vampires. Then Lucian let out a dark chuckle. My nails ground into my palms—too numbed with cold to feel it—and I looked at Drake.

He only glanced at me, but it felt like a warning. Except I had no idea what it meant. Lucian snapped his fingers, his voice like a whip when he spoke in another language, and metal creaked behind me. Nearly jumping out of my skin, I whirled on the suits of armor that I'd assumed were empty decorations. My eyes widened, tracking their eerily fluid movements. Like the dozens of pounds of metal weighing down their bodies was nothing at all.

Drake shouted back at Lucian, his words and their significance lost to me while I faced down the approaching suits of armor. The taller of our vampire escorts still held my chains, but I had the element of surprise when I yanked them free from his lazy grip. In strangely steady hands, I held the links before striking out against the suit of armor.

I managed to wrap the chain once around the suit's wrist, pulling down hard to get the person inside off balance. They only leaned over a few inches. Their staggered movement showed they hadn't anticipated my strength, but *I'd* underestimated their reaction time. A metal-clad elbow snapped out, striking my face.

Pain erupted across my cheekbone as my vision clouded with spots, and then my palms were flat on the marble floor. Metal scraped, and shouts echoed around the incredibly large room while my arm was twisted behind my back. Shallow pants scorched up and down my throat, but my vision cleared as I was dragged away and up the stairs by the armored asshole.

Drake was being held to the floor, the taller vampire escort's knee on his back while the dark-haired one held his chained arms taut behind him. My vampire's right fist was bloodied and broken, but that was nothing compared to the armored guard sprawled on the ground. Blood poured from a wound punched straight through their chest where the metal breastplate gaped inward.

Lucian only laughed. A glint sparkled in his icy blue eyes as he turned a disappointed sneer from the dead guard to where I was being yanked up the stairs. Our gazes met, and chills racked my spine while the remaining armored guard hauled my weakened body to the right, through an archway on the second level.

— 11 —

BE YOUR SAVIOR

MY SKULL THROBBED AS MY VISION WENT IN AND OUT OF FOCUS. THE several hallways I was dragged down blended from the last into the next. Nausea built in my throat, but I was pushed through an arched doorway before I could upchuck bile. The room spun as I stumbled only to collapse onto the rug spread across the stone floor.

The closing door sounded distant. At some point, my shackles had been removed, but my arms were still prickling with pins and needles. Except I was too exhausted to move a muscle...

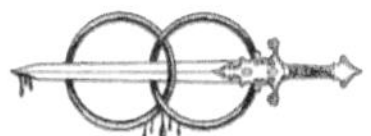

It was the damnedest thing, but I *smelled* water. As I forced my crusty eyes open, instinct took over, and I crawled across the room toward a basin in the shadows. Unable to stand fast enough, I grasped the edge and dunked my head into the shallow tub before gulping mouthfuls.

The water tasted different, almost sour, and the air smelled weird. Stale, like nobody else had been in this room for a long time. When I emerged from the basin, looking around to try and distract myself from my cramping stomach threatening my gag reflex, I frowned at the oddly homey interior.

A large four-poster bed sat opposite the paneled windows—boarded up from the outside. The edge of sparse sunlight surrounding the shutters' perimeter barely illuminated the piles of pillows and blankets adorning the made up bed. Too tempted to resist, and with my thirst finally quenched after what must have been *days* of dehydration, I staggered across the Persian rug to the bed.

Not bothering to be nice about it, I yanked the covers off to surround myself in a cocoon of wool and cotton. Then I sat down on the mattress, and that was a mistake. Immediately, everything came crashing down. The spare moment of rest triggered shivers that racked my body, and panic erupted.

There was no escape, but still I tried the locked windows. I pounded against the glass with everything I had. Tried to pierce it with furniture I'd kicked until it busted into splintered stakes. Shin bruised and throbbing, I went to the door, the only way in or out since the windows were apparently magicked to be invincible.

"Hey!" I screamed, my throat hoarse from disuse. "Let me out of here!" I slammed my palm against the solid wooden door, but it didn't budge. "You can't keep me locked in here forever!"

Suddenly, I stopped. Because they *could*. Nobody was coming for me, and they must have had Drake restrained—locked down tight after what happened in the entrance hall. Tears spilled over my lashes, running down my cheeks in waves I couldn't stop. I covered my mouth with my hand and squeezed my eyes shut.

None of them would have the satisfaction of hearing me cry. There may be no way out, but… Holding on to a shred of hope, I felt my front jeans pocket. *The orb*, it was safe, whole. My tears stopped falling. Devastation turned into resilience, and the anticipation of revenge.

I didn't know what the hell the little golden ball did, but as I glared straight at the door ahead of me, I had a suspicious feeling it might be my ticket out of here.

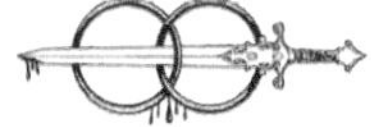

Grayish light darkened around the window's corners while I sat wrapped in several blankets. I'd regained sensation in my extremities hours ago, or at least, that was my best guess for how long it'd been. The watch on my wrist was busted, but I kept it on in case I could use its steel as a blunt weapon in a pinch.

At the slightest creak of the settling manor, my spine stiffened. When the seconds ticked away, I relaxed into stoic impatience. A whole day hadn't passed yet, but my skin crawled with unease. Deep pits in my stomach ached, gurgling so frequently that it became a repetitive background noise. *How long would it take for me to starve to death?*

Focusing was difficult, and my fingers trembled no matter how tightly I clenched my fists. Eventually, the entire room dimmed into pitch black. Time passed in the darkness, and I'd resolved myself for another night in this wretched place when a knock came at the door.

I nearly tripped over my bundle of blankets in my rush to stand at the ready. By the time I steadied, my right foot back and my hands fisted for a fight, the door swung open. Apparently, vampires didn't need a response to barge in on an unsuspecting prisoner.

"Oh." The woman's red-painted lips formed a delicate 'o' while she briefly looked me up and down. Black ringlets fell down the back of her silken scarlet gown, glistening under the candlelight seeping in from the hall as she glanced at the basin by the far wall. It wasn't empty, but I'd already drank all of the water. Her pale nose wrinkled. "You were meant to bathe, *human*." The word came out like a slur, and my eyes narrowed.

At least *I* was alive. While I wanted to tell her 'too bad,' I kept my mouth shut. Her blue-eyed gaze swept back to focus on mine, and her lips pursed.

"Ah well, at least the filthy clothes will be stripped away."

"Excuse me?" Caught off guard, my stance relaxed when she snapped her fingers. My brow furrowed while an armored hand offered what looked like a garment bag to the woman vampire. Without a word of thanks or any acknowledgement to the guard, the vampire strode closer while holding the bag aloft by the hook on one end.

"You will not entertain the gathered court dressed in rags. Remove everything, no one will be impressed by the scent oozing off your undergarments."

"What the hell are you talking about? What is happening?" My fists slowly lowered as I warily eyed the white bag. "Where—Where is Drake?"

"Ignatius Drake?" she tittered, like this was casual gossip between friends, but the shiver that climbed my spine at her hungry stare proved otherwise. The vampire laid the bag down across the disorganized bed sheets, and unzipped it. Within was a shocking gown, at least to me, since it was about as fancy as the one the vampire wore. Green velvet of varying shades formed swirls over the bodice which then flowed down into a multi-layered skirt.

The vampire woman held it up and shimmied it, revealing the loose off-the-shoulder sleeves. *How the hell was it meant to stay up?* Horror dawned when I put together what she'd said. I was supposed to *wear* that thing?

"He will stand trial. It is most enjoyable. The last execution was *ages* ago." Her attention remained on the dress while my stomach knotted. Then those beady eyes turned on me. "Of course, you will be a most helpful material witness."

"Witness?" More like a hostage, but that would be semantics among vampires. The woman either ignored or didn't catch my sarcastic tone because she simply hummed a sound of agreement, and placed the dress back on the bed.

"Your escort will arrive shortly. I hope the dress fits." She eyed my full hips, and I shifted from one foot to the other. "If not, perhaps Lucian will have you taken to his private rooms—nude." A catty smile flitted across her face on her exit. Movement a blur, she left the room with such haste that it must've been meant to unsettle me.

Except as the door clicked shut, locked once more from the outside, I couldn't suppress my shiver. Come hell or high water, I was going to stuff myself into that damn dress. I wiped my sweaty palms on my disgusting jeans and then unbuttoned them.

The orb in my pocket went straight into my sock, held snugly between my foot and combat boot. Alone, and naked, since my underwear reeked as badly as my tank top, I worked on getting the dress over my head. Even with the zipper undone, it was a hassle figuring out which were the neck and arm holes. By the time it was on straight, it felt like my ribs were encased in fabric shackles.

No matter how many times I held my breath, the stupid zipper was stuck only a couple of inches from closing. Flushed and frustrated, I gave up on it. Then I plopped onto the bed to catch my breath from the minimal effort. This wasn't good, and even with the orb up my sleeve—or down my sock—I had no idea what it was meant to do or really how to activate it.

I closed my eyes for a long moment that turned into several more while my heart raced. There was no knock at the door before it creaked, and my eyes flew open. I was on my feet instantly, woozy but determined not to show it. Especially when I recognized who stood in the back-lit doorway.

"What are *you* doing here?" I demanded, and the sorcerer had the gall to look offended by my tone.

"Every respectable young lady needs an escort," Ezra answered, the corners of his lips twitching when my eyes narrowed.

"Very funny," I grumbled, frowning at his offered arm. Undead monsters lunging at my throat, I could handle. Outdated etiquette in the proverbial lion's den was way out of my comfort zone. When I showed no indication of moving things along, Ezra sighed.

"You will fare better if you play your part," he advised, and I scoffed.

"Is that what you're doing? Are you just acting like a traitor to your own kind, or are you really that low?" Despite my vitriol, Ezra appeared unfazed.

"It's the latter. Happy?" His bright smile lit up his piercing green eyes. Gritting my teeth, I stared at his arm.

"Do I have to?" I asked, my voice smaller than intended, and only then did it seem like Ezra's expression faltered.

"It's in your best interest." His tone was flat, but there was something in his stare that made me uncomfortable. Like I was being scrutinized under an x-ray. Then his attention traveled lower, landing on my boot. A frown pinched his features, and I quickly closed the distance between us.

"Okay, fine," I snapped, my pulse pounding, fearing what he might have sensed. Thankfully, his gaze returned to mine when I awkwardly grasped his arm like I did to the handlebars on my first bicycle. "Let's get out of this room. I'm sick of it, anyway."

A sour smile spread across his lips while he adjusted my arm so that it was under and around his. The oddly intimate contact with the man who caused me such intense psychic pain only a few days ago made me stiffen, and I kept my back straight as Ezra led us out into the hall.

There was no guard outside the door to my prison, but Ezra was more than capable of knocking me down if needed. Slowly, I breathed in and out while my gaze roamed the wide hallway. Paintings were hung interspersed between weapons on display, almost like how Caleb had decorated his bedroom.

Except while Caleb collected band posters and Native American artifacts, all of the pointy objects here looked like something out of medieval Europe. Every window was shuttered closed, locked down so tightly that no ounce of sun or moonlight would penetrate. Lit sconces lined the wallpapered hall, emitting an eerie glow over the golden runner we strode down.

"What do these monsters have against natural lighting?" I muttered, bristling when Ezra chuckled. I looked him up and down, from his dark purple suit to the oddly fitting beret atop his brown curls. "What?"

"Oh, nothing at all." Ezra's smiling lips pressed closed momentarily. "All brawn and no brains makes for an interesting combination."

"Yeah, well, at least I'm not stupid enough to turn my back on my own people," I retorted in a whisper, and then jumped when Ezra's arm tightened against mine.

"Trust me, 'people' made me the man I am today." His relaxed features were aloof, but those piercing green eyes seemed to burn behind the pupils. Swallowing hard, I struggled not to shrink from his presence.

"And vampires made me into what I have to be." My voice pitched low, and sweat beaded on my brow, but I refused to show the sorcerer any fear.

He blinked, and the unexpectedly vulnerable reaction emboldened me. Where did he get off trying to tell me that *people* were the problem? Whatever sob story existed in his past didn't justify the hell of my present.

Ezra's brows pulled together curiously, but I faced ahead after we turned yet another corner. A subtly beating drum was growing stronger. It pulsed louder underfoot, accompanied by the cadence of stringed instruments that filtered down the barren corridors. Hairs rose along my exposed arms, and my jaw clenched. Somewhere ahead, the scent of decay wafted closer, and the undead hungered.

"How can you even stand being around them?" I mumbled. "All they are is death and depravity."

"You seem to manage just fine," Ezra replied, tone lofty and superior. *Was he crazy?* I spun to face him.

"I'd kill every single one of those bastards given the chance—"

"I didn't see your *blade* inside Ignatius Drake's throat when I found you two."

Heat rushed to my face, and I opened my mouth only to stammer in shock. "That's not— It's different, I— Why do you care!" My exclamation was followed by Ezra's laughter, but it quickly died when I started to pull from his grasp.

"Not yet," Ezra murmured, still sounding amused despite the severe grip he kept on my arm. It hurt where his suit rubbed against my bruised wrist, but his hold loosened when I stopped trying to move away.

"What's going on?" Real fear kept my voice quiet while the music grew louder as we approached the next bend.

"A performance," Ezra answered, his words nearly lost in the thrum when we turned the corner. Hushed conversations faltered, unfinished sentences fading to nothing.

Vampires stood in clusters of twos and threes along the landing above the grand staircase that had left my hips bruised. An undead man and woman lingered beside an alcove set beneath the archway. Each dressed to the nines in lavish fabrics and gaudy pieces of jewelry. Both caressed the bloodied neck of the charmed human between them, who looked like he was barely able to stand on his feet.

Pale blue eyes stared unseeing while the person held up a silver platter of teetering champagne glasses filled with blood. My stomach lurched, on the verge of being sick, and I stared in helpless horror when both vampires turned their cruel gazes toward me. Chills shook my spine, and I stiffened to keep from bending double.

It felt like I couldn't get enough air, but my heart kept on pumping the blood those freaks of nature were after. Ezra's hold on my arm tightened, his steps seeming unhurried to anyone else while he towed me along. Anger surged for the charmed person between the two monsters, and the sole of my boot scraped against the rug underfoot when I made to turn around—

"Ignatius Drake is downstairs," Ezra said between smiling teeth, barely audible if he hadn't leaned in close to my ear. I met his gaze, my jaw slackening into overwhelmed terror. No matter how slowly I tried to inhale, I couldn't catch my breath. The sorcerer moved us closer to the stairs, past several groupings of vampires and the occasional subordinate human. "If you try to free anyone, you'll die before ever getting to him. And wouldn't that be a pity?"

Hatred boiled up, for Ezra as much as myself. Because the innocent's face was stark in my mind's eye as we descended the stairs. Every step twinged in my ribs, but the ache didn't compare to the pain the man's family would endure when he never returned. This wasn't *right*, and walking away wasn't what I'd been trained to do. If I had a choice, or a chance to—

Would I take it?

If I failed to take down the undead, then it would be me in the man's place.

Which was exactly what I deserved.

By the time we reached the ground floor, my head was woozy, my lungs working overtime, and I shut it down. Guilt was a luxury I could indulge if I survived.

Once the dozen or more vampires loitering in the entrance hall realized I was here, and human, their bloodlust turned to me. Ice seemed to trickle down every bone in my back. I lifted my head high to hide my repulsion while Ezra led us toward a pair of elaborately-carved doors that nearly reached the ceiling.

Before I could ask what lay beyond, a crack appeared between the closed doors on our approach. While the fissure widened, my attention drifted to a display table against the wall.

Beneath an unremarkable painting as tall as me, a glass enclosure was filled with glittering jewels and strings of pearls strung across what appeared at first glance to be a golden tea set. A beating reverberated between my eardrums as the music grew deafening, emanating from the room ahead, but my focus was drawn to the chalice at the center of the case—

"Ogle later, I have duties to attend to." Ezra's voice cut through the buzzing growing in my head, and I blinked. His clenched jaw undercut the smirk plastered across his face, and I grimaced while the enormous doors swung open on either side.

"Bite me," I spat through gritted teeth as we crossed the threshold.

"Not quite the sentiment I'd recommend, considering where you are."

At his whispered rebuttal, I faced ahead and had to snap my teeth together to keep my mouth from hanging open. The room stretched as far as my family's church property, impossibly huge with a tray ceiling revealing carved marble edges and angelic imagery painted across the expanse.

Black and gold colors edged the baroque-style walls, and a pang of nostalgia shot through me at the memory of watching home renovation shows with Aunt Susan. At the center of the room was a raised dais where an empty throne rested at its pinnacle. The marble inlay flooring's pattern was obscured by the packed dancers billowing across its surface.

Nothing at all like the club I'd been in only days ago. The vampires who danced to the instrumental music—being played in the corner by charmed humans—were going above and beyond to display etiquette and grace that degraded the second I considered what sort of foul monsters stepped and swished before me. My fingers itched for my machete, but came up empty in the velvet folds of my dress.

Then I felt a tug on my hand, and was abruptly pulled into the throng. Too surprised to do much except watch my clumsy footwork, I stared up at Ezra in horror while he led me.

"I can't dance!" I almost shrieked. The opportunity to learn for my quinceañera had been stolen by Mom's death when I was fourteen. As if the whole thing hadn't been tragic enough. Dull heartache throbbed in my chest, but it kept me focused on the dance and not on how dizzy the movements made me.

"If you don't play a part, you'll be hooked off the stage." Ezra's demeanor seemed too calm, but his words rang true. Starved and terrified, I gripped his gloved hands harder to ignore the pangs both inside my head and along my body. Because I wanted to *live*. Some selfish, surviving part of me said to hell with everybody else.

After years of saving others, and then nearly getting one of my own killed, I hated the vampires. Most days, I also despised myself. Now that I was faced with the 'easy' way out, a chance to die with the excuse of it being 'out of my hands,' I couldn't let it happen. Maybe revenge fueled me, to get back at the murdering bastards who charmed people into non-consensual service. Whatever the reason, I was going to play my damn part to stay alive.

Even if it killed me—*which it probably would.*

Deafening music beat in my ears alongside the rush of my pulse while Ezra danced us closer to the center of the room. On every spin, I glimpsed hungry glares directed my way. Suits of armor stood positioned equidistant along the wall. Their wolf's head helmets, the breathing vents like black holes that showed nothing within, was a damn more comforting sight compared to the cackling ghouls waltzing around me.

The room spun even after Ezra slowed his pace. Through my pounding headache, I tried to find a familiar face. The only one I cared about seeing. Except the crowd of vampires all looked alike. Some moved so fast that only an after-image was left in their wake. I shut my eyes tight, my hands feeling numb in Ezra's warm grip.

Relief flooded through me when we slowed to a stop, but then Ezra's accented voice redoubled my defenses.

"Damn." The one whispered word made me open my eyes to find Ezra staring over my head. His expression transformed, an almost pained grin splitting his features between his tense eyes and the hard set to his square jaw.

"Prepare the main event, sorcerer."

I whirled when the thick Eastern European accented voice spoke behind me. Icy blue eyes caught my gaze, and a nasty, feral smile spread across Lucian's thin face.

"Certainly." Ezra bowed his head, his hand still in mine as he turned away.

"Leave the lolly," Lucian said, almost too quiet to hear, and Ezra's palm slipped from mine. The last I saw of him was the brief glimpse of piercing green eyes glancing back at me before the sorcerer's purple suit and beret blended into the waltzing wash of colors surrounding us.

Pain trickled down my spine, so stiff from the surrounding bloodlust that Lucian's attention on me started to hurt. Jaw clenched, I faced him with every ounce of dignity I had left. The vampire in charge of this whole charade extended his sickly pale hand, and my fists tightened at my sides. My gut instinct was to tell him *fuck off*, but Ezra's warning replayed in my head.

This was all an elaborate act, and if I didn't play along then I wouldn't be tolerated among these filthy rich undead—their assets stolen from their murdered victims. *I still had to find Drake,* and my concern for him spurred my action, placing my bitterly cold hand atop Lucian's freezing fingers. Instantly, his grip tightened against my knuckles until they burned.

I didn't have time to do anything but inhale a hiss before Lucian pulled me closer. After dancing with Ezra, I anticipated the steps but had to quicken my pace to keep up with the blond vampire. Suppressing a wince when my ankles burned from the strain, I was breathing fast within the confines of my dress by the time Lucian had led me across half the ballroom.

"Such agony," Lucian murmured, sounding like he was talking more to himself than me. Cruel blue eyes bore into mine, seeming intent to scour my brain for secrets left unturned. *At least he couldn't charm me.* "What is the purpose?

To care for something so fragile. A pet that will never last the toll of time."

"Even a tiger can be chained, but that doesn't mean it won't bite your head off given the chance," I spat, and Lucian seemed surprised that I had replied at all. My eyes widened when he yanked me into a twirl which almost pulled me off balance. Biting my lip, I concentrated on my footwork, reminiscent of training with my cousins. My breath puffed out when I hit the solid surface of Lucian's chest, finding there was armor beneath his frilled ivory shirt.

When I tried to move away, Lucian's grip squeezed my knuckles closer to my wrist. I stifled a shriek, glaring up into his icy gaze.

"You willingly refer to yourself as an animal?" His tone was impassive, condescending and unaffected as we stood stock still near the center of the room before the dais.

"If it keeps me alive then you can call me a fucking honey badger for all I care," I seethed, my arm muscles straining under his tight hold that kept me way too close to him. The smell of blood wafted off his breath, and I nearly choked. Instead, I held my breath, counting my heartbeats while others slowed their dancing around us.

The band's final notes were left to hang in the atmosphere, reverberating from wall to ceiling. I subtly slid my left foot back to gain some distance and said, "Whatever you want to call me doesn't change what you all really are."

"And what is that, Descendant?" Lucian asked, as quiet as if he only intended for me to hear despite every surrounding vampire listening in. Any one of them might have been the bastard who condemned Drake to these suckers. Rage at the injustice strengthened my resolve when Lucian leaned closer, and I braced my aching legs not to retreat. "What will your final words be when I devour every last drop of your lifeblood?"

A shiver shook me, and my chest heaved while the bodice constricted my breathing. Somewhere behind me, the shuffling thuds from suits of armor accompanied the rattle of chains.

"You're monsters," I answered, shoving any semblance of fear so far down that I could pretend I accepted this end with whatever pride I had left. "Every single one of you—" My words cut off when Lucian released my hands, his motion fast enough to spin me around one last time despite utter silence surrounding us.

The unexpected movement made me teeter on my boot heels. *Shit, the orb!* Black and gold marble tile rushed up to meet me when I fell to keep the pressure off my foot. The impact jarred my bones as my knees and elbows hit the ground with a loud smack. Metal clinked nearby, and I looked up.

Air rushed into my lungs when I found familiar dark eyes staring back. There he was, maybe two dozen steps between us where he was positioned ahead of the raised dais. Thick shackles encircled Drake's forearms, dragging his posture forward. Vampires didn't *get* tired, but if they were starving him of blood, then he'd inevitably start to slow, lose his strength.

Worry pinched my brow while I took him in. He still wore the same clothes he'd been in when we were abducted. Except his shirt's sleeves were pushed up to his elbows to make sure the shackles' metal bit into his skin, and his dark-wash jeans were coated in grime.

The rest of him seemed untouched, besides the hollows of his cheekbones and dark circles beneath his eyes being more pronounced. Probably a sign of starvation, but it wasn't nearly as gruesome as his visage under the sun. Laughter echoed around us, and I ignored the cackles coming from the disgusting undead. Drake's raven-dark eyes bore into mine, as helpless as I felt but set with an edge I couldn't interpret.

His gaze shifted, and pure loathing hardened his features when he glared at someone behind me. A huff passed my lips, and I counted the breaths that might be my last. For the first time in ages, regret and guilt became a distant emotion.

Noise rose and fell around me, and I heard Drake's voice exclaim through the throng, his foreign words indecipherable. A prickle at my neck made me glance up, and I narrowed my eyes at a lone stationary figure standing against the far wall of the ballroom.

Piercing green eyes stared back beneath a furrowed thick brow. Curiosity and conflict came to mind when Ezra's cheek twitched. Must have been my imagination. Then Lucian spoke, his words concealed by another language entirely. I didn't bother to turn, but rose to one knee while gathering up my skirts to keep from tripping again.

"Death ought not to be delayed," Lucian said, the English clearly for my benefit.

Anger pulsed through my veins, and my molars ground together. If I was going to die, then it was going to be the best fucking show these assholes had ever seen. Sweat-soaked dark curls framed my lowered face as something approached. It sounded heavy, made of metal, and I inhaled through my nose.

The tang of polished steel filled my senses, and I exhaled a slow breath. My eyes opened when the air shifted near my left arm. Anticipation tightened my muscles, poised but waiting until the last moment.

Then I spun on one knee, reaching with blind instinct for the weapon at the guard's side. Chilled metal met my palm, and I pulled with all my might to free the weapon from its sheath. The broadsword swept out in an arc, and I used the momentum to slice in between a gap in the guard's armor where the breastplate met the hip bone.

A startled groan growled from within the armor, but quickly cut off when I rose to my feet and gripped the sword's hilt with both hands. Adrenaline surged, and my survival instinct let loose a shout while I drove the sword through the chainmail covering the guard's left armpit.

The ping of cascading broken chainmail links rang through the silence that descended in the wake of my blade striking true. A gurgle rose as blood ran down the metal breastplate, coating it in red. I yanked the sword free. Blood spurted, soaring to the floor as the suit of armor crashed to the marble tile at my feet.

Through the stillness, the harsh sound of my breathing became deafening as I raised my gaze to greet a room full of enemies.

12

A LITTLE PSYCHO

SHOCK APPEARED TO RIPPLE ACROSS THE CROWD, BUT I DIDN'T WASTE A second to gauge their reactions. I ran, my boots squeaking against the marble floor due to the blood stuck to my soles. My exit was blocked by the crowd of undead, but I wasn't aiming for the doors. Instead, I rushed toward the center of the ballroom where Drake stood stock still before the dais.

Another guard stepped forward, and Drake lurched into motion when its wolf's head helmet turned toward me. Despite the shackles weighing him down, he extended his reach as far as it would go and kicked the back of the guard's knee hard. Metal buckled, and the guard dropped to one knee.

In a lurch of motion that turned out more sloppy than I'd planned, I swung the heavy sword, intent on lopping off the guard's head. An instant of nausea had bile rising up my esophagus, but I shoved it down and shut my eyes tight when blood sprayed from the meaty neck half-hanging off the guard's body. The dead guard's helmet slowly loosened from its face, falling sideways to crash onto the floor.

"Maria!" Drake's exclamation cut through my panic, and I looked up to find another two guards moving in while the vampires all stepped backward toward the walls. The faces of the undead were a blur as I spun, dodging a spear aimed directly for my chest. Stinging pain crossed my ribs when I hadn't moved quick enough, but I managed to turn my momentum into another strike against the second guard.

My stolen blade crashed into a broadsword of equal size and weight. The enemy might have been physically stronger, and I hadn't eaten in days, but all that armor was its downfall. Speed was my ally, and I redirected the opponent's blade with my own before stepping into their space.

A gauntlet reached for me, clenched for additional impact, and I dropped to a crouch. My arm ached as I pulled my sword around to slice behind their knee through the gap in metal plating. The guard stumbled back, and I dove to my left when I sensed as much as heard yet another guard approaching from behind.

Displaced air brushed the skirt of my idiotic dress, and I just barely evaded the spear now skewered into the section of flooring I'd occupied a second ago. The wooden shaft vibrated, its point embedded into the cracked marble inlay. Eyes wide, I rushed to crawl backward and away from the guards now standing side by side.

The one with the sword didn't advance, instead waiting for their comrade to retrieve the spear. I kept backing up, holding tight to my weapon while trying to get my feet under me despite my strained muscles throbbing. A pair of cold hands grasped me beneath my arms, and I shrieked when I was hauled upright.

"Maria." Drake's voice soothed my terror like a balm, and I immediately stopped resisting when it registered he'd helped me up. I glanced back over my shoulder, finding his raven-dark eyes full of emotion I could only guess at—gratitude, intrigue, maybe. The briefest smile graced his lips. *Damn it, this was not the time for my heart to flutter.*

A clanging of chafing metal returned my attention forward. The two guards glanced from their decapitated comrade to where Lucian now sat atop the throne on the raised dais. Lucian's otherwise bland face creased with a condescending smile as he nodded to the guards. Tearing my gaze from him, I assessed our surroundings, and paled.

My legs shook when I glimpsed the sallow white face that had been hidden beneath the dead guard's helmet. Glassy green eyes stared unseeing toward the ceiling, and stubble coated the masculine jaw. Except he lacked the silvery sheen of the undead. Which meant the guard I'd killed must have been human.

I was going to be sick.

"You have to run," Drake whispered into my ear, his breath moving the loose curls hanging limp against the side of my face. My hands trembled, but I gripped the sword's hilt harder.

"Not without you," I replied, my voice hushed while I kept my focus trained on the guards forced into becoming my enemy. Even if I did manage to escape, I doubted I'd get very far on my own. Survival was a matter of making it out together, or not at all. It seemed that sentiment was returned, because Drake's gentle grip on my arm tightened.

The guards' attention swiveled from their vampire overlord, and settled on me and Drake—*not good.* I whirled out of Drake's grasp and angled the edge of my weapon for the keyhole on his shackles.

"They are spelled!" he tried to warn, but I'd already struck my steel through the opening. "It can rebound—"

The metal cut deep, coming away like it was made of nothing sturdier than bread, and the shackles cracked along Drake's forearms. Clearly bewildered, Drake looked up from his freed hands. His gaze focused on mine, a mysterious emotion flitting behind his eyes, and then he looked past me.

In a blur, Drake pulled me aside by my shoulder while he stepped around me. When I turned, Drake had already grasped the armored bicep of the guard wielding the spear. Quick as the tick of a clock, he pulled. His grip on the guard tore through both metal and sinew, leaving only a tangle of shredded flesh bleeding free where the guard's upper arm had connected to the shoulder.

My next blink slowed, adrenaline speeding everything up. The hair at the nape of my neck prickled, tugging on my awareness until my gaze connected with piercing green eyes, staring back from the candlelit corner of the ballroom. All thoughts emptied from my head when the second guard went for Drake, their broadsword aimed for my vampire's spine.

Except Drake was faster, catching the guard's gauntlet while thrusting his stolen spear up and through the guard's throat. It pierced straight out the helmet's opposite side. My brows rose when Drake expertly pulled the sword from the guard's slackened grip only to spin it midair and catch it right-side-up.

Then his focus shifted when a growl reverberated from within another suit of armor. Adjusting his footing, Drake rotated in a semi-circle to block the next opponent's full metal-clad body from bowling him over when they collided. I took a step forward, a strangled shriek clawing up my throat, but then I felt the air shift. All of the crashing bangs from Drake's battle had disguised the guards approaching from behind.

I sidestepped blindly, the air swishing in the spot I'd been standing. The marble floor cracked under the pressure of a spiked mace, and I bolted forward when another weapon swung for my back. My hair nearly blinded my sight as I turned in time to block a strike from yet another broadsword. The zing of the impact reverberated up my arm. I had to back up another step to keep from losing my grip on my sword when the guard pressed in.

Ragged breaths shook my chest while two more guards advanced. The ones now lying dead must've only been attempting to restrain me, because these were aiming to kill. From the recesses of my mind, Johann's advice returned in full force, his words clear as day.

Get it over with, quick and dirty, and you'll make it out with your life.

So I stepped in, bringing my weapon up to deflect a blow from the spiked mace, my wrists burning under the pressure. Again, my speed was my only asset against these people in suits of armor. No part of my brain had the room to think about what that meant, who they were or how they got there. I had to keep moving, and dropped low to avoid the arcing broadsword aimed for my head.

My ankles cracked from the impact of my sudden crouch, and I pushed off the marble floor with the sole of my boot. I bolted up and to the right, directly behind the guard's elbow and out of their easy reach. The next swing of my blade was clumsy, like a baseball bat since I wasn't used to the weight, but the pointy end struck true under the guard's armpit.

A low growl rumbled from the guard's chest, and the other guard started for me—only to draw up short. Within their helmet, a pair of unfamiliar brown eyes creased at the corners. Movement behind me warned me to duck, and none too soon since a fucking ax the size of my torso slammed into the first guard's back, right below where I'd punctured the chainmail.

Howled agony erupted from the guard struck by friendly fire, along with a fountain of blood that made the marble floor slick. I rushed to stand, trying to put distance between me and the new guard that had stepped up to fight. My boot slipped, and I went down hard onto my elbows while the sword tumbled from my grip.

The injured guard fell to their knees, inches from me, and the new challenger yanked their ax free of the now-concave metal armor that the first wore. I looked up, scrambling for my sword and reaching blindly. My attention snagged on the guard with the ax. The damn suit of armor was at least seven feet tall.

They swung the ax back, far over the guard's head, and the other standing with the spiked mace mimicked the motion. *Oh fuck*—I was about to know what tenderized meat felt like. My fingers found the hilt of my sword, just as the kneeling, injured guard smacked my reaching hand with the butt of their own weapon, pinning my wrist. The pain was lost in my terror as the ax and mace hovered overhead.

My vampire appeared behind the two standing guards, his silhouette a blur. With a spear in one hand, and a sword in the other, he maneuvered both like they were only as wieldy as matchsticks. One weapon each protruded from the standing guards' chests. The wolf's head helmets squeaked in the silence as they looked down to their chest plates, dripping blood.

Snatching my throbbing wrist close, I rolled out of the way as Drake withdrew the spear only to stab the final third guard through their visor. It seemed like my body couldn't move fast enough as the ax fell from the guard's slackened grasp, landing inches from my lower leg. Sharpened steel tore into my green velvet skirt as a bang echoed, the mace crashing to the floor right where I'd been.

Another thud echoed when the third guard keeled over, and Drake lowered both his weapons. His stern dark eyes lost all emotion as he glanced from one dead guard to the next before striding closer. He didn't pause before crunching the second guard's head underfoot, assuring their death even if he hadn't delivered a killing blow. Lightheaded at the sight, my eyes closed in a long blink, and a clang from nearby made me jump.

When I opened my eyes, Drake's hand was in front of me, offering the hilt of the broadsword I'd claimed with my enemy's life. Looking up, I met his gaze, but he was suddenly impossible to read. No ounce of humor showed on his face, and I exhaled a slow breath when I closed my trembling grip over the sword's handle.

He straightened, offering his now empty hand. I took it in my left, and Drake lifted me up. Swaying from the sudden movement, I glanced around the ballroom to take in the horror. Seven bodies dressed in armor lay split, skewered, and scattered with missing limbs and heads. Their trail leading from where I'd begun the slaughter when Lucian had spun me to the floor.

On the ground behind me, another four guards lay dead, their blood already cooling despite making the room smell like cloying rust. I gritted my teeth, tasting an unfamiliar tang on my tongue. Surrounding us on all sides, beyond our circle of carnage, were the vampires.

There must have been two hundred of them in this room alone. My stomach sank while chills racked my spine. Hunger glinted in their eyes, each varying in shade and color but all containing the same depraved, murderous intent. I was shivering, and I couldn't remember when I had started or if I'd been shaking the whole time. None of them had attacked, letting the innocents in armor stand between them and me. My throat tightened. It had all happened so fast. Had there been another choice?

The monsters surrounding us made it a fight to the death, and for what—to amuse their unbeating hearts?

All eyes rested on us, me and Drake. His cold fingers brushed against mine. Without a care, I grasped his hand, feeling right in this impossible manor of horrors when his palm pressed into mine. Our fingers entwined, fitting perfectly. For a second, I didn't give a damn about the blood and sweat coating my sticky hands.

Grins and grimaces of disdain surveyed us, the vampires ogling us like this battle for our lives was the best entertainment they'd had in a good long while. What a curse it must be. Maybe Lucian had a point, and suddenly I viewed these creatures in a whole new light.

Because the truth was that their *humanity* was what couldn't last against the test of time.

No remorse existed inside of me for these disturbing beings, the nightmare of thousands, but pity took hold. I'd never thought of them as anything more than animals, an invading species, but they'd all been human once. Now all that was left of them were the hollow shells staring back at me, forcing revulsion from my body in the form of tremors streaking down my back.

My shoulders shook when Lucian spoke in another language. Drake's light pressure against our held hands tightened, and I shut my eyes. Whatever Lucian said made the audience of undead laugh, tittering like the aristocratic snobs they all thought they were.

This was it, as far as Drake and I could go on our own power. Those guards must have been human, weighed down by dozens of pounds despite whatever training they'd endured, and Drake had taken them out in the blink of an eye. If a starved vampire could handle a small militia, then the hundreds bordering our battle-ground could subdue us in a second.

Probably before either of us would realize. We'd be dead that fast if it was what they wanted. The backs of my eyes stung, and a hot tear slipped past my lash line to tread a warm path of saltwater down my cheek.

The pressure of a wet thumb caressed the tear's track, and my eyes opened to look up into Drake's agonized expression. His brow furrowing as his lips pressed thin, like he couldn't think of anything suitable to say while his palm held my cheek, slick from the fresh blood on his hand. He stood weaponless, as assured of our defeat as I felt—but then the orb shifted against my heel.

While the vampires cheered, distracted as they discussed our demise amongst themselves, I subtly pulled away from Drake's grasp to fish the small golden ball from my sock. Covered in my closed fist, I raised my hand to offer it to Drake. He blinked, clearly confused as he stared down at my hand while I opened my shaking fingers one at a time.

The air puffed out of my lungs when his eyes widened. Clear recognition for its use brought his gaze up to mine as his lips parted. The constriction in my chest eased when I found hope reflected in his eyes. Moisture blurred my vision, and I blinked away the tears, not caring an ounce what the lions in this den would think.

I could only stare at Drake, who took the orb between his fore-finger and thumb. As he nodded, a shout rose up from among the crowd. Whatever was being said was lost to me as Drake leaned in.

"Close your eyes," he whispered, the soothing sound of his voice pulling another shiver from my tense shoulders, and I gave in to the heaviness already pressing down on my lids.

Losing one sense should have opened up the others, but I blocked out the eruption of noise echoing around the room. All at once, Drake's hand became a light pressure over my brow to cover my eyes before screams pealed through the space, and light exploded all around us.

13

IN TOO DEEP

THE BARE SKIN ACROSS MY ARMS AND NECK FLARED WITH PRICKLING HEAT like a bad sunburn. Keeping my eyes shut tight, I instinctively raised my hands to cover my face when Drake's touch fell away. Shrieks and screams became tinny background noise to my ringing ears while the harsh light seemed to stretch on endlessly.

I tried to pry my eyelashes apart to see, but couldn't make out a thing. Worse than looking at the sun, my vision turned purple and blue as the wailing abruptly cut off. It took several moments, counting my ragged breaths in the sudden silence, before my sight adapted to find the room dark once more.

White spots clouded my vision, but my legacy's fast-healing genes must have kicked into high gear. My neck and chin stopped burning, and the muscles in my arms slowly loosened enough to let me lower my raised hands. A hissing sound like meat on a grill emanated from all around.

Pained groans echoed off the ballroom's high ceiling, and I blinked. Images soon shuttered into focus while I turned on the spot, and my mouth fell open. Every vampire in the room was laid out on the floor, along with the remaining guards who'd been positioned like static suits of armor around the perimeter.

Smoke unfurled from the slits in their wolf's head helmets, and I understood the sizzling when I took in the downed vampires. It was their skin flaking off from their muscles and bones, one layer at a time, before turning to dust.

Drake—

I looked down, and my heart seemed to stop. His scorched hands were a bloody peeling mess, continuing up his forearms before disappearing beneath his dusty black long sleeves. Not nearly as bad as his bare fingers, flayed to the bone, right where he'd detonated the orb. My hand covered my mouth as I fell to my knees beside him, shivering too hard from the frigid room or my spent adrenaline to stand anymore.

I started to reach out, but withdrew my hand when his eyelids fluttered open. His raven-dark eyes, now stained with blood, stared unseeing up at the painted ceiling. Terror pulsed in my chest, and I clutched the fabric over my left breast.

What the hell was I supposed to do now?

Hot fingers swathed in material dug into the skin around my shoulders, roughly pulling me upward and back. Eyes widening, I was about to shriek when one hand moved from squeezing my collarbone to clap down over my mouth. Warm breath tickled my ear, followed by a British accent.

"Quiet. You don't want them to hear us," Ezra whispered, barely audible, and my whole body stiffened. I turned my head to find piercing green eyes roving over the room of bodies. Then his focus zeroed-in on me. When I inhaled a ragged breath, but didn't scream, Ezra released my jaw one gloved finger at a time.

"What are you doing?" I mouthed at him, too surprised to balk when he took my hand in his. He practically dragged me forward toward the doors in a lurch, but I dug in my boot heels when we passed Drake. Nearly slipping on the bloody floor, Ezra gripped my arm hard to steady us both. It hurt, but the pain only redoubled the rage surely visible in my glare.

"You've got to get out of here," Ezra said, leaning close. "They won't stay down forever. If you have any hope of escaping the surrounding woods then you have to move—*now*."

"Not without Drake," I said, and then startled when strangled gurgling emanated from behind me. Looking over my shoulder, I found Lucian slumped at the foot of his brass throne. Blood trickled from his eyes, his sharp features now charred and flaking. Remembered fear stabbed through me, urging me to run, but then I glanced down at Drake, lying helpless on the floor.

Wrenching my arm from Ezra's grip, I stormed to Drake's side. His handsome features were almost unrecognizable except for his strong bone structure and straight black hair. My molars ground together as I grasped Drake under his arm to lift and drag him. Then I glanced up at Ezra.

Sweat beaded my brow when I heaved Drake a few inches off the ground, almost dropped him, and stifled a cry of frustration.

"You're being foolish," Ezra muttered, moving closer. At first I figured he might try to physically overpower me, and in my current state, he probably could even without the psychic abilities. Instead, he bent to take Drake's other arm, hoisting it up and over his shoulder. I mimicked him, and together we held Drake teetered between us.

My vampire's head lolled, falling onto my shoulder, and my jaw clenched while I forced myself not to cry—*stupid, dumb Maria.* What the hell had I been thinking, chasing after a vampire by myself? Ezra and I shuffled toward the doors, giving the fallen undead a wide berth while trying to keep our path as short as possible.

"Thank you," I mumbled, barely audible under my heavy breaths that I tried to quiet despite my strained muscles burning for more oxygen.

"Thank someone who's earned it," Ezra retorted, his tone filled with so much loathing that I didn't bother to argue.

When we crossed the threshold into the entrance hall, I started for the double front doors made of solid oak. Ezra tugged us in the opposite direction, heading past the display case that I refused to look at. Confusion pinched my brow, and I had to work twice as hard to keep up with Ezra's hurried pace, leading us deeper into the heart of the mansion.

"Where are we going?" I hissed, barely managing it between inhales.

"Somewhere you can momentarily rest to recuperate." His cryptic words rang alarm bells in my head.

"Why aren't we just going out the front doors?" I demanded, and Ezra's bitter laugh made my stomach sink lower.

"Are you mad? You want to try carrying an incapacitated immortal through miles of woods by yourself, in the dark, with no idea of where you are or where you're heading?"

We shuffled further into darkness until the distance muffled the agony ongoing in the ballroom. Feeling blind until my sight adjusted to the gloom, and stupid from Ezra's condescension, I bit my lip and focused on each step onward. In the middle of a long corridor that seemed less insulated than the previous ones, Ezra stopped short.

Staggering, I huffed out a fogging breath while maintaining Drake's weight. *For such a lithe guy, he sure did weigh a lot.* The muscles in my shoulders shook while Ezra whispered a word, and the paneled wall we stared at suddenly shifted. In the blink of an eye, a set of stairs leading downward appeared before us.

Gaping, but trying not to show it, I took a careful step down after Ezra. The two of us kept Drake aloft despite his shoes dragging on the rickety wooden steps. Cobwebs caught in my hair, and I swallowed hard. At least it was too cold for creepy crawlies. Nearly at the bottom, where the darkness seemed thicker, Drake groaned.

The pained sound carved an ache into my chest. It took every last ounce of my willpower not to drop him. Which was exactly what Ezra did the minute we passed through a low doorway. I exclaimed nonsense when I tried to take the full brunt of Drake's body weight, and failed. He slumped to the floor, me along with him when my legs finally gave out. Sconces along the wall lit up with purple flames while I panted through chilled breaths.

As the room became illuminated, an enormous iron oven was revealed against the opposite wall. Nearly attached to it was a long countertop with a wooden surface. A steel bucket rested on a lower cabinet, clearly meant to be the 'sink.' At the center of the room stood a farmhouse-style table, coated in dust but large enough to feed a family as big as—well, mine.

Ezra crossed his arms, almost leaning back against the wall before he seemed to think better of it. Roughly fifteen feet separated him from where Drake laid on the floor beside me.

Piercing green eyes stared directly at me, and a million questions drifted through my head.

"What the hell was that back there?" The orb, faery-made so it would have been equally chaotic as it was deadly, was starting to feel like a mistake. Some *friend* that faery had been. He must've known what it would do, and that Drake wouldn't walk away from it.

Who the hell had I become? First trusting a vampire, and then a faery...

"The sphere Ignatius Drake detonated? I thought I'd sensed something with grand magick potential..." Ezra's gaze studied me, but when I didn't say anything else, he explained, "It contains the power of sunlight. Quite dangerous, and unstable in the best of circumstances. I can scarcely believe it somehow survived your battles with the lycans."

Sunlight—except, vampires weren't damaged like this from just the sun. Had it been so concentrated that it did more than strip their human illusion? Breaking through not just the exterior, but chipping away at their animated death...

Hang on a second—

"Did you just say 'lycans?'" I stared up at Ezra, my eyes wide while bile climbed up my throat. Ezra just looked back like I was an idiot, and apparently, I was. That's why they seemed human, blood the same color as mine, and could move that big hunk of metal armor with such ease. Except, a werewolf's strength was only slightly superior to a human's unless on the full moon. Plus, the way that they were transformed... It was an ugly process.

A bite from a werewolf could turn another person, like a disease spread through saliva and infected blood into a wound.

Nothing like us or the Tsosies, who'd been born with our abilities. Werewolves had been *created* by Dracula and his sorcerers to act as their mindless puppet warriors. Their only will, once they changed into a mockery of a wolf, was to *kill*.

Since they only lived as long as any ordinary mortal man, they should've all died out with the end of Dracula's reign. Which meant the vampires had continued transforming innocent humans against their will.

"I think I'm going to be sick," I mumbled, one hand over my stomach and the other pressed against my lips. My eyes shut tight. I couldn't bear to look at Drake, but I could still hear his flesh crackling. Ezra's scoff brought my gaze up, and he snapped his fingers. The noise it made sounded like a crack, and then a basket appeared a foot in front of me between one blink and the next.

Nestled inside the red and white patterned fabric was a wheel of cheese, a loaf of dark brown bread, and a bunch of red grapes. I mindlessly dove for it, shoving food into my mouth before I could even taste it. Tears burned my eyes, falling down my stuffed cheeks while I chewed and swallowed in quick succession.

Quiet sobs managed to choke out between the snuffling sounds of my eating. This was so messed up. My pace to shovel anything edible into my mouth slowed. Swallowing hard, I wiped the spittle from my chin and looked up. Ezra was staring at me, his expression curious but not concerned. His thick eyebrows lifted when he seemed to notice the tear tracks down my cheeks, and I quickly wiped my face with my grimy blood-stained hands.

"No offense," I croaked, clearing my throat before I continued, "but why are you helping me?" The sorcerer shrugged, and I frowned while he took his time glancing this way and that.

"Apparently, even the lowest of 'traitorous scum' can't stand to see a good dog kicked when they're down." His piercing green eyes bore into mine, and I licked my lips.

"You're the reason why Drake's shackles broke so easily, right?"

"No idea what you're referring to." The cavalier expression he wore implied otherwise, and the corners of my mouth briefly twitched up.

"Thanks." My relief and gratitude faded fast when I finally looked down at Drake beside me. Red welts colored the flesh not peeling, but at least he'd stopped sizzling. The way he laid there, so still and without even his chest moving to breathe, it hammered home the truth of what he was.

Even if that wasn't who he wanted to be.

The thought flitted through my head before I could catch it, and my hands started trembling. "How long until he wakes up?" I mumbled, stifling my unshed tears. *Crying any more would just be a waste of water.*

"Not sure," Ezra answered. "Probably around the same time as the other immortals. But if the hounds heal first, they'll sniff you out and I won't be sticking my neck out to help you a second time if you're idiotic enough to get caught after being given the chance to escape."

My shoulders slumped. "I couldn't leave him."

"Not my problem. I'm telling you now, the moment I hear those mongrels sniffing around, I'll be making myself scarce and leaving you to your consequences."

Right, because everything that's happened so far was my *fault.* Tears stung the backs of my eyes, and I swallowed them down. Maybe the sorcerer felt sorry for me, but I'd never asked him for a damn thing. It wouldn't matter if he abandoned me now. Hell, I probably deserved being left in this cellar with a nearly-dead vampire after what I put my family through last year.

Because it'd been too easy to convince myself it was okay to lie to them. So desperate for their approval, after losing every ounce of their trust, I'd hidden my failure when Drake had both captured me and let me go in one night. All because I'd let down my defenses, made yet another stupid choice that could have cost me my life.

Had I learned nothing? I grit my teeth as painful memories resurged. The disappointment I'd seen in Johann's eyes that day, shattering both of us behind the anger and fear we'd felt for one of our own. Before everything went to hell, I just wanted something to take the edge off.

My thoughts would never stop spiraling, making everyday tasks and errands unbearable beneath the overwhelming panic. Then my breaths would come in too thin, and I'd squirrel myself away either in my room or at the library. The only time the anxiety abated was when I was actively hunting, but eventually the adrenaline couldn't hold off the twisting in my guts.

This damn legacy had lumped on too much pressure. It had sounded so heroic when Grandpa talked about it. I should've known, considering the way that Johann never spoke about the hunts after he and Uncle Alaric came home, that it wasn't a rose-colored dream.

No, it was a red-stained nightmare.

After my first few hunts, the memories of finding bloodless victims made it hard to sleep. Training became a reminder of our duty to the world, the innocent people who wouldn't know how to defend themselves without us stepping in to save them. Andrew, in all his assholery, had probably been the final straw that broke me.

My shrink would have said it wasn't right to blame others for my actions, but his haughty condescension cut too deep, one too many times. When my ex offered a joint to get me 'relaxed,' I didn't hesitate. That wouldn't have been a problem for anyone who was 'normal'—but I wasn't. Soon, the high became my only means of coping.

I acclimated to the drug too quickly, my physiology fucking me over. Then I needed something stronger to make the feeling last. So I pushed him to give me his contacts, trying anything I deemed 'safe' enough. My family barely saw me during that time, but they must have known. We didn't talk about it until it was too late.

Panic had been throttling my throat the day that shit hit the fan, but they were already planning the next hunt. Convinced the 'trip' would enhance my senses, increasing my awareness by not getting caught up in my own head, I took the tab of acid before we hopped into the Ford F-250.

I could barely remember charging the little blue house on the abandoned ranch. Everything felt slowed down, but nobody else seemed to notice. We split up once we got inside, the snarl of waking vampires echoing from all sides. The interior had been dark, with every window boarded up to keep out the daylight.

I realized too late that Olivia had been screaming for help.

Shock took root, made easier by the shit product I'd swallowed, and I became paralyzed. I'd watched as the vampire blocked a blow from Olivia's machete while holding a naked woman by the throat. Cruel eyes swallowed me whole while life was drained from the victim's consciousness. Faster than my drugged brain could register, the human corpse I could have rescued was tossed aside into the dirt-stained corner—and the vampire lunged for my cousin.

I'd tried to make my body move, but the step I took was too slow while Olivia grappled under the undead's excessive strength. Her machete was tossed aside before grayed fingers clamped down on her shoulder and arm. Twisted around until her back collided with the vampire's front. Then the monster sank his fangs deep into the tissue at her throat.

Olivia went limp in the vampire's arms, her attacker faceless in my memory. Blood ran down her chest and neck while her breaths became a gurgle. Finally, Johann stormed in, taking out the undead man with steady, calm precision.

I hadn't been able to speak while Uncle Alaric came in to carry his daughter to safety. Not even after Johann shook me to bring me back into reality. Scathing disbelief had laced his words when he asked if I was high.

The memory shot a phantom ache through my chilled chest. I held my breath while tears leaked out to hit my throbbing cold hands, cradled in my lap atop the folds of the velvet dress. Shame, blame, and guilt tore at me, *and what was even the point of fighting anymore?*

Because of me—because they *trusted* me, Olivia almost died. Left vulnerable for days after the fact, because she survived with vampire venom coursing through her veins.

Nobody let her leave the house for a week. If she somehow died before her body metabolized it, then the venom would begin the transformation, forcing her circulation to pump slow-moving clotted blood for the rest of eternity. Carrying Helsing's legacy didn't make us any less human, and we could become one of the wretched things we faced just like anyone else.

Everybody had a weakness, and my family's had been putting their faith in me.

It all became too much, and to hell with Ezra standing across the room looking like he'd rather be anywhere else. I pulled my knees up, lowered my head, and cried. Ugly, broken sobs racked my chest, but my hot tears were hidden by my arms wrapped around myself.

"Maria…" Drake's voice pulled my face up, and my crying choked off. His eyes fluttered open, the dark irises surrounded by bloodshot sclera. Peeling skin pulled his features taut as concern creased his brow, and the depths of his concern resonated behind his eyes—reflecting my miserable face.

From the beginning, every effort he'd made was to try and save me. It was *my* fault we were both here. Except, with the way he was watching me, and how he'd come to my defense against the guards—sacrificing himself to give me the chance to run—I couldn't pretend I hadn't been hoping for someone to rescue me.

Biting my lip, I lowered my hand to the dusty floor, a bare inch from his scorched fingers. *Had I ever really made the choice to keep my vampire all to myself?* Maybe, deep down, my heart had made the decision before I could logically catch up to why.

"Are you hurt?" Drake asked, his voice rough as sandpaper. Despite everything, I shook my head. His mouth opened to continue, and I leaned closer so he wouldn't have to strain. Slower than I'd ever seen him, his hand nearest rose with obvious difficulty. Until his fingers reached the knotted curls of hair framing my face. All I could do was blink when his cooled fingers grazed my cheek as he tucked my hair behind my ear before letting his hand fall. "What are you…still doing here?"

My face heated, and I breathed deep to hold back another sob. "I couldn't abandon you."

"Because she's a suicidal moron," Ezra remarked, and I glanced up to glare at him.

"That's not helping," I snapped, but Ezra shrugged. He sauntered a few steps closer, pursing his lips when he appeared to study Drake's state before shaking his head, brown curls shifting across his forehead with the movement.

"Well, this certainly won't do. He's too weak to move on his own, and has been starved for at least the past four days. Not to mention, now that he's waking up—" Ezra gestured vaguely with a wave of his hand. "The other immortals will be recovering, with the lycans a step ahead of them. If their sight hasn't already been repaired by their curse."

"So what do we do?" I demanded, already determined to tell him to fuck off if he suggested I leave Drake here to die a second, more permanent death.

"He needs to feed." Ezra raised his eyebrows, and my mouth popped open.

"No," Drake stated, but the finality of his tone was marred by the fact he couldn't even sit up.

My heart pounded. "I'll do it." *This was going to hurt.* As Drake opened his mouth, looking intent to argue, I added, "Ezra's right, it's the only way to get your strength up so you can move. And we need you to move. *I* need you…" Whether any of us liked it or not, I wouldn't escape this place without him.

"She's got a point, mate." Ezra sighed. "No way either of you are making it out otherwise. And if you don't consume fresh blood soon, the calcification process will begin and then you will *truly* be unable to move."

"Stop talking," I ground out, and Ezra raised his hands in a placating gesture.

"Are you certain?" My vampire's tone turned thoughtful, the richness of his accent sending a shiver up my spine—or maybe he was just really hungry.

"Yes." Shaky, but trying to hide it with my grim resolve, I began to wipe the surface of my inner forearm using my palm. It did jack-diddly-squat, just smeared the dried blood that wasn't mine alongside the sweat that was. My vein pulsed beneath the surface, speeding up with my heart rate when I turned to offer my wrist face-down toward Drake's chapped lips.

Inch by inch, his hand rose until he gripped my arm. The pressure was tender, gentle against my bruised skin, and I trembled under the unexpected chill of his touch. When my bare skin pressed against his lips, I resisted the urge to pull away.

The edges of his canines touched my skin, and I inhaled sharply. Then they sliced through my flesh, piercing the vein with practiced ease. My breath puffed out of me, and then my gaze unfocused—*woah*. A rush shot through me, the venom acting fast and taking away the pain like magick, *which made sense.*

My jaw relaxed, and my eyes closed in a slow blink. A strangely ticklish feeling soon spread up my arm as he sucked down my blood, and the discomfort of the pulling sensation ebbed into a dull afterthought. As my breathing evened out, I could suddenly *feel* the expansion of air in my lungs like never before.

Every sense both shut down and erupted into fireworks while warmth spread from my forearm to my aching shoulders, loosening the tension completely. Sure, I'd known vampire venom acted as an analgesic, numbing the victim to make them more complacent, but I hadn't imagined…*this*. Even if I wanted to fight the effects, I wouldn't have been able to—but mostly, I didn't care.

Headrush clouding my thoughts, I involuntarily pressed my wrist harder against Drake's willing mouth—

"That's probably enough." Ezra's voice cut through me, and my eyelids flew open.

Heat warmed my chest, neck, and face as Drake's hand, still holding my forearm, pulled my pulsing flesh away. I startled when he instantly sat up, his visage perfectly restored. His grip on my arm didn't loosen, but it wasn't uncomfortable either. Raven-dark eyes bore into mine, and a ragged breath expanded my chest as my attention flicked down to the trail of my blood dripping from the corner of his mouth.

For some bizarre reason, I wanted to wipe it away for him.

My pulse jumped when he used his thumb to swipe the excess from his chin before licking up the last drop of my blood. *That was unexpectedly…hot.* What the hell was wrong with me?

"You look better." I buried a cringe at my stammered words, but Drake briefly smiled, and my heart thumped. Then he stood, his sudden speed making my head spin.

"Thank you. Take my hand," he instructed, offering both of his. I hesitated for the barest second while staring up at him, but inevitably placed my palms atop his. A moment later, I was standing, and abruptly wobbled on ankles that felt loose and watery.

"Woah." I clenched my teeth to keep the vertigo at bay while Drake caught me by my elbows. "I feel…" Whatever I was about to say was quickly forgotten when I got distracted by the pinch in Drake's brow.

"Are you well enough to walk?"

"I heal fast, so…" I gave my head a little shake, and saw stars. "I-I'm sure I'll be fine."

"We have to leave, and in a hurry, I fear." Drake winced. "My apologies." At first, I figured he was sorry for biting me, but then he picked me up like I weighed nothing more than a sack of potatoes.

"Hey!" I exclaimed in hushed annoyance, but my arms wrapped around his shoulders to steady myself. *So it was a 'better to ask for forgiveness than permission' apology.* Being so close reminded me of our kiss in the park, and tension coiled low. It didn't help when he simpered at me, his face only inches away.

"If we can get a move-on?" Ezra piped up. Both Drake and I looked at the sorcerer.

"I appreciate your assistance, Ezra," Drake said, but the hard set to his jaw made the words come out begrudging. "Name your price for keeping your silence and I will pay it."

"Price?" I asked, stifling a squeak when Drake shifted to take a step.

"Sorcerers are most easily persuaded by bribery," Drake answered without breaking eye contact with Ezra, like he was keeping a predator within sight so he wouldn't lose the advantage.

"I'm sure you will compensate me accordingly, but I won't be gaining a single hair on a mouse's bollocks if you're both caught." Without another word, Ezra strode to our left where another stone archway, set into the framework and covered in cobwebs, stood opposite a decrepit pantry built with bulkhead doors. Except, instead of walking up the stairs through the arch, he turned to the cellar doors set low to the ground.

Crouching, Ezra waved his hand over the handle with a mysterious gesture while muttering under his breath. The doors suddenly opened outward as if under their own power. My eyes widened appreciatively when the hinges didn't even squeak.

Once the sorcerer stood, pulling the lapel of his purple suit straight, he made a grandiose gesture toward the darkness seeping out colder air from below.

"Ladies first," Ezra declared, and I stiffened when Drake moved us toward the descending stone steps. The sconces in the abandoned basement kitchen flickered to nothing on Drake's first step down, forcing my eyes to work double-time to adjust, but the enclosing blackness seemed solid all around.

Drake could apparently see just fine—lucky vampire—since his near-silent footsteps didn't hesitate on our seemingly straight path beneath the manor. Purple suddenly burned my retinas, and I blinked fast at the flames Ezra had summoned to dance atop his palm, the sparks never touching his skin. If this guy only worked for the Cneaz, then just how powerful were the Domnitori's sorcerers?

"Drake," I whispered, and my gaze found his eyes with the help of the ambient glow a few paces behind us. "Where are we going to go?" My voice wavered with uncertainty that I tried and failed to hide. Now that Drake had gotten his strength back, I was suddenly the dead weight between us, making our escape harder.

"I have an associate who will offer you asylum." He glanced pointedly toward Ezra, and I swallowed my curiosity to know exactly where that would be. Then his wording replayed in my head—*hold up.*

"And you'll be there, too. Right?" My heart dropped when Drake's jaw tightened.

"Not likely," Ezra piped up instead. Honestly, I shouldn't have even asked in front of the duplicitous sorcerer.

"And how do you know?" I shot the man a dirty look from over Drake's shoulder, but Ezra seemed immune to my ire.

"Because all of the immortals are marked. How do you think I found you two in that park?"

Truthfully, I hadn't stopped to wonder about that. When I thought about it, remembering how Drake had seemed to expect Ezra's arrival, I felt the blood drain from my face.

"You can't come back to Albuquerque?" My accusation finally brought Drake's gaze to mine, and the corners of his eyes creased in obvious dismay.

"I will do everything in my power to keep you safe. Maria—"

"No." Mimicking Johann's firm diction, I raised my chin an inch. "You've saved my life—twice. I'm not just going to go home pretending like nothing happened." I wouldn't be able to live with myself.

"Even if that means living your life on the run?" Drake retorted, taking me aback. His grimace proved that he wasn't about to budge on this either. "You owe me nothing, Maria. If you believe you do, then I absolve you of the debt. This is not your choice, it is mine."

"So, what?" I snapped, angrily clinging to him while he rose up a few steps to emerge into a small room. Wooden boxes were shoved against the walls, making the space feel even tighter. The iron door across the room was closed, and Drake stopped several steps from it, his focus on me. "You're just going to drop me off at your *associate's* and then run back here to get yourself killed? Like I'm going to let you do that!"

Even if it was his life, his decision, it was a damn stupid one. Frustration became evident behind his dark eyes, and he opened his mouth like he was going to say something, when Ezra suddenly cleared his throat.

"There's always the rings."

I glared askance at Ezra. "What rings?"

Drake scoffed. "The risks far outweigh the possible rewards," he said, but Ezra only shook his head.

"If you went alone, perhaps. The girl on the other hand…" Ezra made a 'voilà' gesture, and the disbelief behind Drake's eyes shifted into speculation.

"What the hell are you two talking about?" I stared from one to the other, growing more irate at being left out of the loop.

"In my time," Drake began, still watching Ezra but clearly answering me, "there was a rumor. Every immortal was marked in their creation so their *voievod,* Dracula, could maintain complete control over his soldiers. However, to prevent himself from befalling the same weakness, Dracula commissioned a ring which, when worn, would shield the wearer from any scrying. Necromantic, or otherwise."

"They're enchanted to keep the wearer hidden from our prying eyes," Ezra summed up, exhaling a breath like he was bored. "But it was never only a rumor. I happen to know they are very real, and exactly where they are."

"Where?" I anticipated the worst at the sight of Ezra's obnoxious smirk.

"Dracula's chambers, of course."

"Which have remained unopened since the first vampire was defeated over two centuries ago," Drake explained, but a certain amount of hope had transformed his expression from grim to inquisitive.

"It's been said that the only magick capable of reopening them is Dracula's own blood." Ezra glanced at me.

Drake's eyes narrowed. "You believe—"

"I would bet quite a bit on it."

"Are *either* of you going to explain what the hell you're talking about before the Earth does another rotation around the sun?" I huffed, and they both faced me.

"You do it." Ezra nodded at Drake, and I bit the inside of my cheek. "I must be returning to my employers."

I opened my mouth, torn between whether I should demand more information or thank the sorcerer for helping us, but then the door beside us swung inward. Cold air rushed into the cramped storage room, and I clung closer to Drake despite him matching the temperature outside. A bluish glow from the moonlight over the grass caught my attention, almost bringing a tear to my eye. We were finally leaving this hellhole.

I looked back, but Ezra was nowhere to be seen. The tunnel we'd walked down was swathed in darkness once more, as desolate and choking in dust as before we'd come through. My focus swung forward when Drake hurried up the shallow stairs to the expansive lawn.

"Will he be okay?" I whispered, unable to keep my gaze off the manor behind us while Drake carried me closer to the treeline.

Before Drake could reply, the quiet night was cut through with a strangled cry. The sound morphed into a howl, raising the hairs along my tanned arms when it sounded like it was outside with us. A growl reverberated on the painfully chill breeze, and Drake picked up his pace until the spiny foliage on the surrounding pines blurred.

Between my thundering heartbeats, I heard Drake mutter, "Time to go, love."

— 14 —

RISE AND RETREAT

DRAKE'S FOOTFALLS ACROSS THE FROZEN-SOLID GROUND WERE BARELY audible over the achingly loud noise of my breathing. So I held my breath, my gaze scanning the woods around us. We were already moving faster than I could easily run, but I had to be weighing him down, holding him back. Still, I clutched tight to him while he avoided piles of soggy fallen leaves and leaped over tree trunks knocked down by weather or decay.

Not needing to breathe, Drake moved quiet as a mouse—which made the growls growing closer sound that much louder. Through the dense pines and sparse oak trees, shapes moved almost as fast as a vampire. Except the glimpses I caught of their furred bodies were anything but human. Spittle gleamed along a jowl, reflecting the moonlight above, but then the long-snouted being faded to nothing when Drake swiftly changed course.

Pulse hammering, I tried to be our eyes and ears while Drake focused on our escape through the woods. Apparently, I'd failed at that, too. His head whipped toward our left, braking his steps so suddenly that the momentum made my insides feel like they tried to keep going while he held me close to his blood-stained clothes.

My eyes widened to take in the shape that launched itself across our path, right where we'd have walked straight into its assault. Too-human eyes reflected the moonlight above, like a nocturnal animal, as the lycanthrope clawed its way to a halt several feet to our right. An oily sheen covered its straggly coat, the texture somewhere between human hair and animal fur.

Even the creature's nails seemed wrong, thin and broken but elongated. Long hind legs let the lycan start toward us with a powerful leap. Before I could think to scream, Drake stepped aside. His fingers pressed into my ribs and outer thigh while I clutched his neck and hoped the lycan wouldn't catch the skirt of my awful dress.

It missed us by inches, but our pause in the small clearing had allowed the others to catch up. Just how many of these things were being kept inside that manor? When Drake tried to turn, my gaze shot over his shoulder, and I screamed, "Look out!"

Another one flanked us, and the beast's jaws opened wide as it leaped off the trunk of a fallen tree—aiming for Drake's face.

"Apologies," Drake murmured, so quiet I didn't have a chance to wonder who he was talking to before I free-fell. My tailbone hit the frozen earth, sending a shock outward through every limb. I inhaled a gasp on impact, scrambling to get my numb-feeling legs working despite the cold cramping every muscle.

The stupid velvet skirt bunched across my knees when I rolled onto all-fours. Luck was on my side since I barely dodged another werewolf pouncing for me. Behind me, the sounds of a brawl was distinctive between the canine yowls and dull thuds of fists meeting fur-clad flesh. Except I didn't dare look, my focus captured by the horrifying *thing* two feet in front of me.

Adrenaline surged, overriding every discomfort. Even my breathing seemed like background noise. Too fast, the lycan sprang at me. Its eyes glowed, despair and pain obvious in its widening pupils, but its open maw overshadowed whatever humanity remained behind the imperative to tear into my flesh. On instinct, I leaned away.

Raising my arms in a cross, I pulled my legs up and out from under me as my back hit the ground. The lycan hadn't expected that, and I kicked out to hit the beast directly in the chest. Pain and terror helped my muscles to work double-time, launching the lycan several feet away.

A wet slap echoed through the narrow clearing, just like when we were in the parking lot across the street from the Two Fools Tavern. I didn't have to look to know a bloodbath drenched the cold earth not far away. Struggling to stay in the moment, I tried to stand but my muscles spasmed when I crouched.

Shit—the lycan had regained its footing. It felt like a ton of bricks weighed down on me when I tried to stand, only to stumble and fall onto my side. *Damn it,* move! Hairs rose along the nape of my neck, and I sensed the shift in air behind me while gurgles slowly cut off to nothing. Then Drake was in front of me, his actions a blur as he intercepted the lycan heading for me.

This time, I didn't have the luxury of my back being turned. Drake caught one of the beast's elongated paws in a fist, his fingers clenching hard enough to break through the lycan's bones. Blood spurted from the beast's demolished front paw, but it didn't make a sound. Instead, its mouth opened wide to reveal pointed sharp incisors.

Drake captured the lycan's snout with his other hand, shoving the snapping jaws aside. My breath caught when my vampire didn't hesitate to lunge for the lycan's exposed jugular. The beast howled as Drake bit deep enough to tear through more than just a few layers of skin. When he pulled away, dropping the body, a chunk was missing from the werewolf's throat.

I couldn't do anything but stare in stunned silence while blood rushed from the lycan's torn open flesh, pumping out its life. Then it went still, the strangely human eyes glassed over, and I looked up as Drake spat out a hunk of tissue. He seemed to hesitate before turning toward me. Fresh blood dripped from the corners of his mouth, covering the entire lower half of his face, down to his neck where his button-up shirt darkened—drenched.

With the back of his hand, he smeared the cascading blood across his chin. Something about it triggered the truth. Never before had I *really* thought of him as being undead. Not since I'd first encountered him at the abandoned warehouse, when my conditioning had overshadowed reason. Now, with his face coated in another's blood and his posture unrepentant, I trembled.

He took a step closer, and I reached behind me, my palms scraping the sharp rocks protruding from the packed earth while my heart raced. Clearly sensing my knee-jerk reaction to flee, Drake halted mid-stride. Raven-dark eyes bore into mine, and the ferocity I'd seen in him a moment ago was nowhere to be found—replaced by an emotion I could only guess at. Disappointment, by the pursed set of his mouth, but it didn't seem to be directed at me.

"Are you uninjured?" His voice hadn't changed, still way too soothing and making me kick myself by how it calmed my rapid breathing but sped up my heart into a fury.

"Y-Yeah." I finally exhaled a breath that felt like it'd been lodged in my lungs since before we left Albuquerque. His pale hand flashed out, and I startled, but he'd only been offering it to me. Drake's stoic features hid the whirling thoughts behind his dark eyes. Hesitantly, I grasped his cold hand a split second before he pulled me upright.

The blood rushed down my limbs, making me sway, but I steadied myself by gritting my teeth. Drake's hand hadn't left mine, and he was already bending to lift me again when I said, "I can walk." It was a statement, not as sharp or prickly as my usual tone—and I blamed the blood loss for my weakened will. Drake frowned like he was about to argue, but his hand only squeezed mine before pulling me along in his wake.

"That is fortunate, because you will require some fortitude to cross."

"Cross where?" I asked, staggering but catching myself before he had to. I refused to glance toward the dead littering the clearing while we walked away. A pang resonated through me at the memory of despair within the lycan's eyes. It must have known it would die, and maybe that's why it fought so hard. *They*—they were people, not things.

Not like the weapon of war they were forced to be.

With Drake's hand holding mine, the pressure gentle enough that I barely felt the rough surface of his palm, it was hard to compartmentalize the version of him that I knew with the unfeeling monster I'd just witnessed ripping apart the lycans. Maybe that wasn't a fair assessment. I had no idea what he felt when he tore apart flesh and bones to save my life, *again.*

Was it so different from what my family and I trained ourselves to do to survive and rescue others? Just because we decapitated and dismembered with a machete to make the process cleaner didn't make Drake using his bare hands any different when the results were the same. Even knowing that the lycans were people, I would have struck them down just as fast if they'd gone after one of my own…

"The Hudson," Drake replied, and my focus snapped back to the present situation.

"The river?" I balked, and then registered the thrum of rushing water not far off. That explained why we weren't running anymore.

"We have to become submerged to prevent them from following us by scent. The lycanthropes may be of little consequence, but the other immortals will chase us as nobles did foxes. Once they have all fed to regain their senses. Can you swim?"

"I know how to, but will I make it? I'm so tired…" The forest became sparser, and through the trees ahead, the wide expanse of sky almost reminded me of home. Except the colors of dawn seemed wrong, more of a bruised-purple that hovered over the hills, visible on the other side of the dark emptiness which must have been the river.

Holy shit, how wide was it? The opposing shoreline was invisible beneath the inky black heavens, with only the tallest trees being discernible under the glow of impending day, each treetop as tiny as a toothpick.

"We will travel with the current to cross, enabling us to move downstream more quickly. Also—" His steps halted, pulling me to a stop beside him. Fading moonlight reflected the silvery shimmer off his striking features, masking what the day would reveal before long. His gaze held mine as we stood on the precipice of the riverside cliff. "I will be there to keep you afloat."

Confidence colored his tone, and somehow, despite the wind off the river chilling me to the bone, warmth spread up from my chest to scorch my face.

"What would I do without you?" I mumbled. *Wait, what did I just say?* My face burned, but it was meant to be taken as gratitude. Except Drake's pained frown made it seem like an accusation.

"Without my involvement in your life, you would still be safe in Albuquerque." He turned away, angling toward the rocky rubble sloping downward.

What the hell could I say to that?

As much as I wanted to tell him that that wasn't true, I couldn't. He was right. Even if I didn't want him to be. It'd be a lie to say that I had no regrets, because after the last several days, I was filled with nothing but confused feelings—my concept of 'right' and 'wrong' so utterly flipped upside-down that I felt like I was drowning well before reaching the water.

Watching my steps carefully, I clutched Drake's hand in mine to keep steady. My boots hit the muddy bottom with a splash, and I shivered at the flecks of water that sprayed my lower legs. This was going to hurt worse than his bite. Drake released my hand only to lean back against the mud-packed wall, and unlaced one of his leather loafers at a time.

I mimicked him, tying my laces together once I'd pulled my boots off, and held the conjoined threads in one hand. When I looked up from the task, I found Drake staring down at me.

His gaze tracked from my chest to my now bare feet—more white than I'd ever seen them. Self-conscious concern made me look down to figure out what he was staring at so intently.

The dress was ruined, that much was obvious. Ripped and torn, blood-soaked and muddied, completely unsalvageable. Not that I'd want to keep any reminder of this disgusting place. Drake shook his head.

"Are you currently wearing any undergarments?" he asked, and I blinked. "The current will attempt to drag you down. If you can, you must strip the heavier material." His hasty explanation seemed self-aware, but I was more focused on the fact that I wasn't wearing *anything* underneath—not even a bra.

"No," I whispered, knowing he'd still hear it beneath the scouring wind pulling at my ratty curls to tickle my shoulders.

"May I tear away the superfluous fabric?" His polite request took me off guard. Honestly, after everything we'd been through, and he still managed to be such a gentleman… *Could I pick 'em, or what?*

"Whatever we have to do." I tossed my dirty socks into the river since there was no way I was wearing soggy socks when we made it across. *If* we made it.

Without hesitation, Drake bent to grasp the green velvet in his hands. Motions a blur, the crisp sound of tearing fabric was stolen by the breeze while he worked. The dress felt significantly lighter when he was done, and the extra material was promptly thrown into the rushing waves. Made sense to get rid of any lingering scents attached to us, but damn it, what the hell were they going to do with the underwear I left in that stupid room they'd held me in?

Orange hues the same color as a camera's glare slowly traced its way across the lightening sky. If I wasn't so freaking cold, and determined to get away from this place, I might have stopped to admire it. *Guess the views up in the Northern states had their own charm, too.* The sky turned a paler shade each passing moment, and Drake extended his hand. His expression was neutral, but doubt flickered behind his eyes as I fastened my fingers over his like they were a lifeline.

Icy water licked at my ankles, and I took a shuddering breath while Drake led me deeper toward the roiling abyss. Only the peaks of each small wave were visible, and it might have looked like a desert landscape between here and the opposite shore if time froze and everything became static.

Instead, the rushing current pulled at my calves even before trudging in a few feet. My knees almost buckled when the freezing water reached them, but I gritted my teeth. I shoved out the inner-voice shouting at me to get back to shore and away from the awaiting torture.

Wind tore at my scattered curls while we waded deeper. The breath in my lungs was punched out by the cold, but I sucked in a short inhale to keep the oxygen flowing. How long would it take for hypothermia to set it? It was too late to worry about that now. I closed my eyes, and took the next step.

Pain iced through my toes and ankles as I slipped on the slimy, pebbly riverbed. The current rushed me, pulling me downstream before I had a chance to start kicking. Clutching to Drake with everything that I had, I felt more than saw when he followed suit. Eyes wide, my head swiveled this way and that to place myself and find the opposite shore.

Rushing water rose to my chin, seeming determined to choke me under. Gasping breaths made my heartbeat pound in my ears as sensation slowly seceded from my limbs while I kicked and clawed my way across in his wake.

"Do not let go. Do you hear me, Maria?" Drake's voice sounded pleasant to my ringing ears, at odds with the urgency and fear lacing his tone. Then the meaning of his words pierced my fogging thoughts, and I tried to nod.

Except the motion felt fuzzy, my focus blurring while my legs either locked up or lost all feeling from my core downward. Every nerve deadened, yanked along by the river against my will. *For fuck's sake, it was March, why the hell was it so damned cold?*

Suddenly my face dipped underwater for a moment that felt like forever. When Drake hauled me closer, his undead existence making him immune to the elements and able to keep kicking for both of us, I coughed on my attempt to breathe in.

"Stay with me," he muttered, muffled to the point that I might have hallucinated it. "Dear Lord, if you take her then I will lose everything…"

His words became nonsense, and my eyes blinked so slowly. The brightening blue sky turned hazy. My wet eyelashes felt too heavy to keep my eyes open. The current was a pleasant brush against my velvet-clad torso, and my head lolled against Drake's bobbing shoulder as blissful nothing took me with a sigh.

"I can hear your heartbeat, love. Please wake up. Please, Maria!"

Something clicked into place, and I squeezed my eyes shut against the dim light behind my closed lids. Renewed aches and painful pins-and-needles prickled across my limbs. My fingers flexed, and I tentatively opened my eyes. The next breath I inhaled was cut short when I choked on a cough. My body crunched inward, and then firm but familiar cold hands helped me roll onto my side.

I kept hacking until every dreg of moisture in my lungs was cleared, leaving me to wipe the spit hanging from my lower lip with the back of my hand. Stomach churning and head pounding like a jackhammer, I groaned while my forehead dug into the damp dirt beneath me. Foreign words were whispered too quickly for me to catch. Drake was still at my back, his palm caressing soothing circles along my spine. That actually felt nice. Too bad I had to ruin it.

"What happened?" I croaked, guessing at the answer despite my muddied memory.

"You fainted near the shore," Drake said, and I dared a glance up at him through my tangled wet curls. His black hair was still dripping, framing the hollows at his temples. Gray skin stretched across his cheekbones, carving out where his cheeks should've been. Bloodshot sclera surrounded the unchanged dark irises which seemed to soften when they met mine.

The sight of his relief didn't help me to fight my rising bile, but I managed to swallow it. Fire scorched down my esophagus, and I exhaled another shaky breath.

"That sucks," I murmured, pushing myself up on my shaking hands. Drake's supportive touch fell away, and for some reason, I suddenly wished I'd stayed down. Really, I knew *why* I felt that way, but admitting it was the hard part. Besides, I'd just survived a manor full of bloodthirsty monsters hellbent on killing me and someone I cared about—

Okay, so it wasn't that *hard to admit it.*

Excuses flooded my mind. I deserved a little comfort after all the shit that went down. Plus, nobody but me knew what was going on inside my head. Then I looked up at Drake again, and my traitorous heart pounded. He was smiling, his canines stark against taut lips, as thinned as the rest of his flesh in the sunlight. A giddy expression lit his macabre face, and heat climbed my neck.

"What?" I snapped, regretting it immediately, but Drake's happiness in the face of my warring emotions continued unabated.

"You are alive," he said, like that was enough reason to be over the moon.

"So are you. Kind of." Damn it, this was why I never tried to be smooth. Drake's chuckle sounded indulgent, and in a blink, he was standing. When his pale white hand extended to me, I didn't hesitate this time to place mine in his strong grip.

"We must continue to flee. Once the immor—ah, the vampires have satiated themselves, they will summon Ezra to scry for me."

"Yeah." I was about to stand, but my legs wobbled. That's right, there'd been other people in that manor. *Innocent* people who were going to be used and discarded like candy wrappers encasing sweets. I'd left them all behind in my selfish escape. "All those people…"

Reclined on my heels while I knelt, my arms felt like dead weight when Drake pulled on my hand to help me up. When I didn't budge, he crouched down to my eye-level, but my gaze was glued to the sodden earth. Something inside me fractured, snapping in half to let out a flood. Tears stung the backs of my eyes, but I wouldn't let them fall. A sniffle or two was unavoidable.

"Look at me," Drake said, quiet enough that I wouldn't have heard him if we weren't inches apart. Cold fingertips touched the curve of my jaw, and I didn't resist when he turned my head just enough to meet his gaze. There was no pity in his stare, only grim understanding. Just how much had he witnessed in over two hundred years? "You are no less for prioritizing your survival over those of others. Factually, I would wager that, had you stayed, they all would have still perished. The only difference is that you would have died alongside them."

"Maybe I deserve to," I whispered, the words out before I could filter them into something less crazy-sounding. Because I didn't want to die. I just wanted the agony to end.

"Never," he said, so strong and sure of himself that it cracked the exterior I tried to maintain. A tear slipped through my defenses, but before I could wipe it away, Drake's thumb traced the track of saltwater running down my cheek. Close as we were, I could see every dark vein hiding just beneath the thin surface of his skin. Could taste the needless breath he'd exhaled with that one word, but then he leaned away.

Like he'd broken a spell, I blinked fast and inhaled deeply to calm down. The pressure clamped around my heart eased a fraction, and I squeezed his hand in mine as he helped me up. My knees shook, but I managed to stand on my own two feet as he released my hand. The absence of his palm against mine felt wrong, but I focused my attention on the birds chirping in the trees, invisible except for their cheery notes.

On silent steps, Drake bent toward the roots of a tall elm nearby.

"These are yours," he said, offering my boots with the laces still tied together.

"Thank you," I said, and secretly hoped his fingers would brush against mine when I took them. They did, and my throat tightened when his touch didn't linger. "For everything."

"I will accept your gratitude when you are finally safe." His gaze scanned the woods around us, and a pang shot through my shivering chest. How had I ever mistaken him for being the same as those bloodsucking monsters?

Unaware of me sneaking glances at him, Drake waited until I shoved my throbbing feet into my boots before starting off on the unmarked path ahead. My fingers still felt tingly and useless with cold as I strode after him, the soles of my boots crunching over the dried leaves littering the ground.

"Where are we heading?" I asked, shivering.

"There is a freeway, or perhaps it is the turnpike ahead. I cannot place our exact location with how far we were swept downstream." Drake slowed his strides when my breathing grew ragged. Damn vampire had all the advantages when it came to physical stamina. *Must be nice, not having to sleep or feel tired.* Then my nose scrunched at the idea of having a desire for blood. I'd rather stick to my naps and calorie-consumption.

"Are we hitchhiking?" I asked, cursing everything when my quads protested on our hike uphill. What was with this state and having so many hills? While missing the flat expanse of home, another ache twined around my still-beating heart. Would I ever be able to see my family again? Was it even safe to contact them? Just how much was *I* willing to sacrifice to make sure Drake would be alright?

"In a manner of speaking," he answered, jarring me from the direction my thoughts had gone.

The thrum of passing traffic interrupted the soft buzzing and croaking of wildlife waking up around us. At the crest of the slope, a breeze pushed against my sticky face. A barrier separated where we stood at the perimeter of the woods from the two-lane road. Biting air filled my lungs when a coupe similar to Andrew's Plymouth Sundance barreled past, going well over the speed limit.

I turned for Drake, only to find him in the shade of a tree that mostly hid him from sunlight. Glimpses of his true face were revealed with each shake of the upper branches in the rough wind. His eyes flickered between bloodshot and clear while his gaze focused on the road with an eerie intensity. I shook off a shiver and followed his line of sight to spot a big Chevy Colorado turning the corner of the pot-hole heavy road.

A man sat behind the steering wheel, his expression changing from surprise, probably at seeing me on the roadside in a ruined party dress and with hair resembling a rat's nest, to slackened nothing. Like when people fell asleep, and all of their features relaxed. Except the driver managed to turn the wheel and smoothly hit the brake, flicking on the indicator to park on the shoulder of the highway before the hazards began flashing.

My mouth popped open as I glanced back at Drake while he smoothly stepped over the barrier. An uncertain smile pulled at the corners of his mouth as he turned to me.

"Your carriage awaits," he declared, and I huffed out a humorless laugh. *Sure, why not?*

"Couldn't we have just asked someone to give us a ride?" I needled, climbing over the partition to join Drake at the truck's front passenger door, which he opened for me.

"Even if someone would stop for us, the nicety is not worth the risk. People often gossip to one another about unusual occurrences—such as picking up two strangers on the side of the freeway—and the Cneaz has many…influential means of gathering information."

Nobody passing us on the road gave us a second glance, and I frowned. Back home, anyone parked with their hazards would have garnered some rubbernecking if not outright assistance. *Northern attitudes must mimic the awful weather.* Sighing, I looked inside the warm truck.

The man seated behind the wheel was getting out, but his weathered face struck a chord of familiarity before I could quash it. Short salt-and-pepper hair matched a beard nearly reaching the man's collar, just like Johann's. The stranger settled into the backseat, his expression dazed and soft green eyes glazed, like he was moving in a dream.

My heart ached while I settled myself into the warm leather seat before Drake closed the door for me. He slid into the driver's side faster than I could buckle myself in. As Drake put the shifter in gear, I directed the air vents my way and then rested my elbow on the door panel before propping my chin on my palm. Guilt squirmed in my stomach, but I refused to glance into the backseat at the truck's owner.

Everything hurt, down to my freezing toes, but my body quickly thawed on our drive into the unknown.

— 15 —

A HEAVY HEART

I BOLTED UPRIGHT AS MY EYES FLEW OPEN, BUT THE SEATBELT HAULED ME back into position. Velvet chafed against my bruised ribs as I gasped for breath. While I clutched the dashboard for dear life, a warm hand touched my forearm, but quickly fell away when I whirled to my left—*oh*.

Drake glanced between me and the road, his worry obvious under his self-conscious wince. At least, I figured that was the reason behind his pinched expression.

"Apologies," he said, "I did not intend to frighten you."

"No, it's okay." My words came out in a pant, my lungs working overtime and edging on hyperventilating until I focused on taking shallow inhales and longer exhales. "I—You're warm. I didn't realize it was you." The heat blasting from the air vents had turned the truck's cab toasty, and I cranked down the dial while stress-induced sweat beaded my hairline. *Yeesh*, now that I had a nap under my belt, I felt gross.

"We are nearly there," he assured, signaling right. Stereotypical small-town Americana surrounded us, complete with mom-

and-pop shops between every other single-story house. All of them seemed to be storefronts, not homes, until Drake took the turn onto a suburban street.

Sneaking a glance at Drake, the tension building in my chest eased from watching his relaxed driving. With one hand on the wheel, his elbow propped on the door, and the other resting against the center console, he seemed as calm and in control as ever. My racing heart slowed, and I frowned. How long had Drake's presence been a source of comfort to me?

Probably sometime between that kiss in the park and running away from the lycans.

Gruesome memories from the woods before the river punched to the forefront of my mind, and my inhale shook. Those lycans had been human once, cursed to endure their transformation. Which meant they must have been brainwashed into service. I really didn't want to know just how many years they'd spent enslaved to those monsters. Just like I couldn't bear to peek into the glovebox to learn the name of the man whose truck we'd hijacked.

I wasn't able to look into the backseat, either, but the stranger's steady breathing was enough of a reminder that he was still there. Facing his charmed unfocused gaze would've made it harder to divorce myself from the abuse of mentally manipulating another human being. Even if it was only for our survival.

Woods bordered the road, thinning out where houses of various designs passed by in a blur as we drove deeper into residential territory. Every backyard seemed to have its own personal treeline, obscuring any neighbors that might live directly behind them. The oppressive dense forestry was another reminder of last night, and I shuddered despite the luxurious warmth cocooning me.

"Are you well?" Drake asked, and I held back a sigh while staring out my passenger window.

"If I never see another oak tree again it'll be too soon." If only oak wasn't such a high-ticket material used in my father and uncle's business. I'd have to steer clear of the woodworking shop for at least a month. It'd been a while since I worked as receptionist there, behind the cozy desk with a great view of the whole shop.

Handmade furniture was our brand, and the entry room had been decorated in a display of Harker craftsmanship. The workroom took up most of the building, through a door just left of the desk, where the raw wood and varnish lived amidst the scent of sawdust.

My insides ached all over again with nostalgic longing, but I shook myself out of it when Drake pulled up to the unmarked curb opposite a yellow two-story house. It looked unremarkable, like any other on the street, but something about it made my blood thrum.

Glancing into the backseat for the first time since getting in the truck, I found the charmed man still seated in the corner. His glazed-over eyes weren't taking in a single thing going on around him. Like the server at the Cneaz's manor who'd been pinned between two ugly undead.

"Will he be okay?" I asked, quiet and defeated. The man at the manor was already dead, *but I wasn't, not yet.*

"He will not remember us in the slightest. No danger will come to him."

Turning to Drake, I frowned. "I mean, will he be able to safely drive himself home?"

Hidden from the sun by the shade of surrounding pines, Drake's stoic features softened with what I guessed was pity at my innocence. "I believe so."

Experience colored his words, more proof that he had a past I knew nothing about. Being around for over two centuries, and with all the abilities that came with being undead to boot, it would be naive to think he'd never charmed someone before. Even more stupid to want to believe he'd never drank another's blood.

Too torn up to voice the issue, I chewed on the inside of my cheek. When Drake unbuckled his seatbelt, I did the same and asked, "Where are we, anyway?"

"Lagrangeville." The thump of the car door closing punctuated his one-word response.

Goosebumps rose along my still-bare arms and legs on my exit. I was already shivering from the mid morning chill while heading around the truck's front to the other side, where Drake stood. By the time I got there, the dazed man was back in the driver's seat, being handed the keys. Hesitant fingers closed around the jingling metal, and the man's brow furrowed.

An instant later, Drake's hand was at the small of my back, turning me to face the yellow house across the street.

"Best to make ourselves scarce as he comes to."

My pulse jumped from the pressure of his palm against my body. "Okay, but where are we 'making ourselves scarce' *to*?"

Drake smirked, the sunlight hitting him briefly to mar his features into anything but handsome—except it was still him, so my traitorous heartbeat didn't seem to care. "Like I said, I have a…friend."

The truck revved into gear behind us, and I startled. Glancing back, my lips pursed as the man made a U-turn, shaking his head. Like he knew where he was, but wasn't sure how he'd gotten there. Urged ahead by Drake, I directed my attention forward as we neared a set of low wooden steps, leading to a front stoop with a small overhang above the white front door.

The knocker seemed more ornate compared to the houses we'd passed, and a wicker chair that would've been fitting outside any grandparents' place leaned against the stoop's railing. All in all, the property looked ordinary, mundane—but something still felt off.

"Will we really be safe here?" I whispered.

"It is the most safe home I know of, apart from the house I own in Albuquerque."

"How so?"

"There are wards in place, courtesy of a generous sorceress practicing witchcraft. They will hide whoever steps foot on the property from being easily found."

Sounded clever in theory, but it meant that the second Drake left, they'd be onto him. Without that freedom, the safe house became a different kind of prison. Still, having a best friend who'd been a practicing witch since well before I'd met her, I tried to picture Everly sprinkling some mumbo jumbo over the church for added protection.

I should ask her if she can—suddenly, my stomach soured. When would I get the chance? More importantly, how was I going to tell my family about any of this—

The door swung inward the moment we stopped in front of it, and I flinched back. My fists clenched, ready for a fight. Except the man standing in the doorway, wearing a navy blue long-sleeve shirt and faded jeans, was anything but threatening. Towering over me, but not quite as tall as Caleb, the man's full lips widened into a welcoming smile.

An attractive array of dark stubble was sparse across his chin, the same texture as his shortly cropped hair. Soft brown eyes gazed down at me first before shifting to my vampire.

"This is the girl, huh?" His deep, resonant voice was soothing, but the first words out of his mouth made me frown. I was forced to swallow my rebuttal at being called 'the girl' when Drake encouraged me to enter by pressing against the small of my back.

Flustered, I crossed the threshold a step ahead of Drake while the homeowner deftly moved out of our path.

"What have you told him about me?" I demanded, staring up into Drake's dark eyes. He had the nerve to look sheepish, which somehow only made it harder to be mad at him.

"Winston is a trustworthy fellow," he replied, avoidant, and my eyes narrowed.

"All good things, I assure you," Winston piped up, and I froze when I turned to him. A chord of familiarity clicked into place, because I'd heard his voice before.

"You were on the phone—with Drake, when I was shackled to his living room sconce."

A burst of laughter filled the small entry space, between the stairs on my right leading up, and the short hallway ahead, but Winston's mirth was totally at odds with Drake's pained expression. My vampire's lips pressed together, his brows drawn.

I frowned, glancing through the open archway to the left of the front door. Where a fire crackled in the living room's hearth.

"I told you I'd like her," Winston said between wiping a tear from his eye and struggling to cut his chuckling short. Then his gaze traveled innocently from my cold legs to the torn dress, and finally up to my knotted, tangled hair. If I hadn't just been through hell, I might have felt self-conscious. "Damn, Drake really knows how to show a gal a good time."

I opened my mouth, but the urge to defend Drake's reputation vanished when I registered the concerned edge to Winston's tone.

"Things did not go according to plan," Drake muttered, glancing down at me with remorse etched across his resigned expression.

"Seems like it. Well, I'll scrounge up some clothes for you both to change into. There's coffee brewing in the pot whenever you feel like it." Winston headed up the hall, taking a right at the end, and the promise of coffee after so many days in withdrawal helped to wake up my exhausted brain.

Silence descended, cut through only by the sound of a clock ticking in another room. Given the moment of peace, my attention drifted over the soft-beige walls. Several framed photos had stained edges, like they were a couple of decades old or more. Winston didn't look older than mid-thirties, but every picture seemed to feature him surrounded by others in his age range at the time of the photograph.

A peek through the open archway into the living room revealed a pair of suede couches with afghan blankets thrown over them. The furniture was angled toward the fireplace against the far wall, opposite a low coffee table and lamp in the corner whose shade widened into a bell shape. Tassels fringed the rim like something out of a Victorian period piece.

My brow pinched, trying and failing to piece together what felt off about the place, when suddenly Drake cleared his throat. In the entryway beside me, he stood with an odd juxtaposition of comfortable ease in his posture, but a look of uncertainty across his features.

"I wanted to apologize—for having chained you in my residence back in Albuquerque on the night we met."

"Oh." Weirdly, hearing him talk about our first encounter as 'the night we met' set butterflies to flutter in my stomach.

"Admittedly, I had forgotten the discomfort they bring to the living. For one such as myself, it merely drains our strength due to the engraved sigils. Wearing them must have been incredibly painful. Had I thought better of it, and I should have, I would not have restrained you in such a way. I am sorry."

I blinked in the wake of his unexpected, drawn-out apology. Concern was clear behind his dark eyes, like he really cared whether or not I forgave him. If he'd said as much right after it happened, I would have told him to shove it. Now, after everything we'd been through, an apology didn't seem necessary.

Hell, he'd saved my life how many times since then? A grin tugged up the corners of my mouth before I realized it, and the tension seemed to dissipate between us.

"I forgive you."

At my response, Drake smiled—like, *really* smiled—and I stilled into stunned silence at the way his honest grin lit up his face. Even with the light filtering in through the windows, no amount of magick stripping away his illusion could change how the sight made warmth spread through my fast-beating heart—

"Getting along, I see." Winston's voice came from right behind me, and I spun. His black eyebrows rose. "Jumpy little thing."

I frowned up at Winston's impressive height, because I was neither little *nor* a thing. Was that how Caleb viewed me, too? *Maybe that's why he teased me so much growing up.*

"Thank you for the garments." Drake accepted the clothes Winston handed over, a matching light blue sweatpants and sweater folded on top of a white long-sleeve button-up and dark jeans.

"No problem. The guest room upstairs is still made up from when I'd been expecting you. Feel free to take it." Winston's final words were directed at me, but his glance at Drake seemed to pry at whether or not we'd be sharing a room. The idea came and went through my head as Drake started for the stairs, but I hung back.

"Thank you." I rushed to follow Drake after a casual wave of acknowledgement from Winston, who then turned to head up the hall toward the drifting scent of freshly brewed coffee.

"Ladies first." Drake waved me on, and I started climbing on aching legs.

"Come here often?" I asked.

"The house originally belonged to me, so, yes."

My brows rose. On the second floor, all three doors—one to my right, left, and ahead—were closed, and I hesitated. Drake smoothly moved past me, angling for the room on the left before opening it. Following him in, I took in the hardwood bed frame and matching nightstands on either side. Against the corner wall with the sloping ceiling was a writing desk not unlike the one I remembered from Drake's house in Albuquerque.

Atop the desk, another black-and-white photograph's frame leaned against its stand, and I stilled when I recognized its subjects. Drake looked the same as he did today, the ends of his straight black hair reaching slightly past his ears. The full lips, high cheekbones and chiseled jaw were identical, unmarked by time. Beside him, dressed just as elaborated in an old-fashioned suit, was a young Black child with familiar bone structure.

"Is that…" Then I glanced at the paisley pattern of the bedsheets, and it dawned on me why the downstairs had seemed unusual. What kind of a mid-thirties guy, living by himself, decorated his house like it was still the 1960s? I turned to Drake, who studied the old portrait picture with reminiscent fondness.

"Yes, it is Winston and I." Drake faced me, and a cavalier shrug lifted his shoulders. "As you may have surmised, he is far older than he looks."

"But he's not a vampire, I could tell."

"Not in full, no."

Oh—a piece of lore trickled back into my brain. Apparently, I'd learned *something* from what we were forced to study as kids.

"He's a dhampir."

Drake nodded, and I exhaled a long breath. Returning to the photo, I tried to find any kind of resemblance between them. They didn't look alike, but if Winston had one vampire parent and one human… I didn't want to pry, and surprise washed through me when Drake spoke without being prompted.

"Winston was a young boy when I took him in from an orphanage, sometime in nineteen-forty-eight." The story didn't roll off his tongue well, and maybe he hadn't told it often—or ever, before now. "I had known his mother prior to his birth, and aided in her escape from the man who I believe was in love with her, but would have destroyed any chance of offspring." A frown creased his forehead, but his thinly-veiled disdain was nothing compared to the horror slackening my jaw.

I should have expected that kind of gross violation of autonomy from the undead, but being around Drake was beginning to desensitize me to them. A deep, integral part of me cleaved in two—having been struggling to rationalize my experiences with Drake compared to what I'd been raised to believe about vampires. Everything I learned about him confirmed that he'd been human once. How he experienced the world wasn't so different from the way I did.

We were both capable of caring for others, putting ourselves in harm's way to protect someone else. Neither of us hesitated to defend ourselves when we were threatened, even if that meant reacting with violence. Vampires were defined by several traits, their strength, speed, longevity, and inception, to name a few—but beyond the bloodlust, and the bodies they'd left behind for me and my family to find, they were fundamentally the same as us.

Was it always so simple? Were they not doomed to commit horrible acts? Drake had proven that change was possible, even for those who never grew older. The thought dawned, rising in me like the sun and warming me throughout. Because the truth was that I'd stopped thinking of Drake as one of the undead. If he was just a man, how would I have judged him?

I wouldn't have. He was too kind, his generosity and patience seemingly endless. Beyond his disarming good looks, there was genuine compassion in his every action. Regardless of what he really was, or how we'd come to be standing here together, I couldn't fight how I felt about him anymore.

Face flushed, my heart throbbed as my lungs filled with relief—*but why did I have to pick the worst time to understand that both realities could be true?* That Drake could be what he was, and *who* he was at the same time. It was never *being a vampire* that transformed them into monsters—it was that they'd never tried to be anything but cruel.

As he continued the sad story of Winston's start to life, I tried to bury the tenderness blooming within my chest to focus on his words.

"The mother rarely survives carrying a dhampir, especially when medicine was more primitive than it is now. Since he was orphaned, and left to face a world that would never understand his slowed aging, I opted to adopt him."

"You guys seem close," I remarked, and the corners of Drake's mouth curved up ever so slightly as he handed me my fresh clothes.

"We often resided in the same household until more recently..."

Before I could ask anything else, he abruptly started to retreat to the hall. "The bathroom is the door on the left here, and you are welcome to use the shower. I will leave you to go about your business." He reached for the handle to close the door behind him.

"Wait—" My hand rose, like I was about to stop him even though I was halfway across the room, but Drake already paused. His dark eyes bore into mine, expectant, and I steeled my courage. "I need to admit to something." After what he'd just shared, it felt like I now knew a piece of him that many didn't get to see. Maybe it was time I started trusting someone else, too.

"Yes?" He re-entered the bedroom, closing the door gently behind him to give us privacy.

"I—I'm not the person you think I am. I mean, I am, but…" Inhaling a deep breath, I blinked slowly and organized my thoughts. "Last year, I did something awful, and my cousin got hurt because of my bad decisions. I went on a hunt with my family, not exactly sober, and nearly got her killed." The tears threatened to fall, but I was done hiding from the guilt.

"You do not have to share anything that you do not wish to, Maria. I did not tell you about Winston, his upbringing, to make you feel as if you owe me anything in return."

"It's not like that," I assured. "It's just—I feel like sometimes you think so highly of me, and I don't want you to think I'm that great when you don't know the truth." *What the hell was I saying?* Flushing hot, like I'd admitted way more than I'd meant to, I averted my gaze to the window. Where lace curtains allowed softened sunlight to illuminate the space.

A moment passed, and to distract from my self-imposed humiliation, I focused on how bright the house was. Compared to the Cneaz's manor, where every window was shuttered closed, and the dwellings of the colonies my family had taken out—where any and all cracks got boarded up—it seemed like the undead couldn't cope with seeing themselves, or each other, the way they really looked.

Drake had never shied away from what or who he was, *if only I could do the same.*

"I was already aware that you held a heavy heart." His voice was too damn tender, and caring. I gripped my crossed arms harder to keep my emotions from welling up. "Blinking hell, you had suggested as much during our evening at the Two Fools Tavern."

The way he said *our evening* heated my cheekbones.

"If I were to judge a person based on who they used to be, then I would never be capable of looking into the mirror."

"Then what do you judge someone by?" Despite my small voice, I looked up to face him head on. He'd moved closer, his steps silent, until I was staring up at him from only a foot away.

"By what they choose to overcome." His smile was heartbreaking, made complete by his heavily-lidded eyes staring down into mine. I swallowed, and took a shaky breath. Desperate to forgive myself, even if nobody else had.

"Okay." It was all I could say, everything in me trying to hold back from throwing my arms around him. Losing myself in his embrace, like I had in the park when we kissed, was too tempting—and the part of me fighting the urge was weakening.

Neither of us spoke. An undercurrent sparked between us, waiting for the other to act while we stood in silence spiked with tension. Then his hand rose, his fingertips brushing my jaw before he tucked a stray curl behind my ear. The simple touch soothed an ache inside me that returned when he pulled away, and a chill caressed my spine.

Drake visibly swallowed, glancing toward the door we'd entered through. "I will be downstairs, enlightening Winston to what has transpired before I tell him of our future plans."

"I'll be down soon." I cleared my suddenly tight throat, which seemed to make Drake smile before he left the room. He closed the door behind him, and I sank down onto the bed. What had almost happened? More importantly, what did I wish had happened?

Slapping my warm cheeks, I shook my head and made my way to the bathroom on wobbling steps.

— 16 —

LOVE IS SUICIDE

FOG COATED THE MIRROR BEFORE I WIPED IT OFF WITH A BLUE HAND TOWEL. Steam surrounded me, and the bathroom sparkled, reflecting the sunlight cascading through the small window over the toilet. I scoffed when I could finally see my own reflection, and then winced. Never before had I ever looked or felt this *wrecked*.

Dark circles weighed down my round blue-gray eyes. A pale sheen marred the olive undertone to my complexion, and the scattered scrapes from my hands to my dimpled chin didn't help. Sighing, I unwrapped the towel around my midriff and grimaced at the bruises across my left hip and rib cage. Taking in every battle wound with idle curiosity, my focus caught on my right forearm.

Two scabbed puncture holes remained over my wrist where my green veins ran to the crook of my arm. My mind's eye conjured up the image of the indents Drake's teeth had created, pressure marks against my skin right after he'd bitten me. The glint in his eyes when he'd first tasted my blood, and then how fast and strong he'd become when it had healed him.

212

A shiver shook my shoulders despite the house's warm temperature. From the mirror, I watched the red of embarrassment spread from my chest and up my neck. It was so stupid to indulge in the memory since it could *never* happen again.

Pushing the romanticized thoughts from my mind, I patted my body dry, and the humid moisture from my shower almost made me break into a sweat. Winston's borrowed sweatshirt was luxuriously baggy across my broad shoulders, but the waistband of the pants had to be hiked up to my waist to sit comfortably above my wide hips.

Cooler air hit my face when I left the bathroom, leaving the ruined dress behind in the wastepaper basket. The woolen socks on my feet kept my steps down the stairs silent as I followed the smell of coffee through the quiet house. At the end of the hall, another three doors were closed to the right, but the kitchen was immediately to the left.

Crisp morning air permeated the space, smelling like pine needles, and I inhaled deeply. Glancing around the kitchen, I raised my eyebrows, impressed by the stainless steel appliances and marble countertop. Goofy slogans were strung up on the walls, and I smirked at *There's no 'I' in 'team' but there is in 'kitchen.'*

Smiling, my attention landed on the empty cup beside the coffee pot—right next to a ceramic plate with the most heavenly-looking sandwich I'd ever set my eyes on. I was already salivating before pulling off the Saran wrap, and poured myself a tall cup of coffee while simultaneously digging into the Italian bread holding together tomato, lettuce, salami and ham.

A moan rumbled in my chest while I chewed fast to swallow and take another bite. The sandwich was half-engulfed by the time I took a swig from my coffee. I swore I could *feel* my neurons firing in bliss. As my chewing slowed, I registered the voices filtering in from the cracked-open window over the sink.

The deep timbre to Winston's words trailed off, and the soothing sound of Drake's light Eastern European accent became discernible as he spoke an answer. Quickly swallowing my most recent bite, I moved closer to unapologetically eavesdrop.

Winston said, "Definitely explains why I haven't heard from you in almost a week. Had the bed all made up and fresh pig's blood in the fridge just for you. Ended up using it to make *blodpudding*, sorry about that."

"Plans had changed," Drake replied, and then inhaled deeply. Cigarette smoke drifted on the breeze, and my shoulders sagged. It didn't smell like the same brand Ethan smoked, but close enough to be a painful reminder of the distance between here and home.

"Clearly." Winston's reply was dry, expecting to hear more. I stood on my tiptoes to get closer to the window.

"Aiden intervened, as he is wont to do without consulting me." Bitterness tinged Drake's voice, but a certain amount of acceptance tempered it. "He manipulated Maria into finding me before I could make the crossing. I had been awaiting Aiden to bring me the weapon he promised. Which he delivered through Maria, much to her misfortune."

The orb, I guessed. I leaned over the sink, careful not to get my borrowed sweatshirt wet while I strained to hear more.

"Ezra caught up to me much sooner than I had anticipated, and Maria was taken entirely unawares. She fought beside me while still reeling from the truth of the Domnitori."

"That's bad luck," Winston commented, taking a long drag from what I assumed was a cigarette.

"Yes." A pause, and then Drake's tone turned somber. "I could not abandon her, either time. If I had, then my survival would become meaningless."

"I know… You've felt that way for a long time. I'm glad the girl has given you back a sense of purpose."

Drake scoffed. "A selfish endeavor, on my part. Keeping Maria safe is now all I hope to achieve after this mess of events."

I rocked back from the stainless-steel basin, feeling warm despite the cool air trickling in. Glancing around the room, I glimpsed the sliding glass doors beside a round breakfast table on the other side of the bar-style counter.

"So, what are you going to do now?" Winston's words faded to the background as I made my way through the kitchen, past the breakfast nook, and grasped the handle of the sliding glass door. It slid to my left, and I stepped out onto the wooden deck, only to immediately stop short.

A cat slinked inside, brushing against my ankles before seeming to realize that I'd only borrowed its owner's clothes. The animal padded deeper into the house, and I closed the glass door behind me, my gaze affixed to the view beyond the deck's pale wooden railings. Seeing it in person was so much different than through the windows.

Bright rays of sunshine filtered through sparse tree limbs, rising higher than any that grew back home. Pines interspersed the naked oaks, their dewy needles reflecting light. Hidden amidst the scenery, a bird's song called out into the still morning. Everything felt slow, maybe because I'd barely slept for a day or more—when the hell had I gotten to that manor?

I didn't even know what day it was, but I wouldn't let the ugly memories of the last few days ruin the serenity creeping into my bones. A deep lungful of air expanded my chest, and I closed my eyes. The chill breeze brushed against the exposed skin on my face and hands, but holding the mug of coffee kept my fingertips warm.

Now that I was properly clothed for the northern springtime, the temperature wasn't painful. Relief seeped in on my exhale, my eyes opened, and my gaze fell on Drake's—his raven-dark eyes already staring into mine. Slowly, a smile curved up the corners of his deathly-pale lips, and I swallowed hard.

To keep my heart from speeding up any further, I turned my attention to where Winston was seated on a white lawn chair beside a glass-top table. A fanciful ashtray rested at the center, smoke curling upward from a forgotten cigarette still smoldering. Winston's breath clouded the air, rising to disappear into the bright blue sky above, and he flicked off the excess ash on his half-smoked cigarette.

My nose wrinkled, but a flush climbed my throat when Winston slyly glanced between me and Drake.

"Tina seems to like you," Winston said, nodding at the house behind me.

"I think she likes the smell of your clothes more than me." I smiled, which felt strained, and then shook my head when Winston offered his pack of American Spirits. "I don't smoke, just a caffeine addict."

"Who isn't?" Winston shrugged, his easy smile still brimming when he turned to Drake. "Speak of the devil, right?"

A sound of reproach rumbled in Drake's throat as his eyes narrowed at Winston. In a placating motion, Winston raised his hands up to his temples, and his cigarette dangled precariously between his middle and forefinger. Clearly appeased, Drake's expression brightened when he took a step closer to where I stood.

"How are you feeling?"

"Like shit." I raised the mug to my lips, and smirked at Winston's laugh, which Drake ignored.

"I can imagine…" Drake's hand rose toward me a few inches, but stopped. His fingers curled into a fist while his lips pressed together. Since he seemed at a loss, and I didn't feel like being pitied, I let it all out.

"All I want to do right now is call my family. To tell them that I'm alive, if nothing else. Which I'm pretty sure is the only thing I *can* tell them because if I explained that our enemies are a lot more organized than we thought—with their own personal enslaved army of previously-thought-to-be-extinct werewolves and untold stolen wealth—then their first instinct would be to track me down and launch an assault on that manor.

"Except, I can't let them do that, can I? Because then they'd all die." My hands trembled, and I tightened my grip on the mug. Jaw unclenching, I said, "I know you want to run off and play martyr, get yourself killed to give me time to get away, but I'm just as embroiled in this fucking mess as you are. Hell, the underwear I spent three days wearing—in a *van*—is still back at that manor. I'm as susceptible of being scried for across the continent as you are.

"Besides—" I took a breath, vindicated by Drake's blank expression, his black eyebrows high, and Winston's companionable silence. "If you tried to go back to that awful manor of horrors, even if you do it while I'm sleeping, then I swear I'm going to follow you back there just to pull *your* ass out this time. And I *really* don't want to do that."

Finally out of steam, I settled back on my right foot, accidentally having shifted into a defensive stance, and glanced between the two men. Winston inhaled a long drag, and when he came up for air, he looked at Drake.

"I told you I liked her."

Drake glanced at Winston, but his attention quickly returned to me. "I have no intention of returning to the regional Cneaz." It didn't sound like he was lying, and I relaxed.

"Yeah, you've got too much to live for now," Winston muttered, soon hiding behind his own mug of cream-filled coffee. Olivia would have approved of that milk-to-brew ratio.

Before Winston emerged from his swig, Drake's form blurred until he stood directly beside Winston's lit cigarette. Almost too fast to register, his forefinger and thumb pinched the burnt end until it went out. He rubbed the black ash between his fingers, the digits stretched tight across the phalanges under direct sunlight, making his short nails seem longer, thinner.

Winston groaned, sneering up at Drake's unapologetic pettiness. I bit my lip to hide a smile. It felt too much like how Uncle Alaric often reacted whenever my cousins managed to get on their father's nerves. While Drake was far from my jokester uncle, the domestic to-and-fro brought on a nostalgic smile, but it faded fast. *Would I ever get to see my family again?*

While Winston was forced to keep his mouth closed in order to relight his cigarette, the corners of Drake's lips twitched upward as he took advantage of the sudden silence.

"My aim going forward is to do as that damned sorcerer insisted—infiltrate the fortress of Dracula, and manage to sleuth my way past the Domnitori and their watchful eyes, where I will then acquire the ring to prevent him or any sorcerer from deducing my given location."

Winston paused in bringing his mug to his lips, slowly lowering it to the glass-top table.

"You want to break-and-enter Poenari Castle?" Winston glanced my way, but I was just as shocked by the new plan.

"That is where the ring resides, which makes it our only option," Drake said.

The dhampir sat up, the emotion behind his eyes hardening with sincerity. "How do you figure you'll get from here to Arefu? It's not like you can travel by boat or air with the damn imperials watching out for you."

"I intend to make the journey by the same means I was meant to travel here without alerting the Cneaz."

Winston blinked, clearly understanding whatever that meant.

"What are you talking about?" I demanded, and Drake turned to me.

"What do you know of the fae?"

"Uh, only that you should never trust one?" My limited understanding of faeries made Winston chuckle, but Drake was serious.

"Have you ever heard the tales where the fair folk lead mortals into the woodlands, never to return again?"

Brow furrowed, I nodded once.

"When faeries were being hunted into near extinction by humans a little over a millenia ago, they did not disappear entirely—obviously." He gestured toward me, reigniting my annoyance with the faery man who'd tricked me. "To escape persecution, faeries bound their magick together to create a realm of their own, accessible from our reality by entrances hidden across the globe."

"Just think of it like wormholes," Winston piped up. "You cross over from our world—here, for instance—walk a ways, and pop back out in the arctic." Drake's nod of agreement cut off short with a frown.

Wait a minute... "When you said 'Arefu,' are you talking about the place in Romania?" I asked.

Without hesitation, Drake said, "The very same."

Suddenly lightheaded, I staggered a couple steps to lean against the deck railing. He wanted to take us into the belly of the beast—to sneak past the Domnitori, the vampires who controlled all others in the world—*and* we had to cross into another realm to do it? Damn, if I survived this, I was never poking fun at Everly's mysticism again.

"You'll need to barter something meaningful for a journey like that," Winston mentioned.

"Then it is fortunate your basement contains a treasure trove or two," Drake replied.

"You've got me there." Winston sighed. "And I've got just the person to help strike a deal. Let me make a phone call."

"Why don't you just call Aiden?" I asked, shrugging when they both faced me.

"Too bloody," Winston answered, waving the suggestion off as he stood. "I don't feel like cleaning up."

Stymied, I opened my mouth to ask what he meant by that, but Drake interjected, "Are you 'game' with this plan?" The somewhat modern term sounded unusual with the way he said it, in the most unfortunately endearing way.

"It's our only option, right?" I shot back, and Drake hesitated before nodding. "Then I'll do it. But I want a weapon."

"I'm sure I've got something sharp and pointy in the garden shed," Winston said, smirking on his way to the sliding glass door. "I'll let you know what your next move is." Shaking his phone for emphasis, he strode inside. The shush of the door sliding back into place gave way to renewed silence.

Even with the chittering of hidden wildlife all around us, the quiet suddenly seemed too full when Drake and I were left standing on Winston's deck alone—together, whatever. To avoid looking at Drake, I tugged on the hem of my borrowed sweatshirt and cleared my throat.

"Since the cat's out of the bag, what *was* your plan originally?" Steeling my courage, I faced Drake with an awkward smile. "I mean, before you got saddled down with me. You said you were going to come here?"

"Ah, yes." Drake's expression cleared, but his stiff posture hinted at unease. "You see, before he sent you to find me, Aiden had originally promised me a weapon worthy of destroying any vampire within its range. At the nature reserve, I had been waiting for him to deliver it to me and then lead me through the Summerland to come here.

"Winston already agreed to my staying for a day or so to plan, and then I would have confronted the Cneaz on my own terms. Although I had imagined Lucian and his fellows would have met a more permanent end than they had." A frown creased the taut skin around his eyes. Somewhere nearby, the trickle of a stream burbled, but my attention was wholly on Drake when the pieces started fitting together.

"You were going to sacrifice yourself for me, weren't you?" I'd already suspected it, knowing he'd only gotten in trouble with vampire law because of saving me from another undead. All because I'd agreed to hear him out.

Instead of confirming or denying it, Drake smiled. "I am sorry for pulling you down with me—attaching my problems to yours." Even marred by direct sunshine, his striking, ghoulish features and soft accent lit up my heart like tinder took to fire.

Vehement, I shook my head and ambled a step closer. "When I went to find you that night—at the park—it was to thank you for saving my life in that damn parking lot."

Surprise cascaded across Drake's expression as he subtly moved nearer, if only by inches. He seemed about to say something, and then changed tracks when he opened his mouth. "You could still notify your family to come for you, it is not too late. Otherwise, I could fund your fare home. Even if Ezra *were* tempted to scry for you, there are ways for a living person to ward against it. Winston could assist you with—"

"You need me there, right? That's what Ezra was implying—a *blood* relative of Dracula is the key. Well, here I am, his long-descended niece. You won't get that ring without me." Saying it out loud only strengthened my belief, especially when Drake seemed at a loss to argue against it. Except, that wasn't the whole reason for why I was going along with it.

"Also… If I did call my family to come get me, it would put you and Winston at risk. I couldn't—I *don't* want that."

My face heated as I glanced up to meet Drake's gaze. He blinked, only once, but it was like something shifted inside of him that extended to the air between us. The space faded as he leaned in, carefully angling closer until we were only inches apart.

"I do not deserve you," he whispered, so matter-of-fact, but his mind melting accent encouraged my eyes to close while I breathed him in. Death and blood lingered on him, somewhere deep in his veins that went beyond washing off what had been stained to his skin. Somehow, it didn't smell so unpleasant anymore.

Heart racing, my thoughts a mess, I slowly opened my eyes and said, "Well, I'm all the backup you've got. Hope you don't mind." It was the last thing I wanted to say. *Why was it so hard to express what kept pulsating under my skin?* Like revealing too much would break all the trust I'd built up, even if I'd already run out of excuses for why I shouldn't embrace how I felt.

His chuckle sounded genuine, but the resignation behind his eyes seemed too sad to reflect his lingering smile. The same sentiment I'd glimpsed when I found him in the park. Almost like he had his own doubts. Just beneath the surface, and hidden by his calm exterior.

Leaning away, he started for the door and said, "Yours are the only reinforcements I shall ever need, love."

Flutters ricocheted through my chest as I followed a few steps behind him, and then my brow furrowed. *When, exactly, had he started calling me that?*

WITHOUT A TRACE

THE WORLD OUTSIDE THE KITCHEN WINDOW SHIFTED ANOTHER SHADE darker, revealing a speckle of stars against the plum sky. When the cloud cover let up enough to see them, anyway. With my elbows resting on the breakfast nook table, I chewed through my third slice of pizza, careful to keep the garlic powder from sliding off.

Since dhampirs were pretty much just humans that aged slow as molasses, and with no daylight restrictions to boot, Winston was well-acquainted with all the best eateries in town. Warmth closed in all around, from the fire in the living room hearth—visible through the wide open archway—to the air vents creating a low thrum as they pumped out hot air.

Honestly, Winston kept the place warmer than our church back in Albuquerque.

I placed my burnt crust onto my plate, situated right beside the sharp and pointy instrument Winston had scrounged up. The machete's blade had a dull sheen, but since Winston claimed he'd only bought it to tackle a snare of poison ivy about a decade ago, that was expected. The point sharpened up just fine with a little elbow grease, and I smirked at the memory of when Johann taught me to use a whetstone back when I was eight.

All that cheese and dough became a rock in my stomach, and I exhaled a sigh. Winston looked up from his seat on the stool beside the counter, his brow raised, and I shrugged. Having only woken up an hour ago, I hadn't taken the time to debate over whether or not to send a message to my family. Would it hurt them more to get a postcard post-mortem, or to never know what had happened to me?

They probably figured I'd gone off on another bender, anyway. My lips pursed. *Maybe it served them right to never know what happened to me.* By now, they'd have found my car, seemingly abandoned at the park close to the Rio Grande. *What if they drag the river looking for me?* I winced, and stifled another sigh. As tragic as it seemed, wouldn't it be better if they stayed ignorant?

Finding out about the Domnitori had changed my worldview completely, but Johann—he was always the man with a plan. He saw our family through thick and thin, and he'd spend the rest of his life trying to take down that evil if he found out that's what took *me.* Even if things were never the same between us after Mom died.

It was at her funeral that I changed his name in my contacts list to 'Johann' instead of just…Dad. I never called him by his name to his face, but it was like I was forcing some separation between us. Considering I'd just lost Mom, it made sense. Instead of coming together to grieve, we'd shut down.

Both Uncle Alaric and Aunt Susan were there to support us, physically and emotionally, but sometimes it felt like I was an outsider looking in. My cousins got to finish growing up with both of their parents, and I didn't. Every time I was around them for the months after, that fact blared in my head alongside the pain in my chest.

On the rare occasions when it was just me and Johann in the room together, what we'd lost weighed heavily in the air between us. The elephant in the room that crushed both of our spirits. Without saying a word, we reminded each other of who was supposed to be there. Which sucked, but we survived. *Too bad our father-daughter relationship didn't.*

During therapy last year, I let loose that innocuous truth, and my psychologist made a huge deal about it. Like it connected the dots, solidifying my trust issues and explaining away every awful thing I'd ever done. Except, that wasn't the whole picture, because I *did* trust my family. It was me that I didn't trust—my ability to do anything right, to make decisions that anyone would be proud of.

I'd spent far too long living under the pressure of expecting myself to fail at the first try. It was why I couldn't pass up a hunt, the one thing I could do that meant something. For longer than I could remember, nothing I ever did *felt* right. Like everyone around me had it all figured out. Their path forward seemingly already paved, but I was lost. Even when I tried following in their footsteps.

Until now, because Drake needed me, and I had the chance to save him.

It went beyond paying him back. I couldn't keep being chickenshit by denying the truth to myself. Ever since meeting him, every choice I'd made finally felt like the correct path. I stared out the sliding glass doors, to where Drake leaned against the far railing, surveying the dark woods beyond.

His sight would be better than mine when it came to night vision. Just how easily could he see through the dim? *Maybe as clearly as he'd seen through me...*

"Can I have a piece of paper and a pen?" I asked through a heavy exhale, my focus returning to Winston. The tall man clapped his hands together, dispersing pizza crumbs, and promptly hopped off the stool. Silent, he moved to a low-hanging shelf beneath a funky ticking clock shaped like a cat—the sort of thing Everly would thrift given the chance.

Winston returned to hand over a pad of lined paper and a black ballpoint pen. Taking them in my right hand, I moved my crumb-laden plate aside with my left—which Winston promptly took—and I sluggishly uncapped the pen. At first, I could only think as far as addressing the letter with '*Dear Dad.*' Then the words spilled out of me, onto the page and inked into existence despite every word being a lie.

Swallowing hard, I signed it off and folded it up. Maybe the best thing I could give Johann if I died was some peace. The tall tale of my running away, decidedly happy but firm that I'd never see them again, was folded up between my fingers. Winston was at the sink, washing up his own plate, but his gaze met mine instantly when I lifted the letter.

"Do you think... If I don't come back, will you mail this for me?"

"Sure, I can do that." Detachment laced his tone as his dark brown eyes glanced at Drake outside before returning to his task. I slumped against the back of the wooden chair.

I was so stupid, bringing up the idea of me and Drake dying when my family weren't the only ones who'd be losing someone. Drake and Winston had been a part of each other's lives for almost a century, and I couldn't imagine what it would be like for one to lose the other. Shoving away the impending depression, I focused on writing our church's home address in Thomas Village onto the outside of the paper.

"Have to be honest, the odds aren't great," Winston said, startling me. Moving away from the sink, but not closer, he dried his hands on a dish towel. "But I've always been a betting man." A plainly impish smile spread across his broad lips. "Anything I can do to boost your morale?"

His attempt at brevity helped ease the weight settling on my shoulders, and I straightened.

"To be honest, I'm not sure how I feel about working with another faery." My embarrassment at the confession abated when Winston's posture deflated a little, and he ambled over to sit in the chair opposite mine.

"You've got nothing to worry about when it comes to Daphne. She's a sweet girl. A little unusual at times, but her heart's always in the right place, and she's as honest as they come."

"Seems like everybody has a faery friend from the, um, Summerland."

Winston grinned. "Not really, and Daphne isn't full faery, either. She's a changeling."

"Is that like…" I shrugged at Winston.

"Like dhampirs? Yeah, one human parent and one faery makes a changeling. Daphne's a bit touchy about her progenitor, though, so I wouldn't ask after it. Still—" He exhaled long and slow, glancing at the ticking clock a second before it chimed, followed by the doorbell. "She's nothing if not punctual."

Grinning, Winston stood and headed through his house toward the front door. The shush of the glass door sliding open and shut, along with the sudden burst of cold air, made me turn to where Drake now stood inside the lit space. Wearing the white button-up and jeans Winston had given him this morning, along with a pair of leather loafers that resembled the ones he'd lost to our river crossing.

Any normal man would have been flushed from the chill outside, but Drake's pallor was unaffected. Although his skin was probably freezing cold. My chest throbbed at the idea of touching him to find out, and Drake's curious smile didn't help my rapid heart rate. A surprised shriek echoed from down the hall, or through the living room, since they both led to the front door.

"Winston!" A feminine voice exclaimed, followed by Winston's chuckle. I leaned my chair over to get a glimpse of the entrance. Winston set down a shapeless figure, who huffed and pushed back the hood of her oversized black hoodie. A whole foot shorter than him, the young woman pouted her plump lips up at Winston, and her crumpled brow looked peeved above large chocolate-brown eyes.

Spiky black hair fell flat against her forehead but curled at the nape of her light brown neck. As she glanced my way, I started to wave, and then suddenly overextended my reach with the chair. Unable to counterbalance it back into position, I flung out my hands to catch myself against the circular patterned rug when a cold arm wrapped around my waist.

An equally frigid hand grasped my upper arm, steadying me mid-fall, and I looked up to find Drake hovering over me. His raven-dark eyes were inches from mine, and I gulped.

"Quit it." Daphne's voice captured both mine and Drake's attention. He still held me while Daphne patted down her hair, which Winston seemed to have unapologetically ruffled. Ducking his second attempt, she spun smoothly, practically dancing out of his reach with a wide smile on her face. "You have too much energy!"

Distracted by their playfulness, I stifled a yelp when Drake physically pulled me upright. The living room became a blur, solidifying as Drake's grasp fell away.

"Thanks," I murmured, and he nodded like it was no big whoop. Straightening out the hem of my sweatshirt, I regained some semblance of composure and snatched my new weapon off the table.

"This here is my old pal, Drake, and his lady friend, Maria." Winston extended a hand, indicating us, and Daphne's attention followed, but her gaze fell to rest on my worn combat boots. "They're the ones I called you about."

"It is nice to meet you, Daphne," Drake said, again inclining his head instead of offering a hand to shake. "I am immeasurably grateful for your assistance."

"Yeah, me, too." My head bobbed while Winston locked the front door before joining us in the living room.

"It's no trouble." Daphne shrugged, her focus flitting across the room but never landing on anything—until she spied Tina. The tabby cat was stretched out on a threadbare pillow by the fireplace, and the changeling strode over in a couple of loping steps. Scratching the cat under the chin, she said, "Actually, and not to disappoint you, um, Drake, but it's not really my help you'll be needing."

"Then whose?" Brow furrowed, I glanced from Drake to Winston.

"That'll be Atticus, yeah?" Winston seemed to accept Daphne's noncommittal nod. "Daphne's new to the whole 'realizing she's a faery' thing, so your tour guide is going to be someone more experienced with the Summerland's landmarks."

"I carry two items of substantial personal, and historical value," Drake explained, addressing Daphne despite her attention being on the cat. "Will this suffice?"

"Oh, yeah," Daphne replied, focused on Tina's twitching ears. "Atticus is flat broke, he'll take anything you've got at this point. Doesn't matter how far you're going."

"And he's really willing to help us?" I asked, dubious, and Daphne glanced up to meet my gaze for a brief second before hers fell to my borrowed clothes. "I always thought faeries didn't like humans much…"

"They are none too fond of vampires, either—usually." Drake smirked, but it slid away to nothing when he faced Winston. "This 'Atticus' appears to be in dire straits, indeed."

Daphne explained, "He keeps losing at the gambling halls. Some kind of swindling game where they throw down dice, and then have to guess the numbers in each other's hand. Anyways, he's motivated, all right." She looked up at the small golden clock over the mantle, and her brows pulled together. "We should probably go as soon as you guys are ready. He won't like being left waiting."

"He's here already?" *Were we really about to do this?*

"Yep, I just left him." Daphne gave Tina a forlorn, final pet, and the cat stretched with a parting mew before resettling on the ottoman.

"And we can actually get to Romania through this—the Summerland?" I asked.

"Not if you run out the clock." Winston moved past me, his hands in his pockets when he stopped beside Drake. "You'll have to time your arrival just right. Wait until daybreak so the imperials will settle down for their nap before you enter the fortress. It might take you a few hours just to get through the Summerland, which gives the two of you a short buffer window, but not by much." His intense gaze was unwavering, deadly serious, and Drake nodded before turning to me.

"Are you prepared?"

Holding in a sigh, I grasped the machete's handle tighter as I slid its blade into the sheath. "Ready if you are."

"Someone's going to have to hold onto you while we're walking, by the way," Daphne said, her words directed at me when she passed.

"Why's that?" I moved to follow, bracing myself for the cold when Winston opened the sliding glass door to the backyard deck. He stepped outside first with Daphne in his wake, and Drake managed to keep pace at my side.

"There's a kind of power in the Summerland. Faeries call it 'manna,' but it's basically everywhere. Even in the air you'll be breathing." Daphne shrugged, her black hoodie and dark green cargo pants blending into the night. "Faeries are immune to it, but for most full humans it causes a kind of, like, drunkenness. Makes it hard for them to function."

"Oh." Before I could wrap my head around that, I was brought up short when Winston held something out to me.

"You might need this."

The gray and blue plaid patterned jacket looked thick, comfy, and I reached for its fleece-lined sleeves immediately.

I stuck the machete's sheath into my waistband, and the material bumped against my thigh while I shoved my arms through the jacket. "You sure? You might not get it back." After wrapping myself up in the renewed warmth, I wasn't sure I *would* give it back.

Winston chuckled. "I can get another one. Can't find another unicorn for Drake if you freeze between now and the fortress." The jab warmed my face, but Drake didn't seem bothered. Concern crossed Winston's features, instantly smoothing into firm acceptance. Drake placed his hand on Winston's shoulder, and the brief contact seemed to be all the goodbye the two needed.

Kind of like how I knew Everly would forgive me for doing all of this, even when I wasn't sure if my family could.

"Lead the way, Miss Álvarez." Drake gestured to the shadowed woods ahead, beyond the reach of the glow from the house's windows.

Retrieving a cigarette from his pocket, Winston lit it up by the time we reached the railing. "Godspeed, man. Give 'em hell." His whispered words carried on the breeze, and Drake turned to flash a parting smile.

"Earlier than they will have anticipated, I expect," Drake replied, and Winston's calm cracked into a smirk.

"Thank you—" I began, but my gratitude toward Winston was cut short when my legs were lifted out from under me. Squealing like a sissy, I clung to Drake when he picked me up like he'd done inside the Cneaz's manor, bridal style. Then he leaped over the railing, and weightlessness took me for about fifteen feet before he landed on Winston's sloping back lawn.

Bearing my weight, he straightened up while gazing at me with amusement. Daphne hopped over the railing in a similar fashion before lithely hitting the ground—only to fall onto her rump. A mildly disgruntled noise came from Daphne as she stood, patting off her backside, and Drake lowered my legs until my boots reached the grass.

"What was that for?" I huffed, and Drake lifted his shoulders.

"I prefer not to dither with prolonged goodbyes."

"It's this way, guys!" Daphne called, already at the treeline, and I swallowed down my complaint about being hauled around like a sack of flour.

The crunch of dead leaves underfoot seemed especially loud in the dark while we followed Daphne deeper into the woods. Maybe I was reading into it, but it felt like Drake walked closer than usual. Then again, how often did we actually walk anywhere together? Run away from bloodthirsty monsters, sure, we'd done that a time or two.

Our hands brushed when I stepped over some overgrown roots, but the contact was brief—probably accidental. Clearing my throat, like it would dispel my awkward feelings, I said, "I'll try to get you back in one piece."

Surprisingly, Drake laughed, and I frowned when his composure returned, but his curious smile seemed strained.

"I apologize. I ought to be the one reassuring you, not the other way around."

"It's the twenty-first century." I shrugged. "My gender doesn't make me any less heroic." No matter what Andrew kept implying whenever Olivia or I joined a hunt…

"Yes," Drake murmured, still bemused, "I am aware."

"This is it." Daphne halted before a very wide and extremely tall oak. Hands on her hips, she hopped from one exposed root to the next, not once glancing up at the barren branches coiling up into the black night sky. Whispered words passed her lips, foreign and too quiet to overhear, then she placed one hand against the trunk.

A low rumble reverberated underfoot. The packed earth between the trunk and two intertwined roots suddenly caved in. Desiccated leaves tumbled into the fresh hole spanning three feet across, falling out of view, and I let out a low whistle.

"Interesting entrance…" I peered over the edge, and my stomach dropped at seeing nothing but darkness below.

"I hope nobody minds getting their hands dirty." Quick as the squirrel I'd glimpsed out the window earlier, Daphne sat and scooted to the ledge. Lowering herself into the hole, she grasped the root system beneath the surface to descend. Her head was at ground level when she glanced up, expectant.

I sat, groaning when my hands touched the cold earth. Dirt got under my fingernails while I found my footing above Daphne's head before following her down. Aside from the gritty earth, it really wasn't too different from rock climbing at the local fairgrounds when Caleb and I were kids. Breath held, I dug my hands into the soil below to grasp the next hold.

"I will follow swiftly." Drake crouched at the ledge above me. Determination set the stiffness to his jaw, but his brow pinched with concern. Offering up a weak smile, I nodded and continued down.

The skin at the back of my neck prickled, but I forced away the thought of insects crawling into my clothes. As darkness closed in when Drake descended above me, my vision distorted, trying to adjust but failing. I glanced up, but everything was hazy. Bright spots flecked my sight, and Daphne called out, "Not much further!"

When she spoke, it sounded like her voice came from above and below simultaneously. A streak of blinding brightness scoured my eyeballs, and I shut my eyes tight. It was like I'd been flipped upside-down as I reached toward the light. A small warm hand grasped mine, and I followed its tug upward. Grappling one-handed with the suddenly dry hot dirt, my fingers brushed over what felt like soft grass.

I inhaled deep, the air tasting like honeysuckle as I was pulled over a ledge. With flat ground beneath me, I rolled onto my back and wiggled my fingers over the smooth earth before opening my eyes. High above was the picturesque image of a crystal blue sky. No clouds marred the view, allowing the brilliant white sun at the centermost point to shine down unimpeded.

Raising my hand to block its rays, I glanced to my left at the nearby rustling. Except the majesty surrounding me made it impossible to focus on the two people standing upright beside me, or Drake lifting himself up from the crevice scarring the earth. Tears blurred my vision, but I quickly blinked them back so I could take in the endless rolling hills across the horizon.

My mouth popped open as I gazed at the distant fields of tall grass and flowers—every color, shape and kind. The overpowering juxtaposition of foliage danced in a pleasant breeze.

Strangely, I wasn't hot in Winston's jacket under the direct sunlight. The wind scattering dandelions and pollen in its wake made the temperature comfortable, like the perfect summer's day. Soft footfalls behind me pulled my attention over my shoulder. A lush patch of four-leaf clovers sprouted over where the hole in the ground had been, right where Drake now stood.

His bloodshot eyes were fixed to mine, and his grayed skin stretched tight over his angular bone structure. A soft gasp passed my lips, but I couldn't figure out why—I'd already known what he looked like in the sunlight, right?

"Oh, pity." Irritation laced the stranger's deep tone, enough of a distraction to make me tear my gaze from Drake's to discover the voice's beholder. "You've made it."

Beneath a slim white tree bearing succulent fruits stood a man that wouldn't have been much taller than me if I was standing, but he'd be hard to miss considering his vibrant red hair and pale blue eyes. Not to mention the ears, as pointy as I'd glimpsed Aiden's back in the club. Beside him, Daphne's round ears stood out in contrast, but their differences went beyond that.

Compared to the changeling's dark-colored ensemble, the full faery stood out like a sore thumb in loose yellow capri pants and a pastel green vest, left unbuttoned to reveal most of his freckled white chest.

"Atticus." Daphne waved toward where I sat and Drake stood, her gaze on the neon green grass. "This is Maria and Drake."

"I don't need to know names." Atticus expelled an exaggerated sigh. "One of them looks dead, anyway." He sniffed, like he took personal offense to the black circles beneath Drake's sunken eyes and his corpse-like coloring. The faery waved his hand in a circular motion. "Alrighty, payment first. I don't do the tour guide thing for free."

"These objects ought to hold more than enough value for our safe passage." Drake pulled out two items from his jeans pocket, handing one to Atticus but withholding the other. "You may have the second once we reach our destination."

"What are their stories?" Atticus swiped the brooch Drake offered, and I marveled at the strange sparkling trail the accessory left in its wake.

"The brooch belonged to a woman who traded it for cash at a pawn shop during the Great Depression of the nineteen-thirties," Drake explained, and suddenly his old-timey way of talking sounded funny. Clamping a hand over my mouth, I held back a smirk. "She walked with a cane, an injury suffered from contracting polio as a child. This was an heirloom, her most valued possession."

The tone of Drake's story turned melancholy, like he'd searched for the woman for years after buying it—intending to return it, but never finding her. *Maybe I was just making stuff up.*

"It will suffice." Atticus bobbed his pointed chin toward the second treasure. "What of that?"

"This comb…" Drake paused, glancing down at it with regret. "It belonged to the daughter of a French Duke, proposed in secret to a member of the royal family in the United Kingdom, during their Regency era. However, I overheard the plot of her assassination by a family opposed to the union. I was the one to rescue her from the fire meant to kill her, and received the trinket in her gratitude." His expression hardened, voice strained, but Atticus didn't seem to notice, only huffed in agreement.

"A befitting trade. I commend you, dead-thing." The faery placed the brooch into a pocket, tapping it once while smirking in greed. "This will teach those pixies to poke fun at my funds. Now—" He clapped his hands, making me jump. "Where is it you wish to go?"

"Arefu, Romania. The ruins of Poenari Castle, specifically."

Feeling like it was time to stand up, I made the effort but wobbled immediately. A large warm hand took my arm, but I only recognized it was Drake's when I found him standing right beside me, his expression troubled.

"Do you think the living one will last long enough for me to get my full payment?" Atticus muttered, quiet with detached speculation, and Drake shot the faery a glare.

"It'll be fine," Daphne assured, but her brown eyes seemed anxious when they met mine. "You'll be fine. We'll take care of you. Just try not to run off on your own, okay? The longer you're here, the less coherent you'll get."

"Wouldn't be much use to feed her, would it?" Atticus whispered, and Daphne frowned.

"Then she'd be stuck here, and you won't get paid." She took my free hand in her surprisingly firm grip.

On my other side, Drake's hand trailed down my arm to grasp my hand. The subtle touch felt like sparks along my skin. Floaty sensations drifted through my head, and I sighed.

"It was only a suggestion." Atticus shrugged, turning on his heel. "Alright, best be off."

"She *will* be alright, yes?" Drake asked across me, his raven-dark eyes revealing a brighter ring of brown in the light of day. Even surrounded by bloodshot streaks, his eyes were beautiful—like the smoky quartz that Everly had on display in her psychic shop. Mesmerized, I stared intently at his eyes until his gaze flickered to mine.

A grin spread across my lips as my head tilted, taking in every minute detail of his bone structure. Vampires appeared more decayed in the sunlight as they got older, but their human illusion in the shade would've been identical to how they looked when they died. Every subtlety, scar, or wrinkle frozen in time. *How old had Drake been when he was transformed?* In the dark, he didn't seem much older than I was—

"I think so?" Daphne offered, her words almost dulled to the background behind a soft buzzing filling my ears. "She's not the first human to come to the Summerland and then leave."

"Do you call it that because it's so sunny?" I asked, and then giggled at the musical sound of my own voice.

"I, um—" Seeming at a loss for words on our stroll through flowery fields—the petals soft as butter against my hands' bare skin—Daphne said, "I'm not entirely sure, but maybe. The sun never sets here, so the day never ends."

"That's silly," I pointed out, smiling wide when Drake raised his eyebrows at me. Wow, it felt *so* good when he looked my way. What were we talking about? Oh, right— "When would you sleep if it never gets dark?"

"We are fae," Atticus stated. "We don't sleep as frequently as humans. Also, there is such a thing as a curtain."

"So, you're like vampires. You don't need to rest?" I tore my gaze from Drake to balk at Atticus's strangely elongated strides, his graceful movements contradicting the sharp disdain on his pale face.

"Don't compare us to the undead, human girl. It belittles our great race."

"Why? If Drake can have a friend that's a faery then how are you all so different?" I wished I could swallow the statement down when Drake suddenly squeezed my hand. Lips pursed, I gave him an apologetic grimace. Then we passed a leaf with a little yellow caterpillar on top. It waved when we walked by, and I tried to wave back, but Drake and Daphne were still firmly holding onto me.

"Let me guess," Atticus began, but I'd forgotten what we were talking about when I faced ahead. "It's that pesky little court merchant. Aiden."

"I have no idea who—" Drake's toneless rebuttal was cut short by Atticus's bark of laughter.

"I thought as much. Acting as your guide is one thing. Selling faery-made wares to mortals, or the undead, is a form of heresy. If I wasn't so far up debt creek to the cretin I'd be telling Queen Titania. She'd put a stop to it. Unfortunately—" He glanced at Daphne. "King Oberon is not nearly as severe."

"Queen Titania?" The name struck as familiar, and then my designated reading assignment from high school flashed back. "You mean, like in Shakespeare's play?"

"Oh, yes." Atticus cheered, his exhale nostalgic. "I remember the days of Shakespeare. A brilliant court jester, if you asked me. Bit heavy on the ale, but most entertaining. All of us alive back then placed bets on whether or not he'd return to the human lands with his liver intact."

"Which side of the bet were you on?" Daphne hedged, a hint of sarcasm coloring her cadence, and Atticus's expression soured.

"Never-you-mind." Sticking his nose in the air, the faery walked on.

Somewhere between when we set off and now, we'd climbed one of the hills I'd seen in the distance. The valley below overflowed with tall yellow grass like wheat or barley that pricked and pulled at my pants. I completely forgot the previous conversation until Atticus kept talking.

"Anyhow, the Seelie court moves on with every changing tide. As it had when Daphne arrived in our midst."

"Why?" I demanded, my curiosity piqued by Daphne's reddening face. "What happened?"

"It's just that the court doesn't think very highly of changelings..." A pink and gold shimmering aura appeared around Daphne's silhouette, and I leaned in to study it. "Nobody likes me being here, very much."

"Nonsense," Atticus retorted. "Prince Lysander thinks very highly of you. I have heard it."

"From who?" It felt like my heart would explode if I didn't learn the answer, but why had I asked?

"She's a nosy one, isn't she?" Atticus addressed Daphne, and my nostrils flared at being spoken over.

"She is not normally like this." At the sound of Drake's soothing voice, all my irritation drained away. *Man, that accent would be the death of me one day*—I'd follow it into hell. "The manna must have a hold on her."

"What *is* manna?" I blinked up at Drake, but Daphne answered on my other side.

"I told you, it's the magick of the Summerland. A wild sort of energy that most faeries are born able to manipulate to some extent."

"It is one theory as to why the fair folk live so much longer than humans," Drake explained. "The manna here is so concentrated compared to where we are from."

"You know a lot about us." Atticus glanced over his shoulder, his tone flat. "For a dead man."

Drake said nothing in response, or maybe I just stopped paying attention. Our location had changed again without me realizing it. Weirdly, my lack of awareness wasn't worrying, because I was entranced by every step I took over the smattering of pebbles we crossed.

A creek carried golden waves downstream, the color reminiscent of champagne. Sparks danced across the glittering surface, but I couldn't blink fast enough to catch them. Whispers seemed to echo all around, and I strained to listen, but the words were just out of reach. Frustrating, until it wasn't.

The sudden urge to break away took root. Sprinting in any direction would've been fun, but the hands on my arms only tightened their grip. The ground molded into a firmer surface, coated with trodden cherry blossoms. Dewy, discarded petals were gone in a blink to be replaced by crunchy grass that smoothed into moss a heartbeat later.

When I tried to stop to think, I was only pulled harder by Drake's much greater strength. A powerless feeling surged, along with the desire to scream, or cry, but the emotions soon faded to the recesses of my mind. Butterflies crossed my vision, rushing closer. They were closing in, and I struggled. The smaller hand on my left fell away when I slapped at the flitting bugs.

Then I was being spun, the motion repeating like an after-image until it slowed and I stared straight into Drake's blood-shot eyes.

"Maria?" His voice sounded sweetly melodic, and I felt my mouth crack into a grin without a reason. Gasping for breath, I tried to focus despite my stinging hand.

"You alright?" Atticus sounded distant, but he was only a few feet away, staring down at Daphne. She nodded, rubbing her cheek with her palm. Understanding dawned as my face fell, and I opened my mouth to apologize, but nothing came out.

"I'm fine," Daphne assured, her gaze briefly meeting mine before falling to my feet.

"The human won't be able to make sense anymore, not until she leaves. And that should be quick if you want her sanity to return." The full-blooded faery sounded bored, leaning away from a stocky leafless tree.

Its long branches sagged under its own weight, and the ground surrounding it was pale and barren. The gray flaking grass circled us, the space devoid of vegetation except the tree at its center. I glanced up to peer at the highest branches.

"What kind of tree is that?" Daphne asked.

"A hornbeam," Drake said, his expression forlorn but certain.

Daphne stared around us. "Why is everything here so…"

"Dead," Atticus supplied, his gaze on Drake. "It's the vampires. Ever since Dracula spun his cursed magick, this access point to the human world has been infertile. A scar, like the marks that boils leave on healed flesh."

"How do we leave?" Drake demanded, holding me with an unwavering grip.

"You should be able to just climb the tree," Daphne answered. "I had to get us to where Atticus was waiting before. That's why I needed to cast the spell in Aelvyn—the faery language—"

"My compensation, vampire," Atticus interrupted, holding out his palm. Daphne pinked, and the sudden urge to sock the faery man in the jaw sparked to life. If I had complete control of my limbs, I would have.

Instead, Drake managed to keep me pinned to the side of his torso, with one arm around my waist, while handing over the comb. Atticus pocketed it swiftly, a superior grin stretching his features into ugly greed. "Much obliged."

"As am I," Drake said, but his kindness was directed at Daphne. "Winston keeps loyal companions, and I am indebted to you."

The changeling smiled sheepishly, her gaze averted as her hands fidgeted inside the oversized pockets of her hoodie. I wanted to say something, to apologize for having slapped her when the memory swept through my head, but all I could manage was to open my mouth. Then I was being pulled toward the emaciated tree, and swiftly given a leg up to reach the lowest branch.

On instinct, I gripped it and wedged my booted foot into the crook of the trunk. My stomach swooped when I nearly slipped, so I hurried to climb higher up the gnarled and blackened tree. The sky above darkened one shade at a time, until it felt like I was scaling into the expanse of the night's sky.

Stars twinkled overhead between clusters of charcoal clouds, moving through empty air at a glacial pace. A cold gust of wind caught my clothes, and I clutched close to the tree's trunk. A warm presence neared against my back, and I turned, finding Drake standing right beside me. The last week returned to my living memory, and I nearly choked.

My heart pounded, and all at once, I wanted to go back. Where the entrancing manna's power kept me mindless. Because the short reprieve from reality made our next task seem even more impossible.

Until Drake placed his palm against the side of my face, his fingers trailing across my cheekbone to tuck my windswept hair behind my ear. Suddenly, whether we made it out of this alive or not didn't matter. There was something I needed to tell him before it was too late—and I held on to that purpose as Drake turned to face our left.

Following his gaze, I inhaled a sharp breath. The ruins of an ancient castle were nestled into a steep hillside overlooking a dense forest valley. Their discarded, dilapidated stone structures appeared deserted, but something in my bones spoke otherwise.

A wholly different sentiment ignited the fluttering in my stomach when Drake took my hand, and our fingers intertwined. Flecks of moisture hit my face while I held tightly to him. Thunder boomed through the treetops, and rain fell across the land from the storm clouds above.

— 18 —

FREE FROM FALLING

HARSH WIND RAKED OVER THE SURROUNDING FOREST, HITTING MY FACE WITH the force of a smack. Leaves rustled, branches shook and the hornbeam's trunk swayed. I clung harder to Drake, who positioned himself between me and the howling wind. Rain pelted down, spraying my hands and face like icicle pellets. Dense clouds overhead hid the phase of the moon, and concealed the stars beyond.

"We must descend," Drake whispered, his mouth close to my ear. "Are you capable?"

After what I'd just gone through in the Summerland, I wasn't sure, but I nodded. I glanced down at the ground far below, where the base of the trunk grew out of the sloping hillside at an angle. Swallowing hard, I reached for the nearest branch with slippery fingers. The coarse wood scraped against the inside of my palm, and I gritted my teeth.

Then Drake's hand in mine fell away, shifting to press against my back while he descended faster than I dared. I climbed down, one slow reach at a time. My boot dangled, searching for the next notch, and then Drake directed my ankle where to go.

It was almost embarrassing to need help down a tree, but between the rain and wind blurring my vision, and the rising haze of darkness from the surrounding forest's dense foliage, I took all the help I could get. The squish of my boots hitting the soft earth seemed loud as I scanned the clustered treeline.

Above, the canopy of branches obscured any chances of fleeting moonlight. I startled when Drake fitted his hand against mine, but my fingers squeezed instinctively. He tugged me into motion, beginning our ascent up the hill.

"Where are we going?" I whispered, barely hearing myself over the rain hitting the ground. A frog croaked from somewhere, and I reached for the handle of my machete. The sheath's material rubbed against my outer thigh with every step.

"Dawn is not far off, perhaps an hour or so? The global time difference has aided us."

"That doesn't answer my question."

Drake glanced over his shoulder, slowing his strides, the silhouette of his features barely visible. Water dripped from the damp black hair over his forehead and just below his ears.

"There is a hovel, once belonging to a gardener of sorts. It is near, but not so close that they would sense our approach while we wait for daybreak." His fingers tightened against mine, urging me forward. Every step he took seemed so sure, while I watched the ground with widened eyes to avoid tripping. How familiar was he with these woods? If he had been alive before Dracula's defeat…

Trust was the word that reverberated in my head, an encouraging, vulnerable feeling that had goosebumps rising up my arm from where he touched me. There was no way back now, so I climbed the damn hill. The trees slowly thinned, and we emerged into an overgrown circular clearing bordered on all sides by more woods, but at the center was the house.

More like a medieval hut, really. Close up, the exterior appeared to be made of stone bricks. Its roughly-built roof looked like it had once been thatched with straw, but wooden beams were now exposed to the outside world while ivy trailed from the rafters, down over a makeshift window.

By some miracle, the wide wooden door was still standing, but its hinges were rusted from neglect. We probably wouldn't be able to open it without making an awful noise. Drake didn't hesitate to grasp the handle, twisting it hard and fast to get the process over with. The shriek of grinding metal followed, and by the heavy sound of the weather-warped door scraping across the stone floor, I reckoned that I wouldn't have been able to trespass with my descendant strength alone.

He ushered me in ahead of him, his hand leaving mine as he quickly glanced over the treeline, still shrouded in darkness. Without a word, he followed me inside before closing the door gently, like he was afraid to break the centuries-worn hinges. In the silence that followed, my heartbeat thrummed in my eardrums while my eyes adjusted.

"Drake?" I whispered, startling when a crack echoed against the stone walls.

"Apologies," he replied, speaking at a normal volume. My shoulders relaxed as the outline of the large single-room space blinked into sight. Drake's figure was at one end beside the wall, crouching in front of what looked like a hearth.

My steps scuffed across the floor, and dust clouded up around my black boots. The scrape of a flame preceded sudden light that made me squint. Drake placed another broken piece of wood into the lowered section of the fireplace. A dismembered chair was upturned beside him, and he replaced a box of matches into his back pocket before using a long rod coated in cobwebs to stoke the embers.

"They won't notice the smoke?" I asked, glancing around.

A worn rectangular table was positioned beside what might have once been a bed, before the mattress had sunk to the floor, taking the rotted wood with it. A mildew-like smell caught in my wrinkling nose. The smudged window near the door probably wouldn't have let in much sunshine.

"Not with the wind blowing it further down the mountain and the rain obscuring even our enhanced sight." Flames reflected against his dark eyes as he glanced up. "The ceiling appears intact, even if the roof is in shambles. We will not remain here long enough to test its stability."

"Yeah…" Bone-deep exhaustion weighed down my muscles now that the manna's effects had worn off, but nerves spun in my bloodstream. This was it, the calm before the storm, and I was spending what might be my last night alive with someone I—

My stomach flipped over, and I inhaled a steadying breath. Drake rose, and my gaze caught his.

"Are you alright?" Concern etched the line between his eyebrows, and my throat seemed to close. So I nodded, my forced laugh sounding weak.

"Just peachy." I crossed my arms, quickly uncrossing them, and moved closer to the fireplace. A question bubbled on my lips, but before I could open my mouth, Drake walked away. He stood in front of the bed, searching through blankets, discarding one strip of moth-eaten fabric after another.

I raised my brows when he began tearing them, collecting a handful of cloth in his grasp. He nodded once, seemingly satisfied, and then returned to lay the pieces out across the floor before the hearth—far enough from the sparks, but close by to keep warm. What I figured were the cleanest remnants of the torn sheets were soon arranged like a patchwork picnic blanket.

Baffled, I smiled when he lowered himself to sit on one side—with barely a scrap separating him from the stone floor—and he gestured for me to take up the rest of the space. I should've been wary, invited to admire the fireside by a vampire, but all I could feel was warmth. It spread from my hands to my heart, where the sensation took root in my chest.

So I withdrew my machete from my waistband and set it beside me as I sat, leaving about a foot of space between us. Where a thousand unspoken thoughts seemed to settle. *Not anymore,* I wasn't going to leave anything unsaid before breaking and entering the fortress where my ancestor took down his greatest enemy.

"Drake—"

"Maria, I—"

We both stopped, our gazes met, and his soft smile made me laugh. Heat burned my face, my heart pounded, and Drake's expression turned curious. Hell, he could probably see and hear it as easily as I felt it.

"What is it, Maria?" The way he spoke my name in his accent, with so much tenderness and respect, was mind melting. Thoughts scrambling, and trying to put them into order, I resisted the urge to make him say what *he* was going to say first.

If I was going to get this out, I couldn't wait.

"Why did you do it?" My voice came out small, so I cleared my throat. "You knew that saving me in that parking lot would damn you, too. I know you said—" I wasn't sure I'd ever blushed so hard, remembering the one kiss we'd shared. Back when he'd called me *beautifully human.* "That you've lived a long time. But we both know what you were going to do if I hadn't stopped you. You would've sacrificed everything—for *me*, and I-I can't figure out why."

Drake watched me, his features thoughtful, and I was almost afraid of the answer. Because I had hope, but nothing was sure in this life. Being a descendant had taught me that. When he didn't respond, hadn't even breathed—not that he needed to—I mumbled, "It was a death sentence for you, Drake."

His eyes slowly closed, opening again only to stare into the flames before us. Whatever he was thinking turned out to be so far from what I'd expected.

"I have not always been a…pious man. Although I suppose one could reason that my devotion to Dracula had been my first system of beliefs. They taught us to revere him religiously as our savior. The one who would cull the weak from the strong. After we were taken from our homes, too young to remember anything else, that was how we were raised."

He took a breath to speak, his gaze wandering as he continued, "Shortly before I was transformed into an 'immortal,' Helsing slayed the being we had grown to believe was impervious to deceit, impossible to destroy—and yet, he was. Order was soon restored among the higher ranks, and they debated on whether or not to transform the remaining recruits.

"In the end, they chose to bolster their numbers one final time, since we were already trained both body and mind to obey them. While those who had served for generations were much too far gone to reacclimate to the world of humans, those of us who were newly transformed were given greater freedom.

"Myself, included." A sardonic smirk curved the corners of his mouth, like he tasted bitterness on his tongue. "It took longer than I would prefer to admit before I understood the truth. That Dracula had perverted our sense of humanity, convinced us that people were cattle for our consumption—pigs we dared not even roll in the mud with. With our abilities to charm, to remove the will of another and impose our own, it became too easy to pretend I was better than my victims."

A chill seeped into my skin despite the blazing fire, crackling as it caught on another length of dry wood. I wasn't stupid enough to think he'd never hurt anyone, not after everything I'd witnessed. Hell, he hadn't hesitated to rip apart the werewolves. Except, he'd only attacked the ones who'd tried to hurt me.

This whole time, I'd been at the center of his violent actions. How long had he lived in peace before walking into my life?

With my thoughts elsewhere, it took a second to realize Drake wasn't going to continue. Vulnerable doubt crossed his features, in the pinch of his brow, the uncertainty behind his raven-dark eyes, and the hard set to his jaw. What he'd revealed could have ruined everything between us. I wouldn't let it.

"But you changed," I accused, as sure of it as I was sober.

"Eventually," he admitted, somber, but honest. "Aiden helped me to find a better way. He assuaged my guilt once I came to terms with how much pain I had inflicted. He has lived many lifetimes more than me, seen worse than I could have dealt, and instructed that the only reparations I could make for my sins would be to continue surviving. Impart some *good* on the world, until it overshadows the evil."

"Did it work?" I asked, and again Drake smiled without mirth.

"In a sense. The guilt did ease, as Aiden promised, yet I never felt that I had truly atoned. Not when I aided others, nor when I brought up Winston. A selfish act, really, because he became my reason—my *excuse* to remain in a world where I no longer belonged. For so long, time has become meaningless. Years blurred into the next, and with every passing day, I wondered why I did not simply end it."

His impassive tone struck me hard, awakening a twinge of sympathy that felt more like empathy. Whatever he'd endured under Dracula's reign, and then in the years after that, must've been a cruel existence. One I couldn't imagine. I'd always had my family, and even when things got rough, they were my reason to keep going.

Unshed tears blurred my vision, but I blinked them back when Drake noticed. Grateful emotion shone behind his gaze while he swiped his thumb beneath my left eye. His light touch was warm from the fireside, and I exhaled a shaky breath.

"Sorry," I mumbled, but Drake shook his head.

"Your kindness is beyond anything I deserve, Maria. It is gratifying that you can feel anything for one of my kind. After what you witnessed before the Cneaz?" Morose acceptance whirled behind his eyes, downcast with obvious regret. "We are monsters, and our monstrous acts are what maintain the illusion that we are above our victims. It is why they congregate in the way they do, and the reason I have been unable to stand being in their presence since before Winston was born."

"You're wrong if you think you don't deserve how I feel about…you." The words were out of my mouth before I could think too hard, and I hurried to gloss over my Freudian slip while averting my gaze from Drake's obvious surprise. "You've saved my life, too many times for me to count at this point. I wouldn't be alive right now without you."

"Neither would I."

Thinking I'd misunderstood, I looked up, and my breath caught at the intensity of his unwavering stare.

"For far too long, I have wanted to leave this world. Yearning to discover what might exist beyond, despite fearing how my soul will be judged. Only recently, have I begun to look forward to every new day. And do you wish to know why?" The hint of a smile quirked up the corner of his mouth when I dipped my chin in a nod. "You, Maria, are where I have found a semblance of redemption—after searching for a century and then some.

"You might believe that I have rescued you from peril, but it was *you* who spared me from a miserable end. Because if my continued existence could produce one good act before I am gone, then I am glad that it was done for you." A humorless chuckle passed his lips, and I remembered to breathe while trying to wrap my head around what he'd admitted. "Even if I have doomed you in the process, I promise to protect you from here on with all that I am."

"So will I." My voice came out squeaky, my heart beating so fast it could've burst. "Whatever happens after this—I'm not going down without a fight. And I *will* fight for you." The confession sounded so superficial compared to how he'd phrased everything, but my jaw was set, silently daring him to try and convince me not to. Except, he only smiled, the beauty of it strengthened by the dim light of the fire while shadows danced across his features.

"You ask me why I have done what I have for you, and yet you do not see yourself in this at all, do you?" His question caught me off guard, but he didn't give me a chance to answer. "You are a light in my abyss, guiding me toward hope that my legacy can leave behind more than bloodshed. In all my time, I have never been capable of carrying the weight that you do. Your understanding of right and wrong, led by a steadfast moral compass. Your strength enlightens, inspires, and it is because of this—despite my better judgment, knowing that I should not want you— that I have inadvertently made you sacrifice all that *you* hold dear.

"The truth, love…" he whispered, his palm caressing my jaw as I leaned in closer to hear. "The truth is that I fell in love with you long before I remembered what it had felt like to do so."

Time must have stopped, because for one endless moment, all I felt was peace. Then it shattered, replaced by my overflowing heart and every thought in my head urging me closer to the man that had become *my* salvation. I leaned in, and grinned like an idiot, even when I caught myself on the hem of my sweatshirt.

Drake placed one hand on my shoulder to steady me while the other held the nape of my neck, his fingers threading through my knotted hair. Any semblance of uncertainty between us was forgotten when he didn't hesitate to press his soft lips against mine.

I wrapped my arms around his neck, pulling him closer as I straddled his lap. The ends of his hair were still damp under my fingertips, the strands soft beneath my caress. His hold on my shoulder relaxed, drifting lower to sweep down my spine. Sensations followed his path, pinpricks of need growing stronger in the wake of his gentle touch.

A moan climbed my throat, exhaled against his mouth as I pulled away just enough to shrug out of the jacket that suddenly felt too warm. Unspent passion reflected in his heavily-lidded eyes when I met his gaze. Drake licked his lips as his hand drifted over my hip, rising up my waist with tentative patience.

My head tilted aside as he leaned in, his needless breath brushing my throat as his hold over my ribs tensed, tugging me closer. A chill tip-toed up my spine, and I shuddered as Drake's bloodlust surged over me. *Damn, that never felt so fucking good.* Heat pulsed to life below my navel, and I nearly purred when my tangled hair was pulled taut as his grip tightened.

"Keep going," I mumbled, my voice thready with want.

"Are you certain?" he whispered against my neck, and my ears warmed from the decadently rich tenor of his accent. There was only one more thing I needed to say, and I dipped my chin to capture his gaze.

"I'm in love with you, too," I murmured, and my heart thrummed when the despair that lingered behind his eyes vanished. A small smile curved up the corner of my mouth. "And if you want this, then I want you. More than I've ever wanted anyone in my life. But if you don't—"

Drake cut off my rambling with a kiss, and my shoulders relaxed. Venom had bloomed in his mouth, tasting sweet on my tongue. When he withdrew, mere millimeters separating us, his pupils contracted against the firelight before expanding to reflect mine.

"Oh, love," Drake breathed the words, and my chest heaved. Pressing into his as he caught a stray curl before tucking the strands behind my ear. His palm touched my jaw as he stared into my eyes, and I could've lost myself in the depths of his. "Never have I craved anyone more."

I inhaled a moment before his mouth returned to mine. His intent was clear as he leaned into me, cradling the back of my head with one hand while the other supported my back as I reclined. My shoulders touched the thin scraps of cloth laid over the stone floor, and our kiss hastened in time with my rasping breaths. Cool fingers dipped below the waistline of my sweatpants, and then he grasped my hips before lifting my ass high enough to pull the material down.

Goosebumps rose along my bare thighs, and Drake's mouth abruptly abandoned mine so he could drag the sweats over my knees. Next he unlaced my boots, his hands a blur before tossing both my shoes and borrowed sweatpants aside. I sat up, hauling my sweatshirt off in one fluid movement. There hadn't been any spare bras at Winston's.

Drake's attention slowly rose, drinking in every detail from the curve of my hips to the swell of my breasts. A breath shuddered from my lungs as I reached closer, my fingers trembling with anticipation as I unbuttoned his shirt. Callused palms traced up the shape of my legs, and my eyes nearly fluttered shut when his knuckles skirted my inner thigh.

Dark eyes met mine, his pupils blown until barely any dark brown remained. My breath seized when I managed the final button, and the rain-drenched fabric parted to reveal the hard lines of his abdomen. *No wonder he'd been so heavy to carry at the Cneaz's manor, the man was all muscle.* Not to mention *covered* in scars.

Grooves of toughened tissue were scattered across his chest and stomach, with more lines disappearing beneath the fabric at his shoulders. One of them must have been responsible for his death, but how many wounds had he been forced to heal without stitches when he was still alive? My ogling was cut short when his lips touched mine, and I redirected my focus to pushing his shirt free from his broad shoulders.

Before I could start on the button of his jeans, Drake shifted us. My back touched the floor, and I gasped as the cold seeped through the thin material separating my flesh from the stone. Except I quickly warmed as his kisses drifted from my mouth to the curve of my jaw.

Following down my throat to my collarbone as his forefinger and thumb teased my nipple. I arched closer, running my fingers through the silken strands of his hair while the path his lips took trailed lower. He'd reached my navel by the time my mind caught up with his actions, and I took his face between my hands to raise his gaze.

"There's no time," I rasped, desperately wishing that wasn't the case. We only had until morning light, and then reality would crash down around us. If this was it for us, then I wanted all of him, for as long as this could last.

Seeming to understand, Drake nodded, repositioning himself over me while I reached low between us. The button and zipper of his jeans were quick work between my fingers, but my hands stilled when his mouth encircled my nipple. Fervor surged to my core, and I bit my lip on a murmured moan as my eyes closed.

Blindly, I shoved the waistline of his jeans lower. Then I grasped him—

Holy shit.

My lips parted as I stroked his hard length from tip to base, and Drake groaned a soft sound against my breast. Warmth hit my face tenfold. Was it going to fit? *It had better fucking fit.* I startled, inhaling a gasp when Drake suddenly hiked my thigh up, opening me fully, and my eyes flew open. Raven-dark eyes bore into mine, but Drake's expression softened as the barest smile quirked up the corner of his full lips.

"You are incredibly beautiful," he whispered, so close that his breath touched my lips.

My voice quavered with a heady sigh as I said, "You're not so bad, yourself."

A full smile graced his striking features while firelight flickered shadows across his face. Then he kissed me, his mouth moving tenderly over mine as a shiver caressed my spine. Bracing myself, I let my legs relax as I lined us up. Rough denim brushed my inner thigh, but the fact that his jeans were still mostly on became trivial as he slid inside me.

My next breath caught in my throat as my eyes squeezed shut tighter. Heat swelled where my center stretched, throbbing with need while my toes curled. On instinct, I held him closer, my hands drifting over the scars across his back. Soft lips grazed my jawline, and his groan was exhaled across my cheekbone.

His palm flatted over my hip, fingers gripping hard. I yelped when he hauled me closer, deepening his thrust until our bodies were flush. At my unintentional squeak, Drake stilled.

"Are you alright?" he murmured, and I nodded.

"Keep going," I urged, biting my lip when he obliged. A moan escaped me in a sigh when my body relaxed around him. Another chill climbed my spine, and the spasm of his bloodlust reverberated below my navel. My back arched as a thrill spiked through me with his relentless pace, steadily increasing alongside the pitch of my strangled voice.

The touch of his lips over my neck sent me over the edge when a wave of his bloodlust echoed the satisfaction that swelled to a fever pitch at my core. Molten bliss washed over me, and I clutched him closer. Every ridge of muscle across his shoulders was hot to the touch, warmed from the fireside and our continued proximity. I exhaled a breathy moan as the aftershocks faded one heartbeat at a time.

After wanting him for longer than I'd dared to admit to myself, being with him was better than anything I could've imagined. The way he moved against me, filling me so completely as his body trembled under the sweep of my tracing fingertips while pleasure coiled low at my core. A tremor shivered up my spine as Drake suddenly slowed, and I blinked fast to bring the dilapidated ceiling back into focus.

His arm had wound around my back when I'd arched, and his hand at my shoulder blade tightened. My chest rose and fell in succession while his forehead pressed against the crook of my neck.

I swallowed, and it took an extra second to find my voice. "Y-You okay?"

He inhaled a breath to answer, and another shiver shook my spine as his head rose.

"You smell divine," he confessed, and his throat bobbed on a swallow as his attention drifted to my neck. "And unfortunately, I cannot stop thinking about how you taste." Lust for my blood shone heavily behind his unwavering gaze, and my heart hammered in spite of the self-deprecating smile that hid the extent of his desire.

Except I could *feel* it, in every uncontrollable chill that racked my spine. Suddenly, the intoxication of his bite was all *I* could think about.

"Bite me," I blurted, my voice clear.

"Maria—" Hesitation smothered his tone, but beneath his concern for me, there was *hunger*. Need threaded the cadence of his unnecessary inhale, the act of breathing me in clearly tempting him further. "I should not weaken you."

His lack of conviction made me smirk.

"I'll be fine, as long as you don't take as much this time." I fidgeted beneath him, and pride prickled inside my heart when his eyes briefly fluttered closed. "Besides, it'll get your strength up, and—" *It improved our chance of surviving what came next.* That truth hung in the infinitesimal space between us, but neither of us acknowledged it.

"You are sure?" His gaze held mine, and I nodded once.

I wouldn't waste a moment of our limited time on regretting what could've been. "Yes."

Warmed fingertips threaded through my hair, his trim nails scraping my scalp as he tugged my head aside. A delectable chill climbed my spine as his canines grazed my throat. Adrenaline pulsed through my bloodstream when his lips touched my skin, bestowing one more kiss before his sharp canines pierced my flesh.

My whole body jolted as the puncture deepened, but the effects of his venom soon soothed the sting, saturating my bloodstream even as he sucked. Airy elation suffused my mind, and I rasped a moan as his pace resumed. His answering groan vibrated along my throat, and his fingers tightened around my loose curls.

Ecstasy spasmed through my middle, and my head kicked back as I bucked into his following thrusts. A tremor of satisfied bloodlust shivered up my spine, echoing the sensation of my release, and I whimpered on a moan. I cried out when his canines slipped free from my torn flesh, but my shriek was hushed by his mouth covering mine.

Iron laced the sweet taste of his venom, coating my tongue with a single stroke of his as rivulets of blood trickled from my neck. Drake's palm flattened over the mark he'd made, his thumb pressing into the base of my throat. Our mouths moved in sync while his rigid chest and stomach pressed into my softer counterparts.

Maybe it was the venom's effects, clouding my thoughts with a surge of dizzying confidence, but I managed to get one foot under me, using the leverage to roll us over. Faster than anticipated, Drake grasped my hips, hard enough to bruise as he secured me on top of him. Our kiss broke as I rose, biting my lip when the shift in our position deepened his next thrust. Blood dripped from the quickly healing puncture wound at my throat, and Drake sat up beneath me in a blur.

The tip of his tongue caught the drop at my collarbone, and my head tipped back as his strong fingers massaged up my aching spine. Then his mouth closed over my nipple, rolling the sensitive flesh between his teeth. I steadied myself against his shoulders while I rode him, and his low moan tickled the swell of my breast.

My breath caught as his thumb slid up my inner thigh, quickly finding my center. Heat swelled beneath the gentle swirl of his insistent touch, and exquisite satisfaction unspooled. My legs shook while I clung to him for support, barely able to keep myself upright. The bridge of his nose brushed my jaw, and then his mouth was close to my ear.

"Maria—" He exhaled a groan as my hips rocked, chasing another kind of delirium as the analgesic effects of his venom wore off. "If you do not slow down—"

"Don't stop," I begged, falling into him as he reclined until his back hit the floor. The low tenor of his accented voice warmed my ears, and my eyes slammed shut. Gratification coursed through me with every powerful jolt of his cock driving into me from beneath. Then his hands seized my hips, and swiftly lifted me off of him.

I yelped at the sudden withdrawal, nearly toppling off his lap, but Drake caught me. A wince of pleasure flashed across his features as he sat up, and I reached down on instinct to grasp him. His low moan ached with relief while I stroked him, catching every jerk that pulsed hot and wet between my hands.

Blissful fulfillment stole over his expression for several long, captivating moments before his posture relaxed, and my hand stilled. The fast breath I inhaled stuck in my lungs when his raven-dark eyes opened, and immediately locked onto mine. Silence surrounded us for one long moment, broken only by the crackling of flames, while we stared at each other in the aftermath of surrendering to our desperate desires.

Then his hand rose, his fingers damp from my sweat as he brushed a stray curl from my face. I leaned my cheek into his touch, my eyes closing as his thumb swept over my jaw only to catch my lower lip. Mirth tugged up the corners of my mouth, and I gave into the grin as a chuckle rumbled from Drake's chest. Vibrant emotion warmed my insides as I cradled my hands in my lap, and then frowned. How the hell was I going to clean up?

"Ah, my apologies," he said, releasing me from his touch only to tear another sheaf from the fabric beneath us. My lips pressed together, trying and failing to hide my smile while he wiped my hands.

"Don't be sorry." I shrugged. "You more than made up for it." My smirk strengthened when Drake closed his eyes, like he was trying to keep from rolling them.

"While I appreciate the reassurance, I was referring to my lack of preparation for any form of contraception." Amusement quirked up the corner of his lips as he tossed the rag into the fire beside us, and then pulled me closer. His firm hold reignited a quiver in my stomach as his arm wound around my back, and I closed my eyes.

The backs of my knees rested over his thighs as my torso pressed against his, warm where our bodies touched. I reached across my stomach to take his hand in mine, entwining our fingers until they fit perfectly.

"Maybe next time," I whispered. Hope for our future battled the uncertainty stabbing into my heart, throbbing like the ache settling between my sore legs. Drake was silent while his fingertips tenderly caressed up and down my thigh. Melancholy hung over us like a cloud, and I huffed to clear the intrusive thoughts.

"Honestly, I can't go a day with you without getting my hands dirty."

My attempt at lightening the mood succeeded because Drake laughed, the easy sound brightening the fragile emotions swelling in my heart. Peace settled behind his dark eyes, gazing into mine.

"I am most grateful for you, Maria," he said, barely above a breath. "Never forget that." Desperation saturated his tone, imploring for more. Like what he really meant was *'Never forget me.'*

My throat constricted, and I nodded.

"I never will," I promised.

Acceptance and gratitude softened his features a moment before he held me closer, clutching to me like he never wanted to let me go. Exhaling a shallow breath, I tilted my head against his. My attention flickered over his shoulder, to where the glow of first light illuminated the outline of the door to the outside world. Suddenly, I didn't want to face the day ahead.

FOUNDATIONS OF DECAY

DAWN STREAKED INSIDE THROUGH THE OPAQUE WINDOW. ILLUMINATING the silhouette of my sweatshirt while the embers glowed in the fireplace. I yanked the material over my head, and the tag caught on my tangled curls. A chill seeped in to raise the hairs along my arms, which I quickly shoved into the plaid jacket's sleeves.

Blowing out a breath, I adjusted the waistband of my pants before retying my boots' laces with a double knot. By the time I looked up, Drake was fully dressed and already standing, his hand outstretched with the machete in his grasp. Smirking, I accepted it before shoving the sheath back through my waistband.

His palm remained extended when I finished, and I placed my hand in his. Once upright, I gauged my balance for a second, but the dizzy feeling from the first time he'd drank my blood never came. *Guess he didn't take as much*, plus, I'd actually eaten recently.

"Are you ready?" he whispered, and I nodded as Drake's fingers entwined with mine.

"As I'll ever be." My hand tightened in his, and while my jugular pulsed against the healing flesh where Drake had marked it, I didn't hesitate to follow him. The squeak of my boots against the stone floor was nothing compared to the scream of the door hinges, but our noisy exit was lost amongst the flock of birds cawing and rising from the surrounding trees.

Over the course of our time here, the world outside had changed entirely. Gone were the dangerous, murky shapes hidden in darkness. Now, the gray sky was slowly giving way to streaks of blue. Light cascaded over dewy grass, still short after the winter but budding violet flowers were sprinkled here and there. Wind rustled the moss-coated branches and my hair alike, forcing me to tuck the strands behind my ear to keep the wonders before me in sight.

"It's beautiful," I murmured. When Drake didn't move or respond, I looked his way. Behind his bloodshot eyes, sunken around thinned skin, a flicker of nostalgic sadness burned. Noticing my gaze, his expression smoothed with a fleeting smile.

"I did not anticipate this part," he said, tugging my hand to follow his steps toward the edge of the clearing.

"What part?" My boots squelched in the damp, natural mulch of broken twigs when we reached the forest.

"That I would experience such a…longing. To be brought up short by merely seeing this place again, after nearly two centuries away."

It was hard to wrap my mind around the idea of abandoning the first place I'd ever thought of as home. Except, after what he'd shared, I reckoned he wouldn't have been eager to return to where he was brainwashed into revering Dracula as a deity.

In a whisper, he added, "I suppose it is because, one way or another, I will never have the freedom to return after today."

"You can't say 'never.'" I grinned through the melancholy, goaded on by the curious amusement he faced me with. "You're immortal, you might not know what will happen, but you'll probably be around to see it."

"Ah, Maria." Drake chuckled, the easy sound making my heart flutter, but he shook his head. "You know as well as I that immortality is a falsehood. My race is as easily eradicated as the tinder I set aflame in the hovel. I daresay that has always been our greatest weakness, to convince ourselves that we are the most durable. In truth, time wears on all—even the deceased."

"Maybe you're right." I shrugged. "Or, maybe not. But if believing you can survive anything gets us to the next sunrise, then I'm willing to have some faith."

A true smile graced Drake's full lips, stealing my breath even with the sunshine trickling through the canopy above marring his image. "There is irony in that, for I am the one who has placed my faith in *you*."

Our pace slowed to a stop, facing a cluster of roots separating two enormous trunks that grew toward each other. Between them, set into the hillside and covered in vines and moss, was an iron door. Stone bricks surrounded the entrance, held together by mortar older than this country. A long oval latch was barely discernible behind the greenery. Drake reached for it before I'd even recognized it as a handle.

My fingers closed around the hilt of my weapon when Drake released my hand. His progress was slow to turn the latch, and my eyebrows rose. Just how stuck was this door? His arms strained to move it, but it eventually gave way with a click that carried on the breeze.

Sweat beaded on my skin, a drop trickling down my neck. My blade was at the ready when Drake pushed the door inward. He stepped back as the iron surface swung away under its own weight. I wasn't sure what I was expecting, but the empty dark hallway beyond wasn't it.

Goosebumps erupted over my body when I breathed in the stale air escaping the depths within. Drake's brow pinched into a frown, but there was no fear or concern in his steady gaze.

"This is how I was brought to the fortress as a boy," he said slowly, like he was struggling to remember. "It was the path they used to bring in all the children whose families Dracula deemed appropriate for service in his army. And it was also through here that I left for the first and final time…"

Lips pressed together, he stared past the open door but didn't move. This time, I reached out to take his hand. With the gentle squeeze of his palm against mine as encouragement, we crossed the threshold into the tunnel together. Exposed wooden beams lined the ceiling, becoming invisible the deeper we went, leaving the light of the entrance behind.

Dust caked the walls and most of the stone floor. The only sounds were my footfalls and fast breathing. I strained to hear anything else, but only silence greeted me in all directions. Before long, the ground shifted from a flat walk into a descending spiral staircase. I gripped Drake's hand harder to maintain my pace and balance.

We must have entered the ruins of Poenari Castle somewhere between the forest door and now. *This wasn't adding up,* and the silhouette of Drake's easy posture put me on edge.

"Where are all the vampires?" I whispered under my breath, barely audible but confident Drake could hear me.

"While this is the most direct entrance to the fortress, it is not one that is frequented often, these days." Except his attention lingered on the displaced dust coating the steps below.

"That doesn't answer my question," I hedged, my grip tightening on the machete's handle.

"Only select immortals, lycans, and the sorcerer of the Domnitori reside within the fortress—and we are not yet there."

"What are you talking about?" I retorted, straining my voice low. "*This* is where Helsing defeated Dracula. My family's passed that story down for generations. They weren't lying."

"No, they were not," Drake agreed. "Although there is a distinction between Poenari Castle—the home to Vlad the Impaler—and the fortress built by his son, the vampire Dracula."

"That doesn't make any sense," I insisted, keeping my guard up.

"Dracula employed powerful sorcerers to strengthen his position. He instructed them to utilize the immortal magick in his blood in order to create a fortress to shadow this one, parallel with the Poenari Castle of his youth."

"Like the Summerland?" I nearly stumbled, and Drake steadied me through the shock. "There's a hidden realm—no, a hidden *fortress* inside this one?"

"In essence? Yes." Drake descended another step, and my footfalls softened when the flooring leveled out.

I followed Drake around one last bend, and nearly ran into him when he stopped. Eyes wide, I glanced over the room we stood in. Across the space, two figures imitated our position, and I raised my blade. When the silhouette opposite did the same, I stopped short.

Roughly thirty feet ahead was an enormous mirror. Its edges stretched to obscure the stone wall behind it, with a gilded frame that glimmered despite there being no light to reflect. I swallowed, shivering from the cold and the eeriness pervading this empty room. Nothing existed between us and our reflection, but the smell entering my nostrils churned my stomach.

A memory flashed, of the days before Halloween following my fourteenth birthday. The funeral service, my crying family members, but I'd already exhausted my own tears by then. Numbed and heartbroken, I couldn't help but focus on the *smell*. Decay staved away only by formaldehyde and the rosy blush on Mom's unmoving cheeks.

Bile rose up my throat, but I gulped it down, focusing on the here and now.

"That's why Helsing spent nearly three centuries searching for Dracula," I mumbled, releasing Drake's hand to take another step. "Because he was hidden, somewhere Helsing couldn't enter."

"There is a…falsehood, for lack of a better term. The myth regarding vampires owning an invisible reflection." Drake walked past me, his silhouette nearing in the illustrious mirror, undamaged by time or the elements. "It is a mistranslation. The truth is not that Dracula was unable to see his own reflection, but that he was concealed within it."

"Why a mirror?" I approached, feeling the room grow cooler with every step.

"Where else would you create a place identical yet inverse to your own?" Drake's gaze traveled along the perimeter of the glass, never quite facing his own image. "This passage is rarely used anymore. When the Domnitori diverted their agenda from conquest to self-preservation, they no longer left their fortress on a regular basis. Instead, their sorcerer communicates with the Cneaz in command of whichever region they wish to contact."

Through the dim, I squinted at the engraved framework. The shimmering metal held vaguely religious symbols, like the ones on the small bell in our church's steeple. Except, these depicted perpendicular lines and infinity symbols interspersed with stars facing the earth.

"How do we get through…"

"It is intended for only the lifeless to enter." Like a demonstration, Drake placed his right hand against the mirror's surface. It didn't stop there, passing straight through the glass like it was as insubstantial as water, but left no ripples in its wake. My heart raced, and I blinked as his pale hand flexed on the other side before he pulled it back to our reality. "In order to gain passage, the enchantment must be deceived. In my day, we were fed the blood of a vampire."

"I have to drink your blood?"

"A drop will do," he explained, but I winced. "I must warn, it may offer some…interesting side effects."

"Like what?"

"The magick running through our veins gives us strength, as it will for you until it is metabolized."

"Like caffeine? Make me more alert?" Damn, a shot of espresso sounded really good right about now.

The wary expression Drake wore wasn't reassuring. "More akin to an amphetamine…"

"Never tried that one," I muttered, and Drake's responding smile was strained.

"I would not suggest it if it were not the only way I know."

"Just one drop, right?"

When Drake nodded, I inhaled deeply. We were running out of daylight every second with my bellyaching.

"Let's do it."

Steeling my resolve, and determined to get back home before Winston had to send that letter, I watched Drake bring the tip of his pointer finger to his mouth. His upper lip curled back, revealing the pointed canine. A bead of blood rose to the surface when his hand lowered, and though he'd already begun healing from the wound, the blood remained.

Grimacing, I hurriedly brought his finger to my mouth and swallowed the sour, gritty fluid. I'd beheaded a number of vampires, but I'd never gotten their blood in my mouth. Sweetness coated my saliva like an aftertaste, strangely citrusy, and not nearly as gross or salty as my own blood tasted.

The single drop slid down my throat, settling in my stomach. My heart thumped, my fingers tingling like electricity danced across my palm. Up my arms and throughout my chest until it burned through my exhaustion.

"Woah." An unwitting smile curved my mouth in the face of Drake's considering gaze. Then he nodded, clearly satisfied.

"The magick will allow you entrance." His forced smile didn't touch the despair behind his eyes, but he offered his hand all the same. An invitation to our damnation, the road ahead paved with good intentions.

His skin felt like a cold flame, the blood pulsing through his veins so much slower than mine. Drake faced the mirror while our fingers entwined, and took the first step. I watched his form disappear one inch at a time, revealing nothing of what existed on the other side. Taking a deep breath, I plunged ahead.

Oh, fuck—

Searing chills crawled over the surface of my skin like an ice cube slipped beneath my clothes. I couldn't suck air into my lungs, like being underwater, completely deprived of oxygen. My lungs flayed with every passing thrum of my pulse. The dark room ahead came into focus, but I couldn't take this much longer.

Was I about to die? Would it all be for nothing?

My eyes bulged as the tempo of my pulse slowed in my ears. The trickling beat grew further away…

Stagnant air hit my face, cold but lacking the excruciation of the mirror, and I gasped for breath. Large gulps of frigid air raked into my lungs, stinging in my chest like an echo of the mirror's entrapment. Drake caught me by my elbow before I could collapse. Bent double, I gagged. Cold sweat dripped down my brow as I glanced up at the concern crossing Drake's features.

"Are you alright?" he whispered, his gaze cautiously flickering from me to the end of the room. Straightening up slowly, I wiped my mouth with the back of my hand.

"I'll survive," I breathed, freezing when I glanced around the old-fashioned drawing room, like the kind I'd seen watching period pieces with Olivia. A wide white-tasseled rug threaded with scarlet and gold took up nearly the entire room. Armchairs were positioned to my right on either side of a low wooden table. On our left was oddly empty space, *a showroom?*

Shuddering, I glanced back over my shoulder. The mirror we'd passed through looked solid behind us. Only the scent of death was consistent.

"What's with the smell?" Imagining a group of children entering through that, led here only to be converted into bloodthirsty killing machines, made the rank atmosphere taste even more bitter.

"A remnant of the spell crafted to create this place." Speaking under his breath, Drake strode across the room on silent footfalls toward a wide black door. "Although intended to be a mirrored image of the original castle, there were limitations. Nothing can grow here, and everything spoils not long after being brought in. Similarly to its inhabitants, the fortress exists in a permanent state of decay."

"This is crazy…" The edges of my vision turned foggy as I tip-toed my way to his side, and I made an effort to keep my breathing even.

"Sorcery is a powerful craft. Some gifted with its aptitude can unlock limitless potential."

"My best friend's a witch, and I can't imagine her accomplishing anything of this magnitude."

"Pray your friend will never be made to, as some who possessed the talent have been." His right hand rested on the iron handle, but he paused, his gaze capturing mine. "Follow in my lead, I know the path we must take. If we come across the guards, hide immediately."

"What if it's too late?"

"Then you run. Retrace your steps back to this room, and flee."

Biting back the argument threatening to break free, I nodded once. Drake was still for another moment, like he was listening for something. Then he twisted the doorknob, and a hush of displaced air followed the door's opening. My hand settled on my machete handle as Drake slipped from the room in a blur.

Fast on his heels, I emerged into a corridor almost identical to those inside the Cneaz's manor—but worse. There were no windows on either side of the stone-brick walls. Oil lanterns were hung at odd intervals, each one unlit, and probably unused since the residents could see as easily in the dark as the day.

A wealth of paintings adorned the walls, perfect and undamaged by time, but considering the gruesome depictions, I was glad they'd become imprisoned here. Another long illustrious rug ran the length of the hall, silencing my steps as I started after Drake.

Without hesitation, he took one turn after another through the desolate castle. Even with his superior senses to guide us, I was uneasy. My blood pounded too loudly in my ears to pick up on anything else. *This long stretch of hallway left us too exposed.* I hurried my steps to bring my mouth closer to Drake's ear.

"How many werewolves are usually here?" I barely enunciated the words, my gaze peeled and darting from ahead to behind us.

"To my knowledge, there may be close to three dozen lycanthropes within the fortress alone."

"Three *dozen*?"

"When the majority of freshly transformed vampires left the fortress, after Dracula was slain, the Domnitori concentrated their efforts on increasing the number of lycans. To serve as security, and whatsoever else they desired."

His explanation brought up more unanswered questions, curiosities that settled into the pit of my stomach like a rock. We neared another corner, and Drake slowed before peering around it. A moment later, his quick pace resumed while I jogged to keep up. Halfway down the next hall, he halted beneath a grand chandelier. More of a decoration, since none of the candles on its spokes were lit.

A click sounded, and I whirled. Drake stood before a set of double doors to my left. Gray wood framed the opaque windows which blended in with the walls on either side. Darkness greeted us when he pushed the right side open, noiseless as the last door's hinges.

Frigid air poured into the corridor as I crossed the threshold from the rug underfoot to sleek hardwood floors. Worried my boots would squeak, I took the lightest steps I could manage, barely making a sound. Once my sight adjusted, my heart leaped.

Long shelves were lined up in a multitude of rows, almost reaching the high ceilings, and well beyond what I could count at first glance. Dimly, I glimpsed a second story balcony high above, and more shelving beyond containing a treasure trove of spines in pristine condition. Marveling at the craftsmanship, I took an awed step toward the labyrinth of stories while Drake closed the door behind us with a gentle click.

"It doesn't make sense…" My unease redoubled, and I finally understood why. Drake strode down an aisle, seemingly at random, and I voiced my newfound curiosity when I caught up. "If this place is a mirror of the castle in our world, shouldn't it be in ruins?"

The hidden entrance through the forest must've been spelled to ward away people from looking too closely, but the magick clearly hadn't extended to the rest of the original structure since it was known for regular tourism, and in complete disrepair.

"Although Dracula is gone, his immortal blood is what this shadow fortress was built upon. And, like he had been, it is incapable of change. There can be no growth, no alteration to the structural integrity. Regardless of what occurs in our reality."

"That's why I'm here," I murmured, watching the books on the shelves blurring from one title to the next as we passed them. "I share his blood, genetically speaking. So I can open the room to his chambers."

"That is the assumption. However, if we are incorrect—" Unblinking, Drake turned in a blur. A soft thud reverberated, and I strained to listen while holding my breath. Then came the distinct whistle of scraping metal. Drake grasped my hand and whispered under his breath, "Run!"

On my first stride, I gripped the handle of my machete and pulled it free from its sheath. My breath came fast while trying to match his strides. Thuds grew louder, approaching in proximity despite our sprint between the lengthy rows of shelves. We reached a crossroads, and Drake pulled me to a stop, then off to our right.

A figure stood at the end of the row. Drake's arm flung out before me, forcing my aching feet to a sudden halt. I turned to run back the way we'd come, but another enormous silhouette was stationed behind us. *Shit*—they'd corralled us like cattle. Our noisy pursuer came up behind us, while their silent accomplice blocked any hopes of advance.

Hefting my machete, I bent my knees, readied for fight or flight.

With my back to Drake, I narrowed my eyes at the lone suit of armor ahead walking closer. Their approach was unhurried, but I wasn't going to bet their armor would slow them down by much. The armored guard's easy grace proved it was one of the three dozen cursed beings forced to serve the Domnitori's ruthless regime.

Whoever inhabited this suit wasn't like the lycans we'd faced before. Effortless ease accompanied their long strides, but the shape of the armor was also different from the ones at the manor. More streamlined, the chest plate narrowed at the hips above a metal-pleated skirt. The helmet went unchanged, that same wrought-iron wolf's head. *What a sick joke.*

Roughly ten feet away, the lycan stopped, staying well out of my machete's reach. A shield on their left arm was engraved, the symbol faded past the point of recognition. The second guard must have stopped, too, since Drake hadn't moved from his position at my back.

My grip tightened on the handle of my machete when the lycan behind me spoke. The dialect sounded familiar, their accent identical to Drake's. While I couldn't understand a damn thing, I didn't need to. Drake answered for the both of us, his response so quiet I barely heard it.

"Now." Then he sprang into action.

The crunch of wood being torn apart snapped my attention over my shoulder. Books cascaded to the floor when the shelf holding them collapsed, the support beam now held like a deadly baseball bat in Drake's capable hands. In my peripheral, the guard ahead withdrew his sword, and I bent to grab a book.

Every part of me screamed blasphemy when I aimed my throw for the advancing guard. The heavy tome wouldn't do any damage, but the guard realized that too late. Raising their shield at the perceived attack, it blocked the view of my actual assault. Keeping to my right and its left, I darted out with a mostly-blind strike toward where I assumed their armpit was, aiming for the thinner chainmail beneath the armor with the point of my blade.

With Drake's blood invigorating my strength, I managed to land with greater accuracy than I'd expected. Fresh too-human blood spurted from the chink between the guard's breast and shoulder-plate. My hope that the pain would distract the guard enough for me to land another hit was sorely mistaken. Emphasis on sore, because the asshole didn't make a sound when they used their full bodyweight to ram me into the neighboring shelf.

Breath exploded from my lungs on impact, my back throbbing and fingers spasming. I clenched my teeth and tightened my grip on my weapon, finding my footing when I dropped into a crouch. The guard tried to hit me with their shield this time, but I rolled aside, missing the blow by inches in the cramped aisle.

More books fell from the shelves while the impact of the guard's shield hitting the hardwood created a boom that echoed through the enormous dark library. Shelves shook—unnaturally, like the wood itself was trying to bend back into its original place. The guard turned, hefting their sword high just as I'd gotten one knee beneath me.

With my right foot planted and my left knee bearing my weight, instinct urged me to raise my machete overhead when the guard brought their huge sword down in an arc. Overpowered, my left hand rose to hold my machete horizontal. My arms shook while keeping the enemy's blade on the central point of mine.

Blood slickened my left palm, cut by my own blade, but I couldn't move under the weight of the pressure. My shocked muscles left me paralyzed as the guard lifted their sword only to crash it back down. A cry of frustration ground between my teeth as my upper body burned, my knee digging into the hard floor.

What the fuck did a girl have to do to get a little help around here?

As the guard's blade rose high above their head, ready to slam back down for a third time, the floor beneath seemed to shift. My knee rolled, and I gave in to the momentum while the guard's sword fell—the blade slicing into the empty floor. Utilizing the shelves for leverage, I pushed my resisting muscles to rise on the opposite side of the guard's shield.

I raised my trembling arm, pausing when I found the guard's sword end was *stuck* between the floorboards it'd pierced. The guard heaved, bent over, trying to yank it from the spot, but the floor wouldn't release it. I hefted my machete, and the wolf's head helmet faced me a moment before my blade skewered through the side of their exposed neck.

Gurgling followed the spray of blood where I'd separated the guard's sinews. Then I slashed downward, opening up the guard's throat, and the helmet snapped against the backside of the armor. The metal gauntlet clutching the stuck sword went slack, releasing the hilt, and the armored body collapsed, dead before hitting the ground.

Then the sword's blade toppled over, its hilt inches from the guard's lifeless fingers. To the naked eye, the floor beneath appeared undamaged. I blinked, but the sounds of a struggle not far off recaptured my attention. Drake was locked in combat with the other guard, who had been joined by two others, now laying dismembered between the shelves while he faced the remaining lycan.

Horror swept away my initial surge of victory. The nerves connecting Drake's left arm had been severed, leaving the limb to hang limp at his side. The sluggish step he took to evade the guard's next swing of their mace meant he was losing too much blood too fast. Even with my blood fresh in his system, he'd need time to recover from a wound that severe.

Pages and bindings flew as the mace smacked against several books, the shelves too close on either side for the oversized weapon. Drake stumbled over a torn-off armored arm, barely catching himself against the shelves opposite the advancing guard. He was weaponless, with the support beam he'd torn away now wedged through a dead guards' chest.

Without a second thought, I reached for the fallen sword beside me. My left palm burned when I grasped its handle. The guard raised their mace, gunning for Drake's head.

"Drake!" I cried, catching his gaze when he glanced over his shoulder. Fear shone in his dark eyes, replaced by determination when I threw the sword.

He dodged the mace, and I exhaled when he caught the sword in his still-able right hand. Drake met the next blow of the battle mace with the sharp end of his stolen blade. I raced down the aisle, hopping over ripped spines and blood-soaked pages.

Raising my machete high, I leaped past Drake to bring my blade down against the guard. My weapon met the resistance of steel, clanging off the enemy's shield. Now they had two opponents. The guard's stance turned defensive, backing up several steps in less than a second. Positioned before the guard, with Drake a step behind, I shifted my weight to my right heel.

Which helped me keep my balance when the entire library started to shake underfoot.

— 20 —

DIE WITH ME

I STAGGERED TO STAY UPRIGHT, FLINGING MY LEFT ARM OUT FOR BALANCE. The guard didn't move, trapped in place by the shifting shadow fortress, same as us. By the time I faced Drake, who gripped the nearby shelf as his gaze darted around the room with clear disbelief, the shaking ceased.

Silence followed in the wake of the disruption, and my head snapped forward at the smallest squeak. The guard backed away, one step at a time, before turning tail and disappearing around the next corner. Maybe I should have followed them, but with Drake injured, defensive action seemed like the better call.

I huffed, slowly lowering my weapon. Wincing at my aching muscles, I turned to Drake and asked, "Can you walk?"

Displeasure soured his features while he tried to keep himself upright without using the shelving for balance.

"You were meant to flee," he rasped, and I took the initiative to shoulder some of his weight to get us moving. "They will surely wake now, our element of surprise is lost. You *have* to leave, Maria—"

"I don't care what I agreed to! I am *not* leaving you," I spat, glaring up into his gaze. Teeth gritted, I hunched under his weight. *He'd heal on our way to the chambers.* "Now, which way?"

"We must turn back." His begrudging cadence convinced me they were real directions and not an argument. "A door at the end of the library contains a passage straight to the floor where the master bedroom is kept."

"Alright." I half-carried Drake as he limped along through the handicap of his blood loss, but the magick in his veins slowly repaired his body during our slow progress around the fallen tomes. My grip on my machete was firm, but the shaking in my wrist was proof enough that the effects of his blood were wearing off. Stupid supernatural metabolism wasn't great for survival.

Under my fatigue, adrenaline pounded a dull beat inside of my skull. Three thoughts kept me moving through the maze-like library, taking Drake's silent indications to turn when necessary.

Firstly, if we left empty-handed then both of our lives were over—Drake would be hunted down eventually, and I'd probably do something idiotic or romantic trying to save him. Sweat ran down my temple, my breathing low but harsh.

Second—I *couldn't* die here. I had to get home. Nobody would know the truth otherwise. Why had I even written that dumb letter? Would that become my legacy, sacrificing myself for my mortal enemy to give my family peace of mind? *What a joke.* No matter how I felt only a couple weeks ago, no death was a good one.

There was no glory in giving up.

Which was the third reason. Because this legacy had lied to me, painting a rose-tinted picture. Promised me a purpose, but only shoved me onto the battlefield. One I would have given anything to stay ignorant of, like everyone else who didn't know to fear the pierce of deadly fangs.

I'd assumed that my family and I were the only ones who stood between these monsters and humanity, but Drake had wiped that slate clean for me. Now I knew the truth, and we didn't stand a fucking chance. Not unless I could get out of here to warn my people of the danger, and prepare ourselves for what might come after.

Maybe then I could be truly free. If, by some means, I could win more than this one day, and eventually find a way to take them all out for good. Except I couldn't do it on my own. Glancing at Drake, whose steps had steadied enough to keep his weight from straining my aching muscles, I recognized what had dug our bond so deep. On our own, we were lost, but together? We had a chance at surviving the hands life had dealt us.

Beyond determination, there was resolve behind his raven-dark eyes. Never again would I question my worth in my family. I might be descended from Helsing, but I wasn't *alone* in this legacy, and the strength that fact gave me had never been more clear.

Drops of blood and sweat trailed behind us between the rows of books that hadn't seen daylight for centuries. Just when I felt like screaming '*how much longer,*' the next turn brought us to an arched door. A cold sensation swept through my bones when Drake stood under his own power as I reached for the iron knob.

Before my fingers could grasp the metal, a click echoed. I raised my weapon, immediately shifting into a defensive stance, but my panic ebbed into confusion when the door opened outward to reveal nothing within. Beside me, Drake's posture stiffened, and his brow furrowed as we glanced at each other. Looking as dumbfounded as I felt, Drake shook his head.

A spark of intuition itched at the back of my mind. It couldn't be a coincidence, and after what happened when I fought the guard… This wasn't the time to wonder idly, so I rolled my shoulders and took the first tentative steps into the shadows. Drake staggered after me, his strides growing more sure by the minute as he started up a series of steps swathed in darkness.

I reached out for a railing, but Drake's cold hand grasped mine, his fingers sticky with the blood of others against my sweaty palm. As I shifted to pull the door shut behind us, I startled when it swung closed without making a sound. Shrouded in oblivion on all sides, I ascended the steps and inhaled a deep breath. *Nowhere to go but up.*

Drake's gentle pull on my arm indicated our direction, but this staircase didn't spiral like the one we'd descended to the mirror room. Instead, it rose diagonally through the castle, cutting straight through the fortress.

Logically, if I had nothing better to do but exist forever, I'd also want direct access from the floor I lived on to the extensive library. *A little light reading would be a great way to pass the time in between planning world-domination.* Man, it was hard to believe I was related, however distantly, to the original inhabitants of this place.

My legs soon felt like jello, while Drake's restitution was only improving. Without warning, I ran right into his back when we reached the final landing. He spun, catching my arms to keep me steady, and his firm touch pulled something from deep within. The fact that he could make me feel anything close to enamored, considering our circumstances, made me smirk. Through the pitch-black, I guessed he could see it because he huffed a note of disbelieving mirth.

"Thanks," I whispered, joining him on the landing but finding that the small square before another wooden door kept us smooshed together.

"Always," he replied. I closed my eyes at the brush of his fingers against my cheekbone when he tucked a stray curl behind my ear, and I focused on the sensation replaying across my skin. "The fortress will be on alert, I cannot guarantee what will come next. We are not far from the chambers now. Are you prepared?"

Swallowing hard, I nodded. The time for talking was over. So I lifted up on my toes, placing my weaponless hand on the side of his neck to give me a clue about where his mouth was before I pressed my lips to his. Sweetness lingered beneath the scent and taste of salted iron, and that sour flavor I recognized as his own blood.

Our kiss was brief, but the gentle way he held me in return—keeping me close but with room to breathe—made my heart ache. Hell, I *really* hoped we made it out of this. There was still so much I wanted to know, and things I needed him to understand about me. When his mouth released mine, our foreheads met, but only my breath fogged the air between us.

This was it, the final stretch. Taking a deep breath, I turned for the door. I didn't bother to reach for the handle. My will seemed to be enough, confirming my suspicions and fears. Soundlessly, the door swung open. Compared to the darkness within the stairwell, the lightless hallway beyond was bright. Pops of color struck my vision from the deep violet of the rug stretching up and down the corridor.

It was a refreshing change from the bloody red, and rather than gruesome paintings, family tapestries depicting status and regal lineage lined the stone walls between more unused oil lamps. Drake entered first, flexing his left hand as the nerves reconnected, but I was fast on his heels. While the door closed of its own accord behind us, I glanced up and down the hall. The start and end was significantly smaller in length and width compared to the floor below.

Drake frowned, then cocked his head to give direction. We walked side by side, my machete low but at the ready. Heart-pounding excitement encouraged my quick steps. Our goals felt tangible, like static in the air, charged by my own hope.

We were almost at the end of the hall when a shiver quaked down my spine. Raising my blade, I spun on the spot. Drake's silhouette blurred on my left, both of us now facing down the opposite end of the corridor. Someone was coming. The odor of death intensified, punctuated by the smell of blood and sweat.

The taste of Drake's blood I stole from his lips elevated my senses, and my eyes widened when the double doors down the hall were pushed open.

"*You*?" Rage burned my synapses when I stared into the icy blue eyes of the North American Cneaz. Four guards flanked him on either side, close enough to act as bodily shields if Drake or I moved in. *Too chickenshit to face us on his own, huh?*

Except Lucian's advance came to a halt with plenty of space between us. A feral sort of smile glinted beneath his ruthless gaze.

"Bravo, Ignatius—bravo, indeed." Unarmed, Lucian slowly clapped and took a single step closer. "Right as I was charged with the duty of locating your whereabouts, you return home to heel. Although, I must wonder, what manner of idiocy compelled your actions?" His gaze held mine, but all I could see in his pupils was my last memory of the human servant at the manor. Countless others owed their deaths to him. "Or *whose?*"

My blood boiled, and I dared a glance at Drake. His jaw was set, eyes narrowed and refusing to look away from Lucian. Years of training kicked in as I assessed our surroundings.

"I have neither the time nor desire to explain myself to you, Lucian." Drake took a subtle step in front of me, and my gaze dropped to the rectangular outline in his back pocket.

"You cannot protect her *and* combat me, Ignatius," Lucian retorted, unashamed glee coloring his thick accent. I moved to stand beside Drake, my left hand quickly plucking the match-box from his pocket and palming it. The slight curl to the corner of Drake's mouth was reassuring, but he turned the smirk into one of derision to continue his verbal distraction.

"I have often wondered if it is in the nature of our undeath to have such a cowardly yellow streak in the face of adversity." Drake took a meandering step toward the wall, and Lucian's pale brow creased. "It is my belief that, no, it is not a trait of our race, but mere complacency on your part. For when this false narrative of immortality is put to the test—" With one hand, I managed to thumb out a single match. "It turns out that you are much too afraid of death."

"You will be forced to embrace the nothingness of a true death long before I." Lucian raised his pointy chin. "None too soon, for my liking."

"No," Drake agreed, and I dropped my machete to fumble with striking the match against the box. "None too soon."

My vampire became a blur of movement when he reached to grasp the wrought-iron backplate fastening the oil lamp to the stone wall. I struck the match, its shush of spasming atoms overpowered by the explosive crunch of metal being torn from stone. Like a brilliant sun in deep space, the bud of fire glowed golden against my fingers.

Glass crashed to the carpet. Slick liquid spilled across its threadwork, soaking in. Armor squeaked, the guards torn between protecting Lucian and intercepting us. They would have been too late.

Flame fell from my fingertips, and Drake's cool, familiar arms wrapped around me to haul me backward. His grip spun me around, and I crouched low to snatch up my machete as heat erupted behind my retreat. A glance over my shoulder revealed the extent of the damage. The dry carpet caught like tinder, eating up the stagnant oxygen permeating the hall.

Lucian and his werewolf henchmen were forced back when the flames followed them. Shifting light ignited the anger in Lucian's eyes, but I was spared from being consumed by my need for revenge when Drake's hand settled on mine. Forced to face ahead or risk tripping, I sprinted in Drake's wake while he pulled me along after him.

Smoke clouded our path, and my eyes watered. Coughing, I clutched to Drake's hand when he suddenly stopped, and the crash of wood against stone followed. I squinted through stinging eyes as two double doors swung inward. Drake pushed me inside, and I stumbled to catch my footing as he hurried to throw the doors shut behind us.

Ash was bitter on my tongue, choking my attempts to inhale the decay-scented air. Somehow, I sensed Drake inches in front of me even before he spoke.

"Were you harmed?"

"I'll—" Swallowing, I cleared my throat and blinked away the moisture obscuring my vision. "I'll live."

Dark-paneled walls surrounded us, lavishly draped in shades of purple fabric that ran from floor to ceiling like gauzy wallpaper. The hexagon-shaped antechamber was grand, but only one piece of furniture rested at the center—if a huge statue made of stone could be considered that.

Atop a marble throne sat the depiction of a man, but no engraving was necessary to know who it was meant to immortalize. It was eerie, and though distantly related, there was something about the square jaw and bridge of his nose that resembled my father and uncle, even my male cousins. I could only guess at what color his eyes had been, but considering the smooth arch of his brow that I'd recognize in the mirror, I was glad the sculptor hadn't painted any irises.

Beyond the statue, opposite the entrance, was another set of double doors. A sixth sense alerted me to whatever magick sealed the threshold. The very one we desperately needed to cross. Drake moved first, disappearing from view around the massive marble sculpture.

The squeak of my boots on the hardwood floor dissipated once I reached the carpet that must have been specially woven for this room since it made a perfect hexagonal perimeter around the centerpiece. Once past the statue, I took in the doors stained so dark they were almost black. Golden handles again glimmered in the darkness despite there being no sources of light.

Drake stood in front of the entrance, his focus on the enchanted handles, but an enormous painting above him caught my attention. He didn't so much as glance up at the woman portrayed in colorful oils. A strange contrast to the room around, since the artist had painted her surrounded by so much vibrant imagery. From her light pink gown to the sunlight streaming into the courtyard setting beyond latticed windows.

Something about her gentle smile struck a chord of familiarity, but not in the same way as Vladislav Dracula the Fourth's immortalized image had. A subtle sense of comfort accompanied my admiration of the deep, dark brown eyes framed by black hair, the long strands half up in a knot while the rest fell straight down over her shoulders. Necklaces adorned her slender pale throat, highlighted by a pretty rose-tinted blush.

Brow scrunched, I found Drake already staring at me when I finally tore my gaze away from the woman in the portrait. Morbid curiosity got the best of me.

"Who is that?" I walked the final steps to stand at Drake's side, but he didn't look away from me when he answered.

"Ileana Petrescu." His accent thickened on her name. "The fourth wife to have been betrothed to Dracula."

"The fourth?" Only three wives ever made it into the stories Grandpa would tell us growing up. Even that was pure speculation, based on what Helsing had uncovered during his nearly three centuries hunting down Dracula.

Except, this was the only portrait of a woman I'd seen in the fortress so far.

Drake offered his hand, palm up. A sad smile pulled at the corners of his mouth, but the effect it had on my heart made it too easy to place my left hand atop his. Unexpectedly, he raised my hand to press a soft kiss against my knuckles. Distracted by his touch, I cleared my throat when he lowered my hand.

"Do I just…open it?" I turned to face the doors when he nodded. An engraving circled the handles, and I bit my lip. Would anything horrible happen if we were wrong? Would it kill me on the spot if the enchantment recognized me as a threat? I had no other choice but to try.

Drake's fingers squeezed mine, and I silently handed him my machete so I could keep holding onto him. When he took the weapon, unease tightened my shoulders, but I slowly exhaled and reached out.

"Whatsoever occurs, I will be here," he whispered.

Encouraged, I bit the bullet and placed my damp palm against the brassy metal. Nothing unusual happened, except a chill climbing up my arm to make me shiver. I tried turning the knob. An audible click cut through the silence, and at the slightest push on my part, the doors swung inward.

Darkness greeted me, and I blinked fast to take in the vast room. Where windows should have been, massive tapestries ran the wall from the ceiling to a few feet off the floor. The room was indeed fit for a king. On the left was the bed, its frame expansive and carved with such expertise that it rivaled anything my family could produce. *Had its maker survived the commission, or was this their final creation?*

Chaise lounges and chairs arranged around a cold fireplace created the sitting area, where a short stack of books were placed on a low central table. Like their owners had forgotten to return them to the library before leaving this world forever. An elongated vanity took up space between two dressers placed against the far wall.

While I stood there in awe, Drake strode ahead. His gaze didn't waver on his way to the vanity, where jewelry and crystal pieces were strewn across the surface, never put away. In front of the vanity's mirrors, Drake's reflection was put into sharp perspective from every possible angle. My first step inside was brought up short when my intuition flickered.

After opening and closing several small drawers, his shoulders relaxed an inch as he removed a maroon velvet box from the rich wooden vanity. He pushed its lid open with his thumb, and nestled within the swath of silk were two nearly identical golden rings. Thoughts emptied out of my head, but I forced my legs to move.

On my approach, I couldn't help but glimpse Drake's oddly nostalgic gaze while he stared down at his salvation. Several feet away, I halted, and Drake looked up. Mistrust built in my chest, and this was *so* not the right time for it. We needed to get out of here, and *fast*. Except I wouldn't be able to take a step outside this room without knowing the truth.

"Who are you, Drake?"

Guarded emotion flickered behind his eyes, and the crease between his brows seemed apologetic. "I am exactly who you know me to be," he assured, taking a step closer, but he stopped when I backed up. "I cannot help who my progenitor was, and I assume you have already guessed. Please, we must hurry to escape, I will explain everything once—"

"Dracula never had children." It was one piece of the lore that could be certain. The man who became the first vampire was barely older than I was now when he made his 'deal with the devil.' If he'd had any illegitimate children before that, then they would have been considered bastards with no claim to the Wallachian throne—hence why Helsing was always the imminent threat to Dracula's seat of power.

That didn't make the resemblance between Drake and the woman in the portrait any less damning.

To my knowledge, dhampirs were immune to the transformation magick of vampire venom. Even if a half-vampire was bitten, they wouldn't turn after death. So what the hell was going on? Drake seemed to recognize my dismay, but he knew me well enough by now that when pushed, I wouldn't budge.

"I was taken from my blood relatives, led to this fortress, and made into what I am." Frustration laced his tone, but I didn't fear his ire. Even with my weapon in his hand, I trusted him that much, and recognizing that fact kept me rooted to the spot when he strode closer. "It was much, much later when I became aware of the fact that my birth mother had me out of wedlock, and the family I lived with in my early years consisted of my grandparents and aunt, the latter masquerading as my sister.

"My family kept records of our genealogical history, and it was not until long after *her* death that I put the pieces together. Recognized her as the kind woman the *voievod* had taken for his wife. She must have requested that I be brought here, and in hindsight, I was favored among the other soldiers. Many, such as Lucian, grew to hate me over their own jealousy." Drake's dark eyes turned pleading, close enough now that he pressed the handle of my machete against the palm of my right hand.

I didn't resist it when he opened my clenched left hand and placed one of the rings there. Too tempted, I rolled the ring between my thumb and forefinger. Calligraphy swirled in a foreign language along the inside rim. Turmoil spun through my head like a tornado. I'd known Drake was set apart, that he had turned out so much differently from the other undead.

Never would I have guessed his history was entangled so thoroughly with my own. Because if Dracula was dead, and his fourth bride was lost to time, I could only guess what had happened—about *who* had killed the woman that happened to be Drake's mother. Strange, nonsensical guilt tightened my throat.

If Helsing had gotten to Dracula earlier, would Drake's mother have still lived in his time? Except, then Drake would have gotten the chance to be human. To live and die like any man, and I never would have met him.

Finally, I understood what Drake found so beautiful about humanity—*choice*.

My eyes briefly squeezed shut, reeling from experiencing too much in too short a time, and I asked, "What does it say?"

"Pentru preaiubitul meu, să îmbrățișăm blestemul eternității." The foreign words pulled my gaze up to meet his, and he helpfully translated. "'For my beloved, let us embrace the curse of eternity.' There had always been two rings. One for the master of death, and the other for the only person he ever cared for more than himself."

Before I could do more than open my mouth, with no idea what I would have said, an explosive bang echoed from the antechamber room with the statue. I spun on my heel, grip tensed on my machete and fingers closing over the ring's cold metal before I shoved it into my back pocket. *We weren't out of the woods yet.* A cloud of stone dust obscured the only exit from the master's chambers, but the deafening stomp of armored boots was becoming familiar.

Drake stepped in front of me, but my view of the intruders past the chamber's open doors was unimpaired. Through the smog, half a dozen armed guards entered one after another. Leading their charge was one truly pissed off vampire.

Soot and smoke blackened his face, his embroidered garb now singed with long streaks as Lucian glared daggers. "I will personally flay you both alive."

21

'TIL I CHOKE

THE LYCANS IN ARMOR ADVANCED, THEIR STRIDES SURE, UNAFRAID. PANIC arced down my spine alongside the chill of Lucian's bloodlust. Drake's stance had already shifted toward the defensive. I was slow to raise my weapon as Drake raced to meet the first guard head on. His fist slammed into the metal breastplate, creating a dent and shocking the guard backward a step, but the damage was nothing compared to his previous strength.

Cold dread twisted my empty stomach. He'd lost too much blood after the library brawl, but there wasn't time for him to feed more to recover. Raising my machete, I ran to cover Drake's flank while the remaining guards closed in. One had caught the first who'd stumbled, but another two had taken their place. Drake's blurred movements were barely dodging the guards' swinging broadsword and ax.

The last two reached me faster than I'd thought possible. A tickle in my ear was all the warning I had to dodge the guard's spear thrust. Sidestepping, I crouched to duck beneath the reach of the second guard swarming me. My drop turned into a roll, and I managed to get behind the first guard before swinging blindly at the back of their knees. Except the son of a bitch twisted around to follow me.

The piercing clang of my machete hitting their metal-plated knee rang in my ears. I sprang up despite my screaming muscles, and backed away, but my attempt at putting distance between me and the guards was short lived. What had seemed like such a spacious bed chamber when we'd entered was now cramped with so many armor-clad lycans.

I tried to spin from their reach, but a cold gauntlet clamped over my right elbow. Air hissed in between my gritted teeth. The pressure made the muscles along my forearm spasm, and my traitorous fingers released my machete. It hit the carpet, lying there only a second before the other guard picked it up.

"Maria!" Drake's alarm brought my attention to where he stood, too far to reach me and not close enough to the exit to escape. The guard holding me twisted my arm, shoving me forward until my knees hit the floor with a smack. Pain shot up my legs, but it became an afterthought when Lucian finally stepped in.

Drake managed to evade the four guards vying for him, with two of them on their knees but no signs of life-threatening injuries. His rush toward me was intercepted by Lucian's blurring figure, too fast for me to cry out and warn my vampire, whose eyes were only on me. A crack reverberated through the chill air when Lucian shoved his elbow into Drake's spine.

"No!" I screamed, twisting my shoulders in every direction, desperate to break free from the two guards now holding me down on either side.

No one else moved as Drake suddenly collapsed to his knees, barely catching himself by his shaking forearms. Lucian's gaze swept over the two recovering guards before he pointedly waved to the other two who were still standing. The backs of my eyes burned when one guard grabbed Drake's wrist, wrenching it behind his back to shove his chest into the floor.

Stone cracked beneath the weight of the guard's knee digging into Drake's back, making the carpet sag an inch under their combined weight. Throat tight, I forced back tears and caught Drake's eye—unfazed by the brutality, but shining with terror I knew deep down was for me alone. Hatred boiled to the forefront as my gaze settled on Lucian while the guards closed in.

"Coward!" I spat, gaining Lucian's attention as the guard with the dented breastplate hurried to restrain Drake with thick iron shackles. "Fight me one-to-one, I fucking dare you!"

"Believe me, little tiger," Lucian said, his voice almost a purr as the gleam behind his icy blue eyes sent shivers down my spine. "Ripping your vocal chords clean from your throat would bring me nothing but pleasure."

"And yet you restrain us." Drake grimaced, trying and failing to get his legs under him while the guards kept him pinned down. *Thank fuck he could still move*, but my flickering hope died with the grating timbre of Lucian's voice.

"Your intrusion has called for a summons," he muttered, then his leg moved in a blur to kick Drake clear across the face. Gritty blood oozed from my vampire's nose while I fought the bile rising up my throat. My shoulders burned, the tendons stretched taut with my arms twisted behind my back. Drake spat dark blood to the stained carpet, blinking quickly like his sight was out of focus, while Lucian delicately adjusted his vest. "One that I would not dare disobey."

Another pair of shackles chimed against its attached chains as a guard strode closer, and I paled. This could *not* be fucking happening, not when we were this close! Cold metal compressed around my numbing wrists, and I shut my eyes. Teeth clenched, I fought the zing of magick icing up my veins from the sigiled restraints.

Faster than a thought, the shackles' power drained away.

Thinking fast, I subtly gripped the iron cuffs between my fingers just-right so they wouldn't fall off my forearms. A relieved sigh started in my lungs, but I bit it back down to pretend the restraints were working instead of hanging loose against my bruised skin. Free, I may be, but whatever loyalty the fortress's magick offered my bloodline clearly didn't extend to Drake. Surrounded by six armored werewolves and one really pissed off vampire, we weren't anywhere closer to escape.

"Follow me." Lucian smirked, motioning with a wave before turning on his heel in a blur. The guard with my machete eased up on my shoulder as the other released me entirely to join the four guards carefully restraining Drake while hauling him up to stand. I managed to get one foot under me to rise. A shove against my shoulder made me stumble. The shackles almost slipped off, and I had to bend my throbbing knees to balance the metal with my momentum.

My back pocket practically burned when I crossed the threshold of Dracula's chambers, and returned to the corridor beyond. *Okay, so things didn't really go according to plan,* but we'd gotten the rings. Hopefully they would do what legend told. I only had to bide my time, despite my fingertips already stinging from the pressure of holding up the shackles. Far ahead, Lucian was flanked by two guards as they took the corner at the end.

A few steps ahead of me, Drake was being ushered along by one lycan on either side and a third following for good measure—all with their weapons drawn and ready if he resisted. The one behind me walked dutifully, but not nearly as concerned. Thumps echoed against the stone walls with every synchronized step the armored guards took, adding to my pounding headache from the spent adrenaline.

No plans came to mind on our steady descent through the fortress, only my circling thoughts that kept repeating *I couldn't lose Drake.* Not now, and if this fortress was hellbent on keeping me alive, then maybe it would give me an opening to get Drake out of here safely.

As long as we survived until then.

Something reassuring flickered at the corner of my consciousness. Like a word I knew but couldn't remember for the life of me. Deep magick created this place, and I didn't understand a lick of the mystical mumbo jumbo, but if I could keep these shackles from falling off after two long staircases and several dark corridors, I had to believe there was a *chance.*

Because nothing would make me throw away my life anymore—or his.

The hallway gradually widened, until the ceilings high above strewn with chandeliers indicated that we'd crossed from the residential area of the fortress into a social political space. Marble floors shone underfoot, like they'd been freshly waxed. My boots squeaked on our approach to the enormous double doors at the centrepoint of the grand entryway. There were no actual exits leading to what would have been the outside in our reality, just unbroken stone walls and tapestries that would have taken a human lifetime to manually weave.

Two massive winged gargoyles stood on either side of the bejeweled doors leading to an equally unlit room beyond. A shiver danced down my spine when we passed their stone faces, chiseled into a depiction of pain and contempt.

The circular throne room inside was surreal, with a long rug woven with blues of every shade and cream colors for accents. Stylized stonework climbed the walls, drawing my gaze to the high vaulted ceiling before my focus shifted to the six silhouettes at the center of the space. Each of them were dressed in lavish robes or gowns, as different from one to the next.

Before their chilling gazes could set off my instincts through their bloodlust, I couldn't help but notice that nobody sat on the *actual* throne in the great room. Built into the floor like a fixture of the fortress itself, a dark throne rose like a pillar behind the six smaller versions of it set onto a spacious flat step, a mere foot above my own standing. Its emptiness felt strange, like a second heartbeat tugging my middle closer. An urge that would only be satisfied by sitting atop the royal seat.

Power emanated from it, practically rippling outward in waves reminiscent of a mirage in the desert. I didn't get a chance to stare because the asshole guard behind me grasped my shoulder in one gauntlet, shoving me downward. Pressure clamped over my collarbone, and I grimaced when my knees hit the hard floor. Drake's familiar voice turned savage, his words foreign, but their meaning obvious.

With a harsh inhale, I glanced to where Drake had also been forced to his knees. Panic iced the breath in my lungs. He was way too far. Maybe ten feet separated us, and the guards' weapons could cut faster than I could move. Wild fear lit behind his eyes, his expression more readable than I'd ever seen, revealing how much he cared about what happened to me.

More foreign words were spoken, this time by an unfamiliar feminine voice. My glare settled on a woman with long black hair pulled daintily away from her pale face. Pearls and sapphires adorned her violet gown beneath the white fur-lined cloak that covered her shoulders, its hem resting at her slippered feet. All of them wore a similar version of the cape.

To her right, a much-taller man's long curly brown hair and full beard appeared even darker contrasted to his silver suit. Next to him, making up one side of the center, was a blonde vampire. Her round face and cutting blue eyes complimented the indigo colors draped over her full figure. Leaned forward on his lesser-throne, the blond vampire beside her seemed washed out in golds—from his hair to his trailing lion's fur-lined cape.

Because of how brightly he dressed, the vampire on his right appeared shorter in stature. Subdued by his hair—equally as dark as the first woman—and the heavy green suit he wore, its deep coloring contrasting his pale green eyes that stood out like some nocturnal animal. The final member of the vampire ruling class, taking the third chair on the right but seemingly the furthest spaced out of the six of them, nearly made me flinch.

Sandy hair a similar color to Andrew's fell stringy and missing in patches over a long scarred forehead. Lines and signs of battle marked the vampire's face, accentuated by the crimson color of his cape, flowing down from his shoulders like blood woven into fabric. While the others' postures were haughty, displaying their prestige for all who came to worship them, the man clad in red seemed more calculating.

It was the way he watched mine and Drake's every move with narrowed eyes, anticipating our next actions before we could think of them. Swallowing hard, but refusing to act meek, I straightened my back the best I could under the pressure of the guard's painful grip. After another flex of their fingers, the gauntlet fell away. As the guard took a step back, my attention landed on the last unfamiliar person in the room.

Half-hidden in the deeper shadows behind the violet woman's throne, a figure with a bent-back stood hunched over a gnarled cane. She hobbled forward on noisy footfalls, her gray eyes blinded by cataracts. Compared to the vampires, her tattered cloak was plain aside from the silver button fastening it around her wrinkled neck.

If the undead before us made up the Domnitori, then the wizened human could only have been one thing—their sorcerer. Looking smug and self-important, Lucian's hastened steps blurred his figure. He fell to his knees before his evil overlords, almost kissing the ground at their feet while he murmured words I couldn't interpret.

The vampire in gold spoke, his deep voice too quiet for me to pick up the vowels on his foreign tongue. Lucian's subservient response was immediate. Meanwhile, Drake stared daggers like he was planning out how to annihilate every single one of them.

Fidgeting to keep the shackles from slipping off from between my sweaty fingers, I whispered, "What are they saying?"

Every pair of eyes in the room was suddenly on me.

"Lucian has revealed our intrusion to the bed chambers of their *voievod*," Drake answered, not bothering to whisper. "He remains clueless as to the 'why' behind it."

Again, the Domnitori member in gold spoke. His steady light brown eyes flickered to me, but he addressed only Drake. My heart raced at the sound of his grave tone, but I jumped when the black-haired woman in violet laughed. Her high-pitched glee revealed a glint of hunger within her expressive gaze. I tensed, struggling to keep still while shivers shook my spine. Drake opened his mouth to reply to whatever they'd said, but I was done with being a pawn.

"Why don't you just ask me why we're here?" I squared my shoulders, wincing from my aching back. The Domnitori stared at me, the emotions crossing their faces varying from unresponsive to disgusted, but the man in crimson looked curious. *Yeah, like that wasn't creepy as shit.*

The pale blonde woman in indigo narrowed her eyes with mistrust before she replied in her heavily-accented voice, "You are English."

"I'm American, actually." That seemed to be the wrong thing to say. The woman actually sneered.

"Doamnă Milica has always loathed the New World, and its inhabitants," Drake murmured, and Lucian's lip curled.

"Domn Nikolai enjoys them." The black-haired woman in violet glanced at the vampire reduced to shadows beside the golden one. Her keen gaze was intent, never leaving mine while she spoke in stilted English. "The blood of the Americans is so… thick."

"*Tăcere*, Doamnă Irina." When the man in gold spoke, Irina obeyed. Not even a hint of displeasure crossed her face at being silenced, and my brow furrowed. These vampires had to have existed alongside each other for centuries. Their allegiance was unbreakable, that was obvious, and once again, I struggled not to cower under the oppressive knowledge that my family and I were more than outclassed by these killers.

The gold-clad vampire paused, like he was translating his sentences ahead of speaking them. "You are a descendant of the slayer, we know this. Have you come to slay *us*?" He didn't sound afraid, and by the slight smirk on Milica's round face, they seemed to think it was a funny notion.

"No, I didn't." Which was true, not that they could tell my truths from lies considering how hard my blood was pumping just being in front of these freaks. I glanced at Drake to gauge his reaction, but he'd shut down anything that wasn't pure hatred from showing on his face.

Surrounded by not only lycans with medieval weaponry, but several vampires—plenty capable of ripping our heads off in mere seconds—our only shot at survival was buying time. Which meant keeping them talking, or at the very least unsettling them. Closing my eyes tight, I made up my mind.

I opened my eyes, wedged my pinky finger into my back pocket, and fished out the ring. It fell from my fumbling hold instantly, tumbling to the carpet on its edge only to roll forward. The vibrations of its centrifugal force turned deafening when it reached the marbled section of floor.

"I came to steal the rings."

Surprise surged across every vampire's face when the realization settled in—even Drake's—but only the unnamed one with the blood-red cape showed a flicker of fear. Sweet satisfaction filled my chest at the dawning comprehension on Lucian's narrow face when his gaze darted from the ring to me, and then Drake. In the blink of an eye, he suddenly stood behind Drake and bent to grasp my vampire's clenched fist.

A flash of irritation crossed Drake's features when Lucian wrenched open his tensed fingers. The second ring fell from his grasp, but before it could drop to the floor, Lucian snatched it from thin air. Startled, I flinched when Lucian's figure made a blurred trail to kneel in front of the vampire in gold. Before the gaudy undead leader could reach for the offered ring, the one in crimson finally spoke.

"Domn Petru…" The rest of his words were too fast to catch, *damn my stupid brain!*

I glanced at Drake, who *could* understand them, but the only reaction I could glean was the curious furrow to his brow. Petru nodded, his expression neutral when he handed the larger ring back to Lucian, who scurried over to drop it in the expectant scarred hand of the crimson-caped vampire. An instant later, and the first ring that I'd dropped joined its pair.

"Descendant of Helsing," the vampire in silver addressed me, his curling brown locks utterly still while he spoke. "Magick has enabled your invasion thus far on the blood which ties you to our *voievod*—long rest his bartered soul." It was tacked on, like the sentiment was rehearsed, but the insincerity of his loyalty to Dracula's memory didn't ease the foreboding that prickled the hairs along my arms. "So shall this become *your* final resting place. Once you have been thoroughly excised for any information you possess that may be of interest."

"What about Drake?" My fingernails pressed painfully into the cold iron of my loose shackles, and my fingers shook. "What's going to happen to him?"

"The rebellion of an immortal is unprecedented." Irina turned, facing her five compatriots on her left. "As *legiuitor*, I propose endless calcification."

My eyes widened. All of Drake's blood would have to be drained from him in order for him to calcify. How long would he be forced to go without replenishing his body's source of blood? Horror took root in me as Drake's jaw clenched, appearing ready for the end.

"No!" This couldn't be happening. I couldn't let it happen. *Damn it, fortress, give me* something *to work with!* "You can't—" Staring down the most influential vampires on Earth, I struggled to come up with anything I could use. "I'll never tell you anything if you hurt him!"

Pain licked across my cheekbone, reverberating into my jaw the instant after Lucian's fist blurred at the corner of my eye. Even if I'd seen it coming, I wouldn't have been able to deflect. A stinging itch radiated down my neck, and I took a shallow breath. With my ears ringing, I glared up at the monstrous bastard as he straightened his embroidered vest.

"How I have longed to do that," Lucian muttered, his words strictly for my benefit considering his thick English. The Domnitori member in black spoke then, and by his cruel smirk, it wasn't in my favor. Drake's shackles rattled, drawing my attention to where dark blood ran from his forearms while he'd thrashed his skin through to the bone against the metal.

"*Te voi ucide*," he spat, seething with every precise pronunciation of each word.

None of the Domnitori showed concern, their cold exteriors unimpressed. All, except the one in crimson. Irina, Milica, Petru, Nikolai… The vampire in silver remained nameless, but his detached, shrewd gaze made beads of sweat roll down my neck. Something unsaid thickened in the stale air, smelling of death.

I itched for my machete, still in the grasp of the guard standing at ease to my left. Petru spoke softly, seemingly addressing his ruling party. They each stood so fast that I straightened up instantly, ready for them to advance on us, but then they left, one after another in a line. They didn't seem to be rushing, but they also weren't trying to conceal their supernatural speed.

My neck craned to follow the crimson one's exit, the rings somewhere on his person, but then he disappeared around the corner where the gargoyles stood guard over nothing and no one. Besides Drake, the only vampire that remained was Lucian. His satisfied sneer was accompanied by a parting line, but I had no clue what he said to Drake, his tone full of thinly-concealed excitement over our predicament.

Really, if I survived this, I was going to have to brush up on Romanian.

As luck would have it, Lucian strode down the long rug after the Domnitori. His departure from the throne room was quick, not having glanced at me once, like I was beneath his notice now. Left alone in the circular space with only the guards and the old sorceress, I did my best to take short breaths to disguise my fast heartbeat.

Whatever they'd planned next had reignited the terror behind Drake's eyes, but when his gaze met mine, his confusion at my calm shifted to understanding. Before the sorceress could raise her hand more than a fraction of an inch, Drake resumed thrashing in his restraints. Two of the guards who'd been standing over him jumped into action to hold him down, but Drake got his leg out from under him. His powerful kick caved in the armored chest of the nearest guard.

More guards rushed in, their attention entirely on Drake. The lycan on my left sheathed my machete using the belt around their breastplate, and reached to grasp their ax with both gauntlets, probably intending to cut off Drake's legs if they had to.

They wouldn't get that far.

Waiting as long as I could—to make sure the Domnitori and Lucian would be far enough away to keep out of earshot—I let go of my restraints. Relief poured through my aching fingers, doubled when I finally scratched that damned itch and reached for the handle of my machete. It pulled free from the guard's belt before the thud of my shackles hit the rug, but I didn't take my first shot at the guards.

Memories of being made helpless by Ezra's magick quickened my strides across the carpet toward the old crone, whose thin, wispy white eyebrows puckered with confusion. Her vision was obscured by the cataracts, but she clearly sensed my intent for 'first kill.' When she raised her hands, I slammed the sharpened edge of my blade down over the thin skin of her forearms. Human blood poured from the dismembered wrist, and the sorceress's mouth opened to form a chord of terror.

Except my blade was shoved through her throat before she could release a note. Utilizing the momentum of my thrust, I spun, and swung my blade across instead of pulling it out straight—just like Johann had taught me. It worsened the damage, and the old crone's head was hanging by half her neck by the time she dropped. Blood flowed over the steps to the thrones, and I kicked the sorceress's corpse down them with a booted foot.

The guards seemed stunned, whether by my newfound freedom or how quickly I'd killed someone, I didn't know. Everything at the edges of my vision was hazy, but I wouldn't let the shivering fear sink in. Weapon readied, I jumped over the body soaking in a puddle of blood, and landed in front of my own warden.

The lycan in armor had to back up to attempt a swing at me with their ax. Twisting the handle of my machete, I shoved the point upward using both hands and hooked my blade under the helmet before thrusting. Squelching accompanied baritone gurgles, blood streamed downward, and I withdrew my blade to face the five remaining guards.

Three surrounded Drake, still trying to subdue him while he twisted this way and that under the grasp of two. The third angled the point of their spear over his heart. Swallowing a scream, I moved in. The last two guards had stood unsure between measuring the danger I posed and helping the other three with Drake, but my action spurred theirs.

Almost too fast, they advanced to get between me and Drake. The whisper of a warning in the back of my mind made me duck at the last moment. A broadsword swung over my head, narrowly brushing the hair at the crown of my skull, and I had to roll aside to avoid the blunt impact of a mace hitting the rug where I'd been a moment ago.

When I jumped back up to my feet, I rushed to parry another swing from the broadsword, trying to force me farther from Drake. Their blade struck mine, and a shout tore through my throat as I *pushed*. Never would I have been able to overpower all of that bulk, but something in the very air of this place strengthened the fibers in my bones.

Especially once I accepted it as mine to wield.

Like the weapon between my hands that forced the armored guard back a step. Slashing my blade free, I ducked under the arm of the second guard. They hefted the mace while balancing their shield, but I snuck inside their space. Where they wouldn't be able to make a clear hit. The back of my neck prickled, and I raised my machete over my head to deflect a blow from the guard's elbow.

Metal skittered off the edge of my blade, but I was past their attempted barricade. I focused on Drake, tightening my grip on my machete when I glimpsed the spear pinned between his ribs. *At least he'd managed to keep them from piercing his heart.* The damage would heal. I didn't have time to think about anything else when I leaped for the now weaponless guard.

My chest collided against the guard's shoulder, and I held on while strengthening my grip on my machete. I climbed using my free arm, my legs gripping around their armored torso, careening the guard off-balance, and I quickly ripped the helmet off the guard's head. Stricken deep green eyes greeted mine.

Wonder and sickening peace settled over their haggard features, but I couldn't stop.

My muscles locked into action, and I slit the lycan's throat straight across, slicing through flesh and arteries. Their eyes rolled back fast, the brain now drained of blood. I scrambled to keep my balance when the body fell from under me. The two guards I'd managed to evade had caught up, both keeping their weapons between us. Neither dared to reach out.

Metal crunched when I awkwardly rolled off the man I'd killed. One of the guards had brought their mace down, right where I'd been on the dead guard's back. To my right, Drake aimed a well-timed kick for the back of one of his captor's knees.

That guard fell, landing hard, and I didn't waste the opportunity. With one of their hands attempting to hold Drake down, the other was clumsy with the sword they'd held to his throat—but I was on the other side. Crouched, I shoved my blade with all my might through the chainmail covering the weak point beneath the shoulder plate. Links of metal burst from the pressure of my thrust, scattering with tiny pings.

Twisting my wrist as I pushed, my machete's blade skewered right through the guard's chest. *Three down, three to go.* Except now, Drake had his right hand back. The chain connecting his shackles stretched taut as he grasped the shaft of the spear. Hoisting it out from him in a fluid motion before he angled the point and shoved it through the eye-hole of the wolf's head helmet belonging to the guard beside him.

Even if these guards hadn't been allowed to use lethal force given the Domnitori's commands, there wasn't time to risk, or hope that they would defect on our behalf. Only to take advantage of whatever luck we had left.

Then the remaining two guards reached us, and I stood to meet them. Calm settled into my bones, my higher thinking shut down. I breathed slow when I dodged a swing of the broadsword. They wouldn't beat me here, not at the steps of my disowned ancestor's throne.

Chest heaving, I bypassed the guard's defenses by ducking around their raised shield. They tried to spin in time, to keep me in front of them, but that damned armor made them slow. I crouched while the guard kept turning, trying to circle me, and then I dove between their legs to pop back up behind them.

The guard whirled, their weapon with them. Raising my left forearm to block, I winced at the sting of the broadsword's edge. Teeth gritted against the pain, I deflected the oncoming blade, slicing off several layers of my skin down to the muscle. A burning pulse seared my flesh in its wake. Maybe they weren't supposed to kill us, but if it was between being maimed or dealing the death blow, I chose the latter.

With a twist of my thrusting hand, the machete's blade scraped under the chin guard to blindly skewer the guard through the face. A slick sound accompanied the withdrawing of my blade. I lowered my weapon while the guard's body collapsed in a heap. Silence descended, and an increasingly familiar shiver caressed my spine.

The sensation drew my gaze to where Drake crouched over the guard he'd taken down. Blood coated his lips and chin, hovering over the torn neck of the lycan whose helmet had been ripped off along with their head. Nausea bubbled in the back of my throat, and I staggered a step away as Drake's figure blurred to reach my side.

Blood coated his fingers, but his steadying hands were gentle. Raven-dark eyes bore into mine, searching for who knew what. Carnage spread out around us. We were the last ones standing.

"Maria?" Drake's palm caressed my cheek, warmed by blood that wasn't his, and I jolted. "Are you injured?"

I shook my head, numbly glancing down at his arms, still encased in sigiled iron. My searching gaze flitted over each guard.

"Maria? Your restraints—" Drake's touch fell away as I retreated to snatch up the keys before shoving them into the mirrored hole.

"They just came apart," I mumbled, wiggling the key until the lock clicked open. Freed, Drake tossed the circlets of wrought-iron aside. His gaze fixed to my face while I averted my eyes from his. "Come on, we can't waste time…" I turned, hurrying to the doors framed on either side by the gargoyles. Drake followed me out on silent footfalls, but then caught my arm when I turned left to follow where the Domnitori had gone.

"Where are you going? The exit will be beyond—"

"One of them has the rings!" I hissed, desperately trying to hold it together. "Where did the scarred one go? Do we have a shot at getting him alone?"

Indecision flickered over Drake's blood-splattered features. "Most likely… Each member of the Domnitori resides in their own turret. To my memory, his wife is in the endless sleep."

I frowned. "Endless—"

"Some of our kind choose to 'sleep' when they are too cowardly to end their terrible existence more permanently," he hurried to explain. Then his lips pursed momentarily, expression grim.

"This does not mean that taking the rings back will be easy. Please, Maria—"

"You can't stop me." I glanced down at where his bloodstained hand touched me. Focusing on my deep inhale, I pushed his hand off. "Either you help me, and we both survive this, or we know what happens next." I refused to save us only to lose him again, not after this—after *everything*.

Tears threatened behind my stinging eyes, but my hope surged when his features softened. Nodding once, the hint of a smile tugged at the corners of his lips, the lycan's blood already drying on them.

"Have I ever once been able to sway your mind?"

"Nope."

His fingers wove between mine, and this time, I returned the sentiment. A tender tug pulled me into motion, and I started running on aching limbs to delve deeper into the fortress of death.

22

BLOOD WE'VE SHED

MY LUNGS BURNED WITH EVERY STEP I FORCED MY LEGS TO TAKE. STONE flooring underfoot became swathed in rich carpets when we crossed some invisible boundary that separated this part of the fortress from the rest. After the breakneck pace, I choked down air whenever Drake slowed to peer around corners, and listened for the sound of more guards.

Our path ahead stretched into shadow, but the silhouette of double doors solidified against the surrounding darkness. Without pause, Drake twisted the right handle and pushed it open. Frigid air poured out from within. Shivering, I crossed the threshold after Drake and stifled a groan. We stood on a level platform separating two sets of spiral staircases, one leading up, while the other descended into pitch-black mystery.

Drake ascended the steps. My haggard breathing kept me moving, but at the cost of alerting our enemies. Maybe that's why Drake slowed his pace. *Must be nice, not needing to breathe.*

"It is not much farther," Drake whispered, his voice like a sigh in the stagnant atmosphere.

"I'm fine," I grumbled, barely enunciating the words. Despite the bloody mess drying down Drake's chin and neck, it was good that he'd fed. One of us needed to be strong enough to face whatever came between us and those rings. Even with the fortress at my fumbling command, I could barely protect myself, let alone him.

As I climbed the stone stairs, I struggled to keep the images from flashing back in the lull. *No*—I had to focus. I could rationalize the morality of mine and Drake's actions later.

"Where in the fortress are we?" Through so many twists and turns, I could hardly believe Drake remembered the way after two centuries of being absent.

"The western turret. It is closest to the underground, where Mihai can most easily preside over the lycans he commands."

"That *he* commands?" I balked, but shut my mouth with a snap when we reached the floor above.

"Yes." Drake strode ahead, soundless across the ruby red carpet stretching the length of a much shorter hallway. Three doors existed on the floor, two opposite each other and a set of double doors at the very end. Vases decorated the low end tables like bookends beside the hinges of each door.

Artwork hung on the stone walls over china dishes and glass sculptures whose silhouettes were too vague in the oppressive darkness to distinguish. Under different circumstances, like warmth and light, the passage might have been cozy. The hairs on the back of my neck prickled, and I raised my machete.

We stood before the doors at the end, its carved trim set with real rubies and diamonds in an abstract constellation, reflecting nothing, but shimmering all the same. Drake silently grasped the wrought-iron knob and twisted. No creak followed the door's swing inward to reveal a sitting room beyond.

Armchairs were poised on either side of a writing desk. A grand piano took up the space by the left wall, beneath a painting covered with a thin sheet. Between them, a makeshift couch was constructed of carved wood, and floral-patterned cushions swelled along the frame. I went to take another step, but Drake's raised arm halted me.

My gaze followed his, to the figure who stood in front of a long tapestry depicting a landscape of rolling hills. His back was to us, with maybe thirty feet between us. When he half-turned, his scarred features deepened the shadows lining his face. His low, gravelly voice spoke in a dialect even more ancient than Drake's.

Weaponless, but never one to show weakness, Drake took a step forward.

"We would not want to wake your *soție*, if she ever stirs from her slumber anymore."

"You provoke me, Ignatius." Mihai's sunken eyes settled on my vampire, not once glancing my way. "You forget your place."

"My only wish is for survival. It was you who taught me the importance of perseverance." A muscle twitched in Drake's cheek, a blink-and-miss-it smile at the irony.

"Survival without a cause is fruitless," Mihai whispered, his accent thick but decipherable. "You risk your blessed immortality for a woman. Has history taught you nothing?"

"Time has been a cruel teacher." Drake's gaze never wavered as he took another step. "Alas, I agree. Without a cause, bloodshed means nothing. I am fortunate to have found such a worthy purpose to risk it all." The corner of his lip curled into a smirk.

"You intend to defeat *me*, Ignatius?" Bleak disbelief colored Mihai's tone. "You truly believe you can?"

"Perhaps not alone," Drake agreed, his right hand slowly clenching into a fist. "Today, I am not."

Those whispers in the back of my head returned, urging my feet to move a split second before Mihai hurled his concealed dagger. It soared inches from my left arm, but it would have hit my heart if I'd been too slow. Something crashed behind me, but I didn't turn to see what. Between one breath and the next, Drake snapped the leg off a nearby low table and wielded it like a makeshift stake.

Mihai met Drake head on, using the couch to gain the high ground when Drake advanced. The older vampire blocked Drake's thrust with the stake, and his gnarled meaty fingers gripped the wood until it splintered. Faster than I'd ever watched two vampires move, the two fought with a combination of skill and familiarity with each other's defensive style that I recognized from having brawled with my cousins.

Forced to stoop to avoid Mihai's knee from hitting his chest, Drake quickly pulled the wooden rim of the couch. It tipped forward, making Mihai leap from his position, only to land on the floor between us. Mihai's crimson cape unfurled, a purposeful distraction as he reached for me.

I ducked aside, raising my machete in time to catch the vampire's fingertips with the edge of my blade. Dark blood dripped down his palm, and his focus snapped to me. Even with the fortress's magick, I was still human. Too fast for me to dodge, Mihai's knee rose to counter my escape attempt. The impact hit my ribs, bone to bone, and I choked.

I swung outward with my machete to ward him off, dimly registering the crash of shattering glass. Drake stepped in behind Mihai, a broken bottle in his grasp, and slashed. The older vampire spun, and Drake's eyes widened as Mihai took the hit across his throat. Blood poured from the new wound, but Mihai's expression stayed neutral, his blurring hands moving to grip Drake's right arm.

In one swift twist, Mihai broke Drake's bones with a sickening snap. His forearm hung at a right angle as the broken bottle fell from his grasp to the floor. I had less than a second, but gravity did half the work for me when I dropped into a crouch and slashed my blade across the backs of Mihai's knees. Only one of his hamstrings was severed, but it threw him off-balance.

He staggered, and Drake took the opportunity to grasp Mihai's shoulder and pull him further from me. Drake's fingers dug into Mihai's flesh while he kicked out the vampire's last leg. Unable to inhale enough air, I fought rising panic and burning muscles to stand and plunge my blade through Mihai's chest.

I didn't hesitate to pull the weapon free, bleeding Mihai out faster to weaken him. Even with his torn heart oozing gritty dark blood down his chest, it wouldn't be enough to incapacitate him. So I aimed my next blow for his throat, but Mihai's hand shot out to grip my blade. A feral sneer contorted his scarred face, yanking my machete—and me along with it—into his clutches.

At the same moment Drake tried to pull him away from me, Mihai grasped Drake's broken arm, and yanked hard. My vampire stumbled, bringing all three of us down in his attempt to keep Mihai's snapping teeth from tearing into my throat. The vampire leader's free hand gripped my arm, and I screamed, the sound strangled and frustrated while I tried to get my feet out from under me. Abandoning my blade, despite everything inside me demanding I hold on, I flung my arm out instinctively to push Mihai away.

Mihai grabbed my blade, and tossed it aside like the weapon meant nothing. Then the monster was on top of me. My head hit the carpet hard, terror jumbling my thoughts while Mihai forced my forearm down to the floor beside my throbbing skull. The arm I held between us felt thin and fragile when he pressed in, but any triumph in his eyes was overshadowed by violent hunger.

Chills racked my spine. I inhaled a sharp breath. Drake appeared behind Mihai, my machete in his grip. In one swift slice, Mihai's head slid from atop his shoulders. Cold grimy liquid splashed down my front, and I sputtered when rivulets of blood hit my mouth. Drake flung Mihai's decapitated body off me, and quickly knelt on the floor beside me to haul me up into his arms.

With a ragged gasp, I wrapped my shaking arms around him and buried my face against his chest. Iron and decay hung thick in the air, freezing my thoughts until Drake pulled back just enough to stare into my eyes, his gaze shifting to look me over from head to toe.

"Are you alright?" He rocked back on his heels, and I sat straighter.

"The rings," I blurted, frowning at Drake with my machete in his grasp. He handed it back before standing in a blur that left me woozy to watch. When he offered his hand next, I fit my equally bloody palm against his before he pulled me upright.

"We have them." He dropped back to crouch beside Mihai's body, and rifled through the vampire's vest pocket without even a glance at the severed head several feet away. After straightening up, his figure blurred to my side, quickly ushering us toward the doors. "We must go, while we still can."

"I'm right behind you."

Without looking back, we fled the room's destruction, pausing only long enough to close the double doors behind us.

By the time we reached the winding staircase, Drake had taken my free hand. He hurried my descent, until I was jumping two or three steps at a time. Whatever noise I made didn't seem to matter anymore. Drake urged me on like we were running on borrowed time. Fatigue slowed me down, no matter how hard I fought to keep my breaths even and footfalls sure.

Goosebumps rose along my arms in spite of the cold sweat beading my forehead, trickling down my temples and making my scalp itch. Too soon, a chorus of clamoring bells echoed through the halls. Reverberating peals of the high alarm made me squint, my eyes watering, and I struggled not to clap my hands over my ears.

If I wasn't breathless from sprinting, I would have asked Drake what it meant, but I could already guess. We'd left just as bloody of a mess in the throne room as we had in Mihai's quarters. It was only a matter of time before our escape was discovered. Our turns began to look familiar, which meant Drake was dragging me back the way we came.

"But the guards—" I managed to choke out, but Drake shook his head.

"Our only route is the way we have come. They will have block-aded all other paths to the exit."

How many more guards could I face before my body gave out? I stumbled over my own footfalls, trying to keep my momentum going. Another bend, and the hallway widened, the ceiling slanting higher. The silhouette of the gargoyles guarding the throne room came into view.

Just as we reached the open space, and Drake pulled me around like he was about to pick me up and carry me, the hammering sound I thought was my racing heart turned out to be getting *closer*. We both paused, listening while the stomping of metal boots across the stone floors was joined by distant snarls.

The lycans had transformed. I looked to Drake, who glanced up and down the hall with such uncertainty behind his dark eyes that I could easily read the truth on his face. When his gaze found mine, understanding passed between us.

We wouldn't be able to fight the next horde and win.

"I'm sorry," I whispered, glued to the center of the space while the enemy closed in. Drake shook his head, his expression vehement as he took my left hand between his.

"Not now. Do not lose your hope, after everything—"

"Drake…" My grip on my machete loosened, my right arm lowering until my weapon hung limp at my side. I raised my left hand to trace the sharp plane of his cheekbone. From the corner of my eye, the first row of guards came into view, their silhouettes becoming solid out of the darkness. Frenzied waist-high shapes sprinted across the marble from beneath swaying metal arms, claws skittering to echo alongside the lycans' growls.

Tears stung the backs of my eyes, and one finally escaped down my cheek despite my best efforts to hold it in.

I didn't want to die—not like this, when we were so close… Rooted to the spot, I raked in a shuddering sob as Drake's cold hand placed something in mine. Looking down through my blurry vision, I found the smaller of the two rings in my palm.

The larger was already placed on Drake's left ring finger, and when I didn't make a move, he slid mine on for me. A flash of light circled the golden band, illuminating our faces in the darkness for one brief second. Solidarity seemed to spread between us when he turned his back to mine, never letting go of my hand.

I inhaled deep and raised my machete. Figures blurred behind the advancing mob of brainwashed lycans. Our execution would have an audience, and it sickened me. Pain mingled with rage at the injustice of our imminent death. Because my family would never know where my final resting place would be.

Even if I did go down swinging, in fabricated glory like Grandpa had always aggrandized, I would never see Johann again. Never again feel the comfort of his big bear hugs, and his rough-hewn pride in me that even my dumbest decisions couldn't expunge from his enormous heart. There was emotional distance between us, but we were always held together by the glue of our family surrounding us.

Uncle Alaric, Aunt Susan, and my cousins, who were more like my own siblings, having grown up in the same church. Their love meant everything, the only reason why I survived not only Mom's death, but the mistakes I'd made last year. If it wasn't for them, and Everly, Caleb—all the Tsosies, as much my family as the people I was related to by blood—I wouldn't be who I was today.

Maybe if I'd been more like Linda, Elias's oldest, and ignored the calling to hunt monsters altogether, I could've survived this legacy. Except, with Drake at my back and ready to fight to our death, the choice to battle for what I believed in or stick to the sidelines had always been obvious. Because that was all it came down to, even if it meant abandoning the warm Albuquerque sunshine for the dark catacombs of this ancient magick fortress.

Saliva flecked to the marble floor as the nearest transformed werewolves ran toward us at full bore, their eerie too-human eyes focused on mine with no hesitation to make the kill. If I could help it, I wanted my last thoughts to be of home. How the heat would beat down, mercilessly drying out the earth until only the toughest of flora learned to survive the desert. I'd taken it for granted.

This time, I wanted to do more than survive—I wanted to *live*.

An explosive rumble of cascading stones pierced the air. My eyes widened, my mouth popping open when the gargoyles on either side sprang to life. On my right, the gargoyle wielding a stone staff whipped its curved edge against the three transformed lycans closest to us.

Blood splattered the walls as tufts of fur were ripped away from flesh by the enormous gargoyle's unyielding advance, leaving crushed canine limbs and caved-in skulls in the wake of its massacre. Behind me, a similar sound of savagery echoed back. My arm holding my machete shook, and I glanced over my shoulder to lock eyes with Drake. His gaze was awed, but not frightened. Then his hand gripped mine, the pressure too firm to be reassuring.

I swung my head back around to stare down the hall, where the gargoyle on my side met the oncoming army head on. Exclamations rang around the room, and Drake tugged me into motion. A resonant crack hit my eardrums, making me stagger. I peered through the doorway to the throne room on my right. At its epicenter, the tall onyx throne behind the lesser six had shifted. A huge fissure ran down its stone structure, leaving the seat backing's highest edges crumbling while a rumble shook the fortress beneath our feet.

"Run, Maria!" Drake's shout zinged through my head, returning me to the moment a split second before a piece of the ceiling broke off in a huge stone chunk. It crashed against the marble behind me, but I didn't look back to assess the damage.

With the other gargoyle now preoccupied by the hall of enemies Drake had intended to face down, a path to escape was slowly being revealed. *This couldn't be happening,* but through the shock, I forced my aching legs to sprint in Drake's wake. Our joined hands had him pulling me faster than I could move, and I stumbled, but Drake's focus was on assessing our surroundings.

Another archway came loose from above when the gargoyle flung an armored lycan into it. Rubble rained down as dust stuck to my sweat-soaked skin, but I held my burning breath to keep from choking on it. Whatever army the Domnitori had at their disposal within the fortress was quickly being decimated, thanks to the gargoyles whose stonework bodies were now coated in a warpaint of blood.

Chaos reigned, but Drake and I were easily obscured by the dust and debris piling up while he led me through the corridors beyond. The fortress still shook, making me wobble until I was clinging to Drake's hand for balance. My next shaky inhale of stale air burned in my lungs, the exertion blazing my stomach by the time we reached the final door.

The hallway on either side was unfocused around me, my gaze trained on the iron handle I recognized. Without delay, Drake pushed the door open with brute strength. Wood slammed against the stone while the door creaked on its hinges, and my breath exploded out of me at the sight of the mirror across the macabre sitting room.

Knowing what was coming, I gulped down air and threw myself at the mirror. After having accidentally taken in Mihai's blood, the enchantment worked its magick and let me through. Ice embraced every inch of my flesh. My nerves screamed for re-lief, but I was mentally prepared for the onslaught. What could have been seconds, or minutes later, I finally fell forward into the barren room beyond.

I flung out my hands to catch myself, and released my grip on my machete an instant before Drake's familiar cool hands caught me around the waist. The clatter of my blade hitting the stone floor echoed while Drake pulled me tight against him. His cold hands clung to me, and I threw my arms around him to hold him equally as tight. Heart hammering, my eyes briefly closed as I buried my face against his chest.

His hysterical chuckle was my only warning before Drake lifted me up into the air and spun us around in a circle. An insane smile spread across my lips, and a giggle climbed my throat by the time he'd set me back down. With his hands on my waist, Drake leaned in to press his forehead to mine.

"We ought to still be running, love." So close, his whisper shifted the tangled hair around my face, tickling my chin.

"We did it." *Surprised* couldn't come close to describing how I felt, but it was probably plain on my face when I looked up to gaze into Drake's eyes.

"*You* did it." When Drake smiled, my chest flooded with warmth.

This—it was all worth it. Tears welled in my eyes, pouring down my cheeks with every blink. Drake's grin slid from his face, replaced by concern. "What—Are you hurt?"

All I could do was shake my head. Inhaling a stuttered breath, I scrubbed the tears from my face.

"I don't know what I'm feeling, but at least I'm alive *to* feel it."

Sympathy and understanding shone behind Drake's eyes, and he nodded. Without another word, I leaned heavily against him as we took our first steps toward the stairs—to freedom. I even let Drake carry my machete as we left the miserable fortress of the undead behind us.

— 23 —

FEELS LIKE FOREVER

SILKEN SHEETS KEPT ME SNUG AND SLOW TO WAKE. ALTHOUGH WARM beneath a heavy blanket, dull aches gnawed across every inch of my body. When I tried to roll over, I winced, and stretched my arm out to find empty space beside me. My eyes squeezed, still closed, as I frowned and felt more freely. *Nope, Drake wasn't in bed.*

I forced my sticky eyelids apart, blinking several times. Compared to the fortress, the darkness surrounding me was thin and easy to peer through. A glance at the closed red and gold embroidered curtains confirmed that it was nighttime, or early morning. How long had I been asleep for? Sighing, I sank a little deeper into the mattress of the four-poster bed.

At the center of the room was a light fixture whose visible bulbs became a comforting reminder of our return to the modern world. Exposed wood panels lined the walls, and the elegant stone fireplace opposite the bed still glowed with embers. Memories surged to the forefront of my thoughts despite wishing to delay facing everything that happened.

To distract myself, I focused on replaying more recent events. Like how we'd gotten from the ruins outside Poenari Castle to this much smaller, and thankfully cozy, castle. It hadn't taken long for us to find a road, and a passing car whose driver was swiftly charmed into giving us a ride. Exhausted and overloaded, the foreign voices filtering in over the radio had lulled me to sleep in the backseat.

I'd woken up briefly when Drake carried me inside this deserted castle. Like something from a dream, the place was perfectly pristine. Grandiose gardens and grasslands surrounded it, almost as ethereal as the vibrant fields of the Summerland. Nobody was home, but that hadn't stopped Drake from entering. Blissful sleep had pulled me back under shortly after getting to the bedroom.

My mouth didn't feel like sandpaper, so I must've woken up at some point to drink water. Except my skin still felt grimy, and the idea of centuries-old dust stuck in my ratted hair finally encouraged me to get up. I inhaled a hiss through my teeth while gripping the sheets to help leverage myself up. Once I scooched to the edge of the bed, my hands fell onto my lap to relieve my aching shoulders.

The ring on my left hand glinted, reflecting the dying embers in the fireplace. Curious, I wiggled my fingers. Somehow, the ring fit perfectly, but maybe that was woven into its magickal creation. From this point on, as long as I wore the ring, no sorcerer could scry for me. Since Drake wore the matching pair, he was truly free. For the first time since he'd died.

I could go home. Better yet, Drake could come with me. Joy flooded my fast-beating heart. Sure, the monsters still knew the region where I lived, but what were they going to do? Knock on every door until they found me? The second we caught wind of the undead within our city limits, my whole family would be on alert, and we'd fry the fucks first.

Smiling, I moved through the thick scabs stinging along my forearm and the bruises smattered over my body. My disgusting sweat-and-blood-soaked clothes had thankfully come off at some point, which meant using the blanket like a cocoon to keep the chill off my skin.

I carefully tested my weight on my sore ankles. Dried blood crusted my socks, but the sensation of the soft rug underfoot was a small reprieve. My soles felt like I'd walked over hot coals, but I gritted my teeth and slowly stood. Past the handcrafted wooden dresser and equally exquisite vanity, I approached the refreshingly plain door.

It opened with ease into a pleasant hall, and the long yellow rug that ran the length kept my feet warm on my walk down. Latticed windows lined the right wall, with nothing to obscure the scenery of lush hills and swaying flowers dancing beneath pale moonlight. A crescent-shaped moon graced the cloudless sky, illuminating the forest beyond the pastures.

It took effort to turn away from the view as I reached a series of stairs, leading down to the ground floor below. I gulped at the thought of descending any more steps, but braved a deep breath before placing my palm along the thick banister. Between the floors, a landing overlooked the story below, and my attention was drawn to the large portrait on the wall beside me.

I gripped the banister as my brow furrowed, taking a long look at the subjects. *Damn, the resemblance was uncanny.* An obviously wealthy family had been painted before a vague backdrop. The older man's tidy beard had wisps of gray showing, but his eyes were painted nearly the same black as his hair.

Beside him, the woman seated on the stool was a head shorter, and her long brown hair was pinned back beneath the bonnet-like hairpiece she wore. A little girl stood prim and proper in front of the woman, her dark hair formed into ringlets and her expression disgruntled. On the floor sat a much younger boy, but he was dressed as exceptionally well as the rest.

Straight black hair touched his ears, but the look on his face seemed unusually mature for a kid so young. It felt like a portal into another lifetime, and I couldn't help but stare at every aspect. From the early 18th century garb to the muted colors in the background, bringing out the family's faces in bright contrast. What it must have been like to be alive then—

"I would offer you a penny for your thoughts." Drake's voice pulled my attention to the floor below. "Though I am afraid I hold no coins." No longer covered in blood, Drake stood barefoot at the base of the stairs, his black hair still wet where it lay flat just beneath his ears. The clean black pants and button-up shirt suited his lean muscular frame, and I stifled a pang of jealousy. *What I wouldn't do to get my hands on some fresh clothes.*

"I was just thinking it's a beautiful picture." I faced the portrait in question, but soon felt his presence at my side even before he replied.

"It was in a time when we did not have flash photography," Drake said. The glib way he put it made me smile.

"So, that's you?" I pointed to the boy in the frame, glancing at Drake as he nodded. Except his gaze was equally glued to the picturesque depiction of his childhood.

"Yes. The Drake family were never quite royalty, nor kings of any nation. Though our family tree has stretched across the European continent, my branch in particular resided in Romania—Wallachia, as it was known then."

"So, this place…" I vaguely waved around us. "This is *your* castle?" Now that I thought about it, it would be pretty bizarre to crash in some stranger's home.

"It belongs to the descendants of my aunt, Adelina." He pointed at the girl in the painting, his tone relaxed when he continued, "The man was my grandfather, Petru Drake. His first marriage had been to a woman named Lidia, who bore my mother. Lidia died not long after. From what, I am unsure, there were many ailments at the time. The woman here is Olga, and Adelina is her child."

"And…nobody will look for us here?" I craned my neck to look over my shoulder, glimpsing the moon between passing clouds through the windows on the floor above.

"We will not stay long enough for them to have the chance," Drake answered, recapturing my full attention. "My forefathers owned several estates, and I doubt any of the Domnitori will have memorized where each child taken had come from. Even if they decide to search the records, ones I am uncertain even exist, we will already have left. Although they will be preoccupied with restoring the fortress first and foremost. And, now that it has been left open, they are most likely snooping through the bedchambers of Dracula."

Images of Dracula's antechamber flashed through my mind's eye, and I glanced up at the portrait on the wall beside us while remembering the one hanging behind Dracula's statue.

"What was your mom's name again?" I whispered, embarrassed at the slip in my memory, but he didn't seem bothered by the question.

"Ileana. Though she did not go by 'Drake' after I was born. The Domnitori only knew her as Ileana Petrescu," Drake explained, and his brow creased. "Dracula often chose his ilk from what he considered superior bloodlines, whether they be his inner circle or the children he stole for his army. I did not learn until after both of their deaths that it was most likely my birth mother who requested I be brought to the fortress."

"Did Dracula know?" My voice came out rough, and I cleared my throat. "That Ileana was your mom, I mean."

Drake's eyebrows rose, speculative. "I cannot be sure. I never spoke with Vlad Dracula as an equal. None of us did."

I bit my lip, remorse and regret for the actions of my ancestor churning my empty stomach. "How can you stand to be around me?"

"What?" Drake faced me, so confused that I could've kicked myself for not elaborating.

"Helsing killed them both, didn't he? I wouldn't blame you for being resentful toward my family for that. Even if it did happen centuries ago. You still had to live it."

Surprise overshadowed his confusion, but kindness won out when his features softened and he took my hand in his.

"Much time has passed since then, and when I have grieved for the family I never had, it rarely included Ileana. I do not hold anything against you and yours. At the end of their existence, they were monsters. Regardless of who they had been before the transformation."

It was hard to imagine the lifetimes that Drake had survived, and the perspective that must've given him. If anything happened to my family… Even if they had become monsters, I wasn't sure how long I'd need to recover from losing them. The realization hit me like a brick wall at ninety-miles-an-hour. *Selfish*—that's what I was for hiding things from them.

Because deep down, I knew they would have gone to the ends of the Earth to get me back.

Disbelief must have been obvious on my face, but Drake's gentle touch as he brushed a strand of curling hair behind my ear melted the tension from my jaw. My gaze returned to the little girl in the painting, and my curiosity resurged.

"Did you ever meet your aunt again? After you were turned."

Drake shrugged, but his lips pursed when he directed his attention to tracing the back of my hand.

"No, never in truth. For years, I watched her from afar. Once, I attended an evening party that she hosted with her husband. Of course, I did not introduce myself. It was enough to know that she was happy, fulfilled."

"How come you never came clean to her about who you were?"

"There were many reasons." His raven-dark eyes bore into mine. "As you are aware, there is a creed of secrecy handed down from the Domnitori. It would have been impossible to enter her life without explaining my absence, or else fabricating a story that would have led to my being reinstated as the family heir."

"What if you just pretended to be someone else? Charmed her, or something? So she wouldn't tell anyone."

The sadness swirling in my heart was met by Drake's genuine interest, but not a hint of judgment showed through his answer.

"If it were your family, would you want them only to know you by a lie?"

Scrunching my nose at my stupidity, I fidgeted on my feet and shook my head. Despite what Drake told me in the hovel outside the fortress, it had been hard to imagine how lonely a vampire's existence would be. For the first time in my life, I sympathized with the undead I've hunted and destroyed. If I'd been cut off from the outside world, brainwashed since childhood and raised into a secret occult society, would I have had the strength to break away?

The alternative was to stay with the only people who'd understand, that I could be myself with. Even if it meant committing atrocities to avoid being lonely.

"Were you really alone? For all those years…" A ridiculous pang of jealousy struck my chest when Drake shook his head.

"Not always. You have met Winston. Aiden has also been a long-time friend of mine."

"The faery solicitor." I scoffed, and Drake openly laughed, the easy sound warming my ears.

"He is far more trustworthy than he seems, although his methods can be a tad…roundabout."

"That's one way to put it," I muttered, but couldn't hold back my smile. "At least his meddling put us together, even if you have had to save my ass every two seconds."

"Excuse me? If not for you, then I would have been drained of blood and left to suffer within the fortress—permanently."

"That was just luck." I shook my head, blushing under his intense stare of disagreement. "If I wasn't a descendant, then neither of us would have survived."

"Is it worthwhile to consider what could have been? I have spent many years yearning for the chance at a human life. Yet, with you, I have felt more like a person than I have since I was one."

"You are a person." I took his hand, and leaned in until our lips met. The kiss was meant to be brief, but when I went to pull away, his free hand rose to cup the nape of my neck and held me in place. A quick inhale parted my lips, and he took advantage of the opening.

Unhurried, I wrapped one arm over his shoulder and around his neck. Space still existed between us, but barely an inch. There was comfort in the way he kissed me, like he meant to savor it. The trail his fingers made down my spine brought on a delicious shiver. His touch glided along my aches and pains, easing every one. The light pressure of his lips moving over mine slowed, and I sighed into the air between us when his mouth freed mine.

"It's hard to believe, isn't it?" I laughed, and the corners of his mouth curved into a smile. "You're free—*we're* free. Finally."

"Finally," Drake echoed softly, and I relaxed into his embrace.

I inhaled deeply, breathing him in, but it was easy to ignore the underlying hint of death coursing through his veins. The ring on my finger caught the glow from the electric sconces along the wall. As I fiddled with the metal, I recalled the inscription against my skin.

So I was human and the man I loved wasn't—not entirely, anyway—*so what?* We'd already escaped the deadliest place on Earth, and *won.* Whatever came next, I wanted to believe we could handle it—together. Nothing was certain in this life, not with the legacy I carried, but the feeling nestling into my heart felt pretty damn close. Because there wasn't anyone else I'd rather fight for my life alongside.

Even if it meant embracing this cursed existence for all eternity, or whatever time we had left of it.

MORE THAN ENOUGH

IT PROBABLY WOULD'VE BEEN QUICKER TO CATCH A CAB BACK FROM THE Albuquerque Sunport—after the five-hour flight from New York— but I didn't mind heading to Drake's place first. Especially since the leather passenger seat of his white 1978 Aston Martin V8 Vantage *was* luxuriously comfortable. If anything, the detour gave me another excuse to put off the impending reunion which had my stomach in a tangle of nerves.

At least I finally learned where Drake lived—a little suburb in San Jose—right across from the Rail Runner tracks, *go figure.* The indicator blinked on, and I sucked in a breath when we got off of I-40 at the 157A exit. Home wasn't far now, and I slowly closed my eyes to prepare myself.

Really, after everything I'd been through, *this* was what worried me?

Somehow, the careful manipulation of airline security— when Drake and I made our journey across international borders—was less stressful. As much as I hated that vampires could charm people, it happened to come in pretty handy. It was also sort of amusing watching Drake go to great lengths to cover every inch of his skin when we traveled during daylight.

Now, with his window tint dark enough to make me wonder about its legality, he was able to relax in the driver's seat with nothing more than a fitted black T-shirt, jeans, and his usual sunglasses and black Yankees cap. Apparently, the baseball team had been Winston's preference, which I'd learned during our two-day layover in Lagrangeville.

Shortly after I'd gotten to Winston's beautiful, hot-as-hell house, I'd asked to use a phone. Johann had picked up after three rings, and my voice almost failed me at the melancholy saturating his tone. Our conversation had been brief, mainly spent reassuring him that I was alive and would be home soon. I couldn't find the words to explain everything over the phone. Right after we'd hung up, I called Everly next. She was my soundboard while I rambled off what happened to me over the last week, since my sudden disappearance.

My eyes squeezed shut as I exhaled a slow breath, and rested my right elbow on the door frame. Damn it, I was already on the verge of tears. Just remembering my promise to be back in a few days was gutting. The cool familiar hand that covered mine helped to ground me, and I blinked fast. Beside me, Drake's compassion shone behind his usual stoicism. His palm caressed my knuckles until my fist unclenched. I hadn't even realized I'd been so tense.

His brow furrowed. "Will you be alright?"

"Yeah. Eventually. Once I get this over with."

The left turn onto Don Fernando Avenue had my heart rate back into gymnastics-mode. Past the park I'd grown up playing on, we seamlessly transitioned onto Don Quixote Drive. My church's steeple rose above the surrounding suburban roofs like a beacon of hope. So why did it feel like I was about to become lost at sea?

"You can stop here." I gripped Drake's hand in mine as he slowed to a stop three houses down. Loud reverberations from the car's idling drowned out my pulse beating in my eardrums.

"Would you prefer that I come inside with you? I could attest to the truthfulness of your story."

It wasn't the first time he'd offered, but now more than ever, I was tempted to accept. Instead, I shook my head. It wasn't whether or not my family believed me that I was worried about. Actually, I wasn't totally sure what had me so scared, but the image of Drake walking in with me only to be attacked by a group of highly trained hunters didn't put me at ease.

"I need to explain things first. Give them a chance to process it all before they meet you." My hesitation at the prospect of introducing my undead boyfriend to my family of monster hunters seemed to make Drake's small, barely-there smile return.

"That is most likely for the best. However…" He leaned in, his hand grasping mine only to pull me closer, and my breath hitched. "If you are ever in need of me, I will be there."

"My own personal guardian vampire." A grin tugged up my lips an instant before Drake kissed me.

The slow, subtle pressure of his mouth moving over mine managed to suppress the panic circling my heart, only to replace it with the kind of desperation that left me dizzy. As Drake pulled away, the sweet aftertaste of his tongue still tingling against my lips, I dreaded whatever fallout I was about to face.

Because the bombshell I would be dropping on my tight-knit family unit might have been explosive—the knowledge that vampires have remained organized despite Dracula's defeat—but it wouldn't compare to telling them about Drake. I didn't care if they believed me about everything else, but the concept of a vampire with a morality complex was a hard pill to swallow.

Hell, I'd been skeptical, too. It took witnessing his actions to protect me, to save me time and again to finally get it through my thick skull. Air conditioning cooled my warm face, moving strands of my hair to tickle my chin. Drake caught the wispy curls like it was second nature, and I smiled.

Whatever happened next, I trusted Drake—with my heart and life both.

"I'll see you later, okay?" It hurt to leave him, but the pull of home was growing by the second. Drake nodded before leaning back into his own seat, and my fingers paused on the door handle.

"I wish you luck," Drake said, his smile more encouraging than a shot of espresso.

Steeling my resolve, I climbed out of the two-door car and started down the road toward the cul-de-sac. The engine to Drake's car rumbled when he put it in gear, but I didn't turn back to watch it drive away. As the white walls of the church loomed closer, I tried to focus on exactly what I would tell everyone.

Thankfully, I'd been able to get those ducks in a row last night during the four-hour long phone call with Everly. It felt good to get the raw, undiluted version out with someone who had only ever been understanding. I would have called Caleb after, but my voice had gone thin from all the crying.

At the chain-link fence surrounding our property, a loud bark startled me just as I touched the gate's latch. Stake bounded around the side of the church from the back garden, and I grinned as the gate snapped shut behind me. Kneeling on the coarse grass in a pair of denim jeans that still needed some stretching out, I accepted every affectionate lick Stake had to give.

My face scrunched to avoid the slobber, but I laughed while patting our Jack Russell Terrier until he settled down. I managed a few scratches behind his ears, while his tail thumped heavily, before the front door opened, and Johann's broad frame emerged.

"What's going on, Stake—" Blue-gray eyes locked onto mine, and I stared back at the man I'd inherited mine from. No matter how much I'd cried yesterday, and kept composed all through the flight, the waterworks started up before I managed to stand.

"I'm home." Damn it, I was blubbering even before Johann raced across the front lawn.

Strong arms wound around my shoulders, pulling me in tight until I coughed through my sob. My arms barely made it around the bulk of his torso, and I inhaled the strong scent of sawdust mixed with lacquer coming off Johann's gray shirt.

"Johann? I was wondering…" Aunt Susan's voice cut off, and I peered through wet lashes to find my aunt standing in the doorway. Her mouth opened as she clutched the crucifix hanging from her necklace. "Oh, Maria! Thank the Lord, you're back." Aunt Susan practically leaped from the stoop to cross the lawn.

Johann took a knowing step back before I was wrapped up in Aunt Susan's warm embrace. Her lean arms hugged around my neck, and I smiled as the sense of homecoming overwhelmed everything else. When she pulled away, her dark blue eyes narrowed in concern. Her delicately worn hands cradled either side of my tear-stained face, looking more closely.

"What happened to you?" Her whispered words were gentle, but I couldn't find my voice for several seconds.

I swallowed hard. "It's a long story." Glancing down, I inhaled a stuttered breath a moment before Johann's large hand clasped my back to steer me toward the church. I scrubbed at my eyes to clear my vision while crossing the threshold, and immediately locked gazes with Andrew, staring back from the family room couch.

"Holy shit, she's back." Without delay, he hopped over the edge and skirted the recliner to run for the door that led into the hall. Poking his head around the corner, he shouted, "Guys! Come into the living room—Maria's back!"

"She's back?" Olivia's high-pitched shriek came before several heavy footfalls. Then her small oval face framed by short blonde hair appeared around the doorway. The messy tangle of her bangs had two curlers in place, but she ran for me without bothering to fix the one almost falling out.

A laugh crackled out of my chest right before Olivia reached my open arms. Her sturdy short arms squeezed me tight around the waist. With my arms over her shoulders, I easily saw over her head when Ethan strolled in from the hall. Uncle Alaric was only a step behind, his smile grand when he went to pat his older brother on the back.

Blinking to clear my eyes, I glimpsed the bit of moisture building along my father's salt and pepper eyelashes. Johann's gruff nod seemed to be all he could manage, but Uncle Alaric smoothly turned to me. "We're glad to have you back, kid."

"It's good to be back," I said, and meant every word. Olivia finally pulled away, her blue-gray eyes wide.

"Where have you been? We've been so worried! Was it another bender, or—"

Unreasonably afraid that she was about to suggest another rehab center, I took her hands in mine, giving them a shake for emphasis.

"It's not like that, I *promise*." I looked around the room, meeting the gaze of everyone in my family. "That's not what happened."

"Then what *did* happen?" Ethan folded his arms and leaned back against the couch that Andrew had taken up residency on again. "Because I had a bet going with Andy about which drugs you were on, and if I'm right, I get a hundred bucks, so—"

"I don't think now's the time, Ethan," Andrew muttered under his breath, glaring daggers at his youngest sibling. Unaffected, Ethan shrugged and raised his eyebrows. Nobody acknowledged the accusations. Everyone was waiting for me to say something.

Suddenly, I was at a loss for words.

"I don't know where to begin," I stammered, drawing a blank until Aunt Susan placed her hand over mine. Releasing Olivia from my grasp, I let my aunt lead me to the nearest recliner where she suggested with a wave that I sit. Then she knelt beside me.

"Well, dear, the best place to start would be the beginning."

Raking in another breath, I stared down at my hands in my lap and told them everything. It started out alright, with the first lie revealed being where I'd actually been during those hours they couldn't find me after our hunt. From there, things became more emotional. I laid my guilt bare and raw, admitting how I'd felt, like they were always walking on eggshells around me, and I didn't want to disappoint them again.

So I'd tried to find Drake on my own, only to end up on the wild ride that started the second I realized I believed him. Judging by the wary glances Johann and Uncle Alaric exchanged, it didn't make them feel better to know Drake had been the one to help me escape the Cneaz's manor. Not to mention the rude awakening that the underground vampire government we'd long thought dismantled had risen from its grave undetected.

I left out Winston's name on purpose, but the gist of our crossing the Summerland was enough of a distraction to keep them from grilling me for more details. By the time I reached the fortress, remembering the guards I'd killed, I finally broke. Ethan left the living room once he seemed to realize I probably wouldn't stop crying for a while.

Uncle Alaric handed me a tissue. Johann's expression had frozen in shock minutes ago. Harsh as the truth was, I couldn't stop once the floodgates had opened. From the horrible mirror allowing passage only to the undead, or anyone that's consumed their blood, to the bizarre magickal dominion I held over Dracula's shadow castle.

Describing the Domnitori had been hard, but necessary. Attentive caution shone from everyone's expressions as they glanced at one another. All of them understood what the repercussions could be, that the undead might want vengeance, and Albuquerque could become a target.

"We won, though." Clearing my throat, I raised my right hand to reveal the shining golden ring. My face stretched tight from drying tears when I forced a smile. "They can't find me now—or

Drake. So it's okay. Even if they wanted to launch a full-on assault, it would go against all of their secrecy goals. They don't want to come out to humanity, and without a sorcerer's magick—"

"You should have told us, Maria." Johann's deep voice struck me silent, and I looked down to my rough-worn boots, the only piece of home to have survived with me. My mouth dried, but I managed to say one last thing.

"I'm so sorry."

The apology was for everyone in the room, but especially Johann. In the following silence, I picked at my fingernails and watched my trembling digits. Then Johann's arms were around me as he knelt on the floor beside the recliner. Surprised, but glad for the comfort, I held him tight. The memory of hugging my dad when he came home from a hunt resurfaced. Back when I was a small child, and still thought this legacy meant the world.

"I'm just glad you're safe now." The broken edge to his voice cut deep, but it was a reminder of why things had gotten this bad in the first place.

All I'd wanted was their trust, respect, and most of all, understanding. Maybe I'd gone about getting it in all the wrong ways, but—held snug by my only living parent—I could only hope change was coming for the better.

THE PROPHECY OF EVERLY NICE

"JERK!" I SWERVED AROUND THE OVERSIZED SUV TAKING AN ILLEGAL U-TURN. Thank the goddess my Chevy Malibu was small, or I'd have been hit by that dingus. I huffed through my clenched teeth, shaking my head until my frizzy red hair shifted across my shoulders. With a glance at the rearview mirror, and a hasty pass of my pasty fingers, my bangs laid straight again. At least, as straight as I'd managed to blow out my curls this morning.

My freckled hands gripped the steering wheel as I smoothly merged into the *legal* U-turn lane to wrap back around Montgomery Boulevard. The building complex I called home was only another two turns, and I breathed a sigh of relief once parked in front of my apartment door.

Stomach growling, I hopped out with my canvas tasseled purse in tow. Sunshine beat down, and sweat trickled down my neck as I hurried to unlock my front door. Bast's welcoming mews greeted me as I slipped inside. The rotund black fuzzball did a cute little trot across the tile toward me, before immediately circling her food bowl.

My shoulders dropped. *Gods, I was battered*, but happy to have my independence. Which of course came with working seven days a week to get my psychic business going. With a resigned sigh, I strode into the kitchen to crack open a can of soft cat food while heavy metal chords drifted down the hall from the closed door at the end.

So, Addison was home. Once Bast was contentedly lapping at her dinner, I bent to give her a quick scratch behind the ears before getting my own. *Leftover guacamole and tortilla chips would have to do.* At least I'd bought the avocados myself and squeezed the organic lemons from the farmer's market without having to resort to pre-made plastic wastage.

The dining table was empty and clean, a perk of living with Addison, but I bypassed it. Headed straight for the couch on aching feet. Even my back was sore from sitting in that awful lumpy-upholstered chair I'd thrifted for the shop. A heavy sigh deflated my chest as I plopped onto the couch, picked up the game controller, and booted up Addison's console attached to my outdated television.

I flicked for the juicy Turkish drama a client recommended, and since the rock music pounding out down the hall made it impossible to hear anything over the TV's crackly old speakers, I turned on the subtitles while crunching down on guac-dipped chips. The typical hetero-pairing being showcased on the screen was in the middle of a mushy declaration, and I rolled my eyes, but grinned.

Honestly, they didn't seem so different from my best friend with her new beau. Considering they'd become practically inseparable since Maria returned home a few weeks ago. I totally called it about her 'vampire problem.'

Smiling, I left the plate on the coffee table to settle deeper into the cushions and tugged the patchwork quilt from Goodwill around my shoulders. Addison's music faded into the background as my eyes grew heavy, and the sun started to set behind our slatted-plastic curtains. My eyes must've closed at some point, because the images behind my eyelids turned strange.

A scene unfolded, pulled into existence one shadow at a time. As if the room itself was shrouded in permanent night, with no lights to give my eyes anything to latch onto. Silhouettes solidified like ink spilled in water, reminiscent of coiling smoke, until human features formed. Four men, two women, each seated on uncomfortable-looking chairs with high backs.

Behind them, a fractured throne splintered the stone it was made from. A hum reverberated underfoot, barely noticeable beneath my bare feet. Chills along my arms raised goose-pimples, and I folded my arms across my chest as my breath fogged the air. It was weird to feel cold in my own dream, but something about the place screamed *magick*.

Confused, and clearly invisible to the people speaking in thoughtful low voices, I drifted a few steps closer. Foreign words sounded muffled in my ears, but something ancient pulled their meaning into my thoughts.

"There must be a means by which we can hunt the descendant." The blonde woman dressed in an indigo gown—with a Queen Anne neckline, revealing plenty of cleavage—frowned. Her full lips pouted in her attempt to sneer.

"I am not concerned with the young girl." The man bedecked in scarlet might've been annoyed, but his scarred face obscured his emotions. "Ignatius Drake has betrayed us, and an immortal who shares our knowledge and secrets may become a dangerous enemy. During his isolation from our community, he has developed a survivalist instinct and contacts outside of our reach."

"The force he has allied behind could destroy us from the inside out. Until now, we believed the descendants to be of little consequence. What did it matter if the descendants of Helsing culled the weakest of us? Those lacking the intelligence necessary to overcome centuries…" The dark-haired man wearing black pursed his thin lips, his expression ugly.

"If we mean to hunt the spider, we must tear off its legs." Another man chimed in, his silver brocade muted by the pitch-darkness.

"Then it is agreed." Golden robes clashed with this man's light hair, but the steadiness of his gaze indicated some position of leadership over the others. "The Helsing line must end—once and for all."

Chill sweat dribbled down my shoulder blades. My eyes widened, stuck to the spot. Like any other nightmare, I experienced the worst of it in slow motion.

A beautiful woman in a violet gown inhaled a short breath to speak, her words ringing like an echo in my ears. "We will summon Belial."

Inhaling like I'd just surfaced from a deep dive, my eyes flew open and I bolted upright. Addison leaned back fast, like she'd been hovering over me, and I gasped two-fold.

"Damn it, Eve." Addison exhaled a staggered breath, as surprised as I felt. "A little warning next time."

"Why were you standing over me?" I stuttered, blinking away the deep sleep my nap had dragged me into.

"I was checking if you were still breathing." Pink blotted her pale cheeks before she turned away, heading for the kitchen. "You were muttering in your sleep, and then all of a sudden went deathly still."

"Oh… Sorry." *Goddess, I felt sick.* My mouth tasted wrong, like wilting flowers—or something rotting. The confusion accompanying my growing migraine was cut short by the notification lighting up my phone. I plucked it up off the coffee table and unlocked it, smiling even before the message loaded.

Courtney must have gotten off work late—wherever she was in the world for her art-dealer job—because the 'good-night' text she'd sent with the cute kissing-face emoji was timestamped at 11:06 PM. Grinning unashamedly down at my screen, I thumbed out a quick response before relaxing into the tan suede couch with a longing sigh.

Maybe Maria wasn't the only one who'd gotten it bad this spring.

"Tea?" Addison leaned over the counter that separated the kitchenette from the dining area.

"Definitely. Herbal." I rubbed at my pounding forehead. Something indistinct nagged at my subconscious, and I tried for the life of me to remember what the heck I'd been dreaming about. Vaguely renaissance-like imagery popped into my head, with a big circular room and a bunch of people in fancy dress-clothes… *Maybe I've watched* The Da Vinci Code *one too many times.*

Addison returned to the living room area carrying my favorite mug. '*Are you kitten me?*' was stamped across the steaming ceramic cup she offered, and I accepted it with a hasty sip. Then Addison sat down on the coffee table, her willowy frame modelesque and her slim face puzzled. I opened my mouth to ask what was up—but she beat me to it.

"So, who's Belial?"

ACKNOWLEDGEMENTS

As difficult as my postpartum experience was, I never would have believed in myself enough to finish a single novel—let alone several—without my daughter, Sabrina. Who inspires me every day to do it scared, and do it anyway. I appreciate my husband for never once scoffing at my dorky desire to write vampire fiction, and my mother for always supporting and encouraging me to keep drafting.

Several beta-readers somehow made it through the early versions of this novel, many of whom offered crucial feedback that improved my craft tenfold. I'd like to specifically thank my critique partners, Lauren Foley and Olivia Danson, for not only putting in the time to give detailed, constructive criticism, but being there for the long haul.

I'm sincerely grateful to my editor, Kait Waterhouse, without whom this book would've been an entirely different beast. As well as Sarah Clark, whose indispensable sensitivity input was incredibly helpful and educational. Rest assured that, if there are issues or discrepancies throughout the book, it is most likely my own error, and not a reflection on the individuals who have contributed to improving the story and how the characters are portrayed.

Concerning the polishing done on the text itself, I have Sabrina Milazzo to thank for her skillful handling of the interior design and typesetting (as well as her endless patience answering my many questions). Nikki of @blkbirdesigns for the beautiful scene break illustration, and Kim Dingwall, who graciously fit me into her busy schedule and brought a stunning cover to life that I had been imagining for years.

Finally, I must express gratitude to my podiatrist, Dr. Zuckman, who told me I would have a better chance at book sales if I "put some dirt in it."

ABOUT THE AUTHOR

MICHAELA CUNNINGHAM is an inadvertent globetrotter and non-binary mother-of-one who consumes way too much caffeine while writing characters that often do the wrong thing for the right reasons. They also have a penchant for run-on sentences. *The Curse of Eternity* is their debut novel, the first installment in the *Descendants of Helsing* series.

CONNECT ONLINE

www.michaelacunningham.com
@michaelawcunningham

www.ingramcontent.com/pod-product-compliance
Lightning Source LLC
Chambersburg PA
CBHW020229010826
48973CB00006B/1442